GW01417399

Please consider rating and/or reviewing this book on Goodreads.com or Amazon.com.

To Fly Without Wings

I remember watching him in the sunlight. He was teaching me how to make fishing line from a horse's tail hair. I can see him now, tying the hook onto the line. His nails were bitten short to the quick, but the hands that wore them were strong and tanned. When our father died, he took over the man's part of the job of raising me. He seemed so wise to me. Always patient, always tolerant of my questions and my mistakes. Where our own father would have been firm, because my brother was young, and because of his character, he always used logic and reason and sympathy.

I remember romping in the woods together. I remember helping in the fields as he drove the cart full of hay. I have no memory of that life where he was not present.

I was the youngest in a family of sons. My three brothers learned to farm, learned to shoot a bow with a string of horse hair. I helped find the small brush growth to make the arrows. Not too small or they would break when stretched against the string. Not too heavy, or they would not fly true or far. I collected the feathers of wild birds as they dropped in the forest. They did not trust me to make the flint tips, thinking my hands too small and lacking the strength to grind them sharp. But everyone had a role, mine as important as the rest.

After our father's death, our mother had to represent the family in the village. Our mother was wise, clever and unintimidated by the men who made decisions for all of us. But she was smart enough to take her two older sons with her, in case any of the elders wished to dismiss her opinions because she was a woman.

The eldest wore his brown hair back with a thong, his face clean shaven. On feast days, small braids on either side of his face would frame it, adding to his already good looks. He was calm, but opinionated and sometimes unable to see through the eyes of others. He would form opinions without all of the facts. But he honestly wished for the best outcome, and his counsel was valued. He was already a man, with children of his own. Not old enough to be an elder of the village, but old enough that his word was respected. He also had a reputation for honesty and for sincerely trying to do the fair thing. He was the sort of man that other men wanted to count among their friends.

The second eldest was the opposite of the first. With his dark hair and pale skin, he would colour to anger and look like his flesh would fly off his bones if he held the anger in any longer. His choice of clothing made from textiles coloured with raspberries or strawberries heightened this effect. He was loyal to a fault, even when the subject of his loyalty wronged him. He chose a wife who did not respect him, and he was cruel to her in return. Neither of them was happy. The only moment when he seemed to find peace was when shooting his bow. He would go silent, all the anger would rush away from him, his only thought on the deer in the forest soon to meet doom by his hand. His dark hair and beard gave him a striking look, drew him many admiring glances, although I know for a fact that his sense of loyalty prevented him from turning his attentions away from his family. He could be funny, and loved games and competition of all sorts.

But my nearest brother ,the one I mentioned first, the one whose name I cannot remember, even though I strain for it, struggle to reach back in time, he was the man I wanted to be. As well as raising me, he learned the trade of the wheel from one of the elders. He knew how to create a wheel for a cart that was perfectly round, so the cart bumped less as it turned. He helped build the big carts that we used to bring in hay for the horses, and wheat and other foods for ourselves. He knew how to fix a cart with a wheel that would not turn. And he made the absolute best libations in all the surrounding villages, having learned from our father. When his brew was consumed at celebrations, men and women alike set themselves free and the result was always a bumper crop of babies nine turns of the moon later. My brother understood that sometimes the village needs release from the drudgery of living, the sorrows and regrets of choices. Even the happy need a change from ordinary life once in a while to appreciate the goodness they enjoy. My brother was always thinking about how to contribute to the lives of others. He once said to me that if he could do one truly good thing each day, then our village, and maybe other villages, would be better when his time came to join our Father where he waited for us.

He would stand with his back against a tree, with his right knee bent and his right foot braced against the bark, both hands behind the small of his back. Other times he would stand with his side toward a tree or a building, his elbow against a protruding branch. It was almost as if, when he really wanted to pay attention, to absorb everything a speaker was saying, then he surrendered the business of keeping his body upright to his elbow or his hands or his foot. I knew when he did this that I should pay attention to my surroundings.

The weather in our land was ideal for crops. The rainy season went from the beginning of winter to its end, and the world was mud, mud, mud. I hated the mud, and the chilblains from the cold rain. I felt the cold seep into my spine during the winter. Even in summer, it would rain for a time each day. The rain ensured successful crops. But then the clouds would clear and a healing breeze would dry out the fields so they did not rot. As children, we spent summer afternoons escaping our chores and running in the woods, observing the creatures there, and discovering ourselves. I once ran off to the forest with a girl from the village. She taunted me, teased me, encouraged me, and then removed my clothes. She touched my whole body, as if it were a magic thing, even my club foot, the foot that prevented me from ever becoming a warrior. When she finally removed her shift and stood naked before me, I could think of nothing else but touching her, kissing her, knowing her body. In family groupings, we all knew the nakedness of the opposite sex. But this was different. The stretched breasts and scarred belly of my mother had nothing to compare with the girl's smooth, soft, magical skin. Once it was over, I was deliriously happy, but I never had any illusion that I would be her choice. A healthy, beautiful young girl would be expected to choose a husband perceived to be as strong and healthy as herself, to ensure the health and survival of their babies. But I walked away with a treasure, one I was surprised to own.

Once I was old enough, it was my choice, and my role, to care for the horses. Our horses were mostly used in our fields, completing the tasks we ourselves were not strong enough for. Ploughing, seeding, harrowing the rows of plants, and carrying away the ripe produce in carts to be stored for winter. I am not sure how I learned to care for them. At least some of it was instinct. I learned how to care for overstrained muscles, how to trim sore work weary hooves. I knew how to use grain poultices to relieve the sores that grew deep in the foot. I could calm and tend to the needs of the angriest or most frightened horse. I rubbed plants on them to keep the bugs away. I pulled knots from their manes and tails and plaited them when the days were too hot. I knew the difference between a horse dying of pain in the belly and a horse that merely had discomfort that would pass. I knew which horses needed grain to bolster their strength and those for which it would prove too strong and heady for them to maintain a manageable temperament. And my favourite thing, my moment of greatest happiness, was to take the buckskin mare down the path toward the next village and to turn her head to home and let her run as fast as she dared. This, I thought, must be what the bird feels, what the arrow feels.

I knew, as only few horsemen do, that if I was calm and silent both inside and out, if I focused, like my dark haired brother with his bow, I could hear the horses talking. I could hear my mare's thoughts as she moved out of the way of the dominant mare approaching to receive a piece of turnip. There was no resentment, no rancour. I knew when a pain in the foot was brewing but not yet causing a limp. I knew when the stud colt's testicle did not drop that he was in terrible pain. I knew that he understood what was happening, and that he begged for death. It was all I could do not to give in to my own despair when I cut his throat. Instead I concentrated on sending him compassion, calm, and reassurance. He went quietly, before our meat man came to get him. I never troubled with the idea of eating the horses I despatched. The soul inside was gone. It wasn't like people, where we died and then waited for the burial rites in order to proceed to the next life. Our bodies had to remain and rot in the ground to give back to the earth what we had taken from her in our lives. The horse meat gave strength and health to our village. The other horses always understood what I was doing, and they never suggested to me that they felt it wrong. They had a wise and beautiful understanding of life.

From my first man hair until I was of marriageable age, our village gradually changed. We had seasons where the summer was too wet, and the winter cold enough for snow. We hung animal pelts in the doorways of our homes sometimes five or six layers thick. The homes were buried in the ground to the turf roof, but now needed more turf to stay warm and keep out the rain.[1] We burned fires much higher, used more wood, ate less, and slept less well. It was a gradual, creeping process, not so bad at first. We could have called each year simply aberrant. That's all right, next season will be better. In a couple of years, at the beginning, next season was better. But then, next season became only no worse. And we became worse.

We began to hear from other villages, our allies, who experienced more than we did with poor crops and bad weather, and people were suffering. They were thin, they could not fight off disease, and they were losing their teeth. They were starving. In the poorest village closest to the coast, the grey ocean now seemed colder, greyer than ever. The storms brought more mountains of water than before, and all the inhabitants could do was hide in their flooded houses until it was over. Fishing was no longer a viable option due to weather and rough seas, and a valuable source of protein was lost. The woods along the shore were beginning to thin, and the game animals had moved inland in search of better vegetation.

At first we sent what little food we could spare. But as hunters from other villages began to hunt in our part of the forest, as foragers took the vegetation that supported the smaller wildlife

---

[1] https://www.orkneyology.com/skara-brae.html

there, the berries were picked over, and the leaves for the reviving tea we brewed were over-picked, there became less food not only for other villages, but also for us.

One night I came in from tending the horses to find my mother and my brothers in a heated discussion. My mother was old now, and she reclined on a bed, covered with skins. Her body could no longer withstand the cold. My eldest brother, the one with the brown hair, was speaking. He was talking about the meeting of the elders from all the surrounding villages, just held. His face was rigid with strain. He said "I do not want these people to starve, and I would help them if I could. But I have begged the elders not to sacrifice our own village to do it". My hot-headed brother began, "we cannot allow them to steal our game, our food! We must stop them at all costs!" In the firelight his dark hair and beard contrasting his fair skin made him look like a god. "Look at our mother here. Do they want us to let her die?" My mother, ever calm and sensible, replied, "It is my time. It is nature's way for the old to die out when food is scarce. It makes room for the younger generations." Her voice was so low we all strained to hear. My next older brother, the blonde one closest to me, asked quietly "is that what you want Mother?" He looked at her directly, waiting for her to voice her wishes. But again the hot-head spoke "Of course she doesn't! " My calm brother repeated, his golden hair shining in the light of the fire, "Brother I hear your own wishes in the way you speak, but I think the choice is our mother's, if choice it is. I do not wish her gone either, any more than I wish any of you gone. I just don't know how we will resolve this situation. My heart is broken that this has all come to pass. And truthfully, it is our Mother's choice and none other when she leaves this earth. We leave when we cease to fight to remain." All this time he held our mother's hand and tucked her skins in around her. I said nothing, having no standing as the youngest brother. I held my arms around my chest, wishing my buckskin mare could fly me away to another place.

My eldest brother sighed, and it was agreed that no more should be said that night, that we would see our way clearer in the morning. My gentle brother and I slept on either side of our mother to keep her warm. She had never snored, but just after the moon had gone down, she made a noise with her breathing, as if her very throat was collapsing. I had heard this sound before, just before my grandsire died. We woke our brothers and we all sat vigil with her, until her passage to the next life was ready and she chose to tread it.

I was filled with despair. My mother's wisdom and will had encouraged my brown haired eldest brother's most charitable, most reasonable self. Her will had dimmed my dark haired second brother's anger and helped him find the calm place he found with the bow. He so wanted what was right, and she helped him find the path to seek it. And my third brother, the one I loved, had drawn strength from her, and courage to be his very best and most perceptive self. She had brought out the best in all of us. Who would we be without her?

The elders arrived at our house as my sisters in law were washing and preparing Mother for burial. Their wrinkled faces were grave. All four of us, my brothers and I, sat to listen, and my sisters in law continued what they were doing in the background. They did not miss a word.

The elders wanted us to burn my mother. It was not our way. Burial with a few of her possessions ensured that she was ready for the next life, and gave back to the earth. If we burned her, she would be unable to pass beyond the veil where she now waited. She would never make it to the next life. She would never see our father again. We were horrified. There were angry words. The elders accepted this; they knew it was a horrifying request. We were absolutely united in our refusal. Until...

The healer, one of the most senior of the elders, spoke. "Reports have come back to us about events in some of the other villages. It seems holes in the ground have been dug where once loved ones lay. This seems to happen within one or two days of the body being laid in the ground."

He paused to let his words sink in. I felt like my entire body had gone numb and my chest hurt. I felt a trickling sensation from the top of my head to my feet. This must be how old men felt when they clutched their chests just before dying. But I was not dying. This was not a heart ending. This was a heart breaking. We were all silent, even my angry brother. I reached and held my gentle brother's hand. He was shaking.

It seemed like forever before anyone spoke. My eldest brother, motioning to myself and my other two brothers, said "We will do as the elders ask. For Mother to become food for starving men would be an affront to the natural way of things. We will say extra prayers to guide our mother to the afterlife. We will ask that the earth accept her ashes as the return of the energy she has taken. You two youngest will build a wooden frame on which to lay her. We can light a fire underneath".

It was odd to me that my eldest brother tasked me with helping to build the pyre. I should have prepared the cart to carry her and I should have walked with the horse, providing comfort to the frightened animal. But one look at my other brother, the calm one, and I could see he desperately needed comfort himself. He was pale and his hands shook. I had to agree with our eldest brother's choice.

My brother and I went to a clearing that we knew our mother loved, where she once picked berries and flowers, and we collected wood from the forest. There was some dead wood despite the increased burning over the last few winters. We cut a small tree to have enough for our task. We lashed the wood together with vines and made a frame that would hold her body off the ground. Then we laid the makings of a large fire underneath. We dressed it with animal fat so it would burn hot and high. We laid extra wood to one side. We watched the sky for rain, but although it was overcast, no drops fell.

All the while my brother and I had not spoken. We sat down together to wait for the others to bring her out. I sat close beside him, put my hands through his arm, as would a girl who was sweet on him. But I wasn't being sweet. He was my anchor, and he was what kept the whole world from blowing away. I had never seen him cry. He was always strong and comforting to me. But now I saw the tears roll down his face fast and thick, as if he were trying to drown himself. I leaned on him, held his hand, and cried my own silent tears.

After a while we looked up. My eldest brother had roped my buckskin mare to a cart, and my mother's body had been placed on it. I regretted, bitterly, that I had not been the one to ask my mare to perform this task. I should have been there for her. Our family and the others of our village were escorting her to the fire. They all looked stricken, knowing what we were about to do. My beautiful mare sensed their heartbreak, and she walked quietly, head down. I could feel the heavy burden of sadness she wore. She was wishing she could ease the hurt around her. So she did what she knew how to do.

My brothers and I laid our mother on the frame that we had built. My eldest brother drew the flame to the animal fat we had placed in the fire, and the leaves and dried plants we put there caught and the fire leapt to life. The villagers sang the songs that would normally accompany a burial, but my brothers stood silent as the tears ran down their faces.

When the fire had burned down after several hours, I took my beautiful mare and the cart and put them away. I stood close, touching the mare with my body, resting my head against her neck. I had precious little grain for the horses, but they had lots of grasses, so I tended to their hurts, made sure their shelter was sturdy in case of a storm, and went home to bed. In the morning when I came back, my buckskin mare had died in the night. I couldn't even weep for her. She showed no signs of dying of a belly ache. I believed then, and have believed in the many eons since, that she died of a broken heart.

About a week after my mother died, and after my mare died, there was a massive rain storm. The clouds rolled in so black they were almost green. They rained down water, hail, lightning and thunder. Water came in the doors of our houses, not enough to flood but enough to complete our misery. The thatched roofs lifted and fell back where they had lifted from. Such storms don't often last long, giving way to clearing as the clouds move along across the sky. When we emerged from our houses, we surveyed our village. The thatch roofs, although mostly intact, needed serious repair and re-anchoring before the next storm came through. Trees had fallen, some blown down and some felled by lightning. Animal skins and pieces of clothing were scattered randomly, blown from wherever they had been when the storm began. There was a shout, and we all moved toward it. During the storm our stock of turnips, wheat, and other produce had been plundered. It was bold. The thieves must have been desperate to be out in such a storm, and with a horse and cart no less. The food had only just been harvested, our first good season in several years. Our position inland on our island had spared us much of the fury of the sea and its storms. The other villages had not been so lucky. And now neither were we.

I checked on the horses, but they were all still there. They were loyal to me and well fed and would be unlikely to tolerate an intrusion. Horses most often react out of fear, but they can and do sometimes react out of anger. Our stallion had plenty of spirit to protect his mares. I breathed a sigh of relief but then immediately felt guilty. There were so many other problems facing us.

I could hear a loud discussion in the center of the village. The men were clustered around the elders, including my three older brothers. My angry brother was shouting, demanding that our men ride to catch the culprits. There was hot blush in his cheeks. They were exactly the same colour as his tunic, dyed red with raspberry fruit in a long ago summer. There was no question of me riding of course. Although I was the best rider in the village I did it with precarious balance, and my foot and my crooked back prevented me from ever wielding a club or a spear in addition to maintaining my seat. So I sat back and listened as the other men argued. In the end the elders prevailed, counselling caution. After all, we only suspected which village had taken our food. We had no proof.

When the discussion was over, scouts were sent to the other villages. All of our friends and relations were now living in tension and sadness. While the scouts were out, the rest of us set about scrounging the fields for any turnips and other vegetables that could have been missed in the harvest. The remains in the food storage house were carefully picked up, cleaned and organized. Some of the women went into the woods to harvest more grasses and roots that could be added to soups and stews through the winter. Some men went in search of thatch to repair roofs. Others went to cut the wind-felled timbers and stack them for drying. We were in for a cold and lean season.

Over the next few days, the scouts trickled home, singly or in pairs. The news was not good. Two villages showed signs of having far more food than they could have harvested. Deep in the night, visits to their food houses, avoiding the sentries, showed large quantities of vegetables and grain. Their hubris was such that even after what they did to us, they did not take precautions against it happening to them. We had seen their fields all summer, how they struggled to produce. If we were going to survive we were going to have to raid those villages in turn.

There were village meetings and arguments among the men almost every night. The tension showed on the women's faces. It was like the air was going to shatter around us. Now all of my brothers were angry. My angry brother was at the heart of the discussion. He seemed unable to take a

17

dispassionate look at the situation, now more than ever. I loved him and his passion, but something in my heart leaned away from him. He demanded that the men form a raiding party, right then, in the light of day, to go to the other villages and take back what was ours. We should demand justice! The other men were not averse to a raiding party – after all, we had to eat and it was our food. But there were two villages involved besides our own. That meant we were fighting against twice our numbers. And that was if the women did not join in the conflict. It had been many years since our village had faced battle, but anyone old enough to have children of their own could remember the year we had been attacked, and everyone had fought. I was not alive then but had heard the story many times of how the women of our village had proved their worth with clubs while three or four hid with the children in a cool dark clearing in the forest. When the battle was won, the same hands that splattered heads on the fields held the children in their skins and stroked their faces.

In the end, all of the men and the single women agreed, with the blessing of the elders, to form a raiding party and take back our food. All of us knew we would seek retribution, but it remained unspoken. Any wrong a man did was between him and his own heart. My job was to bring the horses and keep them behind the fray, available to replace exhausted or injured mounts. I would also serve the injured horses and preserve them as best I could.

We set off to the east when the moon was high. We would attack the weakest of the two villages first, the one out on the cliffs. We rode quietly in the night. The horse who pulled the cart of stones and extra weapons was a big black gelding with a strong steady temperament. I had talked to him quietly and pulled out burrs. I rubbed him down with grass until his black coat shone in the moonlight. I made sure all of the horses got light rations, so they did not feel the weight of their riders. I let them feel my sadness and my anger, but I also let them feel my hope for the raid to come. Only a few were old enough to remember war, but I felt it as best I could, I looked into their eyes, and they knew through my honesty that they might not come home when the sun rose. For myself I chose a white mare who was skittish but strong. She would kick when she was afraid, and that is exactly what I wanted for myself. As we rode along in the night with only a few creaks of the leather the horses wore, I stroked her beautiful neck. I rode with three other horses tethered on a long rope. Enough relief horses, I thought, for thirty strong men and women.

My brothers rode just ahead of me. They spoke quietly between them, and occasionally they smiled encouraging smiles back at me. At one point one of them threw me some dried meat, even now precious in its rarity. I found it eerie to see all the faces painted blue, and the blue symbols on the horses that each man had painted to identify his mount if he fell or had to set it loose.

Many of the women had painted their men's face with magical symbols, and artistic patterns.

As we came to the edge of the wood over the first village, we all gasped as one. The living growth had pulled far away from the edge of the village where it once ended. The village had been visited a matter of months before, and the change had occurred almost overnight. Tree trunks were everywhere, but there was nothing in between them, not a bush or a blade of grass. Beyond the village, the grey sea roiled and crashed against the cliffs. The village itself almost looked abandoned, save for clothing hanging on a line, and the scavenging animals in the midden heap. As our eyes focused better on the midden heap, we saw to our horror that there were pieces of human bodies there. A collective gasp went up, causing the man leading us to turn and scowl us back into silence. I would happily have turned back then.

We sat quietly while the leaders decided how to proceed. Where were the inhabitants? Had they left for good? Where would they have gone? There were low murmurs. Just as the leaders started walking their horses down toward the village, we heard a chorus of war cries coming through the wood behind us. Here they came on skinny horses, skinny men and women swinging clubs and carrying their spears high above their heads. They were all naked, and painted completely blue. Even their horses had blue designs and magical symbols all over their bodies. My mouth hung open. I almost didn't hear my favourite brother yelling at me to take the horses to cover.

I turned to seek egress back into the wood, but everywhere I looked there were more blue faces. I recognized a few. And then I realized that these were the inhabitants of both villages. They had allied against us. In a split second I realized it. They didn't just want our food. They wanted our village and our fields and our wood. And they could only do that if they annihilated us. We were all going to die today. I looked back for my brothers. The angry brother was already dead, his face unrecognizable, but he was wearing a red dyed jerkin that had been my father's. His horse was being led away snorting. No doubt many of their horses had been eaten so this raid would serve to replenish their herd. My eldest brother fought with superhuman strength. I saw three fall by his hand. He swung his club with all his weight behind it, and his aim was as true as ever. Just as the third man fell from his horse to the ground, another rode from behind that my brother did not see. I screamed his name, just as the spear tip ran through his body, right through to the other side.

The last brother, the best, I could not find for a few minutes. But when he saw our older brother speared, he came running from somewhere to be of aid. His eyebrow was bleeding into his eye, and he appeared to be favouring his right leg, but he was otherwise unharmed. He ran with his unbalanced gait to our brother, held his hand, and whispered to him. I was riveted. I had long since lost my three backup horses, but I sat immobile on my beautiful white mare with the blue spiral on her forehead. Everything else but that mare and my three brothers, one dead, was a complete blur and to this day I remember only that in the midst of the melee.

It seemed ages before I dismounted and ran to my brothers. It was probably no more than the time it takes to wash your face, or to eat a few tangy berries in the forest. Once I began to move, I could no more have gone back than I could have made the moon rise at midday. I had just reached them when a club hit the back of my beloved brother's head, killing him instantly. And then it all went black.

It's not that I remember nothing after that. It's that there was nothing.

Of Dogs and Horses

I sat on the riverbank with his Lairdship on a sunny afternoon. The home of the Laird of Keppoch was to our backs, the hive of activity there continuing despite the quiet mood of the master. The fort was neither stone castle nor wooden motte, but both, and repairs and improvements to it never ceased. It sat on the bank at the meeting of the Roy and Spean rivers. The entrance from the river was through a curtain wall around a mound at the lowest part of the complex. A second mound was up higher along the ridge from the first. The curtain wall was of timbers, the bottoms of which were buried in the soil and fortified with rocks. Higher than both mounds was a pie shaped enclosure, in which were the gardens, and the wooden keep. There was a gate at the high end of the complex, it was doubled and bristling with arms. The plan was to rebuild everything in stone as soon as it was possible, but My Laird had to land on his feet when he settled this spot, and a serviceable home base had to be created. The Keppoch that was his inheritance was only newly carved away from the Lord of the Isles, and management of it had to begin immediately lest it be lost to competing clans. In addition, there were a hundred souls living here, and all of them were part of the community that kept everyone fed and healthy, and My Laird oversaw all of it. His grandfather had been the King of Scotland, but the King was rich in grandsons. The inheritance of Keppoch was both a gift and a test.

I had made a decision and I was sharing my thoughts with him, explaining why I was making the choice. He listened and nodded, occasionally touching my hand or my arm to show his understanding. Often he would stand and lean against a tree with his right foot braced against it. We knew when he surrendered the balance of his body to a tree or other object that he was concentrating very hard on what was being said. That conversation reconciled him to my choice, to understand that I was making a choice for who I was, not against who I did not want to be.

There was a light breeze that gently lifted and dropped his fine blond hair, so pale in the summer it was almost white, bleached by the sun. I had once heard him confess that he was not always a perfect man, but if he could do just one really good thing each day, then he might have made the family, the clan, and even Scotland a better place. This was the quality of the man. After I had finished explaining we sat quietly and periodically the silence was broken by some observation about the state of the Clan, or the crops. I had never seen him so pensive, a man usually given to action and leadership. Mechanically gifted, he would often have a small mechanism taking form in his hands as he listened, but today his hands were empty.

I was not born into the house of Keppoch. I came from the home of the Lord of the Isles, and came out to Keppoch when my Laird's father left Keppoch to his son, dividing his estates between the children of both first and second marriages, as set forth by Robert II. I was only a small child then, in my grubby skins and woven linen clothing. I was raised by the people of the Keppoch, clothed and fed generously by her ladyship, Mary of Keppoch, and the servants and residents of the castle. My Laird and his Lady believed that a castle community, even where there is not yet a castle, only works if everyone does their part, and every part is important. All were treated with decency and kindness. This is not to suggest that any of us were allowed to forget our role, our status, and justice for transgressions was swift and appropriate. A punishment was never carried out in anger. When necessary, which was rare, there was a gibbet on the estate.

Until I was old enough to begin the change to manhood, maybe twelve, I only saw my Laird from a distance. I watched as he presided over his territory, here addressing crop issues and adjudicating between his stewards, and those who appealed to him for disputes with other members of the clan. As in any clan, one didn't have to be present in the hall know much of the Laird's character. We all knew that our Laird could be depended on to be fair most of the time, and that once he had made up his mind, he would be annoyed and sometimes angry if he had to readdress an issue. We could all leave at any time. We stayed because our lives were better if we did so.

I saw him when he left for battle once. His leather and chainmail and metal armor made him look bigger than he was. His helm was carried hanging from his hip as he rode the big white stallion that had been a gift from one of his brothers. His massive sword, seemingly too big to be wielded, hung in a scabbard on his left side. His blond hair floated free, the pockmarked face that gave him his nickname Carrack did not seem a detriment somehow. As he rode past me, his blue eyes looked down at me and he smiled. "It's all right boy, all will be well". I smiled back, encouraged by him. In that moment, most of all, I knew that Alasdair McDonnell Laird of Keppoch was a force to be reckoned with in more ways than one.

My parents both died long before my time at Keppoch. My mother died giving birth to me, and the midwife at the time said that she bled to death before she could even see me. She had come from Eire across the sea where the clan of the Isles had land holdings. My father I barely remembered. He died of fever when I was very young. So I became the kept child of my betters, the child who earns not his keep. My Laird brought me to Keppoch when the move was made from the Isles. And when I was old enough, something had to be found for me to do. I had always known and expected that I would clean up after horses, provide muscle and labour to build stone walls, or work in the gardens, these being the lowest jobs.   Indeed I would not have been surprised to be taught to clean the guarderobe.[2] I did not begrudge any of this, but simply accepted it as my fate.

---

[2] Medieval castle toilets, usually where waste landed outside the castle wall. At least one more place where an enemy would not willingly penetrate.

From early on I was fascinated with His Lairdship's hunting hounds. The ones I longed to touch were huge, and could be vicious in the hunt. They were not necessarily friendly toward people, as they were often used to patrol the grounds for intruders. They were impressive, unpredictable, and I couldn't tear myself away.

I had begun to stretch upwards, and Cook would grumble as she dressed me in yet another new set of clothing, a castoff of some other growing child in the clan. She grumbled, but then she hugged me before letting me go. I heard her say once to My Laird's agent as he counted the proceeds of the rents that every child needs the warmth of love, even one who God had seen fit to Orphan. I had been born with a left foot that was twisted so that I couldn't run as fast as other children. But I was strong, I could count the sheaves of oat as they were unloaded from the cart and stored for winter. The stores master often told me I was his best helper, to the smiles of the workers.

On a grey day after the harvest, the hounds' keeper approached me. I tried to duck him – I wanted to go play in the wood with the other children. But he caught me soon enough by the back of my tunic. "Master wants me to take you to see the dogs". I was surprised and alarmed by this – none of the children were allowed near the hounds. One of them had maimed a child at last Easter, and it was not the first time a fascinated child got too close. Of course, my own fascination with them meant that there was no doubt that I would accept his invitation, even had My Laird not called for it. I was surprised too that My Laird had instructed anything with regard to me. I had the lowest status of any member of the clan, why should he be interested in my fate?

The kennels were away from the main house, in a building of wattle against the curtain wall of the centre mound. Nothing was too good for the master's hounds. They were fed the offal of some of the prey of the hunt. Sometimes, if a dog seemed ailing or tired, or if a bitch had just whelped, a proper piece of meat would be served. They also got vegetables left over from last year when the new crop came in. Sometimes they would get warm porridge with the blood of a hart or a pig cooked in. Occasionally there was grumbling from someone that dogs ate better than people at Keppoch home, but the grumbler was usually set straight pretty quickly. Good hounds meant good hunts, and the people of Keppoch ate better as a result.

All this I learned as we walked together toward the sounds and smell of the kennels. There was not barking as much as there were growls and scuffles and a variety of whimpers and groans. For the first time I found out that the hounds' keeper actually had a name, Kin. It was a name often used among the people of the highlands. Kin had started in his service to My Laird as beholden like me, but had worked his way up, and was now a freedman with the honourable trade of Kennel keeper.

The smell of the kennels had an acid tone to it, a tone I was later to associate with dog waste. There was also the smell of stale meat and the overwhelming smell of wet dog.

We entered a sort of corridor between the cages where the dogs lived. I had never been so close to them, and they were much bigger than I had realized. As I stood in front of one of the cages, the dog inside approached me, sniffing the air. His head was level with mine. He continued to sniff until I put the palm of my hand against the wrought iron bar. He considered for a moment that seemed to last forever, and then gave my hand a lick. Apparently deciding I tasted good, he licked a few times more before retreating to the back of his cage and curling into an impossibly small ball and putting his head down and closing his eyes. His name was AilbheFair, which meant White, and indeed his coat colour was lighter than the others.

Another dog I was strongly attracted to was Bearnas. She was very quiet. Kin told me that she had borne puppies, but only two, and they were sickly and had to be destroyed. It was as if Bearnas knew what had happened to her puppies and mourned. Kin said that if there had been another bitch in whelp, they could have moved a few of her puppies over the Bearnas for her to raise. But she was the only one at that time. She was My Laird's favourite, his pet, and he had fervently wished for puppies from her and Cadeyrn. Cadeyrn was pointed out to me as the large, regal looking dark male in the kennel at the end. Looking back to Bearnas, I found her sadness almost to be as if I felt it myself. Kin said that was the way for a true dog master. I looked at him to see if he was smiling indulgently, the way the adults usually did when they said nice things about me. But he wasn't smiling at all.

The smaller hounds were in the kennels in the middle, between the biggest dogs. There were two groups, one group of five that were medium sized and that looked able to run very fast, and a group of four shorter dogs with the biggest noses I had ever seen. [3]

When the time came to meet Cadeyrn, I stood quietly in front of his cage. He growled softly and the hair rose on his shoulder blades and his hips. I stood quietly, feeling his uncertainty about me. He walked stiff legged over to the bars and challenged me with his eyes. He was awe inspiring. His name meant battle king, and I could see that in him. His eyes were a light gold colour, his neck strong, and the fangs were half the length of my finger. I did not flinch but neither did I challenge him. He sniffed the air and then turned and urinated through the bars on my feet.

Kin laughed and slapped me on the shoulder. Apparently I met with Cadeyrn's approval. Or at least, he thought me no threat.

I was introduced to twenty-one dogs that day. All investigated me, and all eventually accepted my presence outside of their cages. Kin explained that My Laird kept the finest hunting dogs in the land, at least as he knew of and defined it. Litters of pups

---

[3] <u>Life in a Medieval Castle,</u> Hunting as a Way of Life; Harper Collins Publishers 1974l; Joseph and Frances Gies.

often were sold for a fine price to other Lairds and wealthy men to use on their estates. Talented hunting dogs improved the provision of any master's table. As he explained this I thought of Bearnas. What could be done for her?

Kin looked sad when I asked this. Clearly Bearnas was not just a favourite of my Laird but of Kin also. Her appetite was not what it should be, and he feared she might eventually die from her sadness. He admitted to devoting much thought to her fate. And then he looked at me. Hard.

The next thing I knew I was being propelled back to Bearnas' cage. As the door was opened she lifted her head, but did not move toward Kin and me. Kin moved easily toward her, and the tip of her tail wagged at him. I was instructed to get down on all fours and move slowly toward her without looking at her, which I did, shuffling across the fresh straw. When I was almost close enough to touch her, Kin passed me a small piece of fresh carrot and gestured that I should move toward her head with my hand outstretched, the carrot offered as a peace offering. I sensed no harm in her, and in fact I felt her curiosity toward me. So I did as I had been bid.

I had the fleeting thought that perhaps I, the burdensome peasant child, was to be disposed of in this way, but I pushed it down. Shortly Bearnas could reach my hand and moved to sniff the carrot. Apparently it wasn't tempting to her, because she left it in my hand and began to sniff my arm. I hoped she wasn't investigating it as a potential meal, but I really didn't think so, and I was right.

She continued on, investigating my body all over, from my hair to my toes in my woolen socks and leather shoes. The longer she sniffed, the calmer I became and the safer I felt. Ten minutes found me sitting quietly beside her, stroking her coarse fur.

"Tomorrow when it is time to feed them, you will look after Bearnas. You will clean her cage, ensure her water to be clean, and you will sit with her as she eats. I want you to become her special friend, you understand? Perhaps you can draw her from her present state. But for now, it is time for your supper and you are expected in the kitchen. Sleep well. Meet me here tomorrow right after Matins and your apprenticeship shall begin"

My feet had wings on the way back to the kitchen. "Apprenticeship" was not a word I would ever have expected to hear in reference to myself. My joy at my visit with Bearnas added to my excitement. A moment of trust with such a powerful and potentially dangerous animal was enough to send my child's heart into ecstasy. I ate a barley soup, and headed for my sleeping place, but it was hours before I slept.

In the ensuing weeks, I devoted myself to Bearnas. Over time she became first tolerant of me and then happy to see me. In between my chores looking after her and the other animals, I spent hours with her, touching her gigantic paws, stroking her ears, and accepting her licks and sniffs. I taught her to retrieve a stick for me, to roll over on command. Kin's solution for her sadness worked. She was sufficiently diverted by me as her companion that she forgot her loss and had reason to look forward to each day.

I worked with the other dogs too, but the dog I most wanted intimacy with, Cadeyrn, was never far from my consciousness. Sometimes I could feel his yellow eyes boring through my tunic between my shoulder blades. Kin was the only one to work with him, coping with the big dog's occasional bad temper and glowering. Kin was the only one who could exercise Cadeyrn except My Laird. The dogs were exercised on a long rope, now walking, now loping in a circle, the way horses were often exercised on a line. Bearnas was easy. AilbheFair made occasional feints toward the woods, testing my authority to hold him in the circle I allowed.

The days passed in a blur of activity and exhaustion. I was extremely satisfied with my lot. Each night I fell into my sleeping place in the corner of the kitchen and slept dreamless sleep until I woke up at dawn.

One afternoon when all of the dogs had been exercised and the grey sky threatened snow, a shadow darkened the doorway at one end of the kennels. Kin rose immediately from our chore of preparing food for the hounds, and pulled my collar until I also stood. As the shadow moved closer, I discerned that it was My Laird. This was the closest I had ever been to him. He looked smaller than he had that day when I had seen him on his horse, probably because he wore no armor, just a warm gambeson and big boots. He addressed Kin warmly, and then asked "So the lad has saved my lovely

33

Bearnas". As he looked at me his blue eyes twinkled.

"We will see how well Bearnas fares, come boy, let us take her to walk with us. Hurry now, fetch her". When I reached for a long line to put Bearnas on, Kin nodded no at me. I was simply to release her and let the Master control her activity. I let her out and stood beside Kin, watching as she joyously joined our Laird, cavorting with him like a puppy. My Laird Alasdair turned and looked at me expectantly. "Are you coming?" To be asked to walk with him was indeed a tremendous honour – many more exalted persons than I did not enjoy such favour. I ran and took a position just behind his right shoulder. He turned and urged me forward to walk beside him.

"Well boy, tell me how you saved my favourite bitch?" After only a moment's hesitation, I started to tell him how it had been that first day, and how I had earned Bearnas' trust, and how she had earned my love and loyalty in return. He listened quietly, but not missing any detail of his surroundings. At one point there was the sound of a small animal scurrying through the underbrush and he signalled casually to Bearnas. She became very serious and intense, bounding through the bush and coming back with a weasel in her mouth. He took it from her, praised her, and gave a small piece of meat from a purse strapped to his belt. To me he handed the weasel, instructing me to include it in our store of meat for the dogs. We continued our walk, Bearnas walking companionably beside us until he signalled her again, and this time she returned with a rabbit, and again meekly handed it to him in return for a small piece of meat. The rabbit was to be delivered to the kitchen. I was dumfounded. This massive dog who could be vicious to another over possession of a dead grasshopper handed over her kill without whisper of complaint. I asked him if Cadeyrn would do this, and he laughed. "Yes, but he demands a little more of a reward".

We walked until it was almost dusk. We returned to the kennels with two weasels, four rabbits and a pheasant. Bearnas sniffed him and licked his face before returning to her cage. She accepted her supper gratefully and then curled up into a deep sleep.

He left me in wonder. I asked Kin about this strange turn of events. "He likes to walk with the dogs and casually hunt when he is troubled or trying to work out a problem. He has always taken an interest in your welfare, including asking that you come to learn with me. His behaviour today is unusual for a Laird, but it does not surprise me. Come, take the rabbits and the pheasant to the kitchen and get your supper."

Kin's revelations gave me much pause for thought. Why did My Laird follow my fortunes? Had he more of a hand in my existence than I had known? Why?

I had no answer for these questions as the days rushed by, then the months. My Laird came to the kennel periodically, and we would walk with the hound of his choice, and he bade me talk to him, to tell him about the dogs. Sometimes it was me who controlled them, sending them to hunt and rewarding them. A year went by in this way, and I had fallen into a contented routine.

During this time, there were several much more formal hunts. The men went into the forest on horseback, and the slower dogs with the big noses sniffed for game. When something was found, the medium sized, faster dogs were set loose to corner it. Then Caderyn and AilbheFair were usually sent in to keep the game, often a hart or a boar, from escaping. One of the members of the hunt was given the honor of killing it. This person was usually a guest or one of My Laird's men whom he felt deserved a reward. [4]

Bearnas was again bred to Caderyn, in the spring. Kin and the Laird and I all fussed over her and worried. We also made sure that one of the other bitches was bred at the same time. It wasn't difficult, in that multiple females in the same kennel often go into heat at the same time.   It meant more work for Kin and me when the puppies came, but it ensured that if Bearnas again could not bear a healthy litter, we could give her some pups from the other litter to ease her heart.

Bearnas got the best food during this time. Entrails of hunted animals, milk from a cow, bones from a butchered pig. When the garden began its early produce, she had of that as well. Daily I rubbed her coat with handfuls of straw, and she even let me

---

[4] Life in a Medieval Castle, Hunting as a Way of Life; Harper Collins Publishers 1974; Joseph and Frances Gies

check her teeth for rot and pain, but I found none. I cleaned the snot from her eyes, checked her toenails for splits and cracks. Kin would watch from a distance and smile.

The other bitch whelped first. She birthed six healthy puppies, and so we breathed a sigh of relief. We watched for Bearnas. She was uncomfortable for two full days before she finally whelped. And we needn't have worried. There were four big pups, two dark, and two grey. She let me help her break their sacs and hand them over for her to lick until they breathed and mewled like kittens. Placed up to her giant teats engorged with milk they all suckled strongly and were soon sleeping against her warm skin with bellies full.

The birth of Bearnas' pups and the way she allowed me to participate is a collection of sensations and emotions that I will never, ever forget. I have felt echoes of it in the many years since, but never have I been immersed in it again the way I was that day.

The next six weeks was busy and fulfilling. We watched over the pups for signs of illness. We watched over their mothers to ensure they continued to produce enough milk to nourish their babies. And as the puppies grew, their individual personalities became more evident. This one would growl and play more with his littermates, and that one was content to snuggle into its mother's body and snooze in the warmth.

When the bitches showed signs of weaning their pups, his Lairdship began bringing guests to the kennels. Most were nobles wanting to add a good bloodline to their own kennels, but one in particular was very different. A man in the fullness of middle age arrived, dressed in a way I thought I had never seen, but that was somehow familiar. He looked keenly at me. My Laird gestured for me to join them.

I did so, respectfully and with my eyes lowered as I had been taught to do with my betters. The man put his hand under my chin until my eyes were level with his. They were blue, like mine. His hair was brown with braids twisted into the sides, grey strands woven through it. He wore a tunic of rich linen dyed with indigo, and under his cloak his belt carried three separate purses, each worked with symbols and patterns. He wore silver rings, but not so large as to attract attention when journeying from afar. He was clean shaven and handsome, and felt to me to be the kind of man men would want as a friend. Around his saddle were rich furs.

I glanced at my Laird, looking for an explanation. Why did this man look at me this way? His face had a gentleness to it when he spoke. "This is Faolan. He is known as the Wolf of Antrim in the land across the sea to the west. He is your uncle."

If he had said the thatch on the dog kennel roof had lifted up to reveal a giant he could not have surprised me more. I had always understood that I was an orphan, and never thought of myself as having relatives. But this explanation furnished more questions than answers. Why now?

Seeing my confusion, Faolan spoke. "It's all right that you be confused lad, for I have not been here for ten years or more. Much has been happening in our homeland to keep me away. I have come to see the finest hounds in the land of the Scots, and to see how my sister's son fares in the hands of his Lairdship".

My head was swimming. I was his sister's son. His sister who had died while bringing me to life. Had he known my father? And how was it that he stood here so confidently when his sister and brother in law had been in thrall of the Lord of the Isles?

My Laird was watching me carefully. "Faolan, he seems a little pale. Tis a shock to be sure. Perhaps we should allow him to sit and have a drink from my flask."

They sat me on a rock nearby and as if the surprise I had already encountered were not enough, the shock of being offered my Laird's flask could certainly be added to it. It had a strong liquor in it, what I now know to be whiskey. I sipped obediently and handed it back.

Faolan said, "I have no wish to detain the Laird any longer. Sir please do not let me keep you from your many obligations. I will bide with the boy until he regains himself. We can talk and he will have time to think a bit. And then I must resume my travels. That is, as long as his friend Kin can spare him." That was the first time I remembered that Kin was there. I suppose he must have been nearby the whole time. He bowed slightly to Faolan and went back to his work with the dogs, returning only to bring two puppies. I was glad for the puppies, as I found they gave me a focus. One part of my brain petted dogs, the rest of it coped with my stress.

Being alone with my uncle was better than being with both men together. With both of them I felt like I was travelling in a strange land and did not know the language. But with just him, I felt better able to get my equilibrium. And he began to talk.

"It is evident to me that you know very little of your origins. I suppose I should not be surprised. My sister did not live to tell you your heritage, and my brother in law did not long outlive her. And those that remain who know of it are in the Isles, not here. The Laird and his family have no doubt protected you from much of the story, as he always wished you to simply enjoy your childhood. Mayhap I will begin at the beginning."

My mother and father were residents of a community on the Antrim shore. In the generations since, it has come to be called Dunluce and is now fallen into ruin, but in the days of my parents, it was newly built and their clan was called McGuigan, and they had status in the clan, as my maternal grandsire was the chief. By the time I was to be born, my parents had moved to the island of Finlaggan, the home of the Lords of the Isles. Why they had left their lives in a grand castle in favour of the home of the Lord of the Isles he did not say.

The rest of the story I already knew. My mother had died giving birth to me and my father had died of a fever not long after. I was the only survivor of the three of us. And not a peasant at all.

Faolan sat with me quietly for a while as I tried to take it all in. It explained so much: why I was treated much better than the average homeless, helpless orphan; why I was being given a vocation, something usually reserved for my betters; and why my Laird seemed to take an extra interest in me.

When he thought I had taken in enough for him to continue, he explained one of the reasons he had stopped at Keppoch on his journey. Yes, as he had indicated, he wished to inquire after my welfare, and he was pleased with what he saw. But I was a noble of his clan. He wanted to ask my Laird if he could take me home.

In the space of two hours or less I had gone from being a well-treated urchin content with my lot to a young noble of the Clan McGuigan, with the freedom to decide my own fate. Nothing in my life had ever prepared me for this. I had no idea what I wanted or how to proceed.

"I see this is much to absorb my young nephew. My journey takes me away to Edinburgh. Tis a long journey, and once my business is concluded, it will take me some months to return. I leave you here until then, to decide your fate, as it is my intention and that of the Laird Alasdair to allow you a voice in the choices that are made about your future. His Lairdship is a fair and good man. If you ask him to advise you, know he will advise you of what he deems right and be supportive of your thoughts during this time. I take my leave of you, until we meet again. May the Lord Bless you. "

And with that, Faolan, the Wolf of Antrim, was gone. I stood looking at his ever diminishing image, his woven cloak over top of his liver chestnut horse, with two puppies in arms, nipping my fingers. Such a short visit but of such import to me. I sat for more than an hour by myself, just feeling the weight of it on me. It was almost dusk when Kin came to me, with Bearnas in tow.

"I thought you could use a wee break from the little buggers", he said, smiling. He picked up the puppies, now fed up with me, and left Bearnas with me. She plopped down beside me and rolled her prodigious body over, looking for a belly rub. I obliged absent mindedly. Her teats were still big from the puppies, and red in places where the remaining two still occasionally tried to nurse, even with their sharp puppy teeth. I put my head on her chest and slid my arms around her. Her heart thumped softly in my ear. It took several minutes before I realized that Kin was wiping tears off my cheek.

For the next several months, things went on as they had been for some time. I worked with the dogs, caring for them, feeding them and training them. I even learned to work with Caderyn and earned his respect. There was another batch of pups that year, and another group of fine gentlemen coming to look at them and take one home. Kin and I shared our tasks. Occasionally, we talked about Antrim. I had found out that the McDonnells in

Ireland did not have a castle or stronghold of their own, but had homes in a settlement on the shore. The Chief of Clan McGuigan allowed them access to their stronghold and they were welcomed as trusted allies. Occasionally small skirmishes broke out between individuals, but for the most part, the two Clans supported one another against aggression toward their shared territory.

My Laird would come regularly to walk and hunt the dogs, and we would talk about my situation. He too explained what he knew about Antrim and what my Uncle had to offer. He maintained a sort of neutrality, not telling me what I should do, but only providing me with the information I sought and helping me to think critically about it for myself. But I always had the feeling that there was still more to the story. I waited for the other foot to drop.

One cloudy morning after Matins, one of the scullery maids from the house came looking for me. I was to join my Laird in the stables. The most interesting fact about this summons was that I had never even darkened the stable door.

When I arrived at the stable, I peered into the comparative dark, not wanting to walk into danger. After a few moments my eyes adjusted and I could see that there were horses in large stalls down either side of a spacious aisle that curved and followed the roundness of the mound and the curtain wall that circled it. At the far end, I could see a large white horse with a head halter on and connected to the walls at either side by short ropes.

He moved as he heard me approaching, and the bunching of his haunches was intimidating to me. I stopped.

"Come along boy. Make noise so he can hear you. Making gentle and repetitive noises will reassure a horse, and serves to help keep you safe. He is already listening for you. Talk to him, and then approach. Even from behind he will not hurt you." The speaker was Angus, the Laird's son, he who would inherit Keppoch. I had only seen him from a distance before now. He was a young man, not yet ready to marry, but old enough to have ideas and responsibilities of his own, and about five years older than me.

I bowed my head slightly to acknowledge him and began to sing one of the songs the people of Keppoch sang around the bonfires at Easter. When I was pretty sure the horse was listening, I felt my way along the wall at one side of the aisle. Presently I was standing in front of him, and Angus was smiling at me.

"First test passed and you still have your balls. Well done." He grinned like his father, but more light-heartedly. I grinned back, but carefully, not wanting to exceed my limits in this fascinating but unfamiliar situation.

The horse, to my surprise, was the stallion my Laird rode when he went out to battle, or at least he had in the past. At closer inspection, he had small scars on the side of his jaw, and a larger one on his shoulder. I could see the black skin underneath his shimmering white hair. He took my breath away.

Angus said "His name is Caesar, like the Roman kings of old. It suits him don't you think?" And suit him it certainly did. "My father suggested we should use him, because he is older than battle age now, and experience has made him calmer and wiser than before." That's calm? I thought. But I nodded. I really couldn't believe this was happening.

"Forgive me, I don't even know what to call you. You are not my Laird, for that is your father. But not through a years' worth of hunting seasons will I be your equal. I wish to be respectful. Why are you here with me?"

Angus grew serious for a minute. Grey eyes surveyed me up and down. "My father perceives you have need of riding lessons. You may soon have a need to ride a horse. But he himself is not free to teach you, having left for the Isles this morning. I am generally called Laird or Sir by most of the people of Keppoch. But in private, you may call me Angus".

That first day passed in a heartbeat. Caesar was haughty, and absolutely knew his power. Angus, who I could not call anything but Sir, showed me how to assert myself with Caesar without arousing his pride. I was to earn his trust before I learned to tell him what to do. I learned to feed him without getting bitten, and how to move around him without getting stepped on. Only once did that powerful back leg lift the foot off the ground, a foot fully the size of my face, and threaten to launch it in my direction. But I began to sing again and backed up to a respectful distance, and the leg relaxed and the foot rested once again on the stone floor. As I looked up I saw a look of alarm on Angus' face that ran away almost as quickly as I had seen it.

Before bed I went to see Kin. I told him all about Caesar, and about Angus, and that I was to be given riding lessons and I had no idea why. Kin listened as my words tripped over my lips and with my hands I showed him the things I had learned.

"He teaches you as his father taught him. He has Lady Mary's laugh and her humour, but he can be serious as a broadsword when required. It is interesting that Angus teaches you and not one of the grooms, and using his Laird's own horse. I suspect that young Angus has much more to teach you than one of the grooms ever could. I believe his Lairdship expects you to go to Antrim with the Wolf of Antrim. And should you not, you will be equipped for more than the duties of a dog handler. "

He looked sad, and I realized that he too thought I would go. And even if I stayed he thought I would become beyond his reach.

By the time My Laird returned from the Isles, I could mount Caesar and ride him around the field that sat outside the curtain wall. Caesar did as I asked, provided I asked respectfully, which I always did. My Laird watched us approvingly but I could see there was one thing about which he was not happy. He and Angus exchanged knowing glances.

"If he is going to ride any faster than a walk, he will need the left stirrup adapted" acknowledged Angus in a low voice I think I wasn't supposed to hear. My Laird's saddle maker was called for.

When he arrived, the saddle maker watched me, not entirely approvingly, and looked at the angle of my left foot.

"My Laird, if the lad were to ride with any frequency, I would need to turn that stirrup on an angle so that he would have use of the foot. I can have it done in a few days, if it pleases your Lairdship." He hesitated, looking at me on the big horse and trying not to eye My Laird too directly. But there was defiance and discomfort in his stance.

My Laird looked at the man with one eyebrow raised. "Is there a problem?"

"Well, My Laird, it's just that there are questions being posed here and in the village as to why a peasant is being taught to ride, and such a fine horse at that."

My Laird turned to face him head on and the atmosphere between the two men turned icy cold. I could see Angus bracing himself for what might come next. I squirmed in my seat, wishing I could just get down, hide myself somewhere.

"The boy will be experiencing a change in station, and will need to ride. The horse is old but is apt in temperament for this task. Even the fine horses of gentlemen grow old. Not that I am accustomed to acquainting tradespeople with the business of my house. "

The harness maker's face was beet red and downturned at the rebuke. I could see by his body language that the issue was not settled. My position here was apparently much in question.

After the man left, I asked leave to get down from the horse. Angus helped me, and I bowed to them both and made to leave. I felt something akin to shame at the oddness of my social position. I wanted nothing more with this haughty horse, and this charming young laird. But My Laird called me back.

"I am sorry" he said softly. "I knew this problem with arise eventually. I have a story to appease the townspeople, and even those within our walls here. But things have to come out naturally. This has to be handled carefully. Go now to your rest. It has been a long day for you".

He waved at me leave to go. I ran to the kennel, crying hot lonely tears. Kin was just checking all the dogs before he went to bed. Seeing the state I was in he walked me to the kitchen. The cook gave me stew and she washed my hands and face with warm water and a cloth. Once I was calm, they both listened as I told them the whole story from start to finish. I confessed to them that I had no idea why any of this was happening to me. And silently I thought surely if I had been born into such a noble house I would have been treated differently all along. And why did I stay with the McDonnell clan? Everything I understood about myself was now in question.

As I spoke, one of the maids came into the kitchen from having cleared the big oak table in the hall from the supper dishes. She listened also until I had finished.

She muttered under her breath to one of the other maids." Yes, and this is what happens from being soft on peasants and servants. This whole family are soft, that's all. Imagine having your son and heir to teach a peasant something far beyond his ken. "

The words were barely out of her mouth before Cook had heard her and flown across the kitchen and slapped her hard on the side of the head. The girl reeled as she was pushed onto a chair. I was shocked by the violence of this woman I had known as a gentle soul all my life.

"Stupid girl! You don't know what you're talking about! Who do you think you are shooting your mouth off to, based on the few paltry things you hear from listening at keyholes? What do you know about this?"

Cook was vibrating with anger and the girl was crying and cringing in the chair. My mouth hung open and I wasn't sure whose side I should be on.

"If you ever say anything so stupid again I will have you turned out into the wilds, or even across to Eire for your trouble. Or have you forgotten that you yourself are the product of this family being soft on servants?"

The girl ducked her head against the blows and cried. Cook turned to Kin, still shaking and red in the face. "You had better go to Master Angus. Tell him we have a problem that warrants his attention."

I had experienced many revelations of late about my origins, but this was the first time I felt something more sinister. I couldn't make sense of the things Cook said, but I knew Kin's face, and he was very alarmed indeed as he trotted up the stairs to tell the family...what? What exactly had been revealed here? There was obviously something much deeper here than I had ever been aware of and Cook and Kin were extremely protective of it. Cook could have dealt with that situation just a little differently and no one would have need to be summoned. Everyone's reactions seemed so out of proportion to what I understood.

Angus came into the kitchen shortly, wearing just his chemise and a robe. Like all of us, he had wool socks on his feet, and his hair and beard were in disarray. The chemise he wore was fine linen, with embroidery around the neck, but I could see a very small fray where it hung to his knees. Clearly he had been roused from sleep. This interested me, because whatever he was about to address was important enough to rouse him.

First he approached the servant girl. He pulled her up from the chair, wiped her tear stained face with his hand, and kissed her forehead. Then he invited her to sit again. His kindness quieted her sobs, and hopefully loosened her tongue.

"What's your name again girl? I'm sorry, I've forgotten."

"My name is Daisy Sir."

"Good girl. And tell me Daisy, how did you come to be working here for my family? " Angus' voice was low and even in tone.

"Me Ma brought me here, three years ago this spring and asked for the Laird to assist". Her eyes darted around the kitchen. She had been deftly and quickly maneuvered into a position she did not want to be in and it had happened almost before the introductions were over.

"Yes, that's right, I remember now. And what happened to your baby?" His mien was more direct, a little harder now.

Tears started rolling down her cheeks again now. "She is now with a family in the village Sir, they agreed to raise her as their own".

"And does anyone outside this household know that you are the mother of that child?"

She started to sob again. "No Sir".

"Good girl. And then we accepted you into our household, so that you could earn a wage to help your mother, and put a little by for yourself by way of a dowry to attract a husband of better calibre than the blackguard who left you in the first place." Daisy was nodding.

"There was one condition of your situation, one thing you had to remember above all. Do you remember what it was?"

"To not question the actions of my betters and to not share the goings on of the household with anyone, not my Ma, not my friends." This among wails and wiping of her now snotty nose with dirty handkerchief. With a wave of his hand, Angus had cook provide her with a fresh one from a drawer.

By now, aside from poor Daisy, everyone else was calm, because Angus had approached the entire situation with calm. A sort of dangerous calm. I kept waiting for the real subject. But I had to let Angus spin it out in his own time. My teeth were grinding in frustration.

"All right Daisy, now, calm yourself. I'm not going to hurt you, although Cook may have overreacted just a bit (flicking a glance at Cook). But you have obviously had conversations with other people about the way the family is treating the young boy", nodding toward me. "I would like to know every person that discussed this with you, and what they said. I want you to tell me everything you can remember. And you will sleep here at the house for a few days until I can iron this out and you feel better. "

Once again calm enough to speak, Daisy talked about an evening two nights ago at the ale house where she sometimes helped to pour beer.

Someone started a conversation about the orphan peasant boy who was being given much better treatment than his station merited. Several men in the village, and their womenfolk, knew that the boy was being trained as kennel master for when old Kin died. They felt it was a job above his station, better taken by one of their sons. (Absolutely correct, I thought.) But then the saddle maker spoke up about the boy learning to ride, a skill that was not allowed to any but the most ranking servants, except certain stable hands. And on the Laird's horse, no less!

There was a throat clearing, and we all realized that My Laird had come down into the kitchen during this exchange. His wife the Lady Mary was there as well. Our voices had carried up through the hall and to the family sleeping quarters above.

My Laird looked at his son and there was a silent understanding between them. I knew that the saddle maker would either be joining us here or joining someone somewhere else, and it wasn't going to be pretty. But why? Angus disappeared back upstairs, and momentarily he reappeared fully dressed only to leave out the kitchen door.

To Daisy, My Laird said "All right my dear girl, if anyone asks you about the boy from now on, you're to tell them you overheard me say that he was my son. I cannot acknowledge him publicly, and so I favour him against the day I may be able to own him. Do you think you can do that for me?"

She nodded energetically, of relief I thought. He hugged her, gave her another clean handkerchief and the Lady Mary came forward and ushered her upstairs.

I didn't realize it, but during this little meeting my arms had crept up to cross my chest. My Laird looked at me and smiled.

"You are not my father" I said. "I don't know how I know, but however kind you are to me, and I am sincerely grateful, you are not my father. This is the second story I have heard about my origins. What I want to know is, why is anyone taking notice of me? When I was a child, playing in the forest with the other children, no one cared. But now I am receiving special attention I do not understand, and its making me the subject of gossip. People are now feeling hostile toward me. What is it about me that makes this the path you have chosen for me? The story you and Faolan have told me does not justify what is happening here." I had spoken clearly and without tears, but I was feeling far more emotional than I let show.

My Laird sighed. He spread his fingers out across his lap to distract him while he sought the words to explain. The fingernails, to my surprise, were bitten to the quick. I had never noticed before.

"You know that your mother died giving life to you?" In response to him I nodded, in a way that I hoped would encourage him to go on. "What you do not know is how you were conceived."

"My Laird, I don't understand. I believe I was conceived in the way of most living things, like the pig, the cow, or the horse ". I didn't see how my conception affected the life I was to lead now.

Kin chuckled and touched my back. Cook groaned and rolled her eyes, "Laird he is too young", she said.

"Boy, some fourteen years ago, the King of England, Richard he was, made to visit across the narrow sea to the west. He fought battles in the south of the country, but during that time, he also made a journey to the north. He came to Dunluce and remained there for some days.   Your mother spent her days with the other ladies, doing needlework, spinning and the like. She and her husband also sang beautiful songs in the hall about tribal stories. Her voice was so beautiful. King Richard would have met your mother in the hall – it would not have been difficult for him to find her again in the sleeping quarters. He determined to take her to his bed, and for the good of the McDonnell family there she would have simply submitted. But she fought him for the love of her husband and out of pride for herself. In his heart he truly believed that his rank and position entitled him to anything he wanted and so when she resisted he reacted in anger, he beat her so badly he destroyed her face, so that she would nevermore be regarded a great beauty. And even as he impregnated her, he hurt her enough that she could not hope to deliver the child without much bleeding. We know not if a blade was used, or some other thing. A crone could have been found to dispose of the child, but your mother refused. The child she carried was an heir to the king, and well she knew that this could be a great boon to both Eire and Scotland. And so she sacrificed herself for you, and the hopeful future you represented, knowing that bringing you to life might mean the end of hers."

I was now audibly crying and holding my arms around my chest. This was the most awful thing I had ever heard, and it concerned my fate. My mother should have disposed of me, and I would have counselled it so had I been there. This was also the third story I had been told about my birth, and I tired of the different versions.

He continued. "After you were born we brought you here, raising you as an orphan child in order to escape the notice of anyone who might look to see. In order to protect your identity, we told you very little of your origins. And I moved you to the kennel to give you something to learn, a challenge, to let your own self shine through, and to see if you can handle the life you might lead. That would be a life of responsibility to others, much the way you feel responsible to the dogs and Kin. You have succeeded beyond our wildest dreams. Faolan came to see the boy you became, to assess whether you were ready for the changes to come. He thought if he moved you to Eire, we might have secrecy a little longer.   Seven years ago, the same English king was arrested and imprisoned. Dark words are spoken about how he died, whether it be murder or starvation. At the time we seriously considered making a claim for the throne on your behalf, but we judged that there would be too much peril for you and all of us who support you." His ice blue eyes begged a response.

"And I lived in ignorance all this time. Even of the King's death I knew nothing, even though I might have had to become his heir with no knowledge, and no preparation. And even now, reared as an orphan, I have no idea how to rule, I barely even have the skill to ride a horse. And I know I have no choice. "

My Laird had a way of listening that could be unnerving. He sat so silently, absorbing every word, never taking his eyes off me. He sat for a long time after I had finished speaking, intently regarding my tear stained face and sensing my emotions.

"I agree that the story is terrible and sad. Your mother's sacrifice, her husband's loss of her, and the deceit of the men who are caring for your welfare, all must seem grievous. Your mother did not just make the choice she did out of political ambition for you, she made it out of love. And I did not make the choices I have out of political ambition. I knew that if your existence became public you would be in utter peril. This is a game of Kings. If Henry of England knew of you he would send assassins to kill you, lest the crown revert to Richard's bloodline. And whatever his attempts to keep relations with England positive, King Robert of Scotland's Lieutenant could seize you for his own purposes. I am not a perfect man, and my judgement has often been called into question, but I have done what I did to give you the safety and joy of childhood for as long as I could, as well as trying to prepare you to think for yourself, and if the need arises, for a kingdom".

He rose from his seat, and came to sit beside me on the bench. He put his arm around me and pulled my frail boy's shoulders so that my head rested against his chest. I had never been so close to him. The softness of his chemise was like nothing I had ever felt. He hugged me close and rocked me back and forth as I cried, and I thought, this is what a father does. I forgave him all in that moment.

While we sat, I asked him quietly "Do I look like him?" He answered, "King Richard was a tall man with pale skin and dark hair. The boy I see before me favours his mother, with her auburn hair and blue eyes".

Angus had already returned with the Saddle maker in tow, and had left the man standing with a man at arms. He had listened to the last part of the narrative. He stood aside for a moment with me and My Laird. "Papa" he spoke low, for the first time using the word in my presence. "I have been hearing the boy's story in various versions all my life, but there is one thing that stretches credulity." My Laird turned his blue eyes on his son. "I have always heard it whispered that Richard II was a sodomite. How does such a man carry out such a terrible act if the love and softness of a woman do not excite him?"

My Laird sighed and somehow seemed to have aged so much in a mere second. "I am not sure', he ventured, "Richard was married to Anne of

Bohemia, and they say it was a love match. But he also had an unnaturally close relationship with Robert de Vere. When Anne died he was devastated, and she died without issue. De Vere became ever closer to him over time, a favourite over all others, and it was a matter of great resentment among the other powerful men, including Henry Bolingbrooke, now King Henry. Had Richard been more guarded in his affection for de Vere he might still be King.

"It seems de Vere was with him during the attack, and that both de Vere's presence and the violence were things he enjoyed. This enabled him to perform the act."

Angus and I both stood with our mouths agape. Aside from boys casting taunts at one another, I am not sure either one of us had ever heard anything like this before. Angus looked sick. I was thunderstruck, and destroyed. My mother. My poor beautiful mother.

"I am his son. Am I a sodomite too?" I whispered. But it wasn't just sodomy I was afraid of inheriting.

"Boy, you may or you may not be, but I think it matters not. There have been good and bad kings, good and bad men of all stripes. What made Richard II a bad man was not his relationships with other men, but his need to indulge his own desire and his own will above his duty and above what was best for his subjects. The world frowns on sodomites. I cannot claim a kinship to the way they live. But they are men, with the same responsibility and joy in the world that we all have. I have known very good, sincere and responsible men, who were secretly sodomites, some of them men of God. I suggest that if they are good men, then the morality of sodomy is between them and God. And it does not follow that because you are of his blood you will be as evil as he was. Who you are is as much a matter of choice as a matter of your blood inheritance. And regardless, I feel your mother's beauty of soul made up for anything you might have inherited from the King. Does this ease your heart Boy?"

I sighed and leaned against him again. I wasn't fully satisfied, and my mother's story would be with me the rest of my life.

After that night in the kitchen, my riding lessons continued with more intensity. I began to know the big beautiful stallion well, and the two of us together began to find a rhythm. The saddle, having been altered for me, made it all easier. A slight move on my part could cause Caesar to change which of his feet he led with. I could encourage him to speed up with slight pressure from my knees. I could spin him around by pushing a foot on his side. And tension in my body would rise tension in his, his proud head up, his ears erect. I fell in love with this feeling, and so fell in love with the horse. At least, in the saddle I did. When I was on the ground we had a respectful, formal relationship. That's the way he wanted it. I could almost hear him telling me this. Sometimes after working together for hours, we trotted down the path away from the castle, the one the travellers take, and then at a distance we would turn and run back home. And for those fleeting moments we forgot the nature of our relationship and shared the magic of flying.

With the riding came other lessons. My lady sat with me in the hall and taught me how to use a spoon and fork in a more dignified way than the "stoop and slurp". She acquainted me with the cloth I could use to wipe drips from my chin, discretely. Clothing more befitting a nobleman, even a bastard, was found for me. Tunics of finer wool than had ever touched my body, chemises of linen, pants of heavier linen. Belts both fine and heavy. I felt I was to be in some sort of mummery, these fine things could not possibly be mine.

Up until that point in my life, a bath consisted of a series of buckets of water and soap made in the kitchen beneath the hall. And they only took place in the summer. After one of my days riding and working in the kennel, I arrived in the kitchen to find a wooden tub there. It was lined with a kind of heavy linen, the kind used to catch water for drinking in the forest. Several large cauldrons of steaming water were dumped into it, along with a few buckets of cold to get the temperature just right to cause the dirt to scream off my body and leave behind nothing but pink skin. I was reluctant to bathe in front of Cook, but when she threatened with a rolling pin, I relented. The soap she gave me was much nicer than any I had before. It smelled as if lavender had been infused in it, and when I asked, I was told that it had.

And while I was naked, I was taught how to use a knitted cloth to give myself a sponge bath. This I was to do every night. I was told, in no uncertain terms, that nobles don't smell like dog shit. Horse shit, maybe, but not dog shit.

And finally, after I was squeezed out of this process to make me over from what I was into the noble I was to become, I was given a fine linen chemise with four leaf clovers embroidered around the neck and on the sleeves, a gift from Cook. She blushed when she gave it to me and her eyes swam with tears. I guess I wasn't the only one who was worried about this. I hugged her and thanked her for the beautiful gift.

Since I was now to be owned by the family, I was to commence sleeping upstairs in a sleeping area shared with Angus. I was pleased, as I had come to know and admire Angus well. Perhaps I should have reconsidered my admiration, as Angus could snore and moan as loud as a cow needing to be milked. In the year we were to sleep in this shared space, I learned to sleep through earth tremors, the villagers singing and arguing going to river (and more than once the sound of lovemaking on the river bank), and arguments in the hall downstairs. I had never heard these things sleeping in the kitchen.

There was a cost to Angus in this arrangement. With me there, he could not sneak women up the back stairs and into his bed. I was just at the right age to appreciate this, as I was developing my own interest in women. I wasn't bold enough to sneak them up the back stairs, and truthfully, I didn't have time. I fell into bed exhausted, and rarely had time during the day. So Angus and I developed a system. If the tassel which held the curtain was tied up, no problem. If it hung limp, go sleep in my old place in the kitchen.

My next set of lessons was in the use of weapons. I was given a broadsword in a scabbard that hung on a big belt around my hips, a bow and a quiver of arrows, and a dagger. These had belonged to the man I considered my real father, my Mother's husband. Angus gave me lessons in how to use my weapons, how to thrust, parry and stab. Some of the men at arms also would spar with me until my arms drooped and I could barely hold my sword. I shot bows into far away targets, until at least half of the time they landed. In the space of four months, working at the kennel with Kin (I insisted), riding Caesar every day, sparring, shooting arrows at targets (some moving) , by Easter that spring I was strong, nimble, and could hold my own in the hall with the rest of the family. I still felt like fraud, whatever was in my blood. It was like contraband I carried next to my chest.

With all of the exercise I was now getting, and the work I still did with Kin, and the fact that much of my growth into manhood was now virtually complete, my shoulders broadened, and the beard almost appeared on my face. I was taller now than Angus, and could boast a strong arm and a solid fist. When I went into the village, I knew that none dared challenge me. And as the gossip that I was My Laird's bastard son had now spread, there were few angry glances any more. As the bastard son of a noble, I would not exactly be a unique character in Scotland at the turn of the fifteenth century.

One cloudy afternoon, someone came and told me to report to the kennel. I was busy with Caesar and not due at the kennel until afternoon, but something about the message got my attention. When I got there, My Laird and Kin were already waiting. They had brought Bearnas out on the grass. Her belly was distended and she was obviously in great pain. I dropped to my knees beside her, touching her face. She licked my fingers, but her eyes were glassy, and she was drooling. Kin explained that as they aged, the great dogs were more likely to suffer from intestinal torsion where the stomach spun on itself. What I was seeing were the symptoms. The words "but she isn't old" dropped from my lips, but even before they were out of my mouth, I knew the truth of it. Bearnas was in agony. And the two men looking at me, my father figures, I knew what they wanted from me. I pulled my dagger from my belt and kissing her and holding her, drew its sharp blade across her throat. I stayed with her there for a long time, until the men came for her. My Laird explained that he saw to it that his dogs were never disposed of on the midden heap. The two men were there to bury her. With the muscles I had developed I picked up her body heavy as a grown woman and carried her to the spot they indicated, and I took the shovel myself and dug her grave. Once she was laid in the hole, and the dirt covered her, I sat beside her and rocked back and forth. The loss of Bearnas opened a place where I had been hiding my grief. The sadness about my mother; the gratitude for what My Laird had done to protect me and to furnish me with the skills and belongings I would need in the world; absolute fury at the English King, Richard II, who thought his rank gave him the right to destroy my mother before her life had really begun. I curled in a ball and cried, loudly, so everyone could hear me, and I didn't care.

After that I knew I was leaving. Maybe not tomorrow, maybe not next week, but I was leaving. I had to face the world and find my place in it. And I wasn't going to let anyone push me into challenging for the English throne. It just wasn't where I was meant to be.

It was about another three months before Faolan returned. I am sure My Laird apprised him of all that had occurred in his absence. He openly talked of the Scottish Crown and how the Lieutenant to the King had flatly turned him down when he asked for support to challenge England. He had hidden my location, lest the lieutenant send assassins. He cursed the Lieutenant and said that Richard III of Scotland would have supported me in the old days but now he was a doddering man, placing the business of kingship in the hands of clerks and servants. The whole family was sitting at the eating table, and after a long time, I quietly put my eating utensils down, accidentally making the spoon clatter on the table. My Laird nudged Faolan, who stopped talking. My Laird pointed at me, and I realized that his hands had become dry and fragile, with dark spots on them. How had I not realized how old he was? Both men looked expectantly toward me.

"I am not a king. I'm not going to be a king. I want to go to Dunluce to meet my other family." Faolan's lips formed the word "but", but he never cobbled together a sentence. My Laird looked surprised, but proud too. He knew this was my first real step into myself.

Much talk followed, including that wonderful afternoon with my Laird in the sun, but the conclusion was that Faolan and I would leave two days hence, and Angus would accompany us to the Isles. He would carry messages there, and it would allow us time to spend together. We were not brothers, nor had we ever been brothers before, but we had become brothers and I knew that we now had a link that would never sever.

The day we left, Kin appeared as we were readying, with a little bundle in his arms. A puppy, one of Bearnas' grand puppies. This was truly a grand gift, of great value to one of my Laird's noble customers. He and Kin both had tears in their eyes as Kin handed her to me. I might have had tears in mine too. I allowed Caesar to sniff her, to know that he would carry her along with me. He sniffed and blew air out his nose, and the hair on her head lifted.

My parting from the people who had become my family was almost enough to make me take Caesar back to the barn and resume my duties in the kennel with Kin. But I didn't. I hugged them all, even Lady Mary, and Cook. Kin and My Laird were standing together when I came to them. I held My Laird's hand and looked back and forth at him and Kin. "Thank you", I said. "Thank you for doing what you thought was best, and thank you for teaching me and providing for me. Thank you for setting such a high example for me. I love you both". Finally, when Angus and Faolan were waiting for me on their mounts, I swung myself up onto Caesar's back, and held my beautiful little puppy, and turned toward the road for the Isles.

Riding Anyway

I woke in the morning and my eyes were hurting, burning from the sun I could see through my eyelids. [5] But my headache, and the pain in my arms and legs was mostly gone. I opened my eyes and found the curtains around my bed drawn back, and the window shutters were opened. I felt well enough to try getting up, so that Meg did not have to bring me the pot. I knew I had been ill but I didn't remember much about it. I sat up in bed and made to swing my left leg out and down to the floor. Except that it didn't quite follow the instructions the rest of my body was sending it. Confused, I looked down at it and beheld that it was not as I remembered it. It was skinnier than I remembered from the knee down.

The door to the chamber opened, and Meg, upon seeing me attempting to get up, called "Mrs. McGuigan! She's up!"

Mrs. McGuigan was a relative to my father, a cousin of some sort, and she had helped run the affairs of our household with my mother since I could remember. She bustled into my chamber, pushing Meg aside, and behind her came my mother, who also being Mrs. McGuigan, was generally referred to by non-family members as Madam. All three

---

[5] https://www.mayoclinic.org/diseases-conditions/polio/symptoms-causes/syc-20376512

women charged to my bedside at once and in their earnest desire to help me so interfered with one another that I pushed them away, and then signalled Meg and just Meg to put her arm under mine and around my back so that I could slide across the feather tick to the side of the bed and slide down to the flagstone floor. Once my feet hit the cold stone, she helped me arrange my left foot so that it could bear my weight.

I gently pushed Meg away and then stood looking at them all. "Who took my foot?" I said to no one in particular.

Had my question been interpreted as insolence it would normally earn me a swift slap to the side of the head, but since I had slumped to the floor by the time any hand could reach me, Mother, Mrs. McGuigan and Meg all worked together to get me back up on the bed, change my nightgown, bathe me, and clean up a wet spot on the floor. I couldn't make sense of that, couldn't figure where the puddle had come from. I was suddenly extremely tired again. Mother brought me a bowl of broth from the cauldron downstairs and fed it to me. It tasted really good, and I felt stronger after I ate it. Just when I was beginning to doze off, Father entered the room. He rarely entered any bed chamber besides his own, but it soon became evident from the quiet conversations around me that he had been here beside me for multiple nights, holding my hand and praying with the priest. I cried when I saw him. He had left his duties at the castle where he helped to run the Earl of Desmond's estates to come tend to me. When I asked him in a whisper how he had been free to do so, he told me that all the Earls in Ireland could not keep him away from me, the eldest child he thought lost for ever.

Within a week I was sitting beneath the willow tree just near our home and enjoying the fresh air. The surgeon Father had consulted and the crone Mrs. McGuigan had consulted both advised that fresh air and shade on a sunny day would be beneficial. Apparently three other children had fallen ill on the same day as myself, two dying of the fever and one recovering as I had done. The four of us had been together on that last day, fishing for tadpoles to use as bait. We had been using a net made from very fine fabric sewn to a frame that our local blacksmith had put together out of drawn wire. We stood in the pool in bare feet, impervious to blooms of algae and dirty water. I suppose that was the very last day of my childhood, coming home as I did, refusing supper and collapsing into my bed. That was the last day I remembered, but Meg told me in bits over time that I had entered such a deep sleep that I rarely roused, and I was so hot to the touch that the adults all feared I had brain fever and would die. As time went on both the surgeon and the crone, working together, puzzled out the nature of the ailment. The simultaneous illness of the other children, my occasional moments of wakefulness (I didn't remember those) allowed them to expect some paralysis when I woke up and watching my limbs over the period of my illness allowed them to predict the extent of it. The fact that these two healers worked together was, I thought, an indication of both their regard for my family, especially since crones were officially banned by the church and had to be careful not to offend anyone, or to be seen by any of the clergy. These women worked only in the shadows, using age old wisdom to fill in the blanks left by the medicine sanctioned by the Church.

My father's position with the Earl of Desmond at Lismore Castle certainly earned him regard in our neighbourhood. He was a calm voice and a steady hand, exactly the sort of man the Earl required to keep his estates in order and his staff with their eyes on the aims of the Earl. My father was the sort of man that other men respected. He was good looking with thick brown hair, and solidly built.

Before my father had ever taken employment with the Earl, however, he held some status of his own. My great grandfather had come from the north of Ireland, in the neighbourhood of Dunluce in Antrim, but in my grandfather's time, the family had moved south to Lismore. Before the family left the north, my great grandfather had begun to breed beautiful white horses. The original horse had been a gift from a Scottish Chieftain, and this ancient equine had passed along his white colour and kingly bearing to many generations. The skill of choosing which mare to cross to which sire to perpetuate the white coat had been passed down by the men who made breeding choices for over a hundred years. Painstakingly taught by each father to each son, the family lore and the stunning breed of horse which my father sold all over Ireland was our family's treasure and the stuff of our reputation. As my father had no sons, much of this lore had passed to a nephew and to me.

I sat quietly under the tree, dreading the return of Meg and Paddy, who would bring the litter to take me back into the house. But while no litter came, I watched the children of the village playing on the grass under the big oak in the distance with my younger siblings, three girls. The oak was on the far side of our pastures, off to the west. The childrens' play showed that they were still adjusting to the loss of their playmates, me among the rest. In order to see them I had to look over the backs of some thirty white horses on the flat just below me. One of them was a stallion and the others were mares in various stages of the breeding cycle.

While I watched, a man on horseback appeared at the gate in the wall on the far side of this large field. He entered the gate and closed it behind him and then remounted and progressed on the margin of the field toward the house. His horse was huge, maybe 17 hands or more, and black. On his saddle , I could see that decorating the leather were studs of silver, highly polished but not ornate. The overall effect was simple, but perfect. Even when far away, I saw the sun glinting on the silver.

The man himself appeared to be very tall. He was dressed, like his horse, simply but with great taste. His hair was dark and simply pulled back from his face, too long for the style of the time. He was of fine colour and his full beard emphasized the contrast between his hair and his skin. He did not wear a doublet, but a sort of over tunic in wool. An older style of dress, it was elegant as the rest of his clothing. His tunic was the only part of the ensemble that had colour. It was the colour of raspberry and bore embroidery around the sleeves and the hem.

As I observed the gentleman, he and his remarkable steed arrived at the front of the house. My mother had emerged from the front door and bobbed her head several times. Perhaps this was the Earl of Desmond then, as she seemed to have met him before. [6]

The man, now dismounted, and mother walked toward me. The horse was led by the gentleman with Paddy behind to take over at the right time. The horse was the one of the group who interested me the most.

When the three of them reached me, Mother spoke. "Your Lordship, this is my eldest daughter, recently recovering from a terrible fever". He took my hand and kissed it. Well that was new. Nobody had ever done that before. "My Lord, how kind of you to come visit me", I said with one eye on my mother, checking for that little tic around her left eye that meant I had said the wrong thing. No tic. Oh good.

"Well young lady" he said, smiling at me. "I am thrilled to see you looking so well after your recent illness". I smiled back, broadly, and watched that tic

---

[6]

https://en.wikipedia.org/wiki/Maurice_FitzGerald,_9th_Earl_of_Desmond

twitching away merrily. I should have glanced down and smiled with my mouth closed. Bah.

"My lord, I am fascinated by your horse. Used as I am to the white horses of my family, his beauty is particularly striking to me". Now I thought my mother would go into a full body twitch, because she had long taught me that all conversations should be led by the gentleman, and that I should be demure and passive at all times.

He smiled broadly (he had excellent teeth) and said "do you like him? He came from Burgundy. I'm quite taken with him myself. Perhaps when you are better we can go riding together and you can see him in action."

"I would like that very much your lordship. "

With a flick of his hand his Lordship had Paddy move the beautiful animal close to where I sat. I put my hand up and allowed him to sniff. I stroked his face, rubbed his chin. He was spotlessly clean and as soft as ermine. His mane and forelock were tightly braided. I would have let them fly free.

After the Earl and his exceptional horse left, Mother went on for some time about my forwardness and how it would drive the Earl away. Or that it would attract him inappropriately. She talked while I sat under the tree, she talked while Meg and Paddy carried me inside, and she talked all through supper, for which Father was not present. And then she talked as Meg helped me up the stairs to bed. I was quite amazed. I asked Meg what could possibly justify the extremity of her reaction. It was a few casual sentences with a neighbour, albeit an august one. What could he possibly see in me, a girl who was crippled and who had only just started bleeding in the last year?

Meg looked at the floor and made nondescript responses. As she busied herself around my chamber, fussing about bed curtains and dirty clothes, she continued to avoid my gaze.

Something was definitely afoot.

Over time, I was gradually encouraged to walk on my own legs, placing my feet carefully to overcome the numbness in my lower left leg. It took months, but I got so that I could walk as well as anyone, even though it looked kind of wobbly. I didn't run much, but Mother assured me that no fine lady ever ran anyway.

Mother had a new wardrobe of gowns made for me out of rich dark reds and yellows, and rusts, with touches of black velvet that was worth more than the whole rest of each dress it touched. I had never cared about gowns before, but I loved these dresses, their textures and their shapes. What I loved the most was the way they looked on me. The undergarments and the shape of the dresses pushed my breasts high and hinted at full hips under the skirts. The colours Mother had chosen played beautifully on my auburn hair. I was nothing much to look at, even in my youth, but Mother's skill played on my strengths and produced an image in the polished metal mirror that at least was passably pretty.

I wasn't stupid. I had been prepared for this process for years and as it developed I began to understand my mother's reactions that day months ago with the Earl of Desmond. All her fussing truly wasn't for nothing. For women in the fifteenth and sixteenth centuries making a good marriage was critical. The more demurely you behaved, the prettier you were, and how well you were able to make do with less, even for a rich man, all determined how well you lived out your life. Your individualism, your independence, this you worked out by how you ran your home, not by how you ran your man. And you had better be good at it, if you wanted contentment.

I spent weeks learning how to get my paralyzed lower leg in and out of a carriage with delicacy. I endured endless hours watching Mrs. McGuigan managing the kitchen and the activities of the household with my mother, and was passed some small responsibilities of my own. My three younger sisters were part of that responsibility. I both cursed them and loved them, but I saw to it they were well cared for, clean, and obeyed their tutors.

And then it was time for me to choose a horse that would be my own and I would take with me no matter who I married. This was a tradition of my family and not a dowry, but a deeply personal gift. Both my parents fussed over this process, sure that I would fall when I rode. But I insisted. My siblings would all select a mount and every lady of quality could ride and so should I.

I chose not a white horse (my father called them greys), but a bay. This pleased Father, as the bay was worth far less than any of the white ones (that only stung a bit). Funny how people are colour blind when it comes to horses. He wasn't large, but plenty large for me. He had ample mane and tail, and he was well muscled. Best of all he was steady and quiet, and I hoped my odd way of mounting with my paralyzed foot would not spook him. I called him Cian[7] and began forming a relationship right away.

Much to Mother's horror, I insisted on tending to Cian myself. I gave him hay, a little bit of oats, clean, cool but not cold water. I kept him away from other people and horses so that his only source of food, water and love would be me. And love him I did. And Mother and Mrs. McGuigan cursed the horse shit on the hems of the simple kirtles I wore in the barn, even though they were several inches shorter than my regular gowns.

When the day finally came to try riding him, Paddy brought a block for me to stand on, and I stood on it beside Cian, with my hands on the saddle for a long time. I was waiting to be absolutely calm, so that when my body felt strange to him, he would simply accept that all was well and await my commands. I made everyone but Paddy go away, because I didn't want him to sense their anxiety.

As I stood there, Paddy said 'Don't worry Miss, there's nothing to be afraid of. You've prepared

---

[7] Sean or Shaun

him well. He won't fail you.' I loved him for that. I wasn't afraid, but his support when everyone else had been so negative meant a lot. I turned and saw them all watching me through the leaded glass. Wouldn't have surprised me a bit if they had a priest in the house leading them in prayer for my safety.

'Now or never Paddy' and I carefully fitted my foot into the twisted left stirrup at an angle away from Cian's body. When I put my weight on it, the stirrup spun back to its regular position and propelled my lifted right leg over Cian's body. I landed my weight onto the saddle and fit my right foot into the right stirrup. And then I sat down. Cian didn't react. His ears indicated that he was very interested in the proceedings, but otherwise I was quite safe. I petted his neck and cooed at him, delighted.

Over the next few weeks I worked with Cian some every day, and I sat on him a few times through the day. Each time his ears swivelled in my direction, but he stood quietly, probably wondering what on earth I was thinking. Are you going to ride me or just have a statue made?

And the fateful day came. I didn't just sit on him. I pressed in with my knees and gave him a little kick with my right foot. Well, maybe more of a nudge, an urging. And he began to walk within the small enclosure. We walked around several times, criss-crossing, circling, and backing up. We were ready.

The next day Father and Paddy rode out with me. Well, Father rode and Paddy drove the big mare and the farm wagon, in case they had to bring in my lifeless body back when I was thrown. Father and I were both rather relieved when I wasn't thrown, and we were even able to ride at a canter for a while. Eventually Paddy and the mare went home, and Father and I took our time riding behind him, laughing to one another about how MOTHER had thought I would die with 'That HORSE'. I didn't point out that he had been just as afraid as Mother. And when he looked at me with tears in his eyes and told me how proud he was of my determination and my methodical work with Cian, I had tears too, and I was grateful.

A few days later, while preparing to go out again with Cian, and humming as I did, I turned to pull the blanket off the rail, and there was the Earl again. He was immaculate as before, this time with a rust brown tunic. He was smiling at having caught me in a relaxed moment.

'I'm sorry, I should have told you I was here, but you look rather nice working away there. That's a nice mount you have chosen. He isn't white. '

Now, it was one of mother's great frustrations that she could not, could not, teach me to be demure around gentlemen, even after all her months of work with me. Couldn't look down and blush, couldn't smile without showing my teeth, which were quite good I daresay.

I didn't answer the Earl's question, but instead said "I believe you owe me a ride my Lord" with a broad smile. "But I also believe I am not appropriately dressed for the company of a gentleman. And my mother would be greatly relieved if you would apply to her for the company of Cian and myself on a day that suits you". I grinned and said "this would improve my existence with her in that quarter". The Earl smiled broadly, nodded his head toward me, and moved off toward the house.

I was returning to the blanket for Cian, when Meg came from the house at a run, with Paddy following. By order of my mother, I was to return to the house immediately and don my rust coloured Burgundian gown, with the pink under gown, as I was to ride with the Earl of Desmond. I snickered, and returned to the house.

Mother fussed as she and Mrs. McGuigan dressed me, pulled my breasts into position so that an onlooker had a hint of their presence – "Your tits are one of your few virtues dear"-pulled the layers of skirts into place so they didn't bunch up. Mrs. McGuigan braided and tied up my hair, fixing it in place with combs. I drew the line at the hennin with its fussiness, and its absolute refusal to sit still with layers of silk veil that got sat on, fussed over and caught in everything. Mother muttered that she wasn't sure about the Earl courting me in such a way, that she wasn't sure of his intentions, she didn't like this one bit. We said nothing, but Meg and I exchanged glances.

I returned outside to find Cian brushed, again, saddled, but with his mane and tail loose as I liked them. He looked glorious. Nearby were the Earl and his beautiful black horse. He invited me to come and inspect the horse. The Earl told me about him as I ran my hands over his muscles, inspected the crest of his neck.

"These horses were originally bred in Friesland. But I found him from a man I know in Burgundy. He has enthusiastically taken up breeding them. You notice he is sturdy enough to carry an armed knight but light enough to be a pleasant riding horse. I have found his temperament to be extremely compatible with my own." I nodded as he spoke, taking in the nostrils, the ears and the wise eyes. I saw small scars barely visible on his shoulders and his flank, but I did not comment. Unfortunately there were many men, even those who professed to know much about horses, who did not possess the skill or the love for the animal to train it without pain or fear. The only man I knew who could do so was my father, and I worked to emulate his almost magic ability with horses every time I came into contact with anything from a dray horse to a riding horse to an ass.

I stepped back from the horse and asked "Does he have a name?"

"His name is Dante, after the author of an Italian poem I have been reading".[8]

My mother could see me getting ready to talk about the Inferno, the same poem I had been reading obsessively during my convalescence, struggling through one Latin one word at a time. Mother

---

[8] https://en.wikipedia.org/wiki/Inferno_(Dante)

swore no nice young woman should read such a terrible poem, so full of frightening and unpleasant images. As it was she felt we should hide that we were taught to read. But Father allowed it, insisting that all education could be good education with the right guidance. As I took a breath to respond to the Earl, I saw Mother nodding frantically NO over his shoulder. I saw the logic in her objection and so did not speak. No man wants to think a woman as clever as he, as worldly as he.

I looked at him and said brightly "Shall we?"

Paddy brought my stool and I could feel my face hot with the shame of having to use it. But use it I did, and shortly I was mounted and ready to go. As we rode off, I could see Mother wringing her hands, and a worried not altogether pleasant look on her face. I wished Father were there. I resolved to ask him for his counsel the next time I saw him.

We crossed the fields to the common road, and turned toward the village of Lismore. We talked as we rode, of inconsequential but pleasant things. He told me of his travels, and his properties, how Lismore Castle was one of the estates owned by his family, but not the family seat. He talked of how his tenants raised cattle, sheep, pigs and goats. They grew grain, corn, and a variety of vegetables. I realized that he was listing these things for my approval, so I nodded periodically and provided verbal approval where it seemed to make sense. I really didn't care about his estates. I wanted to know about himself and his pursuits.

"Do you have men at arms my Lord?" I asked this purely to shift him to a new topic.

"Yes, enough that I can mount an army, if I wish. I currently am working on a campaign that I hope will improve the situation of those in my demesne. I think that this will take a very many men". I concentrated on Cian's mane and tried not to show my reaction to this assertion. Oh yes, I needed to talk to Father.

Why did he feel the need to brag to me in this way? I was a gentleman's daughter and of good name, but he was an Earl. I could not help but be impressed with his estates and his men at arms. I was annoyed.

For the remainder of the ride, we talked horses and dogs. It was a topic we found we both enjoyed. We both loved big horses, and neither was concerned about colour, both of us content to see beauty in all that nature provided. I told him how I loved big hunting dogs, and that I had some skill in taming them for the house. He told me about his kennel of dogs, and how many of each kind. He told me of hounds he had seen in Burgundy, with long ears and low bodies. He had found them deeply comical, but gifted with a nose that was incomparable. I found this interesting. The hunting dogs I was familiar with stood almost to my face and had ears that stood upright.

When we arrived back at the stable, both of my parents were waiting. They both saw the look on my face, but did not comment until after the Earl had entered our small hall and been given refreshment before heading home. The last thing he said before leaving was to Father. "You were absolutely right McGuigan. She is a cracking girl!" Mother and I turned to look at him, our mouths open, our eyes all astonishment.

The ensuing row between Mother and Father was Epic. I sat, quietly horrified as they fought. Mother said things I had never heard before, that his first wife Ellen had died under suspicious circumstances. That he was known to have an incredibly foul temper and was unyielding and unforgiving of family and staff. That he was given to emotional extremes and was inconsistent in his decisions. Father countered that Ellen had died of a dead baby in her womb, and that he was confident in my ability to sway a man to my way of thinking. That he was mostly away from Lismore. But he didn't look at either of us when he said it.

He spoke quietly then. "She is a pleasant young woman of a good family. She has a physical limitation, and a not particularly attractive face. When the Earl told me that he hoped to yet have another son to protect his bloodline and asked about my daughters, I did not feel I could turn him away given our relative positions, and given the unlikelihood that another suitor would present himself".

"And so you betrayed me. You sold me like a horse."

I rose and slowly mounted the stairs with my physical limitation and my not attractive face and went to bed. Later, when the whole house was quiet, Mother crept to my bed and climbed in with me. She held me and cried. And I knew there was nothing I could do.

Father was gone to Lismore Castle in the morning when I rose. I thought grimly that he and the Earl were toiling away on the plan of insurrection against me. As soon as I had eaten I went out and took Cian for and unsanctioned ride all by myself. Paddy looked dubious as I rode off, but I wasn't in the mood to placate anyone, not even a dedicated and adored household servant who had no axe to grind. I took him out a good ways from home, turned him back the way we had come and gave him his head. He flew with me on his back the whole way home, as if sensing I needed to feel the wind in my hair.

When Father came home in the afternoon, he bore a message with a wax seal addressed to me.

Miss McGuigan

> *I have secured permission from your father for you and your Mother that you may attend Lismore Castle tomorrow for a tour and refreshments. Your father is arranging for your man servant to bring you in appropriate conveyance, for your Mother's comfort. Please plan to arrive around the hour of noon to allow you to see Lismore's gardens at their most attractive.*

> *Maurice Fitzgerald*
> *9th Earl of Desmond*

I glared at my Father. "Why must you persist in this?"

He looked at me steadily and replied "And what would be the result if I refused? The Earl can have any bride he chooses, have her kidnapped, have her killed if he chooses. What would happen to this family if I told him that my daughter does not want him? Would he not be incensed that the daughter of a lesser gentleman who would otherwise become a spinster should turn away his interest and his generosity? I would certainly lose my employment with him, which feeds our family, a feat not currently accomplished through horse sales. If he were truly piqued, perhaps he would prevent the sale of our horses, or perhaps have the entire herd poisoned, a life's work lost. And the law could not touch him, he being the magistrate in effect for the county. I do not suggest that he WOULD do this, but merely what considerations might be in just such a situation. Please remember that the Earls of Desmond are a lesser branch of the Fitzgerald family, whose power in Ireland are second only to the Church. I suggest that you might consider the effect of your prejudices on the rest of us before you indulge them. This marriage could be very good for your family. And very bad if it does not come to pass."

I was speechless. I had not considered the thing from this perspective. I felt a bit like I had been punched in the gut, and my stomach hurt. I picked up my walking stick and walked out the back door. I spent the rest of the day with the horses, rubbing their foreheads and reclining against their bodies as they slept. I had known these beautiful souls since my birth, and theirs, and I accepted their comfort and their wisdom.

The next day dawned sunny and glorious, but not too warm. Mother laid out a deep red kirtle and a deep blue cotehardie in silk velvet brocade. This time I didn't have a choice about the hennin, in the same blue as the cotehardie with a veil so white I could not imagine how it became so. Meg set my hair in a bun at the nape of my neck. When the hennin was set on my head, the pins to keep it in place cut into my scalp.

I was allowed some dry toast before we set off, the only food I could have that would not stain my clothing. We climbed into the wagon, a sort of litter affair but with horses. I didn't know we owned it, until I realized a new body had been set on to a wagon we already owned. Two white stallions drew it, with Paddy as their driver. Their names were Roman and Caesar. I knew them well. Paddy wore a heraldic tunic that I did not know he owned, half yellow and half green. The McGuigan family crest that I had never seen before was embroidered on the left shoulder and a gorgeous white horse pranced across his right shoulder. There was a tiny piece of tartan at the top of one shoulder. Then when father appeared out doors and nodded his approval I realized that Mother and Mrs. McGuigan had stayed up all night producing it.

Our home was north of Lismore, toward Carrignagower West. The road to the castle ran through a dell southward that came out on the Blackwater River, with the castle being on the far bank. The trip usually took about an hour, assuming there was no problem with the road. Coming across the bridge we saw the castle at its very best advantage, a Norman style castle with its brave towers and strong walls, pennants flying in the breeze. As we came around the gate, we saw the gardens. There were crops of fruit trees, corn, nuts, and the most exquisitely perfumed flowers. Waiting for us was his Lordship and his household staff. As we dismounted he held our hands and assisted with our skirts until we were safely on the ground. I grudgingly admitted to myself that his manners were delightful and the castle and its grounds were like a latter day Garden of Eden. It irked me to have to do it.

We were standing on flagstones, and a small step took us up to the main gate. An older woman stood there, perhaps in her 50's. Her hair was fiercely drawn back under a St Brigid's cap. Her dress was of a dark brown, and when I looked at it carefully, I realized it was very fine undyed wool from dark brown sheep. She wore an apron gathered across her chest. She might once have been pretty, but now she had a habitual look that suggested she always expected the worst to happen. The Earl introduced her as Mary, and I wondered what her last name had been, and where she had come from.

The Earl's steward was next. Like Mary, he was older, and he wore a brown tunic very like her dress and made also of undyed wool. He wore a leather apron, and he had apparently come from the garden to meet me. His name was Tom, and his surname that he had apparently been allowed to keep was Butler.[9] He would have worked directly with my father, who was not here, presumably regaining his sleep from the nights work. Glancing at Paddy, who showed no sign of exhaustion, I turned back to the staff.

I met a group of serving girls, none of whom met my eye but two of them giggled softly. A small group of men whose roles were apparently unspecific and who worked for Tom, shuffled past, stiffly bowing as they did.

---

[9] Fitzgerald and Butler families were sworn enemies. Tom was probably captured in a much earlier raid and came to live with the family.

"You had asked me about my men at arms, and so I arranged for you to meet some. Allow me to introduce (pointing at the first) James of Portsmouth, (the second) Francis of Tipperary, (Third) Jean of Agincourt, and Archibald who only admits to being vaguely Scottish". Archibald rested his elbow on the wagon beside which he was standing. As if the proceedings had been deeply interesting and he was resting his body so he could concentrate fully on the conversation. The men chuckled, and Francis slapped Archibald on the back. He had blushed full red but was smiling at the Earl. There was history between these two. Archibald had light blond hair and wore a full beard as they all did. I immediately noticed his blue eyes, and as he resisted the shoving and back slapping of the others, I saw that his fingernails were bitten so short they almost were invisible. All of the men wore tunics of linen or wool with gambesons cut down for every day wear, and all of them had weapons of the sort a man would use in close combat, knives tucked into boots and belts. They all wore scars on their forearms, their faces, even their necks. No doubt they bore more grievous marks that were hidden by their clothing.

A small hound dog just bigger than a house cat had been running around us the whole time. This was the Earl's dog, casually called Digger. I felt Mother freeze when I bent down to him and petted him when he ran to me.

The Earl, dressed for the first time in a raspberry doublet and black hose, gestured for me to lead the way into the castle, or the house, as he called it. A heavy wooden gate with wrought iron curls stood open, inviting entry and intimidating the guest all the same. Through the gate was an inner courtyard, large enough to muster about than 200 men and their horses, or so I thought with my inexperienced eye. The castle walls that surrounded the square had slits for archers to shoot out at unfriendly guests. At various spots were stairs that allowed defenders to rise to the top of the wall, gaining an advantage over attackers below. Across the square diagonally was another set of heavy oak doors with wrought iron hardware. As we walked, the Earl explained that there were more than 30 rooms, including two halls, two rooms used as private day rooms, a kitchen with two fireplaces, and a larder. From the inside, there seemed to be windows everywhere, angled in such a way to prevent incursion of arms or men. Inside each window, heavy shutters on either side could be closed to protect the room within. To the north, the castle overlooked the Blackwater River and the view from almost all of the windows was spectacular. As we walked down the upstairs hallway, each room proved to be beautiful and light, despite the presence of stone and dark wood. Large canopy beds had rich trappings, and the rooms all had chests and chairs. The Earl told us about the building as we walked. It was over four hundred years old, and had passed into Fitzgerald hands some two hundred years past. It had been occupied as an abbey and later as the bishopric.

"Any spirits?" I asked with a smile. He responded with a soft laugh. "Of course. Don't all the *good* houses?" I could feel Mother's eyes boring between my shoulder blades.

We stopped in one of the halls for bread, excellent cheese and pickled fish. The food was very good. I made sure to tell Mary, who had joined us, to compliment her excellent cooking. She bowed, and looked surprised.

On the west side of the house were more buildings which proved to be lodgings for the men at arms and some of the servants, and storage for equipment, wagon and litters. A reinforced curtain wall protected the area from attack. The stable was at one side of this area, and there was Dante and several other very good quality and beautifully cared for horses. I patted Dante's nose on the way by, and he knew me. There was a kennel to one side of the stable, and it held a variety of hounds in different sizes. The Earl and I had a conversation about the dogs, especially the big wolf hunting hounds. He found them intimidating, but I found them challenging and rewarding.

Throughout our time at the castle, my misgivings had been pressing on me. I felt I had finally to speak.

"Sir, I have some questions to pose of you". He was only a little surprised at my forwardness. Mother, of course, would soon be foaming at the mouth and rolling on the ground. He nodded for me to continue.

"Your home is beyond anything I could otherwise hope for, your taste in horses is exquisite, and your staff appear capable. If you wished for me to approve the tour of your home, you have it. But I know nothing of you yourself, I have no idea why you seek the company of a gently bred but somewhat disadvantaged and very young woman. Please mother, stop. (Mother had made a choking sound). I have heard disturbing rumours of your first wife and her death, and wonder if I might have a similar fate. What is it that makes you interested in me?"

The Earl paused to hand smelling salts to my Mother while his staff sat her on a bench as she had suddenly and inexplicably swooned, and then gestured me to another bench, overlooking the garden. He waved the others to stand back.

"My wife Ellen and I married when we were both very young. We learned about estates and responsibilities together. She gave me two sons, one of whom has now died. James, who will become the tenth Earl is twelve, and is in Kinsale, acting on my behalf as I am rebuilding a tower castle in the name of my birthright, Desmond. Ellen was carrying a third child, a girl, when the child died in her womb and in turn poisoned her. I may never recover from the loss, but I am impressed by the importance of having more children in case something happens to James.

"I have business interests throughout England, Ireland and in Burgundy, as you no doubt suspected. Your father assists me to manage those business interests. I am away from home a great deal of the time. My servants manage the castle and its lands in my absence but they occasionally require a unifying authority. I hope that a strong wife might supply that unifying authority.

"And as for you, the young disadvantaged woman, that is not what I see in you. I see a young woman who beat swamp fever and therefore must have a very strong constitution. I see an extremely intelligent young woman, one not afraid to speak her mind, much to your poor mother's chagrin. I saw your face when I told you about how I named Dante. Someday I hope we can discuss Dante's Inferno and its meanings. You are not typically beautiful but you are very attractive to me. You would be a strong partner to me in my business and family dealings.

"Have I answered your questions to your satisfaction?" he finished.

I began slowly, "My Lord, I am so sorry if I have caused offense. Sometimes I am far too forward. I--".

"You have not caused offense", and seeing that my mother was now facing the other way, no doubt smelling the salts, he leaned over and kissed me. At least, I thought it was a kiss. It was soft and wonderful and involved lips and tongue, it made me very warm and damp under all my layers of clothing, and I wanted him to do it again. But the others were now moving to rejoin us, and he rose, with his hand under my arm causing me to rise too.

"It is time for me to return to the affairs of my estates. I wish so much I could linger longer", he said quietly.

"Mrs. McGuigan, thank you so much for bringing your wonderful daughter to my home. Do not distress over her directness. I prefer it to false modesty. I am delighted to have both of you here. Sadly, I ride tomorrow to transact business in Waterford. I must see to my preparations, and I see your husband is awaiting my attention" (a glance to my right and there was Father no longer at home but returned to work, nodding no, discouraging me from addressing him). Tom is bringing your horses and your vehicle, and your servant Paddy is coming from the kitchen where he has been given refreshment. If there is anything else I can do to ensure you a comfortable journey home, please name it and I will be delighted to oblige".

After the requisite curtsies and bows, he moved off to talk to Father as we boarded the wagon and made ourselves comfortable for the journey home. Father did approach us briefly, just long enough to say he would see us at home. The Earl smiled and waved as Paddy urged the horses into movement.

Huh. I certainly had a more complete view of Maurice Fitzgerald the 9th Earl of Desmond. I thought dreamily that I could be the mistress of that gorgeous castle, managing Mary and her team of young girls. There would certainly be room for Cian in the elegantly appointed stables. And surely there would be children. I thought of little ones running through the castle, playing with little wooden swords and dolls. But I forced myself to go back to our horse ride on our own. I had found him boastful. But if I allowed for him wanting to impress me so that I would accept him, it did not seem so bad. I thought that everything I had seen had been carefully managed for my benefit, but then I had to admit that the substance of the place was every bit as impressive without any management.

Father found me in the stable yard getting Cian ready for a ride. "Shall I join you?" He saddled a white mare that he had been training for what seemed like months but was probably only weeks. As he tightened the cinch, she jerked her head up. He murmured lowly to her, stroking her neck. She settled, and allowed him to insert a gentle bit in her mouth. When he was mounted, we turned at a walk and headed out onto the road, riding north toward the Sliabh gCua. [10] The view of the low lying mountains was restful and we rode for a while in silence.

"I would be honored if you would share your thoughts dear daughter. I have felt our estrangement terribly, and would prefer if we could solve these problems together. "

I flicked the hem of my kirtle down over a naked ankle and sighed as I sat back up in the saddle.

"You provided me with a wonderful childhood. I grew up believing that people by and large did the right thing, and that you, my father, were the most righteous of all. My mother, though prone to worry and nerves to the extent that she annoys me almost more than I love her is at least sincere. I have always viewed my family as kind and giving. The

---

[10]

https://en.wikipedia.org/wiki/Knockmealdown_Mountains

year we gave money to the miller as the crops were short and he had no trade. The servant who disgraced herself with the hand from the Dougherty farm, and we helped her to set up home with her chosen, and Mother was even there when the baby was born. These were examples of the me who I wished to become.

"I suppose it is part of growing up that one should come to a point where one's parents are suddenly human, and not idealized. Where one's father ceases to be a hero, but merely a man. This is that moment for me.

"I have asked about the Earl's character of almost everyone I know. I don't have a wide acquaintance, but I asked the tradesman who delivered last Friday. I have grilled Meg, Mrs. McGuigan, and Paddy. I also asked the stable hands and the man who came to buy a horse last week. All were careful how they responded, which in itself is a bit worrisome, but all were kind enough to give me some indication

"Maurice Fitzgerald is a manly man. He is known outside his home estates as valorous, brave, and a powerful soldier. He is admired far and wide. My visit to his estate was delightful, carefully managed to give me the very best impression. I don't know why it mattered. You both know I have no choice. He has selected me as the mare on which he chooses to base his herd. I suppose it is desirable that I not scream on the way to the barn to meet the stallion.

"The visit today did impress me, but I also formed the opposite impressions from what you had hoped.

Although the serving girls give the impression they are happy with their working conditions, their mistress gives the impression that she does not feel safe to speak or be silent, to decide or to ask permission. Her skulking look reveals this. Praise surprises her. Tommy likewise looks like he expects trouble all the time. The Earl's horse shows signs of having been treated cruelly, or at least trained with cruel methods. This could have happened before he owned the animal, but then it would be true that he bought Dante from someone whose methods were questionable, which he shouldn't have.   His men at arms have the air of not having loyalty or bond to any master, except he who fills their pockets with gold coins. Their true natures would be revealed with very little prodding, but I would never be permitted or unwise enough to prod.

"And when I saw you there, I suppose I saw that you, too, are a mercenary of sorts. And don't tell me again that the horses do not sustain us. In my training to become the mistress of Lismore Castle, Mother made sure I learned, and practised her method of tracking the revenue and expenses for our estate. We could easily do without the Earl and his Castle. Your employment there then is either from ambition or duress, and I don't know which displeases me more. If there is one person in this whole situation for whom I have new respect, and who I woefully underestimated for my whole life, it's Mother. She is tough, courageous, and she maintains her own ideals in the face of yours with which she often disagrees. I believe that this is the source of her anxiety.

"I know that I am naive, young girl that I am. But I have read, and have heard many stories of the world, and I understand that neither you nor the Earl are unique. And perhaps neither of you are so very wrong, given the way of the world. But I was raised to believe so much more of you. I am disappointed, my heart feels weary and sad.

"Of course I will marry him. As I said, I have no choice. My fate was sealed the minute that you suggested to him that he might consider me, and I am certain it was your suggestion, not the other way around. But I tell you this, his tolerance of my free speech will wear out, and what side of him might I experience then? What if I cannot produce a child? I ask you this Father, where might I be a year from now, and what portion of that outcome will be your responsibility?"

I turned Cian toward home and urged him on, leaving Father far behind.

The final detail to be settled before the Earl and I could marry was the question of dowry. Often the bride does not know specifics, negotiated as it is between the groom and the father of the bride. But I had won some sort of a victory with Father, and thus had some power to influence the package to be presented to the Earl.

The initial request from the Earl, ran thus:

The Stallion known as Roman, two grey mares, the bay horse known as Cian, and the collection of linens and heirlooms inherited by the bride from her family.

By the time we were finished, after three or four negotiations, by letter, the final list was thus:

Three white mares, all the offspring of the Stallion known as Roman, with lifelong breeding rights with the stallions of the bride's family. Three bolts of linen to be purchased in Waterford in the weeks before the union. The horse Cian and the bridal chest belong to the bride and only the bride. This is family tradition and is not subject to negotiation. (I'm sure he knew that this last was at my insistence).

Frankly he did not push the negotiations hard, and I had the feeling that even had I no dowry he would not have cared. I didn't entirely trust that he loved me so much; he barely knew me.

The final draft of the dowry was accepted easily by the Earl, and the wedding date was set in a month's time, the middle of June. We were to be married at the cathedral at Lismore, with its beauty and long history. Roman and Caesar, on loan for the day, would pull the Earl's most beautiful conveyance.

Three weeks before the wedding, the whole family loaded into our wagon and drove to Waterford. Each of my sisters was excited for her own reason: hair ribbons, delicacies, books (we were an unusual family), and of course, fabric for new dresses and cloaks.

The journey took a long time. We departed home at eight o'clock in the morning, with Meg and Mrs. McGuigan waving as we drove away. We had cloaks and blankets and pillows to comfort us, and we each had a satchel of fine bread and cheese and a small skin of wine. Father and Paddy both did the driving, sometimes walking the horses, and sometimes trotting them. We stopped at each waystation to water the horses and to fill our skins if necessary. Travelling in this way, the journey took until after supper. We arrived at the inn about sunset, our satchels of food empty, our skins gone dry, and our sense of humour used up.

Father was driving as the horses touched their noses to the stable door of the inn. But almost immediately they began to back up. Noises could be heard within the stable yard, yelling, whinnying, and squealing. Paddy took the reins of the horses as father jumped down. There was a small man door to the right of the big wooden door that hung on iron hinges, and Father went through it.

There was some yelling while the horse noises continued, but then all was silent. And finally, the big door swung open, its weight resting on a wheel that ran on an iron rail buried in the stone driveway to keep the weight of the door from sinking it into the ground. It revealed a man on the flagstones being tended by others, and father holding a big grey, its eyes wide, its sides heaving, blood flecking the saliva on its face and its flanks. Father spoke quietly to it, stroking its neck, pressing his body gently against its shoulder, and with each passing moment it calmed a little more.

I jumped down and took our horses from Paddy, doing with them as Father was doing with the big grey. Horses are prey animals, and when they experience firsthand the terror of one of their kind, they share in its emotion, and therefore in its fear, a phenomenon that gives them warning and contributes to their survival in the wild. So although our horses were confident, well treated animals, they were still uncertain they should enter into the stable yard where their compatriot had clearly experienced something terrifying. I sang little songs to them, I talked to them and leaned in toward them. As the big grey calmed, so too did our team.

Paddy took the frightened horse to a stall in the other side of the yard, and from what I could see, was watering him and rubbing him down with straw. This has a further calming effect, further assuring the horse that he can trust the person handling him. Seeing glimpses of Paddy's elbows, his back and his shoulders, there was something about the way he was moving with that particular horse.

Father was now moving toward the injured man. He swiped up a riding crop that was laying on the flagstones and stopped at the feet of the man. He was conscious, but by the behaviour of the inn stable hands he had taken some pretty vicious kicks. One was attempting to splint a lower leg. Another was supporting ribs. And a third was cleaning several abrasions with water. Father stood there, with the riding crop quivering in an ominous way. He was shaking with anger.

"You see what a dangerous horse you sold me", said the injured man. "Look what he's done to me".

Oh no. I knew now why Paddy moved so tenderly with the grey. I recognized him, the way his top line was so strong and straight, the shape of his eye, and the attitude of his tail. His name was Goliath. He had been born in the foaling shed on the edge of our paddock, black as night. He was so large he almost didn't make it, and his mother died the next day, presumably of internal bleeding. We committed him to the care of a wet nurse, a large gentle mare who took him willingly as her own. By the time he was a two year old, he was huge, and just starting to turn from black to grey. He was so sweet we could trust him completely, and I and my sisters would run through his legs. Oh Goliath.

"When I sold you this horse, you swore, you SWORE that if there were any problems you would bring him back to me and I would re-train him. And a part of the contract that you signed, YOU SIGNED, was if you mistreated this animal in any way, an errant flick of the whip, a bruise, your ownership of him would cease and I would take him back". I didn't think I had ever seen father shake like that before.

"The Common Law…"

"You know as well as I do that a signed contract supersedes the Common Law. Or would you like to take it to the magistrate?"

He turned to one of the stable hands, and pulled out the purse that hung under his cotehardie. "Here is enough money to pay for his convalescence, and the attendance of a surgeon. This ensures that I can be held blameless in this matter. Now I wish you could take this man to the midden heap where he belongs, but take him to a room and keep him out of my sight. Now attend to my family and my horses. The big grey is named Goliath, and he is to be treated with kindness and gentleness until he returns home with us the day after tomorrow."

There is nothing like the sick feeling in your stomach when you know an animal you loved and let go with reluctance has been mistreated. As anyone to whom it has happened will relate, you suffer the fury, the righteousness, but mostly the self-loathing and the absolute knowledge that you have failed that animal that trusted you and depended on you. It was in this mood that we accepted our evening meal and then went to bed. Father checked on the horses and I knew he would be with Goliath.

Unable to sleep, I put my travelling cloak over my chemise and tiptoed down the stairs, toward the back of the inn, through the carriage room where our carriage sat, and out to the stable yard. As I thought, there was a lit lamp in the stall where Goliath rested. Father and Paddy were there with a bucket of warm water and two cloths. They had also found some liniment to rub into his sore muscles.

Father looked up at me as I stepped into the light. "Do you judge me for this too?"

"No. I have been unable to sleep knowing that he is frightened and in pain. "

Wordlessly, Paddy handed me another cloth, so I pushed my cloak back over my shoulders and started wetting his front legs with warm water, massaging as I went.

Casting an eye at the cloak that now lay partially in some horse manure, father's eyes twinkled as he said "Your mother will be furious."

I smiled, just a little, before saying "I'm proud of you. I think I would have killed him."

Goliath tolerated our ministrations as long as we would continue. I thought he would have shown more fear after the way he had been treated. But I guess he knew us, and perhaps the hay and carrots and mash in front of him didn't hurt much. It was very late when we each in our way wished him goodnight and returned to bed.

The next day, after we had all visited Goliath and found him to be much happier and healthier, we ventured out into the Vikings triangle on a day most unseasonably cold for the end of May. [11] Here and on the Mall which formed one side of it, we found many shops selling beautiful things. There were tailors, butchers, jewellers, and sea captains selling wares from all over the world. And there were plenty of textile merchants.

We bought a bolt of linen dyed in indigo, and two natural. While we were in a shop, and I was distracted looking at the silks and wools there, Mother called my name. She was in the corner with the merchant, and holding a bolt of silk. It was white, the purest white I had ever seen. It took my breath away. The look on my face was all she needed, and she began to bargain with the man. To

---

[11]

https://en.wikipedia.org/wiki/Waterford_Viking_Triangle

get the price she wanted on the silk, she agreed to also buy a fourth bolt of linen, and a bolt of wool. Whatever she was going to do with all that fabric, Father didn't seem to mind.

We hired a man to help us carry our purchases back to the inn. We tumbled in the front door and up the stairs, laughing and giddy with the rush of what we had spent, and had the man put all six bolts of textile at the foot of Mother's bed. Then we went downstairs.

There was a roaring fire in the fireplace downstairs, and the mantel was blackened with years of just such treatment. It was a comfortable and attractive room with padded benches and dark wood tables. Father went out to check on Goliath and the team. He returned to rejoin us he looked pleased, but then the man who had beaten and hurt Goliath, came into the room, using a crutch to support his broken leg, the leg Goliath had broken in pain and fear.

"There he is, that's the man who is going to steal my horse, and me injured and all", he said loudly enough that the twenty or so patrons could hear. Father turned to face him, ready to defend himself and us at least as well as he had the day before. But before he could open his mouth, a dark, beautifully carved shillelagh (made of blackthorn– funny how things go through your mind at odd moments) slid under the man's chin, and from the other side, another man pushed his cheek so that he faced the holder of the stick. A very familiar voice said, "Do you know who I am, Sir?" The man's mouth came open as much as the stick under his chin would allow.

The man nodded "no".

The Earl's face was alabaster save for the redness of anger in his cheeks. "I am the man who would hear your case for horse theft. I have seen the contract you signed as I know it to be the contract this gentleman uses when he sells a horse. I also know that regardless that the fault is your own, this gentlemen has paid for all of your expenses until you recover. As things stand I might be justified in throwing you into the dungeon of my castle and throwing away the key for slandering him over a situation of your own making. I suggest you cease and desist and take yourself elsewhere". The hand that patted the man's chest wore a ring inscribed with the Fitzgerald family crest in negative, so it could be used to finish a wax seal. It was conspicuous; it was evidently pure gold and the work was very fine.

The man was shown to a table by himself by the Earl's companion. Due to his actions on Father's behalf, we asked the Earl to join us. After all, he was my betrothed. But there was something about the bald use of power that made me uncomfortable. After we had ordered food and wine, he addressed us all.

"I hope you did not find my approach to be too heavy handed. Indeed my betrothed currently glares like she sees in me all the finesse of the highwayman. However it is my experience that some men will never understand simple concepts like justice and legality. They simply take whatever they can get for themselves regardless of who it hurts. Sometimes a heavy exertion of the power of wealth is the only way to teach a lesson. "

As the food arrived on the table, the Earl's man returned and explained quickly in French that the man had tried to take Goliath from the stable once more and had been repulsed. The Earl's man had arranged for the brute to be taken to Lismore the next day and that he would be under arrest until then. He turned to my father, who had gasped, and said in English, "monsieur the cheval is safe and will be ready for you to ride home with your family tomorrow." With a nod to the Earl, he departed.

We were all silent for a few minutes, thinking of poor Goliath, and frankly of the ease with which the Earl wielded his power. Much as Goliath's assaulter was a monster to be sure, though it was suppressed, there was something monstrous in the Earl as well.

"So, I trust you have had a productive shopping trip here in Waterford? "He ventured. To which the eldest of my three sisters gave us all a delightful recitation of what she had bought with her three pennies, and that her sister was getting married and she would get to wear a pretty gown. By the time she stopped talking, we were all smiling and the Earl had one eyebrow raised in delight. She had done an excellent job of relieving the tension in the group. "McGuigan", the Earl said, "you have a talent for delightful daughters". He looked at me and winked and I blushed, not altogether pleased.

That night, Father and I, Paddy and the Earl all spent time with Goliath again. He had indeed developed an abscess in his rear hoof that made him very lame, and this had been the initial reason for his beating. The stablemen of the inn had cared for him expertly and the abscess was fully drained. He seemed to be completely sound when we brought him out to the stable yard and drove him in a gentle circle. He had lost much of the confidence in his stance and his head hung somewhat. But his cuts from the whip were scabbed over, and the welts he had suffered had healed.

The Earl seemed genuinely saddened by what had happened to this still very fine horse. He confused me. The same man who bullied and had Goliath's previous owner arrested here gently stroked his neck and murmured to him. Where was the bully now?

Both Paddy and the Earl's man stayed with Goliath for the rest of the night.

In the morning the Earl explained that he had business in Waterford with his nephew, but that his man would travel with us home to Lismore. Father rode Goliath, who was afraid after his bad experience, but in Father's expert hands he calmed and was once more a gentle if not confident mount. It would take a long time to ease the betrayal Goliath felt, and the fear that it might reoccur.

From my place in the wagon, I watched the Earl's man. "Excuse me" I said, "What is your name?"

He didn't look at me when he spoke, but said "Gabriel de Blois".

"May I call you Gabriel then?" He nodded. I would have watched him the whole way home, but two nights up tending to an injured horse had left me tired, and I drifted off. I woke up when the wagon stopped in our yard, and he was long gone. I was disappointed as I had wanted to ask him some questions.

Preparation for the wedding rose to a fevered pitch. Women from the entire district came to our house to work on my gown, now forming from the perfect white silk. Nimble fingers worked tiny holes for lacing at the back, tiny even stitches for seams and felling the seams on the inside of the garment. They worked well and fast, and my wedding gown was ready four days early.

They helped me put it on and stand in front of the large metal mirror in the hallway upstairs. Clustered behind me they all gasped. It was sort of like a Burgundian gown, but the neckline ran to the side and my shoulders were exposed. There was fur trim all around the neck line. It had a self-cape attached along the rear of neckline, which given that the lacing was at the back meant that this was not a gown to be gotten into and out of easily. A beautiful gem, dark in colour but opalescent with many colours[12] that had been bought in Waterford when my attention was elsewhere hung between my breasts and was affixed to the dress. The sleeves fit my arms, with buttons that ran all the way up under the arm to the armpit. The body of the dress was layers and layers of white silk that

---

[12] Labradorite

flowed like milk into the separator. When the seamstresses realized I was crying, they all stepped forward, mindful of the silk, to dry my tears lest they stain the dress.

I looked at Mother and she too was crying. I mouthed "thank you" at her through my tears. She put both her hands over her heart and made a motion of rocking a baby. That made me cry even harder.

My wedding day dawned grey but the sun was valiantly trying to burn through the clouds. My trunks had been sent to the castle the day before, complete with the exquisite white chemise Mother had made me for my wedding night. She had been fussing for some time about whether I would bleed on my wedding day, but so far it had not been a problem. She herself did my hair with a braided crown filled with delicate wild flowers woven into it, leaving the remainder of my hair hanging down almost to my knees. She fitted a veil over the top of my head, under the braid, and down almost to the ground. (When did she find time to make that?) She worked a dark powder around my eyes. She combed my eyebrows and fixed them in place with a tiny bit of egg white, joking that too much would be like having breakfast on my face. She worked a tiny bit of red cream onto my cheekbones and my lips. She gave me mint to chew for my breath and in case my stomach was uneasy. Meg and Mrs. McGuigan helped me down the stairs and out to the wagon, the same that had taken me to the castle over a month ago, with Paddy once again in his finery. Father would ride Goliath behind us.

Mother came out the door in an exquisite gown of the most vibrant blue, the indigo linen. Like mine, it showed her shoulders, though not to the same extent. She wore a butterfly hennin in matching blue, her hair hanging down in a braid under the veil at the back. The gown brought out the blue of her eyes and the auburn of her hair where it peeked out. I almost cried again, but I didn't, to spare the dress. I looked at Father, and unlike me, he was crying. Not over me, but over her. And I suddenly understood something. Theirs was a love match.

For the journey to Lismore, I was lost in my thoughts. I thought about my misgivings, but I thought about the Earl, soon to be more intimate to me, to my body than anyone on earth. I had no idea what to expect. I was afraid I might disappoint him. I thought about my parents, my sisters. About family and traditions. I thought about the changes in my life since I played in the water and became so ill. I had reworked my opinions of my parents over and over again. I watched Father riding, and how much improved Goliath was under his influence. As I did, I noticed a small detail about the way Father was dressed. His robes were as rich as Mother's, with a beautiful belt and cloak. And the tiniest piece of tartan affixed to his collar. I puzzled over it for a minute, trying to identify the pattern. McDonnell. Yes, I thought so, red with blue and green. I had seen it on guests to our home over the years. It was worked into the tunic that Paddy was wearing and that he had worn a month ago. That was interesting. But when we arrived at the cathedral, it slipped my mind to ask him why he wore it.

Father helped me down from the carriage and Meg and Mrs. McGuigan picked up my dress from behind. They laid it out on the ground behind me as I stood on the flagstones ready to enter. Mother and Father stood on either side of me and we all walked in together. My little sisters were at the front, dressed in simple but beautiful little gowns the same colour as my mother (accomplished against odds by the army of seamstresses). The cathedral was full mostly of people from the Earl's household and estates, but also people who knew our family.

The Earl was there, with his hair carefully combed and pulled back in his preferred style. This was the second time I had seen him in more formal clothing. It showed his physique to better advantage. The hose showed his leg muscles, the doublet the width of his shoulders. He wore a chain wrought of silver crests across his shoulders and chest. His belt was wide and was studded with silver and had a large silver buckle. The fittings were also silver and from them hung a broadsword in a beautifully tooled silver scabbard. Around his calf a thong held a knife in a similar silver scabbard. And every inch of his clothing was scarlet red. It became him. A lot.

My parents dropped back as he took my hand.

And I have to tell you that is all I remember about the wedding. We were married by the Bishop, there was a lot of Latin, but mostly I just stared at him, both afraid of him and fiercely attracted to him, which surprised me. At the end, when he kissed me, I am afraid I swooned.

"Could someone get my wife some wine please?" asked the Earl, now Maurice, with his arm firmly around me. I looked up at him, and although he swam before my eyes, I allowed him to pull my head to his shoulder and hold the goblet as I drank. "I hope this is not an omen" he said and his gentle smile betrayed the lines of concern on his forehead.

In a few minutes I recovered enough to be helped into his wagon, much grander than ours, and pulled by the two stallions. I sat with him, his arm around me. He held my hand and kissed me, more kisses of the kind he at given me at the castle that day. This time I began to return them. Who needs lessons?

He had a small wine skin with rich red wine in it. He gave it to me sparingly. He gave me the most wonderful piece of white bread that had obviously been stowed in the carriage. By the time we arrived at the castle, I felt much, much better.

The wedding feast went on for hours, and there was much music, dancing, storytelling, and the most wonderful food and wine. The hall was hung with banners, some with the Fitzgerald Crest, some in the McDonnell tartan (Why?), and some merely coloured beautifully. Shortly after the feast began, a handsome youth, not quite old enough to be considered an adult, approached us. Before he was introduced I knew he was Maurice's son James. He had that same highly contrasted colouring.   We only exchanged pleasantries, but he seemed genuine and honest. I couldn't wait until I had time to talk with him further.

When my stomach was full, I had too much wine, and I began to feel drowsy, Maurice stood and also took my hand asking me to do the same. Immediately his men at arms that were present began to chant, most of it in French. I couldn't quite follow it, but its intent was clear. It was time for Maurice to bed me. Suddenly I was wide awake. And Mother, Meg and Mrs. McGuigan were suddenly there again, straightening the train of my dress for the walk to the bed chamber. It seemed everyone knew this was coming but me. Maurice nodded to me to begin the walk, and the men at arms followed us, chanting and singing. I caught Maurice looking at me and rolled my eyes. He was delighted.

At the door to the bed chamber, one of the men announced in Irish and English, in case I might not understand, that it was tradition in their group that each of them should kiss the bride before she went into the bedchamber. They were all laughing but I thought I should do something before any of them took the chance. I bent over, took the knife from the scabbard at Maurice's calf, and held it as if I was prepared to fight them. "Who's first?" There was a chorus of laughter, and they all began shaking Maurice's hand and dispersing. Gabriel was there, and then so too was Archibald, the reluctant Scot. Once he had shaken Maurice's hand, he took mine, kissed it, and wished me every happiness before turning away. When the last man was gone, Maurice turned to me, and nodded at me to enter the chamber.

The room was larger than any I had ever slept in. There was an unusually large window, but it being night the shutters were firmly closed and barred. There were trays full of freshly lit candles in several places in the room. The floor was wooden, but there were flagstones around the large fireplace where a roaring fire blazed. The bed was large and the bedding matched the deep burgundy canopy and curtains. There was a large chest at the foot of the bed, and another by the door. There was a bench covered with thick red upholstery on the other side of the room.

Maurice motioned me to stand in the middle of the room, then held up a finger and said "wait". As I watched he removed his weapons, the silver chain, and he pulled the thong that held his hair. He began undressing, and presently he was naked to the waist. I didn't know men could look like that. I realized I was panting, but I don't think he noticed. He had me sit on the bench.

"I think you are the most courageous person I have ever met. This could not have been an easy day for you. And yet you got through it with good humour and gentility. "

He was taking the braid out of my hair, taking each faded flower and setting it aside. The veil fell to the floor, and he picked it up and draped it over the back of the bench where I sat.

"I know you don't entirely trust me. I hope we can work together to change that". He was lifting my hair and kissing the back of my neck. "Tomorrow we can get you more acquainted with the staff, and the castle. It's yours now, the same as it is mine". He had slid a hand under the self-cape and was undoing the lacing down my back. He stood me up and turned me to face him. He reached in the neck of the dress and pulled out my breasts, kissing them, kneading them. Now he was moaning. I couldn't have spoken if I tried, but I was very interested to see what happened next. He reached his hands under the billows of silk, and slid them up my legs. I froze, but he ran his hand over my withered calf without stopping, seemingly without noticing. Then all of a sudden the dress was gone, whisking over my head on onto the bench with the veil. He picked me up and carried me to the bed, urging me to the centre. Now I REALLY wanted to know what happened next.

Insistent hands parted my legs, and insistent lips the inside of my thighs. The appearance of a unicorn couldn't have surprised me more than when a thumb went in between my legs, and a finger just barely entered my back passage. And then his tongue licked the little knob that I had found long ago on my own. It didn't take very long before I felt something somewhere between a thundering, a gushing a roaring and a tingling that started at my back passage and ran all the way to my navel and up inside me. Everything was wet and I thought I had wet the bed. Maurice was standing now, dropping his hose and braies. The only penis I had ever seen ready for coupling was on a horse. His penis surprised me at how long it was, and how incredibly hard it was at this very moment. When he put it inside me, I felt a momentary pinch, but then it felt good. Really good. And when he moaned, I felt that roaring feeling again.

How many times could you do that before you died? Or before God struck you dead with a lightning bolt? Each time we did it that night, I expected an angry nun to storm into the room and put a stop to it. Something this good could never be sanctioned by the church.

In the morning, there was a knock on the door. Without moving, Maurice said "go away."

Mary's voice responded, "You did tell me to bring you food My Lord. Your bride must be hungry." She was almost pleading, asking not to be scolded.

He didn't notice my surprised reaction, but jumped out of bed and threw on a chemise that I hadn't even noticed was there. He ran to the door and opened it.

"You are right Mary, I am sorry. Thank you, this looks wonderful" he said, taking a tray from her. She shot a glance at the bed, presumably wondering if this performance was for my benefit.

He closed the door as she walked away and brought the tray to the bed. It held fruit (strawberries!), some of the fine bread that came from the castle kitchen, boiled eggs, and some kind of preserved apple that was delicious.

Following his example, I had put on the beautiful chemise Mother had made me for just this occasion. It was in my box that was in the corner, lost in the shadow last night.

"That's beautiful work", he said, eying the embroidery around the neck.

"Maurice – I presume I am to call you Maurice" – he smiled "there is something I must ask you. Must discuss with you. I want to understand".

"You want to know why the servants are afraid of me."

You know that feeling when you are so surprised at the response that your mouth drops open, your mind goes completely blank, and you forget you actually spoke in the first place?

"You're not the first person to ask. I thought your father might have told you, since he certainly knows. I suffer from melancholia. After Ellen died it was so bad I thought I might follow her. Some days I am happy, useful, in control of myself. Other days I am black. Angry. One of the reasons I often travel to France is that the change of scenery can sometimes pull me out of a bad period."

I sat looking at him motionless. What did this melancholia mean? My mind was processing and trying to imagine what he might be like in the throes of an attack.

He looked back at me and continued "The simplest things can throw me into days or weeks of despair. Often I cannot afford to darken my chamber and sleep though I long to, as it is often the restorative I require. I have estates to run, obligations to fulfil. Your father often steps in for me, but sometimes only my own presence will suffice. In these situations I can be bitterly angry. I hurt the people around me. I sometimes make bad decisions. And then one day I see a small detail, or the weather changes, and I am myself again. It is a piteous existence.

"There is only one thing that will always dissipate the cloud above me, will allow me to rid myself of the anger and sadness totally for a time. "

I raised my eyebrow, hoping that he was going to tell me of something I could do, that I wasn't powerless in the face of this dark monster that took over his body and soul from time to time.

He continued "Battle. Killing in battle. I can feel the anger running down my fingers and through my sword. Battle is the one time in a man's life that he can lose all restraint, can forget the bonds of sin and sanctity, and just follow the urges of his soul. My men at arms think I am a valiant soldier and leader. We all share this same flaw, that we loose our souls from their mooring and go mad, and it is sanctioned by the world around us. We are monsters in full view, we are praised for our villainy, winning a battle is simply a measure of who can kill more men. Men who prayed to God at the beginning of the day and are dead at the end of it. "

I was frantically searching my mind to turn this conversation around, lest he plunge headlong where it felt he was going.

"Are there things that help?" I asked, looking for a positive aspect.

"Yes", he said carefully, "none miraculous, but some that ease the extremity of it. Mary has a tea she sometimes makes that helps, that allows me to go out into the world and carry out business without doing too much damage to the others around me. Sometimes a simple but pleasant activity, like a horse ride, a particularly lovely piece of cake —"

"Relations?"

He smiled a wistful smile. "Sometimes. Especially with a woman who loves me and truly appreciates what I do. What I am. How I am. I'm not sure I'm making myself clear."

"Then perhaps I am not making myself clear. On this score at least I can give you comfort for the rest of your life. If you do at least some of what you did for me last night, I will always appreciate what you do, who you are and how you are. I've never had any experience like what you did. I liked it. A lot. "

By this time he was laughing softly. "But you must listen one stroke more. I have this monster that lives within me. I should have told you before we married. Can you ever forgive me?"

"Maurice I knew there was something, something important. I knew by the aspect of your servants, by the way people avoided something when I asked about you. I could well have been walking into Hell itself. I did it. I'm sorry it was not for love, not for love of you anyway. I did not know you well enough to decide if I could love you. I did it for the love of my father, my mother, and the rest of my family. I hoped that my marriage would benefit them in some way through the years. And I hoped that when brought into intimacy with you, that I would find you to be as wonderful as you are now, and that whatever it was would be something we could surmount together. I am sincere when I say that I want children with you, I want to make this house my home, with your permission. And I want to understand you so that I can enrich your life."

A tear ran down his cheek. He studied my face, and stroked my cheek with his thumb.

And then I said "there are still guests in the castle, but would it be wrong to do that again first?"

Ever so gently he raised his chemise and exposed his naked torso. I was disappointed to see that his penis was flaccid, but he started pulling it up and down with his hand, and pushing my head toward it, whispering "put it in your mouth, and see what happens". I did so, and was delighted to hear him moan. I put my hand on his hand, the hand moving up and down, and soon my hand was the only one there. He whispered for me to move my head up and down, and so I did. And he was absolutely right. Shortly it was very hard, very erect, and he pulled me away and rolled me on my back. He spat into his hand, and then rubbed the spit all over me, and then penetrated me. His thumb teased the little knob, and shortly I had that unbelievable wave of feeling again, and after, he made not so much a moan but a sort of yelp. He collapsed in a heap beside me but his head was on my shoulder. He sighed and held my breast through my chemise. And I laid there with my husband and thought that I could never tell a priest what I had just done. And I didn't care.

When we emerged downstairs in the hall, there was a smattering of applause. The hands that had just held my body, tightened the laces on my gown, and pinned my veil in place shook hands with all of the men in the room. Women approached me, hugged me, touched my cheek and told me how wonderful I looked. If I was to believe them, relations became me.

Mary and her young ladies had seen to it the trays of food were on all the tables. Digger the little hound was ever-present under the tables searching for scraps. I picked him up and petted him, and his tail wagged hard, but he struggled to get down again.

Between greetings and hugs I worked my way over to where Mother was sitting. She hugged me warmly. I whispered in her ear "you didn't tell me about that!"

She responded "I most certainly did!"

More whispering "no, you didn't tell me about THAT. " She looked at me with brows raised and a smile on her face. "Indeed?"

I smiled enigmatically and worked my way through the house again. Soon the person in front of me was young James. I motioned for him to follow me and went to find a seat that I could share with him. He sat beside me reluctantly, this twelve year old boy learning to be an Earl. He was only three years younger than me, but it seemed so much more than that.

"How long will you be staying with us?" I asked.

"Not long", he said, "for I am back to watch the construction of the tower. I am not certain why Father wants me there. I know nothing, and I am still too young to have any real authority. What can I do?"

I smiled at him and suggested "You can learn to be an Earl. Watch, make sure all the workmen know you are there. Ask questions, not in such a way as to meddle, but to show them you sincerely want to understand. Make it your business to learn how a customs castle is built. Then they will know that if there is a problem, you and your men at arms will convey the information to your Father forthwith. You are the assurance that the Earl is paying attention. And you are learning for your time as Earl."

He looked puzzled, but nodded at me. "If you have a son, I will not matter so much. Maybe I won't be the next Earl after all."

In alarm, I said "No! That is not true! I know he treasures you from how he has spoken to me. If there is another boy, it's true, that child would inherit from you until such time as you have your own son, but I know that no one intends to replace you! Have you spoken to your Father about this worry?"

"No. He gets angry, very angry, so I am careful not to disturb him unless I have to. Did you know he had my Uncle killed so he could become the Earl? Why would he hesitate to kill me?"

I was trying not to cry. I was desperately trying to find an answer for James, and one for myself as well and my mouth opened and closed. I did not know this. Where was my Father?

Out of nowhere Maurice swept in to rescue me, although he had no idea from what. It was probably a good thing he didn't.

"Come dearest, we're to dance. Look, the players are assembling". As he led me away he looked back at James, a questioning look.

I didn't see James again for quite some time, though my heart ached to comfort him.

Within a few days, we departed for the house in Youghal. It was not as big as Lismore, but was grander and more refined. It was set off the road, with abundant stables and doors for receiving supplies for the house in the back. I had my own suite of rooms, left over from the last Lady Desmond. There was a bedchamber, a receiving room, private sitting room, and a bathing room with a big wooden tub. I was given a large sum of money to redecorate the rooms, but the first Lady Desmond had obviously had excellent taste. I did little but to order new bedding.

Maurice also made sure that the best tailors in Youghal attended on me. While the gowns my mother had ordered were acceptable, the Lady Desmond should wear the very best. Bolts of Silk brocade from Italy, the finest wool, and much finer linen than I had ever seen. These fabrics were not available on the Mall but were ordered specially for the Earl and brought directly to the house. I felt a little like a fraud in my grand new wardrobe, like I had forgotten where I had come from. But Maurice's face glowed with pleasure to see me so attired. So I thanked him, genuinely for providing for me so beautifully.

Our lives were so busy. Maurice was attended by debtors, clergy, tradesmen and supplicants every day. I sometimes overheard his conversations with these people, and rarely did I ever hear him raise his voice. Those with whom he met seemed to leave our home satisfied, with the exception of those he deemed to be asking for something for nothing. There have always been grifters around powerful men, and powerful men have always had to encourage them to make their own way.

My own schedule was as busy as my husband's. I received all manner of women, some just to pay their respects and satisfy their curiosity on the looks of the new Lady. But there were others that wanted money, some that decried their husband's lot in life. I would occasionally help a student attempting to gain access to St Mary College, established by my deceased father in law. If they had the academics but not the fortune to attend, I would talk to the master on their behalf. I had to be careful. If the master deemed a student I supported to be unworthy, he would go to my husband to have me overruled, attempting to sow dissent between us.

We held balls in the hall, we visited the college and the friary, we went to mass, and we smiled and shook hands with everyone.

Not every night, but regularly, Maurice would come to my chamber, dismiss my Maid and lie with me. It wasn't always the way it was on our wedding night, but I always loved it, and loved even more the mood between us when it was over. We would doze and touch and talk and then have relations again. I lived for those nights, for the smell of him, the sight of him and the sound of his voice. If he was stern in the daytime, at night he was tender and gentle and I couldn't get enough.

During one of these wonderful nights, he sat up on his elbow, leaning over me.

"What were you and James talking about the day after our wedding? It seemed a very serious conversation for a son and a step-mother at a wedding. "He smiled but there was something serious in his eyes.

"My Lord, he fears that by you keeping him at a distance that perhaps you do not value him the way he hopes you should".

"Oh?" It was the response of a man who did not entirely believe what he was hearing.

"Indeed My Lord. I asked if he had discussed this with you. He said he has not." I paused. "Maurice, he fears your anger should he broach the subject."

He had wrapped himself in pillows and blankets and lay semi-prone. I was very sorry the subject had ever come up. He was frowning, not in an angry way, but as one considering how to proceed with the subject at hand.

"If I may….." I began. "Does James know how to play chess?"

He raised an eyebrow. It was as if I had asked if James had a third foot. Who cares?

"My point is, it would teach him reasoning and patience, but it would also allow him to interact with you in a..." I paused, looking to see how he might take my words, "a non-threatening way. If he is frightened of the anger you have shown in the past, this is a way to show him what you are at your calmest."

He sat up now, seemingly energized. "I knew I had chosen my wife well, and not just because she is fun to fuck".

Laughing, he pushed my body back down on the bed, and sucking my breasts, took me again, urgently.

Of course, with all of these intimate nights, not only were we exhausted at least some of the time, but I fell pregnant just in time for our return to Lismore. Like all mothers, I wondered over the sex of my child. Would he or she be like Maurice or like me? Whose hands would the baby have? Whose feet? And then, with anxiety, would all be right with the child? In the bath and in bed I surveyed the shape of my growing belly, wanting to identify head and feet.

Maurice was all affection and servitude. Upon our return to Lismore at the end of the season, he and Mary spent hours together ensuring that I had the best food, the right amount of fresh air, that my chamber was well prepared for the day. My Mother came to the castle many times, bearing precious little clothes for the infant, including a baptismal gown made from the remnants of my wedding gown. The stitches were tiny, and the design was beautiful. I thanked her for everything she and Mrs.

McGuigan were doing for my child. Father came to work sometimes bearing gifts of his own. A silver rattle, a wooden toy, a set of beautifully made blocks. I never did get to talk to Father about James and the extraordinary assertion he made about the death of the 8th Earl.

During the second and third trimesters Maurice did not come to my chamber. He said the midwife told him it encouraged miscarriage. So we became in a very small way estranged, lacking our quiet and very private moments. He went to England and to Burgundy. I was lonely for him. Sometimes I saw him at the breakfast table. We would talk and laugh at one another's jokes. But he remained distant, and even though I had been very unsure of him initially, I was very saddened as I thought I might have lost his esteem.

About the time I was sincerely wishing for the pregnancy to be over, and I could not see my own feet, Maurice arrived at my chamber one night. He smiled sheepishly and told me that the midwife's advice was now to bed me, as it would make the fully grown child come.

"I don't care why you're here, I'm just glad you are" I said with tears in my eyes. "I've missed you".

"You feel up to it then? "He asked, touching my cheek.

In answer I pulled my chemise up over my head.

He laughed and put his hands on my breasts. "They're so big."

He backed me up to the bed, laid me down, and took me ever so gently. After he laid beside me stroking my belly. "Such magic the way a woman brings forth life. Just plant a seed and it grows and grows".

Then all of a sudden he sat up and said "Why did you not tell me that James had told you he suspected me of killing my brother?"

"Because I did not credit it as true. I took it as something he had misunderstood from pieces he had overheard. I was trying to formulate some kind of answer to comfort him and dispel his worries when you came and took me away to dance. I wish I could have dispelled it for him in a way that would have spared your feelings. As his father I knew this would break your heart".

His brows drew together. "Truthfully I have stayed away from you all this time not just because of the child, but because I suspected you of colluding with him in this". He was challenging me. "I have had you both watched to ensure you were not".

I rose to the challenge. "Maurice he is a BOY. Not a man. He craves your love. He has lost his mother, has lost his Father to a new wife close in age to his own, and he is all at sea over things he imagines and is afraid of. All he needs is for you to reassure him. And I, only three years his senior, what power could I have to collude with him. You are my whole world, and I do not regret it. I love you, I trust you to be fair, and I live for our nights together. Take me again now and I will show you!"

I never voiced how betrayed I felt that he had me watched. But I knew he was capable of it, I had seen in it Waterford.

His face relaxed and he said "ever the woman, win me over with the power of your body". As he took me again and again that night, I never noticed that he hadn't said that he accepted my explanation.

The next day, the baby was born. (The midwife was right about that). It was a baby girl, and I survived the birth with only a little tearing. I was afraid when I saw she was a girl, but despite her sex, Maurice was in love with her the first second we saw her. We baptized her Joan, but I nicknamed her Pádraigín after the great Saint of Ireland[13]. She was perfect. We counted toes and fingers, stroked the dark hair on her head, the pale skin on her cheeks.

We had a glorious summer at Lismore. It rained enough for the crops but not enough to make us miserable. We spent afternoons under the trees, where I played with Dragon, as I called her from the English and for her spirit, and fed her, and she was visited by some loving person almost every day. As she grew she was exquisite. Her hair never fell out but grew thick and curly, almost black with dark hints of auburn, like her father. Her eyes were hazel, her lips cherubic. She showed signs that she would be tall like he was.

By the time Dragon was two, she tottered around Lismore on her own. When Maurice approached her she would squeal with delight, and he would hold her up in the air and they would both laugh.

---

[13] Saint Patrick. This is an Irish spelling.

We played blocks with her and we played elaborate games with her doll that involved long conversations in unintelligible baby talk. I could not have been happier.

I did, however find time for Cian every few days to explore the estate and to have our hair blow in the wind.

When it was time to go back to Youghal that year, Maurice had two new horses that he had purchased from my father. They were two gorgeous but young mares, and although Father had been breaking them as a team, they were not nearly ready. But Maurice refused to listen, as he wanted their glorious good looks in town to impress everyone. This was the team that pulled Dragon and myself and her Nanny to Youghal while Maurice rode Dante alongside. The roads were quiet and they did well, and Maurice felt the long distance would be enough to settle them as a team. As my Father's daughter I knew this to be folly, but as my husband's wife, I knew my counsel would be unwelcome.

In Youghal Dragon's nursery was in a room beside my own. I could hear her if she cried, and though her Nanny was there for her, I was invariably there very quickly, so that I could comfort her. I was pregnant again, and so I would take a nap in my room at the same time she napped in the afternoon.

One afternoon I was lying in bed, just drifting, when I heard footsteps in the corridor. Maurice would often sneak a few minutes to sit beside her as she slept and watch her dream. I loved that he did that. I heard him leave a few moments later. And then hoof beats as Dante carried him out of the yard. I thought he did an excellent job of closing the door silently, so as not to wake her.

My window was open, and as it faced the back of the house, I heard men's voices what seemed only a few minutes later. They sounded urgent, using words like "WHOA" and "STEADY". I knew what I was hearing. It was the sound of horses being unruly and men starting to panic at their lack of control. I got out of bed and looked out the window. Sure enough they were trying to hitch the young team. One of the mares reared up, breaking the harness and hurting one of the men with her hoof. I said "Stop! I'm coming!" I intended to throw on a kirtle and run down. I could calm the horses and have them ready to harness again in a few minutes. But then I saw something out of the corner of my eye. It was small, and tottering. At that exact moment, one of the men below hit the rearing mare with a whip. She screamed in terror and both horses lurched forward, uneven with the broken harness, and pulling the wagon behind. Everything was happening in slow motion, and I screamed "DRAGON!" She turned and waved to me just as the horses trampled her.

I remember NOTHING for a long time. They say I ran out in my chemise, my almost see through chemise, screaming her name and that I got to her before Archibald could stop me. I saw her crushed face, her broken body and screamed, and screamed and screamed. Archibald pulled me away, held my arms from hitting him, and took me back upstairs to my room. When Maurice came, having been summoned to the chaos at home, he saw his child, and immediately killed both horses. The poor horses, it wasn't their fault.

The servants and the men at arms worked together to gather Dragon's broken body, have someone come for the carcasses of the horses, and washed away the blood. The servants and the men at arms made sure Maurice and I were present for the funeral which was at the friary. And then they took us home to Lismore to recover and to await the birth of our second child. Neither of us took control of the situation. Because neither of us could. We were broken and catatonic. We could not reason.

My Father took over running all of the Earl's affairs. He even went to Youghal twice a year, with Mother to help him. He did very well by Maurice, making sound decisions and fair judgements. But it took a great toll on him and as he was now in his old age it was not easy.

I don't know how long I moved through the fog of my grief. Mary fed me, washed me and sat me out in the sun in the hope that its warm rays would rouse me. She would put a book in my lap in the hope that I would read it. Occasionally I would look at her and acknowledge I saw her. Mother would come and talk lightly of my sisters and the servants whom she knew I loved. Until one day I asked to help Mary plan the meals. I was heavily pregnant by then, and it had occurred to me to think of the baby. I was never the same, but I was rallying.

I never lay with Maurice again, because he never recovered. The melancholia that he had been free from for the entirety of our marriage so far struck him with a vengeance. He was always angry, always accusing people of things that just weren't true. He accused stable boys of stealing hay, was sure my Father was stealing from him until it could be proved that he wasn't, and that I was having an affair with his son. I had not seen James since our wedding. How could I lie with him?

He drank all the time, and always stank of alcohol, even in his more reasonable moments. He spent days in his chamber without emerging. I grieved for him. I cried all the time.

My own grief was always there, causing me to stare off into space and forgetting what I was supposed to be doing. I cried in my bed at night, wishing that Maurice and I could grieve together. I suffered horribly, but after a while I had to continue to run our home, to keep the servants in control of their own activity. One of us had to be strong, and it ended up being me.

When our second child was born, another girl, I called her Ellis.[14] Maurice didn't seem interested in what she was called. She was a redhead, with pale skin, and big lungs. She looked like one of my younger sisters. I didn't bother with a Nanny. I looked after her very well, but I did not take the delight that I had in Dragon. It was as if I could not give my heart again. Maurice did not show any interest in her at all, probably for the same reason.

---

[14] A root of the name Alice

Sometimes I only heard rumours of Maurice during the day. Yelling at the servants, throwing pieces of furniture. One day Mary told me that he had throttled the dog. I cried. I prayed for recovery. For forgiveness. For a miracle.

One evening he appeared at the door to my chamber and asked to come in. Ellis was already asleep for the night. I nodded and opened the door wide to give him leave to enter. He stumbled on the way in, but that wasn't unusual.

"I've.....I've been thinking......." He said.

I raised an eyebrow and waited, trying to look sympathetic.

"I...I would like Ellis...." (He knew her name!) "To have the finest education".

Surprised, I nodded, and waited to hear what exactly he meant.

"Soooo....I think she should go to Burgundy".

He looked at me to see my response.

"When she is old enough, I think that is a fine idea" I said, wishing I knew what he was driving at.

"No. Now. "

"Why?" I had to say something, to absorb the shock. I needed to buy time to figure how to convince him that this was preposterous.

"Because, I am her Father and I want what is in her best interests"

"Maurice, you think it's in her best interests to be torn from her mother at the tender age of two?"

An exaggerated nod. "Yes".

"No. Get out of my chamber".

I turned my back to get ready for bed. I saw Mary hovering in the shadows in the stone corridor. The slap hit the back of my head and made me lurch forward.

"You have NOOOO right! I am the Earl! I am the sole arbiter about what is best for my family". He was weaving. Mary had disappeared.

And stupidly, I said, to a drunken person who was not talking sense, "You know so well what is best for your family that you are the one who left the nursery door open on the day Dragon died. You allowed her to walk out into the stable yard. I know because I heard it, although I did not know what I was hearing at the time."

I thought he had only landed a few more blows before help arrived. He was still screaming invectives at me as the men at arms took him to his chamber and guarded over him until he was unconscious from the drink. Kind hands touched my face. My jaw was dislocated and I had a black eye. A cool cloth was applied to my eye, and strong hands relocated my jaw. I was surprisingly calm. I had been tiptoeing since we were married, and now the tiptoeing was over. I knew his black side now.

The strong hands belonged to Archibald, the others were Mary's. They guided me to the bed and put me in it without removing the blue linen kirtle I was wearing.

"My Lady, you must listen. You must leave Lismore. You are in grave danger." Archibald was very much in earnest.

"This is my home, it's Ellis' home. I will not allow him to chase me out" I responded. I would have clenched my jaw but it hurt.

"My Lady we should have told you before now. He will escalate from here. You are not the first woman he has done this to. Lady Ellen, Lady Ellen died because he kicked her in the belly and the child inside her died, poisoning her. And there was a mistress after she died. She was found beaten so badly that she will never be the same. Please, he will kill you and the child".

I was crying. I had worked so hard to form a life with him, to do all of the right things, and I really did love him. And I am only a little ashamed to say that I regretted that I would probably never have relations like that again.

"Archibald, will you do something for me? In the morning, tell the Earl that I am not well and that I mustn't be disturbed. And right now, this instant, please fetch my Mother. If the Earl asks, she is looking after me. I crave her counsel."

As Archibald began to get up, I said "He picked a fight with me so he could beat me. He doesn't care about Ellis. He just wanted to beat me"

Archibald tilted his head to one side and nodded doubtfully. "My Lady, I think he wanted to send Ellis away to protect her, and had you suggested it, he would have sent you too. It is characteristic of the way he gets that he couldn't make the intellectual transition from one to the other on his own. So instead he got violent."

Archibald left and Mary stayed with me, bathing my face and giving me sips of water to drink. After a while she said" He does care about Ellis. He knows his own darkness. That's why he wanted her removed to Burgundy. My Lady I have known him and served him a very long time. His own violence terrifies him. "

Realizing that she and Archibald were right, that the Maurice I knew would try to protect his child, I wailed and wailed, with Mary caring for me, for a long time.

Mother arrived in the wee hours of the morning, Archibald himself having ridden for her and ridden back. I found out later he took Dante, who had been unridden in the barn for some time. Poor horse.

Mother entered my chamber quietly, so as not to wake Maurice down the corridor. We hoped he would sleep late to recover from the night's exertions. Archibald, Mary, and Mother and I had a war council in my chamber. Always after one of these violent outbursts Maurice always had a lucid phase, as long as for a few weeks. So we had a little time. Mother would look after me for a few days, and some ruse would be found to get Maurice out of the way. Once Maurice was away Archibald and I would take Cian and another horse, and ride for the abbey of Saint David's across the sea from Wexford. Maurice would expect us to head for Waterford or Youghal. At Saint David's we would find sanctuary to decide our next move. Ellis would of course come with me. The servants and men at arms would misdirect Maurice as best they could to give us as much time as possible for our escape.

In the morning, after we had all slept, Maurice arrived once more at my chamber.

"My Lady, Mary tells me you are not well, I......."

He stared at my broken and bruised face. In a moment he was beside the bed with his head in my lap, begging forgiveness, and looking up periodically to see what he had done to my face.

"Tis no great loss My Lord, as I was never a great beauty". My attempt at humour fell flat and he cried all the louder and would not leave me.

"Please My Lord, all has been done that should be done. And you see my Mother is here to care for me. We can talk about this when I feel better, please."

He calmed a moment and then nodded, backed away and left the room.

Mother was astonished that he did not remember beating me. Mary said, "In time My Lady McGuigan, he will find a way to blame her for the beating and beat her again in retribution. All of us who work for the Earl are on her Ladyship's side, if side there be. While we love the Earl, we know this dark side of him, and we dread that our neglect might lead his Lordship to exact a mortal injury. We should have told you. We should have told you all."

Mother touched Mary's hand. I noticed she did not seem to be suffering from her usual anxiety.

Possibly because the anxiety was the product of her having suspected all along. She saw me looking at her as I thought this. We were of an accord.

Within minutes the Earl was back at the door. "Why are you wearing your kirtle in bed?"

I looked down. I had forgotten about the kirtle. I decided honesty was the best policy. "The servants found me My Lord. Wanting to spare my modesty they put me to bed as I was. In fact it's beginning to be quite uncomfortable. I think I should like to get out of this kirtle. Maman, will you find my chemise? I'm feeling a little dizzy."

Mary unlaced me at the back, and she and Mother peeled the kirtle off over my head. The loose under gown came next, and then everyone gasped, including Maurice. There were bruises all over my torso. Maybe he landed more blows than I thought.

I said "My Lord, I really think I need to lay down again. I promise I will seek you out when I am feeling better. Mary would you bring Ellis to me? She can stay in here with me today." I pulled my chemise over my head. He was still watching me from the door.

"If you are going to stare at me at least sit down and ease the tension in this room Maurice!" He did so, and so I put my head down. I was asleep before I saw Ellis, and Maurice was gone before I woke.

It was actually closer to a month before Archibald and Ellis and I left Lismore for ever. I vacillated between staying and going depending on whether Maurice was having a good day or not. And then Maurice had a really bad night. He told me that he had in fact ordered his brother's murder, but that although many knew of it, none dared accuse him. He had planned the murder with his nephew, his brother's son with whom he still had a close alliance born more out of mutual suspicion than love. Of course, he somehow found a way to blame others, and broke one of my teeth in the blaming. It was the last thing for me, the last thing to decide me. All of my friends, and friends they were, were right. I had to take Ellis and go.

Forgoing more elaborate plans, we gave Maurice a sleeping draught in his whiskey. When he finally passed out, we tucked him into bed, and I arranged the blankets around him tenderly. I kissed him and whispered "I love you" in his ear, turned and walked out the door.

I had packed a bag with two kirtles, a cloak and all my jewels, including my gold wedding ring and some gemstone necklaces Maurice had given me. My father had also seen to it that I had money. I didn't ask where from. I also had two changes of clothes and a blanket for Ellis. She wore her little cloak when we lifted her up on Cian. Archibald led Dante out, and Father was there with Goliath. I was glad to see them both.

We rode away from Lismore Castle, and I steeled myself not to look back.

We rode north across the river, and in an hour or so we passed my childhood home. There, Father left us. He felt he could do better if he continued to serve the Earl, if he could. I begged him to be careful, kissed his cheek and turned away. We kept riding into the foothills, and by the time the sun was rising we were well into the forest.

Archibald was a veteran traveller and veteran warrior. He knew how to travel without being noticed. Each time we stopped to rest, we collapsed into bushes or dark forest, and even the horses were invisible. No one bothered us all the way to Wexford.

But in my sleep I was plagued by worry. Would he come after us? Did I hear hoof beats from the road? Would he pounce on us while we slept or while we ate? Could I keep Ellis quiet enough to avoid detection? Should I have left home at all? Maybe he was too ill and I should have stayed to care for him? I was wrong, surely I was wrong. It was a relief when that part of the journey was over.

We camped outside the city of Wexford and Archibald went to see about passage across the sea to Cymru. Ellis and I lay in the bushes and played little games with our fingers until he came back.

When he did come back, he was vibrating with energy and ducked us down and bade us be absolutely silent. "He's here! He's bloody here! We've been followed!"

The three of us lay on our bellies and looked toward the road. And there was Gabriel. As we watched he sat on his horse and looked toward town. Ellis was remarkably quiet, and we held our fingers to our lips and pointed at the man on the horse. She put her pudgy little finger to her lips too.

As we watched, Maurice rode up on one of my Father's white horses, and the two men spoke for a minute. And then Gabriel pointed off to the south away from where we were. There was nodding and gesticulating, and the two men rode off to the south. As they left, Gabriel looked back in our direction over his shoulder and gave a slight salute with his fingers. I almost cried at this evidence of his protection of me, as he obviously knew exactly where we were.

It was interesting, Ellis did not call out for Maurice when she saw him. She simply watched as if he were a stranger. How sad.

We waited until dark, and then Archibald took us to the docks. A boat was waiting. I had never even thought. "How do we put the horses on the boat? Do we put the horses on the boat?"

Archibald took a small vial out of a hidden pocket. He gave each horse a sniff of the vial, and they calmed down and were almost sleepy. We walked them across a sort of gangway, and we were on the boat. The horses were taken to the bottom of the hold and put on cross ties. The sails were raised and we were underway. The journey was surprisingly smooth, and the swells were not very large. The horses occasionally showed the whites around their eyes, but I rubbed their foreheads and sang to them, and they calmed.

I heard the anchor drop while it was still dark, but Archibald said we were to wait until daylight.

"Where are we" I whispered.

"Porthlyski Bay "came the answering whisper from above.

"Oh, well then" came Archibald's whisper.

"Just south west of the Abbey my Lord" and a muttering from above.

When daylight dawned, we could see that the boat was floating some distance out. There were other boats too. Archibald explained that these were pilgrim ships, and indeed now that we could see, there were other people on the boat carrying bundles and with the expectant look of someone about to disembark. Ours were the only horses. One of the sailors indicated that we should bring the horses up a ramp to the back of the ship. A door had been opened. We had come down it the previous night in the dark.

We were to simply walk out and jump into the water. My mouth hung open. It was only about six feet, but it was a possibility that I had never considered.

"Look, Dante has done this before. I will go first with him. Cian will see him do it and follow "said Archibald.

"We do this while we're riding!!" I said, clutching Ellis very tight.

Everyone was assuring me it would be all right. Archibald took Ellis. "I've done this before".

And so Archibald and Dante and Ellis went first, and when they landed in the water, she squealed with delight. A sailor slapped Cian's rump and down we went. To my surprise, Cian did really well. I got pretty wet, but he was a trooper and he worked hard to catch up to Dante. At the shore, the rocks were the size of your fist and round. We let the horses pick their way out.

"Now all we have to do is follow all the people!" He was right. The road ahead of us was full of people walking, all headed for the Cathedral and the Abbey. Some had crutches, some were on litters. They were looking for cures at the holy place created by Saint David. Others were headed to the Abbey for different reasons. Some carried packs, bags and even trunks. Many were stopped at the side of the road trying to dry out their belongings, however few those might be. We were conspicuous with our beautiful horses and beautiful cloaks, but as we needed them for later in the journey there was nothing for it. I wished we could bring some of the children to ride for a time on the horses, but it would have increased our conspicuousness.

We rode for about an hour, sometimes faster, sometimes slower depending on the crowds. When we came in sight of the Cathedral and the surrounding complex, we and all the pilgrims around us gasped. The morning sun was shining on the cathedral, over five hundred years old. The whole complex actually sat in a hollow, with a ridge that ran around one side. The cathedral was so large that it emerged from the hollow and towered over the surrounding countryside. The bishop's palace was very large and ornate. The abbey to one side was smaller, and it was there we were bound. Fields surrounding the complex were bursting with crops, and immaculately tended. We rode past gravestones of monks long dead, some of the writing on the stones erased by weather and time.

It was the sort of place that made you speechless, and that had the magic of the saint, the accumulated vibrations of hundreds of years' worth of prayers. As we walked our horses and Ellis slept against my chest, exhausted, Archibald told me about the monks of Saint David's.

"These monks practice extreme deprivation. They plant their crops and harvest them without horses or oxen. One monk wears the yoke, the other guides the plow. They drink no wine but only water, and their food is simple but healthful. The bishop of the cathedral leads a much richer life, but he does take cues from their lifestyle. They trade with the surrounding countryside for the things they cannot make. It is a magical place". It was clear he had been here before, although perhaps a long time ago. I wondered about the story behind Archibald's taciturn exterior, where he had been, of what his life had consisted.

When we got to the abbey gate, Archibald told the monk there that we needed to speak to the abbot on a matter of some urgency. He motioned us into the abbey. "We will care for your horses while you are here", and another monk came and allowed me to hand down the still sleeping Ellis before I dismounted and then took Cian and Dante. The horses were dirty and tired. I hoped the monks would be kind to them. They were led into the door of a low building. On the opposite side was another low building, sturdy and with baskets of herbs hanging from the eaves. A man emerged, another monk.

This man had lines around his eyes that made him look as if he laughed a lot. His tonsure was neat and fresh, and his habit was clean, in contrast with the first two men. The abbot looked right at me, and said "Please come in, Lady Desmond."

My stomach sunk.

As we entered, he motioned for us to sit on a bench, and he pulled up a chair. "I can't remember a time when I have had so much correspondence" he said with a gentle smile. I almost didn't understand when the monks spoke, because although they spoke English, it came out of their mouths as lilting, singing beauty, like nothing I had ever heard. It made it hard to hear what they were saying, because of how they were saying it.

I was full of trepidation. I didn't know what I had been thinking. Monks had no tolerance of women, and women had no status. They could have held me until Maurice arrived to take me home. Maurice had rights as my husband. He could beat me, rape me, kill me, and the monks had the right to do nothing but sit back and watch. But I stuck with the instinct that I would get better care among them than that.

He clapped his hands and we were brought wine and small cakes with butter. Ellis had wakened when we entered and sat on the floor, eating her cake smiling.

"These letters have either come for you or about you in the last week. There is one here from the Earl of Desmond" he raised his brows and looked pointedly at me, "there are two from a Mr.

McGuigan, esq, two from Mrs. McGuigan, but it seems these are two different women, and now you arrive all wet and with a small child."

I took a deep breath and began to explain. This man made we want to talk, to hold back no secrets in spite of my misgivings. I told him about my marriage, about my initial misgivings, but how I had come to love Maurice. I told him about the death of my first child, and how Maurice had changed. I told him about having been beaten, and finally how the servants, the men at arms and my family had conspired to smuggle me out of Lismore, and how the Earl had followed us to Wexford but had been thwarted. I told him about the death of Ellen after she was kicked in the womb, and the injuries to the mistress in Youghal.

"I need to rest for a few days to determine what I should do next, where I should go."

"And this gentleman?" Nodding at Archibald.

"This is Archibald (I faltered) of...Scotland. He is one of the men at arms from Lismore and he has guided me thus far. Without his kindness I would not have escaped Lismore or survived the journey here."

The Abbot sat back in his chair.

"Hmm. My Lady, I hate to say it but you are not safe here". When he saw me begin to protest, he held up his hand and continued "Which is not to say we can't help. The Earl is a powerful man, and he wrote directly to the bishop. You are his wife, and by law we must return you to him. However, no one here wants to lead the Earl further down the path of sin. We may be able to carry out some sleight of hand, or to act as intermediaries, for the greater good of God. "

"And as for you, Sir Archibald McDonnell, I have been warned of your identity too. Do you not think her Ladyship has a right to know with whom she travels?"

My mouth hung open a little, and I looked at him in surprise. I thought of my father on my wedding day, of the banners of the McDonnell clan in the hall for my wedding.

Archibald responded directly to the Abbot "Father Abbot, I am a simple man at arms. I gave up my name McDonnell after a disagreement with my father when I was young. I have not been that man for many years". He glanced at me. "I'm sorry. I didn't think it mattered." The Abbot looked for several seconds at Archibald before he looked back at me.

The Abbot continued, "The Earl has been searching all of the south of Ireland for days. I estimate you have about two days here before the Earl realizes that here is where you are. It won't be hard. You travel with valuable horses in elegant clothing. Word of your whereabouts will travel quickly. Soon you should depart again on your horses, for speed. I will send a monk with you who knows the road. You will ride to Fishguard, where you will hire a boat to take you east to Merseyside. From there you can travel up to Scotland, and then wither ye may. Scotland is in my experience an excellent place to disappear. Sir Archibald both you and the Lady have ample resources that ensure she can go wherever she will be safe and can do so in obscurity. We will give you monk habits as disguise in the hope that they will aid you to escape the area undetected. As you know, our monks don't ride horses for our work here, but monks who work for the bishop will often ride when their errand requires speed. Should the Earl arrive here, we will give him comfort and succor. But we will not reveal your destination. Presuming of course that he does not arrive before you depart". Tears of gratitude and surprise ran down my cheeks.

"Now, follow Brother Justin and he will show your to your accommodations and furnish you with your habits". The man was smiling broadly. He was having fun. Archibald didn't look very happy though. We would have to talk about it later, in private.

As we left the Abbot's receiving room, for that is what it was, he handed me the letters he had received in care to me. I could read the one Maurice sent to the bishop, but he did not advise it.

Brother Justin took us to another long low building of wood. Despite not being made of stone it was solid, and had a dryness and warmth a stone building would never have. He showed us to two cells normally used for monks. Although the monks normally slept on the floor, beds had been fashioned for us from straw and blankets. There was even a little bed for Ellis. All three of us had one of the monk habits laid on the bed, Ellis' one a beautiful little miniature.

Brother Justin explained where the refectory was, where to find water to fill the ewers in each of our cells, and he directed Archibald to the monks' library, should he wish to read. I wasn't offended at the omission, as I felt little desire to read. As he spoke, the cathedral bells chimed from the hill above the cathedral itself. Brother Justin explained that the ground in the hollow was too soft to bear the weight of the bells, and so a bell tower had been built along the ridge surrounding it. We were welcome to pray with them, and then he excused himself to run to the cathedral.

Archibald also excused himself and followed Brother Justin, which allowed me quiet time to spend with Ellis and read my letters. I fished out Ellis' blocks, those that once belonged to her sister, and sat her on her little bed. I pulled everything out of the bag I had brought from Lismore and allowed the dresses to dry. They were watermarked, but they would cover my body if I needed them to. I thought drily that the monks' asceticism was rubbing off on me already. I lay down just for a moment and was surprised by how comfortable the straw bed was. I was shaken awake by Archibald and found there was no light coming in the cell door. Brother Justin was there holding Ellis and allowing her to touch his tonsure.

"You must wake up!" said Archibald. "An emissary has come from Lismore. No, it's not him. But I think you might be surprised at who it is. Brother Justin will take Ellis to the refectory. You have both slept long."

I rose, and was suddenly conscious of the state of the kirtle I was wearing. I waved Archibald out of the cell and changed quickly into one of the other kirtles, now dry. I cursed the buttons that ran all the way up my sleeves and into my armpits, but I had dressed myself for most of my life without a maid and knew how to do it quickly. I rebraided my hair and emerged, ready to face this emissary, whoever he was.

When I entered the Abbot's receiving room, there was a young man there, and his elegant clothing stood out in contrast to the simplicity of the room. He was dusty and had obviously ridden a long way. When he turned toward me, he had Maurice's face, his dark hair, his height. My stomach lurched and then I realized who he was.

"James!" The shock of seeing James there, the young boy I had so worried about at my wedding, the boy who had been sent to Burgundy for education and learning, had become like everything wonderful that his father was, made me suddenly burst into loud sobs that wracked my body.

"Stepmother, I am so very sorry. I tried to tell you when we sat together at the wedding, but I failed. I am so, so sorry". He held my hands, and looked earnestly at my face.

"Tis true then? The Earl is in the grip of evil?"

James looked at the Abbot and said "my father is two men Abbott. He is the handsome, capable clever Earl, full of charity and patience for all around him. But then an event will send him into the most terrible melancholy, such as the death of my baby

153

sister. He cannot seem to rouse himself from the dark place he inhabits. When he adds drink to the situation, he becomes warped, single minded and dangerous. Everyone who loves my father knows of his affliction. My step mother did not know any of this when she married him. Her father did, however, and so I was surprised he did not prevent the marriage."

"My father did not believe he could say no because of his status relative to that of the Earl. So he helped me as much as he could, including aiding me to escape and providing me funds to do so." Looking back at James, I asked, "How is he?"

James sighed at looked at his hands. "He weeps. He sleeps for days and then does not sleep for as many days. He rides out looking for you. Then he drinks again. We called a surgeon who advised a strong sleeping draught slipped into his food or his drink. He suggested that if we could get him to sleep for a long period, he might awake freed of the melancholia. Mary grinds the herb that sometimes helps and puts it in his food, but he seems out of control now. He does not eat much. He looks ragged and tormented. He sent me out in search of you, and now that I have found you I will have to tell him". A tear trickled down his cheek. "I don't know what to do".

Another voice spoke from a dark corner of the room. A man in the robe of a high ranking cleric emerged from the dark. This was obviously the bishop.

"My son, you have done much. It is obvious to me that all of you love the Earl, and that the power of Christ is in you, and that he is possessed by the twin demons of melancholia and drink. I was not certain until now though I have heard rumours for years. I will offer this. We can never find justice for the wrong he has done, but we may be able to heal him for the future. I would still recommend that Lady Desmond continue on her journey to keep her child and herself safe. It seems the Earl cycles in and out of melancholia, and the death of a child is a horrible thing. Perhaps an even stronger man could not have withstood it."

I stood up, now angry. "I withstood it! I kept moving despite the loss of Pádraigín who we adored". I was yelling now. "He was the one who insisted on using a team of horses that was not ready. It was a WASTE! It was not the horses fault! It was his fault that he left the nursery door open, and she got out and walked in front of those horses! I never held it against him, never mentioned it but once. We shared the same devastating loss, and we should have walked that path together, but he FAILED ME! HE FAILED ME! How could he do that to me, I needed him!" My screaming began to degenerate into unintelligible wailing and I was now down on the floor. All of the weeping and grieving I had held in because of Maurice's illness was now exploding out of me and I couldn't stop it.

Archibald knelt and put his arms around me. He had never touched me before, had always been proper, been somehow withheld. He pulled me to my feet, bore my weight, and walked me across the compound to my cell.

"Ellis…"

"She is fine. The monks adore her. They will care for her for a few more hours. You lay down. I will stay with you for a while. You shouldn't be alone".

He lowered me down onto my straw bed. He lay down beside me and held me while I cried. It seemed like forever.

I was still sobbing softly when a monk came from the infirmary. "My Lady, will you take a sleeping draught?"

I took it gratefully. It smelled of herbs and had honey in it to make it palatable. I handed the cup back with a nod of thanks and put my head once again on Archibald's shoulder.

I remembered nothing else until morning.

I awoke in my cell, and neither Archibald nor Ellis was there. My bag was once again packed, with my gowns, Ellis' blocks. My cloak was hanging and so was my disguise, the habit of a monk. I stood up and brushed the straw off my clothing. As soon as I exited the cell, Brother Justin approached me, having obviously been waiting for me.

"My Lady, judging that women have different sensibilities, the bishop has arranged for you to take a bath, if you wish it. "He smiled gently. "A moment of gentleness and recuperation perhaps. The Bishop regrets that he misspoke and wishes to ease your distress."

The sudden idea of a bath widened my eyes and warmed my heart, not to mention that parts of me were crustier than a sugar coated pastry.

"Oh yes please! Please tell the Bishop how I appreciate his thoughtfulness."

"You can tell him yourself Lady Desmond. I will accompany you to the Palace and everything you need will be provided to you ". He smiled at me and I saw that he had very bad teeth. With the excellent diet of the monks I would have thought his teeth would be better. But then I knew nothing of his life before he became a monk.

We walked through a cool rain to the Palace and entered through an impressive wooden door. Two women were there and they led me to a quiet room toward the back of the palace. There was a large marble tub there, with a drain in it to carry the water away when the bath was done. I had never seen anything like this before. This was opulence of the highest order.

The women helped me out of my kirtle, and the chemise underneath which had seen nothing but ocean water for two weeks. They took my clothes away and left me to soak. Beside me on a little table was a silver bell to summon them if I needed anything. I slid down in the tub until my head was under water. I washed my hair with a wonderful smelling soap, and I soaked all the road dust off my body. Oh it felt so good!

I still felt very fragile from the events of last evening, but it's amazing how a good bath can make one feel stronger and saner.

The women dried me with fine linen and when my clothing returned, my own chemise was neatly folded, and a fresh one was offered. The dust and dirt had been beaten out of my kirtle and even the water stains had faded. It would take a good wash to get them out, but these ministering angels had addressed my ills with the time they had available. I hugged them both before I left, something that surprised them greatly.

I made my way to the refectory as I was powerfully hungry. I had bread, berries, milk and cheese and was soon feeling much better. When I left the refectory I went to the stable to check on Cian and Dante. They were happy to see me, but not sure they ever wanted to leave. There were a few other horses there, including a large grey that looked a lot like one my Father would have bred. It even nickered at me. The monks that tended them smiled at me as they daubed ointment on little nicks, cleaned hoofs, and sang the psalms to them in their glorious language. Dante looked like he had died and gone to heaven. I thanked the monks sincerely, and went to take my chemise back to my cell.

Everywhere I went, the monks were watching me out of the corner of their eyes. I nodded to them each, and continued walking. Did they all know of my disgraceful behaviour the night before? Or was it just because they were unaccustomed to the presence of a woman?

Archibald met me part way across the compound. He had obviously not had the treatment I had. He looked tired and worried. Perhaps he needed a bath too.

"You are wanted My Lady. All concerned parties are to meet in the Bishop's Palace to discuss the situation. And there is something else you need to know. Maurice is there."

So this was the reason for the excellent treatment and the way the monks had been watching me. And the grey horse. I could feel the blood leaving my face. And my head and most of the rest of my body for that matter. Archibald caught me and held me up for a moment until I found my feet. He took the chemise from me and we walked to the cells. He deposited the chemise in my cell and we turned toward the Palace.

The room in the Palace looked like a dining room, but the places had been set with water and fruit. James was there, the Abbot, and there, standing at the end of the table was Maurice. He was well dressed, his hair was clean and tied back, and as soon as he saw me, the tears ran down his cheeks. But he was terribly thin, and his hands shook.

"My Lady. I am sorrier than I can say. I do not deserve your forgiveness."

"Have you come to take me home?" I asked in a whisper.

He nodded no.

I was confused.

The Abbot said, "Why don't we all sit down."

He began, "Sometimes love in a marriage is not enough to make it peaceful. Even as clergy we must admit this. It is obvious to everyone here that there is much love in this marriage. However, the Earl is very ill. It could be the work of the devil, but we don't think so. Sometimes the only devil that really counts is the one inside each of us. The Earl puts everyone around him at risk. He has lost a great deal to his illness. His brother, the 8th Earl of Desmond. His first wife, and the mother of his son. His daughter Joan. And now his second wife. And I believe there is a woman in Youghal whose care will be paid for the from the Earl's estate, until either she dies or he dies, whichever comes first. The Bishop and I agree that no one is at fault except Maurice himself.

"The Earl has undertaken to remove all alcohol, wine and spirits, from anywhere he resides. He understands that the melancholia visited on him by the devil is only made worse when he drinks. However, it is the melancholia that drives him to drink when he is in its grip. The Earl has requested that we undertake his care. In return he will work in our fields and to help maintain the abbey until he feels stronger.

"This is our offer to the Earl. That he stay with us, for as long as it takes, to find an herb remedy to at least ease your melancholia attacks. This is something most men with this condition lack. While you are here, you will immerse yourself in our way of life, in prayer, and in confession and forgiveness. You will not declare yourself healed, for there is no cure, but we will send you on your way when we feel you can cope with your presence in the world.

"As to the arrangement between the Earl and Lady Desmond, it is obvious to us that domestic harmony eludes Maurice Fitz Thomas Fitzgerald. And therefore, while we cannot make a choice for her Ladyship, I suggest that she remain separated from his Lordship, for her own safety and the safety of her child. While the Earl is obviously in control of himself now, he may not be at a time in the future.

"And finally, Sir Archibald McDonnell. Your father is very old now, and has repented his offence to you. You have been needed in the Keppoch for some time. I urgently suggest that you go home. The Keppoch needs its heir. You cannot shirk your responsibilities anymore. And given her Ladyship's bloodline I suggest she go with you" I watched Archibald's face as he listened to these words. He looked sad and resigned. I was confused by the reference to me, but chose to keep my own counsel for the moment.

Maurice remained at the abbey and accepted the hospitality and healing the monks offered. I made sure that he spent time with Ellis before we left, and she stood in his lap and pulled on her Papa's beard. We spent two wonderful, tentative days together as a family, including time between Maurice and me talking and apologizing and understanding. I left the abbey with agreement in writing that although we would be separated, I would remain Maurice's wife and Lady Desmond. Ellis would receive all of the advantages of her station, including an excellent education and an advantageous marriage. I also would continue to receive financial support as his wife and I would continue to work for the education of the poor and other causes with my influence. It was a novel but not unheard of arrangement amongst the nobles of the time. He approved the idea of me going to Keppoch with Archibald, whom he had known about all along. The parting between us was desperately sad, but necessary. He also took a keen interest in Ellis' future, and gave her gifts that he had brought from home.

At our parting there were tears, there were kisses and hugs, and the promise to write to one another often. And we did write, long loving and informative letters, for the rest of his life, until he died in 1520 in battle at Tralee.

Looking back, it seems strange that we could have that happy time after all we had been through, and given that we were about to part as a family forever. But it made sense too. It was a safe place, in isolation from all that had gone before. And Maurice was a sad version of his old self, the man I had loved so much before the accident. And any woman who has been beaten by a man that she loves can tell you of the honeymoon of relief that occurs when the violence stops. It's tempting to think it has stopped forever, but I had lots of support and old bruises and injuries to remind me of what Maurice was capable. I was for Scotland. I would not return to Lismore.

James returned to Lismore to run Maurice's affairs with my father until he was well enough to return. I sent with him letters for everyone I could think of, assuring all of my friends that I was well, that I had finally read their letters, and their efforts on my behalf had not been in vain.

Two days later, Archibald and Ellis, the monk Justin and I set out for Scotland. As we rode, Archibald told us the long story of the Keppoch, his place in it, and mine.

"So you see your great grandsire actually refused the throne which he could have rightly taken. He maintained his relationship with my great grandsire until the end, even though they lived at a distance from one another. Your Father's line began with a truly brave man. Your great grandsire had several children but their lines have all died out, all except yours. Because of the story of our two families, though we are not related, the Keppoch is a natural home for you. The story has been kept alive in our families for a hundred years. I have no idea how Maurice knew, unless your father told him."

After a few moments thought, he said "You see Maurice knew of your bloodline and wanted it for his offspring. That thing your great grandsire was brave enough to reject, Maurice wanted to bring to life. I knew of course, and so did your Father. It's odd that no one ever explained your heritage to you"

Huh. "And my father often wears a small piece of McDonnell tartan on his shoulder. I never knew why, and I never thought enough to ask him"

After riding for a few minutes I said "So that is why he wanted a woman so plain, inexperienced, and crippled." It made me feel so sad and disappointed. I had loved him so very much.

"Oh, it impressed him that the blood of the man who had the courage to refuse the throne still ran strong in your veins. You fought off a swamp fever, and lived. You defied your parents and the accepted order when you demanded to know his intentions in front of everyone. Yes, the bloodline was the initial motivation, but Maurice was so impressed by your character and determination that he loved you from the very first moment he saw you even in spite of your youth. He told me of meeting you as you were resting under a tree, watching over the horses. He said everything about you took his breath away." He was very gentle in the way he looked at me as he told me this.

I wiped a few tears away. I missed him already, in a way that the excitement of escaping clandestinely and running away had not allowed.

"And incidentally, whoever told you that you were plain has never seen you angry. " He grinned.

We rode on, talking of things we knew and places we had been, which in my case wasn't many. When we ran out of things to say to one another in our little travelling party, Brother Justin began to sing in his tenor voice and his beautiful accent. Then Archibald and I joined in with harmonies. Ellis laughed as we walked our horses down the road. [15]

---

[15] By all accounts, the 9th Earl of Desmond, was an honourable and upstanding man of his time. Three of his four children reached adulthood. His second wife, Honora, appears to have been a love match after his children were beginning to mature. He was lame for at least part of his life, and earned the nickname "Vehiculus" because he was carried in a horse litter much of the time. Whether his lameness arose at birth

or through through injury, or through early onset arthritis is unclear. I have assumed the latter here. In 1497 he took part in a small rebellion with Perkin Warbeck, a pretender to the British crown. He was both forgiven and rewarded by the King, which suggests facts that have not persisted into the present. He died in 1520 during a skirmish with Fitzgerald rivals, the Ormonds, and is buried near their stronghold in Tralee.

Carried on the Back of the Horse

Early on the morning of the 19th of April, 1828, I emerged out the main gate of the Royal Citadel in Plymouth, England. I walked under, and turned and looked at the arch above my head, especially the date, 1670, carved into it. Imagine the hands that created that arch 158 years before. Since becoming a member of the King's Royal Engineers, these historic constructions fascinated me. Because of my basic training and my training in the military engineering school, I knew what it took to produce what I considered to be these works of art. I imagined many hands putting the stones in place, and what it took to form the arch so evenly.

Walking down the hill, the City of Plymouth stretched out below me. The Plymouth Citadel was surely the best defended Citadel in the world, with guns that could land shot well out into the harbour, or anywhere in the city for that matter.

Earlier that morning I had attended Mass at the Church of St. Katherine upon the Hoe, completed in 1671. As some thirty men sang the hymns, I cast my eye upwards and admired the construction of the roof and the placement of the columns. The symmetry pleased me. The church was slated for improvements, but I found out after the fact that galleries and transepts were not added until 1845.

My steps led me down through the city. I had lots of time. The tide would not turn until lunch time, and my orders specified that I should board the brig Amethyst by eleven o'clock. That gave me two hours to wander and explore, and I was delighted.

As I strolled through town, with my pack and my weapon, complete with bayonet, over my shoulder, I drew a few stares, but not many. Residents of Plymouth were used to men in uniform.

The market was in full swing, even though at this time of year the seller's wares didn't include much in the way of fresh foodstuffs. There were pickled, dried and salted foods however, and some of them made my mouth water. I bought a jar of pickled green beans and tucked them carefully into my pack.

I wandered through Finewell Street and was impressed by the beauty of the very old houses there, especially Prysten House, identified by a sign on the door post. Imagine the quality of stones and mortar, not to mention the skill, to construct a building still sturdy four hundred years after its construction, like the castles that still dotted the countryside in England and in my Irish home. I admired the arches built over the window to take the strain of the stone wall above. I loved the second story bay windows and imagined looking out of them when the building was newly built. As I stared, a man in the clothing of a merchant emerged from the front door. He walked straight toward me, and looked perturbed about something.

"Are ye at summing?" he said in broad Dorset dialect. Well, I have surmised since that must be what he said.

"Sir I am very impressed with your house" said I.

"Imprest? His voice had raised considerably. "I'll not be imprest!" Now he was yelling. "Ye git out a here!" and now he was charging toward me. I am embarrassed to admit that I began to fairly trot away from the man and his lovely old house.

Once I got further along, and common sense took over, I realized the mistake I made using the word "impress". Although Press gangs had not been officially used by the King's military since it was outlawed in 1707, it was clear that in a navy town such as this one, the local memory was long. It was also not beyond my imagination that sailors might have since been recruited from the town with some prejudice, regardless of what their navy enrollment papers might say. The Napoleonic war had ended in 1815, and I doubted not that there were many here who had just such an experience and were loath to forget.

Still, I was a grown man in my prime, a military officer, and armed no less, and I had been chased away by an older man with no shortage of short ribs around his middle. I resolved not to tell a soul.

I decided to make my way down to the docks, as an hour and a half of my free time had now elapsed. I nodded good morning to all whom I passed, occasionally doffing my cap to the ladies. I loved my uniform, loved it before I had ever put it on. I loved the red wool serge, the white straps across the chest, the wildly impractical but crisp white trousers. All made more splendid by the gold braid. But my favourite of all was the boots, made in such a way that they gave a very satisfying click when I walked. My steps were only very slightly uneven, a condition caused by a broken left ankle I suffered as a child. The rhythm of my step was self-regulating, such that when walking, I invariably arrived at my destination more quickly.[16]

When I arrived at the docks and was directed to the Amethyst, I stood and analyzed her for a moment. She was a brig, her two masts naked until the sails were set for departure. Named after HMS Amethyst, which sailed during the war of 1812 with the United States and later ran aground and was foundered, this ship was a bit smaller, but still impressive in her perfection, her excellent trim.

As I stood and watched, ship's crew loaded wooden crates and boxes addressed to W. Price and Co, Quebec City. She had already loaded some cargo in London before calling in Plymouth, and her next port of call would be Quebec City on the St. Lawrence River in Lower Canada.

I loved every block and tackle, every rope. I had never been a sailor, but as an engineer I could see the work accomplished by many parts working together. She had copper sheathing on her hull, presumably to strengthen it. The deck rails were

---

[16] https://www.pinterest.ca/powercampbell/royal-engineers-uniforms/

freshly varnished. I supposed they would have to be so every time she came into port, a protection against salt water and salt air.

I felt a frisson of excitement. My journey from Londonderry across the Irish Sea had been my only voyage to date. The Amethyst was larger and the journey to Quebec much further by far. The weather was cold for April but sunny and clear, and the mood was perfect.

Boarding the gang plank, I was greeted on the deck by a hand whose muscles were intimidating, but whose teeth were non-existent. His face was weathered such that I could never have dreamed of estimating his age. He had apparently been warned of the embarkment of a military officer, because he gestured toward the upper deck with his thumb. I nodded, proceeding as instructed.

A man sat at a table with a pen and ink noted my presence immediately, and greeted me with my full name and correct rank (lieutenant)[17]. He had a list of passengers, of which I was the first to embark. He placed a check mark by my name and gave me a small piece of paper.

"Welcome aboard the Amethyst Sir, this is your berth. Now mind, this isn't no roomy army mess. It's snug, but it's comfortable. Let myself or the mate know if you need anything". I supposed all of the crew would have these weathered faces and

---

[17] https://en.wikipedia.org/wiki/Lieutenant for a young officer in the British army, this rank would be pronounced **LEFTenant.**

hands chapped by sea water and well-muscled from work.

There were to be 35 passengers including myself. The hold was very laden with cargo. Additionally there were ten crew, for a total of 45 souls aboard for the crossing.

The berths had carefully painted numbers on their sliding doors, and when I slid mine to, it exposed half of the berth, the remainder still hidden behind the doors. There was room for the bed and my kit bag and me, each thing with its assigned space. When I clambered up into it and closed the door, I discovered it was snug, warm, and extremely comfortable. I may have been unconsciously comparing it to less comfortable army digs, but be that as it may, I would be comfortable for the month long journey.

Feeling no need to sleep, I left my little nest and explored the ship. Below deck was the galley and the dining area, scarcely large enough for half of the souls on board. We therefore would eat in shifts. The smell of burning coal filled the galley. The cook was already working, preparing stew and bread for the evening meal. I introduced myself and then moved to the upper deck where most of the crew now were.

Most of the passengers were now on deck, children running around and teenagers pretending they were much too refined for such games. There were three families in all, each intending to find new homes in Upper or Lower Canada. Robert Elliot, with his family hoped to travel to the naval base at

Kingston. The Elliots also travelled with Mr. Elliot's brother and his family. The Price family had relatives in York Factory. Mr. Price was a wealthy merchant, and most of the cargo in the hold belonged to him, merchandise to be sold to the residents of York factory. I wondered idly if they knew exactly how hard it was going to be to get all of that cargo to York Factory. The rest of the passengers were men, some travelling to make a new life in the colonies, but there were 12 persons employed by the Hudson's Bay Company travelling throughout the colonies to take up their stations in outposts from Montreal to the far north.

Presently the cry went up to unfurl the sails on the rear mast, and although the passengers were allowed to stay, we were herded fore so that we did not get in the way of the crew carrying out their task. The bow and stern lines were released from the dock, and men pulled each of them in and coiled them on the deck. The ropes were fully one inch in diameter, and rope of such thickness was surely very heavy and difficult to coil, but the men made it look effortless.

With the mate at the ship's wheel, the ship caught wind in the rear sails and pulled away from the quay. She edged away and out into the bay, picking up speed as she went. Soon we passed Mount Edgecumbe in the bay and sailed out into the open ocean. The sails on the foremast were now raised quickly and smoothly. The breeze across the deck picked up, and most of the passengers disappeared below. But I stayed above, exhilarated by the swells and the wind. It thrilled me to imagine that we were in a giant bowl of water, the swells created by the stirring of a giant spoon.

After an hour or so above, I asked one of the crew if the swells were getting rather large.

"Oh aye" said he, in a tongue that might once have been a Scottish brogue but which exposure to languages and dialects all over the world had rounded into a sort of blended accent.

"Well is that not bad?"

"Och no Sir, this isn'a bad. Now tomorrow when we meet the storm causing these swells, tha' might be a bit bad".

I gaped. "Bad? Well do we not have to go back then?"

"Och no Sir, every ship's journey has at least one storm"

"Oh. So you're used to it then. Very well, we just get through the storm and then it's smooth sailing."

"Nooo" he hesitated. "Then we run into the ice coming south from the north. As long as we are not scuppered by the ice, THEN it should be smooth sailing."

He looked at me. "If you don't mind me saying Lieutenant, you look a little green. Why don't you retire below decks?"

I nodded and headed toward the aft hatch. When I reached the bottom, I was handed a bucket.

"Put it on the floor outside your berth Sir. Crew will empty it from time to time.

Without a word, I took the bucket and installed myself in my berth.

For the next three days I knew neither night nor day. I was sure that I had vomited my toenails by the time I began to feel better. Bad dreams of drowning and sore abdominal muscles made my misery complete. After three days, the door of my berth slid open, and the Mate instructed me to get up and get dressed. It was time to eat.

I was absolutely not sure I would hold food down, but cook had prepared a delicious pea soup and I found I was not just hungry but voracious. In talking to the others, it seemed that none of them had eaten for two days, seasickness or not. Cook had been unable to cook in the storm. Bread and molasses had been served, but it was no substitute for meals. We compared our experience of waves and the rising and falling of the ship, and when we made room for the rest of the passengers, most of us retired to the deck.

The sun was out, and a fulsome breeze kept the sails full. It felt as though we were racing across the sea. The crew had laid out deck chairs so that we could sit and enjoy the breeze and the sunshine. Around us, crew members carried out maintenance and repairs necessitated by the storm. One fellow, the one with the big muscles but no teeth I had met when boarding, sat in a chair beside me repairing a rip in a sail. The sail was thick, heavy canvas. I watched as his massive hands maneuver an equally massive needle through the cloth and tied a knot with each stitch. The fibre he used as thread was also very heavy and he rubbed it with a block of beeswax regularly to keep it moving through the canvas.

"Excuse me" I began "What cloth are your sails made of, if you don't mind?"

"I don't mind at all sir. These are made of hemp. It is a much stronger fibre than cotton or linen, weaves up heavier, and wears much longer." He answered good- naturedly, although I am sure he had answered the very same question for many passengers before me.

"And what is hemp, if you please?" I asked. I had never heard of it.

"Grows in warmer climes, harvested and shipped to mills in the civilized world to be woven. It is also made into rope. Our bow and stern ropes are made of hemp. It doesn't seem to rot in the salt."

"Thank you so much for the information." As I thanked him, he heaved up out of his chair and called for another to help him fold the sail ready for hanging when needed.

Someone sat in the chair beside me, and looking, I found it to be a young lady about my own age. She had very dark hair, done up in the fashion of the time, and the sort of high colour that usually leaves the face pale until anger or embarrassment rises in rich red colour across the cheeks. She was in fact uncommonly pretty. She wore a lovely red dress, and a matching red hat pinned to her dark curls. I was at least as captivated by her as I had been by the sail repairs.

Once she had settled her skirts and underskirts on the chair, she settled back and happened to notice me.

"Oh, I'm sorry! Do you mind?" gesturing at the chair.

"Of course not! I am delighted for the company. "

I gave her my name and reached for her hand.

"Yes, I was admiring your fine uniform. Elizabeth Elliot. My husband and I are headed for the New World. He wants to try his hand at settling. You know, cabin, farming and such. I thought I might write about it." She said these things with an airiness, an ease that suggested she was either very brave, or very ignorant.

"I mean no disrespect" I responded, "but I think what you propose is extremely difficult. Are you well prepared do you think?"

She laughed. "Oh yes, once we get settled we can hire men to build our home. "

"Oh I see. Where will you live while your house is being built?" I asked.

"Oh a hotel I am sure. Wherever one goes, there is always a hotel, even if it is of an inferior standard."

"And have you and your husband decided where you would like to settle? When I met him the day we boarded, he spoke of Kingston."

"Oh yes", she said, "they hope to build a fine university there. It must be a wonderful place, don't you think?"

I nodded and smiled. I could find no more inclination to participate in what I felt was a very silly conversation. I had read everything I could find about Bytown, and about Kingston at length. I had heard that there was a naval base at Kingston, and that some people had begun to settle there. There might be rooms for rent, but I seriously doubted that there was what this lovely young woman regarded as a hotel. No marble floors, not debutant balls for her daughters. Having spoken to her husband, I thought his grasp of the living conditions in Kingston were quite good, but he had sadly neglected to explain them to his wife. He obviously expected that she was simply obliged to trail along behind him on his adventures. I was truly sorry that she was to be disappointed and had no control over what was coming to her. I suspected that if I were to see her in a year's time, she would be a very different woman.

The voyage progressed on until some two weeks had elapsed. We all tired of time on deck and sleeping in our very small quarters. We knew the proper names of every individual sail and every part of the ship. There was no novelty left, however fascinating all of the moving parts were.

One evening as I left the mess, I heard a very different signal up on deck, and some running and shouting. I emerged into the night air to find that the sails were down all but one, and in the distance both to starboard and to port there were huge white ghostly formations. Ice.

A bundle of long thin poles that had been strapped to the inside of the ship along the deck was being broken up and one pole handed out to every able bodied man. I took mine and following the example of a crew member took a position along the starboard side. A man in the crow's-nest watched as we approached the giant bergs. There were many of them stretching into the distance on either direction. There became a deafening silence on deck as the floating mountains came near. Close up they were much larger than they had appeared from afar.

Very slowly we sailed between two of the biggest bergs. When the call "starboard" came, I followed the example of the men around me and used my pole to gain purchase on the ice and to push it away from me. In the cold salt water I could see that the ice bergs were much more massive below than they were on the surface. No matter if pushing or not, I could use my pole to touch ice right beside the ship at least some of the time. Sometimes terrible groaning noises echoed against the ice. Crew members leaned over the side, checking to make sure the copper armor was still intact. Their bodies were taught with tension, their faces white with fear. The calls of starboard and port went on for hours, sometimes punctuated with "gently!" All through the night, the white shadows floated by. All of the men poling were tired in varying degrees. A pole was dropped, and a boy of about 12, who was probably an apprentice, swung down on a rope and retrieved it. Exasperated faces turned to the man who had dropped it.   It wasn't until the sun began to rise that we could see the bergs were dwindling in frequency. Soon we had sailed entirely free of the ice field, and we surrendered our sticks.

My shoulders, back and neck were terribly sore after the long night, not to mention the tension of waiting for the horrible bone-breaking sound of ice tearing copper and wood. I rested for a long time, woken only the next evening by the cry of "ice!"

Once more we assembled on deck with our sticks prepared to push away the crushing ice from the hull. But there were only three bergs that we could see, and those were avoided with a deft turn of the rudder.

I stayed on deck to talk to the crew, an inclination enjoyed by other passengers as well. The captain expressed his gratitude to all of the passengers who had helped with the ice. He said we might yet encounter ice, but hopefully anything we saw would be small and easily avoided.

"Tis a poor captain who allows his vessel to hit a lone iceberg in calm seas."[18] His opinion was apparently shared by the crew around us, who all nodded and smiled.

He leaned over the port side and showed us the copper sheathing meant to help protect against the saltwater and any obstacles we might hit, such as ice. It wasn't perfect, but it was one small piece of armor against a hostile sea.

As it happened, we didn't see any more ice. And eventually we heard "land ho!" It was explained that this was Newfoundland, where Irishmen had been fishing for many generations. I had not known

---

[18] 84 years later the Titanic would hit an ice berg and sink in these same waters.

179

this. Sure enough, we did see a vessel with nets over the side. She sat low in the water, and one of her nets bulged heavily with silver wriggling fish and the men in the boat struggled to pull the load aboard. The men aboard wore canvas coveralls and light coloured sweaters with complex knitted patterns like those from the Aran Islands. Not Irishmen per se but still a long way from home. Huh.

The rest of the journey there was land in the distance on the starboard side. It didn't look very hospitable, being mostly rock and scrub vegetation. Once we saw a huge animal, like a deer but bigger than anything I had ever seen before. It had a massive appendage on its head, so big I thought it must be too heavy for the animal to carry. THIS hadn't been in any of my readings! One of the Hudson's Bay men was amused at my reaction, and explained that this was a moose, usually harmless except in the fall. He said they were good eating. I responded "People HUNT that??!!" and he laughed.

Another animal that all of the passengers enjoyed was a black bear. The Mate explained that they slept all winter, living off the fat stored on their bodies. They emerge in the spring very skinny as the one we saw through the spyglass. It had a glorious long black coat, but it did indeed look rather thin. The same Hudson's Bay man said "Hunt that too" and grinned. I grinned back.

There had been porpoises and dolphin that had appeared alongside a few times in the journey. They swam in the wake of the ship along the prow. It was a joy to watch them as they clearly enjoyed themselves. But then another air breathing fish showed up, when we were in the Gulf of St Lawrence. It was white and much larger than a dolphin or a porpoise. What magical sea monster was this? It had a very definite blowhole in the top of its head, and it seemed equally as friendly as the other cetaceans we had seen. Apparently they would sometimes follow a ship all the way to Quebec City, not so much for food as for the sheer joy of companionship. The ship's mate tossed a piece of bread to one swimming on the port side. It spat out the bread, but a dozen other little fish nibbled away at it until it was gone. Then the Mate tossed a fish to it and it leapt up out of the water for it. It was delightful. I looked for the Hudson's Bay man to ask if he hunted that too, but he wasn't around.

While I was enthralled by how much I was learning, and by the animals, I was beginning to worry about my fitness for accepting a post that was essentially in the bush. I could shoot, and indeed in training I had won shooting competitions against the other cadets. But I had never hunted anything in my life. How would I know what to hunt and what to leave alone? I suspected the bear indulged in some form of retaliation if you shot at it and missed, or worse, injured it. I sincerely wished not be retaliated against.

Finally May 17 arrived, and we sailed into Quebec City. I was surprised at how civilized the place looked. The docks were busy with people of all shapes and sizes. From what I saw ships from all over the world docked here. Men of all different colours and shapes and sizes. I was quite speechless. Many of these people were of races I had never seen or knew existed. I hadn't seen a lot of them in the Parish of Dunvegan. And oddly, not in Plymouth either, despite its worldliness.

Quebec City was a major sailing port that ranked among the greatest in the world at that time. It was the front door to the colonies of Upper and Lower Canada. Shipments came there from all over the world of tea, manufactured goods, and immigrants. This time in history was the beginning of a river of immigration that has been the building of Canada throughout its history.

When it was time to disembark, and I carried all my kit to the gang plank, the Mate showed me where the wharf was for the steamship that was to take me to Montreal. I thanked him heartily for his hospitality and his kindness, and turned to walk down the gangplank. He wished me well and I waved back at him.

On the dock I stopped to look up at the Amethyst. I had spent a month of my life with her as my home. I had learned so much and I felt I was already so much changed from the young man who left the manor at Limavady so long ago. I knew privilege, I knew how to help run my father's estates, I could run work crews, and I had been trained to manage military men. But the Amethyst had made me realize how little I knew about anything.

The Elliot family soon joined me on the wharf but there was no occasion to bid them goodbye and good luck. Mrs. Elliot was crying piteously upon realizing she was to travel to Kingston in a Durham Boat in full view of the American coastline. The canal I would be helping to build would have made her journey both more pleasant and easier, but in 1828 it was still only under construction. I wondered if I would ever see them again.

I made my way to the steamer dock. Her name was the Chambly. I couldn't pronounce it, but the crew informed me that it was French. That made sense, since this area had in fact been French territory for a long time. She was a relatively new ship, and I was to find out later that this was only her sixth voyage. There was a steady stream of passengers climbing the gang plank. I climbed it in my turn, and again was given a number. I was assigned to first class, but the division was not a rigid one. Apparently there were 99 passengers for that voyage. They ranged from new arrivals like myself to families living in Quebec that were going to Montreal for a visit, to business men and soldiers. Families of all forms and shapes strolled the deck as she pulled away from the dock, the wheel turning slowly like a Titan newly roused. She was elegant, and there was a large well-appointed salon, but I was tired. I found a seat, and for the first time on my journey, pulled out my letters from home.

I had picked up my letters from the adjutant at Plymouth the day before I left. There was one from my Mother, written in her beautiful hand and on expensive stationery, expressing love for me and alarm that I was removing so far from her. There was one from my father, on much more business-like stationery, with lots of advice about the damned French and not taking any nonsense from the heathens. And then there was one from Josephine Connolly.

Josephine and I had known one another since we were babies. We played on my Father's estate, went through the childhood diseases at the same time, and were devoted companions almost until I left for England. It seemed we were a match meant to be. She was a distant cousin and we had lived our lives in the same milieu. I thought she was absolutely lovely, from the colour of her hair, to the colour of her lips. I could not imagine spending my life without her.

Until the day when she commenced to pout about what she took to be my lack of love for her. I had never once attempted to be indecent with her (her words) and she took this to mean that she did not arouse desire in me. I can honestly say that it never once occurred to me that she should. I mean, we were not married, not even engaged. Was I supposed to? I thought such behaviour would be frowned on. In my upbringing, being frowned on was bad.

To ease her mind, I agreed that we should meet somewhere very private and attempt to consummate our relationship. I'm not sure how she engineered it, but she procured a small cottage for us where we could be utterly undisturbed. When I got there, she had enough candles burning that an entire fire brigade of horses and men and hoses might be required to put them out. There was a beautiful intricate quilt on the bed, and she wore what I took to be a nightgown, all softness and lace.

It was some beautiful soft fabric and I could see the shadows of her body underneath. Her breasts were full, her belly rounded, and her ass was so firm and well-shaped it made me moan. When she had me naked, however, it was immediately evident that I was not rising to the occasion. She smiled slyly and sat me on the bed, dropping to her knees. She took my cock in her mouth, stroking with her hand as she did so. Where did she learn to do this? This was a whole side of her I had never seen before, and honestly I didn't know if I liked it. Nevertheless, I enjoyed the ministrations of her tongue, her mouth and her hands.

I was just at the precipice of a thundering climax when she pulled her mouth away and mounted me. She was slippery and wet and she slid onto me, and she started bouncing up and down. I tried the best I could to stay in the moment, but sure enough, I lost my erection long before either one of us really enjoyed it much. I didn't know why this didn't excite me. Perhaps I loved her too dearly, too long, to think of her in such a base way.

We both cried after. I held her, as I had always longed to do. The safety of being naked in a bed with this person who knew me so well and accepted me for myself without question was precious. But perhaps I had mistaken her acceptance, as she had mistaken what I was. We talked about it. She suggested that maybe she had done it wrong, that if the approach had been my own it might have held more appeal.

So we started again. I slid the nightgown off over her skin and stroked her with my hands. I touched every inch of her body. She had the most perfect woman's body. Everything looked right, felt right. I worked my way down and spread her legs. I knew how to do this. A maid had taught me to do this when I was about 13, one of my deepest darkest secrets. I did it and I did it well. As I did I penetrated her backside with my finger. When she came she practically levitated off the bed. I mentally congratulated myself.

But Josephine cuddled next to me and cried. I was surprised, given the power of the orgasm she just had.

"Don't you understand?" she sniffled on my chest. "I can't have babies through my mouth or my backside. You have to want to take me as a woman. And it's obvious that is the sex act you are least attracted to."

I saw her a few times after that, but clearly we had become broken. It felt like nothing would ever be the same. With the loss of her I had nothing really left to tie me down to Limavady and the estate of Drenagh. As the fourth son of a wealthy landowner, I would inherit no property. The estate would go to my elder brother, and I would have to make my own way. That was when I joined the Royal Engineers.

You might think that a young lady of Josephine's age and social class should not have known the things she did, but it didn't surprise me at all. As with some women in all times, Josephine made it her business to know what to do. She knew what she wanted.

I read Josephine's letter. It wasn't long. She had married and was now pregnant, due in midsummer. I was genuinely happy for her, and I resolved to send her a letter to that effect at my first opportunity. I was surprised that I didn't feel any regret at the idea of her having a life and children with another man. I missed her, and sometimes wished I could see her and talk to her, but I felt no ill will toward her husband. Huh.

I dozed a bit as we cruised toward Montreal. A mountain island in the Saint Lawrence River, it had originally been settled by religious orders of the Roman Catholic Church, or Papists as my Father used to say. Interestingly, there was already a significant Irish community on the island, both Catholic and Protestant. I had a cousin there who I had not seen for some years, since he left Ireland to make his fortune.

I remember my first drill instructor on the art of wearing the uniform. One must never sleep, dance, vomit or kiss a girl, not necessarily in that order, while wearing the uniform. One must not touch anyone in a familiar or intimate way. And one must never allow meanness or stupidity to exit one's mouth at any time. At the time, I wondered who was to judge what stupidity was.

I could not seem to rouse myself from my stupor, so I went in search of my cabin, pulling the little slip with the number on it from my pocket. The berth was a little larger than the one I had on the Amethyst, the bed was reasonable, and there was room to set down my kit bag and my weapon. I hadn't allowed the purser to bring my things to the berth, as another one of those military rules was that I should never relinquish my weapon to anyone, for however rational a reason.

I climbed into the bed and slept until the purser knocked on the door the next morning to rouse me for breakfast. I told him I would wait for second sitting, and took the time to wash, shave, and attend to the wear and tear a month at sea had inflicted on my tunic and trousers. One thing that surprises many people when I tell them about my time in the army is that we were expected to mend and clean our own uniforms. An officer considerably more senior than me would have a batman, a valet who performed these tasks for him whom he paid out of his own pocket, but I certainly couldn't afford it. I kept a little sewing kit with red and white threads and two or three preciously expensive needles in my bag.

When I arrived for breakfast, I was thrilled with the food that was presented. Apples, nuts, eggs, fried ham, good coffee, bread, and a selection of jams and pickled vegetables. The Captain had eaten at the first sitting, but the Mate explained that this was a very common breakfast in Lower Canada. Sometimes, he said, there would be sausages. I found the food so much more wholesome than what I was used to at home. Perhaps it was the inclusion of the fruit and nuts that made it seem so.

I spent the day strolling on the deck and watching the wilderness roll by. Dark green pine trees, blue spruce, poplar and aspen in places. Occasionally I saw wildlife like deer and moose, much closer than the view from the Amethyst had been. And periodically in a cleared space, a farmer and his horses, usually blacks, plowing and seeding the land. Once we saw another bear, a sow with two little cubs. The cubs were fat and funny, but the sow was still recovering her weight from the winter and nursing her cubs. Her eyes looked up at the steamer as she passed, not in alarm, but perhaps in resignation that man with his technology had invaded her private world.

Of course I couldn't put names to most of these things yet. But I listened to other men on the deck, some of whom dressed in various costumes of leather ("deerskin son, isn't it soft? Best breeches you can imagine"). Some of these men had been here for all of their lives, learning from settler parents. Some had come as young men, and the adventure and hardship they had lived showed in the lines on their faces. One man showed two ladies that he was missing two toes from his left foot and said that they had been frozen one winter when he was checking trap lines. When one of the women fainted, I shook his hand but pointed out that his display might have been a bit much for ladies new to the Canadas. He grinned and showed a mouth full of rotten teeth.

Both nights after the ladies retired, I sat on the deck with these same adventurers. With the need for manners or bravado gone, they passed around an excellent bottle of rum and told stories of their lives. As I listened to them in the dim lamplight, they talked of the beauty of snow and silence. One told a story of killing a bear in the fall, and finding she was pregnant, carrying triplets that would have been born in the den. He cried over her body, wished he had killed the male he had seen earlier and spared. They talked of living with the Indians, and scorned the word savage. One man said living with the Algonquin for a year had taught more about survival and decency than he ever could have imagined in his Scottish home. After listening for a while I asked a question.

"If life in the wilderness is so magical, why are you all travelling in such a civilized way as a steamship bound for a settlement?" To a man, they averted their eyes, searching their hands for sudden miraculous discoveries.

Then I realized that one hand had a wedding ring. I asked the wearer "you left the life you loved for a woman, is that it?"

He looked at me sheepishly and said "I love her more". The others nodded, smiled, shrugged. I fervently wished that I could enjoy such love and fulfillment and full sense of self as these men had found.

We crawled off to bed, tired and a bit drunk, for our second and last night on the steamer.

In the morning and after breakfast, I stood on the deck and watched the forest go by. Settlements were more numerous here, villages clustered around large churches. There was a lot less wildlife, and more farms, what I had learned were called seigneuries, a strip of land starting at and leading away from the river. Most of the seigneuries had docks of some kind built at the river. Their main conversation with the rest of the world was often by boat. And everywhere, at least some of the horses on every farm were those same blacks.

We steamed into Montreal by lunch time.

There is a painting of Montreal painted by James Grey in 1828, at precisely the time of my visit. It shows quite accurately what I saw. On the far bank, cattle and sheep grazed. The Island of Mount Royal was so large that it wasn't immediately evident that it was in fact an island. The Mountain lurked in the background, with the settlement in front comprised of wooden dwellings and a few masonry buildings, including a very fine partially built church that I could see in the distance. It merely awaited its steeples.

At the bottom of the gangplank, there were two women, one white and one with beautiful skin the colour of caramel, and the way they greeted two of my friends from the previous night, it was immediately obvious that they were the reason for leaving life in the wilderness. One pulled a cake out of her bag and gave it to her man. The other kissed her man in a very wanton fashion. He didn't even notice me watching.

Bemused, I turned away. My passage on the Amethyst had been booked by the army, and I had been instructed to seek out the steamship line in Quebec City. But here, my instructions simply stated that I was to make my way to Bytown and seek out Colonel By. I looked around at the confusion of boats and people and cargo and animals and truthfully I felt a bit bewildered. Especially when the cacophony of multiple languages was added to the mix. French, English, and something else spoken by dark skinned people also moving on the dock.

As if summoned, I heard a voice somewhere on the dock calling my name. I stood on my toes and looked all over the docks. In the distance, there was an arm waving. Hearing my name in a strange place where I was beginning to feel alone was such a heartwarming occurrence that I would have moved toward the voice and its arm even if a dragon might be attached to the arm. I pushed through the crowd in that direction.

When I finally found the source of the arm, I was delighted to find that it belonged to Thomas McCausland, my cousin through my Uncle Maurice on my father's side. I hadn't thought I was homesick, and maybe I wasn't, but the sight of him brought tears to my eyes, and I hugged him tightly.

Thomas was a good ten years my senior, and like me, he was a younger son, only his father was a younger son as well, so there would be no sizeable inheritance from that source. He had left for Lower Canada more than five years before I did, seeking his fortune. He still looked like an Irishman, with his vest and cap, and a full blond beard clustered around his jaw. Apparently my father had written him of my approximate date of arrival. He had looked for me on the docks for the last week. We repaired to an inn a little away from the docks (leave the sailors to their own, he said).

The ale and the whiskey flowed and we were joined by some of the dark skinned men I had seen on the docks. Their clothes were deer skin, like the men on the steamer, and their hair was long and braided back out of their faces. These were the Algonquin, the native peoples of the Ottawa River Valley. Their muscles bulged under their tunics and their trousers. I would not have wanted to meet those men alone without a friend to recommend me. And as they surveyed my red uniform, my pack and especially my weapon, they didn't look thrilled to meet me either. I smiled awkwardly and toasted to their good health, swallowed all of my whiskey and wondered what Thomas had got me into.

Once a few rounds of whiskey had been drunk, and Thomas had spoken with them in their own tongue, nodding and gesturing at me, the intimidating men did seem to accept me better. When we finally parted company, all of us with at least a few ounces of liquor on board, we were jolly friends.

Thomas shook me awake early the next morning, and my head pounded. I could hear Irish voices, some from our home in the north, and others from the south. I could smell fried food, probably eggs, bread, and some kind of vegetable – a good old Fry. My stomach turned at the smell and I found myself heaving into a chamber pot. When I felt a bit better, Tom cajoled me into getting dressed and fed me some of the food. There was a woman in the kitchen of the house, clearly a very good friend of my cousin, judging by the way he touched parts of her anatomy that I thought she should not admit she had around a stranger. I thanked her for the food and the tea, and I really did feel much better.

Tom started ushering me out of the house, saying "Come on, come on, you're going to be late". This surprised me as I had no idea I was going anywhere.

We hustled down to the docks, quiet at this hour of the morning. As we trotted, Thomas was talking. "Now the thing about the Algonquin, they follow their own time, you know. They simply leave when they feel it's time. And if you're not there, they'll leave without you."

My head pounded as my feet hit the dock, and I was trying to make sense of what he was talking about. I had no idea why I was at the docks so early, with a fine rain beginning. And then I looked up.

There were our friends the Algonquin, the one who seemed in charge standing on the dock, and two in a vessel that was at least as long as four men. I was captivated by it. I greeted the men, but then spent several minutes looking closely at it. I had never seen a canoe before but I had heard about them. I looked at the formation of the beautiful rounded ends, the bow larger and more exaggerated than the stern. I had heard that these vessels were made of birch bark, part of the Algonquin's natural inheritance of the land. I reached out my hand to touch the bark, when Thomas cleared his throat strongly. Oh. Don't touch.

I looked at these Algonquin men, who bore me no love, and said "It's magnificent".

Then Thomas picked up my pack and my rifle and tossed them to the men waiting in the canoe. Then he looked significantly at me. The rule about touching my weapon echoed in my head. I heard it go "snap!"

"Remember cousin, we talked about this last night. I called in a favour from these lads to get you to Bytown. It's a great favour for which I am very grateful" he said in a singsong voice, nodding at the men.

My throat went dry. "How long will it take?" I croaked.

The man standing on the dock said "Depends on the flow of the Ottawa River. The worst of spring rains are past, if we paddle well, three, four days".

"Paddle well....."

Thomas looked annoyed. "Yes, you are to provide the fourth paddler, to make up for the man who lies ill in the Jesuits Infirmary, as we discussed last night". His eyes bugged out a little at the "discussed last night" part. He looked at the others and shrugged and said "Whiskey".

Accepting my fate, I shook Thomas' hand and nodded to the Algonquin. "Before we begin" I started doubtfully, "what do I call you all?"

I gave them my name and turned to each man in turn. The big fellow on the dock, who seemed to be in charge, identified himself as Pierre. The other two were Ahanu and Jean. I shook each of their hands as I shakily got in the canoe, a formality they accepted reluctantly, and sat down where I was pointed. They seemed to accept me begrudgingly. Ahanu started explaining in excellent English how to paddle and how the paddle could be used both as propulsion and steering. As he spoke, I understood it in engineering terms, the way the angle of the blade gave force to the stroke, and I was very pleased suddenly to take part in the journey though my training in the art of it was somewhat scarce. I looked up to wave goodbye to Thomas, but he was already gone, and the Algonquin were already beginning to paddle.

Since Ahanu was in the back, he was the steering wheel. After a short while we approached a canal to our right that appeared to cut right through the island. I asked what it was and Pierre told me it was the Lachine Canal, although he offered no further explanation.

We paddled continuously since we were travelling against the water which flowed toward the Saint Lawrence River, and beyond it the Gulf of Saint Lawrence.   I realized all of a sudden that the entire journey would be upstream. Oh. Great.

On either side of the canal, there was industry of many kinds. Horses worked along the bank, and barges floated here and there that the boats, and our canoe, had to navigate around. Occasionally there were pipes that dumped fluid into the canal. The Algonquin muttered among themselves. When I asked what they were saying, Pierre answered that the industries were poisoning the water, and that the Algonquin believed it was wrong. I agreed with them. It seemed very wrong. [19]

---

[19] https://iaac-aeic.gc.ca/Content/A/4/2/A421C8F2-FEA0-40A0-A584-2C8DDFCDB497/report_e.pdf Lachine Canal Decontamination Project

Coming out of the Lachine Canal, we entered Lac St Louis. The day was calm and sunny, so we made good time. When we reached the Ottawa River and turned north, the flow was a little stronger and so the paddling was harder. I barely noticed the brush that grew up to the banks of the river as I was devoting most of my energy to my paddle, I had a notion that it was pretty dense but nothing more. Once a steamer passed us. I looked at it in surprise. Pierre looked back at me and merely shrugged.

It was starting to get dark when Ahanu steered us into the shore. I could hear a loud roaring in the distance, and I asked about it. Pierre merely said "falls".

The others got out of the canoe, so I grabbed my pack and my rifle, but Pierre stopped me. He showed me how to strap my bag and my rifle into the gunnels of the canoe, so that it would not come loose. I thanked him, but I was not even sure he heard me. Then one, two, three, we picked up the canoe and turned it upside down, balancing the cross members on our shoulders. Pierre led us through the bush, and suddenly a narrow path became apparent under our feet. We walked in this way for some time, certainly until it was very dark. In my position behind Jean and Pierre, I couldn't see where we were going, so I just concentrated on the placement of my feet. There were rocks on the path fairly regularly, and I decided that it would not do to break an ankle whilst out in the bush. I remembered the break in my ankle that caused my uneven step. It ached sometimes during a cold rain, but most of the time it didn't trouble me. But having experienced the pain and inconvenience in the past, another broken ankle was even less attractive. The Algonquin barely seemed to have any respect for me as it was.

After we had walked for about 45 minutes, suddenly there was light off to my right. On the count of three we put the canoe down on its side, and turned toward a camp fire. There were women and children, and more Algonquin men. There was the smell of food, and evergreen trees. A few dogs trotted around. In a clearing behind the campfire area, there were large, conically shaped tents that appeared to be made of skins and more birch bark. I tried not to stare but to take it all in.

The others sat near the fire, so I did the same. There was much talk and gesticulating and pointing at me. Pierre seemed to be explaining to one of the women why a British soldier had just climbed out of a canoe on the nearby riverbank. It was pretty clear that British soldiers were not popular among the Algonquin, at least, these Algonquin.

The woman looked at me and walked off. I felt like a skunk at a garden party. But she came back with something in her hands. In perfect English, she spoke to me. "You take these clothes, put away your fine English uniform before you ruin it. You will also find it easier to talk and move around our people if you don't look like the instrument of everything bad that has happened to the Algonquin for the last hundred years". Second military rule: never be out of uniform. "Snap!" But her advice made perfect sense.

I rose immediately and took the fine deerskin breeches and tunic from her, almost in tears for her kindness. Why was I emotional about this? I was an officer in the King's army, not meant to be emotional ever. But I was suddenly very tired, and the stress of travelling with Pierre, Jean, and Ahanu when they clearly wished me elsewhere caught up with me all of a sudden. And truth be known, I was also still a teensy bit hungover, but don't tell anyone.

The woman told me her name was Alona, and she showed me to a tent and bade me change there. Her black hair was down and shone in the firelight. It didn't arouse me as much as I envied the freedom she showed in letting it down. She also asked me to give her my uniform so she could clean and mend it for me. I stared at her for a moment and decided to trust her. She was being so kind.

"Why do you not dislike me?"

She had begun to turn away with my uniform in her hands, but she turned back and looked hard at me. I was suddenly very conscious of my underclothes, but she paid no notice.

"Our people have lost their land due to manipulation of elders and ensnarement using alcohol. They tried to wipe us out by spreading smallpox among our people. The Jesuits and the nuns took us as children and tried to make little white children of us. We got a white man's education but we lost so much in exchange. We have good reason to distrust any white man. But it is clear to me that you are very young and inexperienced. You as an individual have done nothing to us. And my brother says that you worked as hard as any of our people today. You have earned his respect."

I didn't know what to say besides "Thank you".

Pierre came into the tent after she left and explained how the garments I held should be worn, and that as a white man I might be more comfortable if my soft cotton undershirt and under breeches remained close to my body. He was matter of fact, but again, I found him extremely kind.

As soon as I was dressed, I approached the fire. Pierre handed me a wooden bowl with some stew in it. They were also passing around a water flask. The stew was delicious and like nothing I had ever tasted. I wondered what I was eating, but decided not to look a gift horse in the mouth.

They began to talk amongst themselves, but Alona, plying a needle and fine white thread on my trousers, cleared her throat significantly. They switched to English.

The next day we would continue to portage the canoe for a good part of the morning. The passengers on the steamer we had seen were most likely resting in an inn on the other side of the river. They would take a carriage or walk up the other side of the river to meet the next steamer above the falls.

"The steamers take the river in parts, and their passengers have to change boats two times. Their journey takes almost a week, but they do not have to paddle". Pierre explained with a smirk. I smiled back.

Presently we all retired to our tents, mine being the one I had changed in. As I was headed to my tent, Alona approached me with my uniform. "You really should put it in your pack to keep it clean. Keep the skins I have given you. They are yours. A gesture of goodwill" she smiled.

She hesitated before turning away. "The sick man left behind in Montreal is my husband. He has a white man's disease, I don't remember the name. I don't expect to see him again." It was as if she didn't know why she was telling me, but she wanted to tell someone that didn't already know.

My mouth dropped open, and I said "I am so very, very sorry. I hope my arrival in his place does not cause you more pain." She nodded no and walked away.

That night I dreamed as I hadn't done in a long time. It was one of those times when everyone I ever knew was in the dream. Josephine and Mother and Father, my cousin Thomas, my drill instructor from basic training, and all of the Algonquin. And there was a man there, whom I couldn't quite see. When I looked down at myself my fine red uniform was in tatters and I didn't know why.

The next morning, Alona had a meal of corn and jerky ready. I asked her what animal it had come from, and she said it was bear meat. I told her about seeing the bears from ships, and not being able to imagine hunting for them, and she smiled.

"Perhaps while you live on our lands you will hunt only carefully and not indiscriminately as a result of your awe of the bears". She pronounced the word indiscriminately as if she had not learned it in speech but by reading it. I found her tremendously interesting and sad.

"What will happen to you, without your husband I mean?"

"Are you going to marry me white boy?" she laughed. But seeing me blush red, she said "The tribe will look after me. I have always had a role to play here separate from my husband". I had never known any woman who could say that. I was in awe of her.

My fellow paddlers and I picked up the canoe and resumed our portage. As we walked there were fewer and fewer rocks and eventually it was a dirt path, and soon we were lowering the canoe again at the water's edge. We all took the opportunity to relieve ourselves (the Algonquin were completely unselfconscious about this), then took our places and paddled once more. Pierre said "Hurry up White Boy" and everyone chuckled.

The day was cloudy and grey and the clouds affected my mood. My sore muscles from yesterday lost their stiffness as I paddled. Well, except maybe that little pain, just there in my armpit. After about an hour, it began to rain, and it didn't just rain. It poured as in the story in the book of Genesis where Noah saves the animals from the fate of the evil humans. And that's what it felt like, that some force of nature was trying to exterminate us. Ahanu tossed me a bailing bucket, like so much Algonquin ware, made of birch bark but surprisingly hard and sturdy. I bailed as fast as I could but Pierre made the decision to make for shore. We pulled the canoe onto shore and turned it over, and then squatted underneath it. I was sure everything in my pack would be soaked through.

The four of us were quiet for a long time, but the rain kept on. The noise on the canoe was deafening. Rivulets ran underneath us.

I turned to Pierre and said "I have been thinking about Alona all morning"

He looked me square in the eye and said "White Boy, I would kill you before I would let my sister marry you. ". The others snickered, but the kind of snickers that indicate the joke is not that funny.

Such was the intensity of my interest that I didn't miss a breath. "No, no, you mistake me. The sadness of what is happening to her has occupied my mind. What has happened to her husband? What illness has taken him in its grip? Why do you all assume there is no hope? Why did you leave him in Montreal?"

Pierre sighed and looked down at the ground. Then he looked around at the others, and finally, back at me.

"White Boy, you are not one of us, and it goes against my instincts to tell you these things. They are private and belong to my sister. But I know she likes you, and we also like you, so I will tell you. When we were younger, Alona's man was a good person, smart and kind. He was a good hunter and a good provider. He and Alona were one, the way lifelong partners sometimes are. But then times got hard for a few winters, and we started working with some white fur traders. They were not really bad men. They were respectful of our ways, and fairer than other traders. But in their company he learned to really like whiskey much more than he ever had before. Over time, years, he became worse and worse, unable to wake up in the morning, sometimes not remembering what he had done the night before. He would stay drunk for days at a time. Two weeks ago his skin began to turn yellow. He was sick, not just from the drink, but his body began to rebel. We took him downstream to Montreal to the Jesuits, with whom I still maintain a relationship. They said it was unlikely that they could save him, but if we left him there, they would try. "

What was it about these people that their stories raised tears in my eyes so easily? I began to understand that the pall that had hung over my time with them was not just that I was white and wore a red uniform, but was their sadness over this man they had left behind.

"Cirrhosis of the liver. Why is she not with him? Why did she not go to Montreal with you" I asked into the silence. I realized there was silence because the rain had stopped.

"We are not sure that either we or Alona would be welcome. There are many white men in the room with him. They barely tolerate him because he is not a white man. And even white women are not really welcome there" answered Pierre.

I said "Look, if he had died in the camp that we left this morning, would she not have been with him? Would it not ease her to be with him at the end?"

"The Jesuits would not be happy to see a woman there" Ahanu said from my right.

"Well then, I suggest that we should turn back and pick her up and take her to her husband. It would help with the Jesuits if a British Officer accompanied her. We can also stop at the Garrison in Montreal if necessary. I feel strongly, this is the right thing to do."

After a short discussion it was agreed that it was worth a try. We put the canoe back in the water, this time facing downstream, and paddled back toward Alona in bright sunshine.

Distance that had taken two hours upstream took thirty minutes downstream with the rushing rainwater to add volume to the river. Alona was surprised to see us portage our canoe back into camp again. Pierre explained our idea to her, but she had a doubtful look on her face.

Looking at me she said "But you have to be in Bytown. Your commander will be angry."

"What's a week, here or there?" I asked, raising an eyebrow and smiling. I did have misgivings, but I felt strongly that I needed to help this woman.

It took only a short period to convince her and get her into the canoe. She had her own paddle. It surprised me, but then I realized it shouldn't have.

We were back in Montreal by nightfall, walking through St. Anne's quarter (known as Griffintown) with our canoe above our heads. A few Irish stared as we passed. A white man and four Algonquin carrying a large canoe in the Irish district. Yes, I suppose they stared for good reason. In another part of the world we would have been beaten up. But in this port town I suppose even the Irish had gotten used to seeing strange things. I arrived at the place where I had slept under the hospitality of my cousin Thomas and asked after him. After stowing the canoe behind the residence to be watched over by a cow and a pig, we proceeded to the shebeen[20] where he was said to be spending the evening.

I went in and fetched him, leaving my friends outside. When he joined us all, I explained what we were trying to do.

"You want to make demands of the Jesuit?" was his initial response. But when I explained that I would attend the garrison in uniform and ask that another soldier accompany me, his eyes really widened.

"You want to enlist the help of the garrison to make demands of the Jesuit on behalf of an Algonquin, and a woman at that." He blew out a large breath, and looking at Pierre said "He talked you into this? You know the Jesuit better than any of us. Are you sure you want to try this?'

Before Pierre spoke, I chimed in "we could enlist the help of the bishop. The church is trying to convert the Indians, right? Would this not be a goodwill move? " I raised an eyebrow.

---

[20] AN IRISH HEART: Sharon Doyle Driedger: A Phyllis Bruce Book, Harper Collins Publishers, 2010: p. 135

Now Thomas had his head in his hands, like it might explode. He took off his cap and messed his hair, then plopped his cap on top of his head again. He smelled of whiskey.

"All right. We can but only try. But how about I go get you a soldier. I know one that might be willing to help, on the quiet like" and off he went, all of us agreeing to meet him at a tavern at the end of the road.

I changed into my uniform in an alley. It was wet and a bit out of shape, so the Algonquin, under Alona's direction, pulled and pushed it back into its original form. I put my helmet on, pushing and shoving my hair under it. By the time Thomas had arrived back, I was in fair form and had an ale under my belt in the tavern.

The man who accompanied Thomas was a corporal whose name was, predictably, Smith. I rolled my eyes when he introduced himself. "Sir, all due respect, you want me to use my real name? In the event this all goes wrong, I would be flogged. I want the garrison commander to continue not to know my name. If there's a problem with that I can go back to my bunk. Sir. "

I sighed and nodded, clapped the fellow on the back. The time was now 2 AM. It would take an hour to walk through the silent streets to the Hotel de Dieu. We agreed we should arrive there after 5 AM, after matins. In the ample time on our hands, we wandered the streets of Montreal, admiring churches, in awe of factories, and walking along the shore of the island that overlooked the Saint Lawrence River, all under a starlit sky.

At the residential door of the building we knocked at precisely 5:30. A nun answered the door, a Sulpician by her habit (Pierre and Thomas at least were familiar with the habits of the different orders in Montreal). When they explained that they wanted to see the bishop, her eyebrows rose.

"I think you mean the auxiliary bishop? The diocese has been divided into four parts for some time in order that all of its faithful receive the attention they require".

We all nodded, shrugged, and smiled. I thought we looked a bit like a group of village idiots. My stomach was starting to sink. Her black habit, with the rosary and the pendant she wore, felt very intimidating to me.

The sister welcomed us into the building and showed us into a sitting room that would have been bright and attractive in the daylight. There wasn't room for us all to sit down, so the corporal and I stood, and Ahanu and Jean simply sat on the floor. Thomas took his cap off, and Alona and Pierre sat on the settee.

Presently a man who, by his clothing, could only be the auxiliary bishop, also Sulpician, entered the room. Cordially, he welcomed us all and equally. The sister returned and offered coffee or tea to each of us, but we none of us accepted. What had I gotten us all into?

I cleared my throat, and began to explain about Alona, her husband (merely ill in my explanation), and my relationship with my Algonquin friends. I explained that there was some expectation that the Jesuit would not allow Alona in to see her husband, who we understood was near death. What we wanted from him was his intercession to ensure that she could see him again before he died, and stay with him if she wished.

He looked at Alona. "Madam, if this be your situation, I would agree that it is difficult, to say that least. I have found that no matter your people or your faith, the bond between a husband and wife, even when their hearts have strayed apart somewhat due to circumstance, strains terribly in times of trial. I will see what I can do for you."

I could see that as a Sulpician the opportunity to one-up the Jesuit fathers was not unattractive. I didn't care, but I hoped that it would make him more sympathetic to our cause.

He looked at me next. "Lieutenant, you are not from the garrison here in Montreal, I take it?"

I replied that I was enroute to a posting in Bytown, working for Lieutenant Colonel By on the building of a canal.

"Oh yes, the Rideau Canal I believe it is to be called. It is my understanding that Lieutenant Colonel By struggles much with the unwieldy funding formula imposed by his superiors. He is stressed and requires the help he requisitions from the ordnance group here in Montreal – or the North of Ireland, in your case. I suggest that although I believe what you are doing is noble, he might not be impressed when he finds you have taken a week's extra leave in

Montreal. I will provide you with a letter explaining that your services were required by the church and that we are deeply indebted to him for his indulgence. Corporal, I will provide you a similar letter to give to your garrison commander, as I believe you are concerned with being flogged for your actions here this morning."

By this time, I was too astonished to speak. Never doubt the power of the Church, or at least its command over the information in its demesne. How did he know about things said in conversation between us in the dark Montreal streets just hours ago?

We were all invited to a dining room for breakfast while the auxiliary bishop worked with his staff to find out about Alona's husband.

Thomas leaned over to me and said "was that too easy? Are we all going to the magistrate?" I honestly had no idea, but we might as well eat the delicious breakfast laid out before us. It was excellent. Fried potatoes, wonderful fresh bread, oatmeal, berries, tea with the best cream, and sugar from the Indies.

When we finished, two nuns arrived to collect Alona and take her to the infirmary. They were equipped with a letter that overrode the authority of the Jesuit priest who ran the infirmary. Alona looked a little frightened to be leaving with these two strange women, but Pierre nodded his encouragement and she went.

The rest of us were left to wait in the room we had been in initially. Shortly a nun asked me and the

Corporal to join the Auxiliary Bishop in his private study. I knocked on the door I was shown, and we entered.

"Ah, Lieutenant, Corporal, please sit down. I have here the two letters I have written for the corporal and yourself Lieutenant. They make absolutely no mention of the Algonquin or any other tribe. I mention only a task of great delicacy to be undertaken on behalf of the church. I apologize for detaining you both from your duties and I offer the succour of the church to His Majesty's troops at any time in the future."

I thanked him, sincerely, both for his help and for his diplomacy in the matter.

He sat regarding me quietly for a moment. And then he spoke again.

"Why did you do this thing?"

Surprised, I raised my eyebrows and said, "Because it felt like the right thing to do."

He ran his hand along his brow and sighed.

"Young man, you have a soul that truly echoes the teachings of our Lord. This is why I helped you. But you need to understand that we don't live in the world of our saviour, we live in this world. Everyone here thinks they know what the right thing feels like, but each man's sense is different. And as a soldier, I caution you to refrain from diverting yourself from your duties again. Lieutenant Colonel By and his garrison of Royal Engineers will not thank you for it. The Indians are viewed by the crown as, if not an enemy, then certainly not an ally".

I sagged. His speech reminded me of home, where as a member of the gentry, it would be unseemly for me to spend too much time with a Paddy from the group of workers who worked my father's land. My mother would regularly send the midwife to help birth babies in the little cottages where the Paddies lived. But she would never go herself, would never take a personal interest in any of them. Right there in that comfortable private study, I realized how badly I had wanted to get away from the hateful values of my parents.

And as a member of the King's army, I and those like me had brought this same sad and lonely set of values to the new world. It was a pivotal moment for me and a memory I would return to again.

Regardless how I felt, I knew the Auxiliary Bishop spoke sense. If I was to get along here, I should do so amid the values espoused by those around me.

"I thank you, sir, for your kindness and wisdom. It is not lost on me. It breaks my heart, but it is not lost on me."

The Auxiliary Bishop gave me a ticket on the steamer system to Bytown. He advised that I would be there in a week. He promised to care for my friends until they could return up the river, and to ensure the corporal was returned to the Garrison with no repercussions. I accepted a salute from the Corporal and wished him luck.

"And one more thing", he said as I was leaving.

"How well do you know your cousin?"

I laughed gently. "He's a rake, but he's a good man. As a teenage boy if I ever wanted something my parents would disapprove of, he would get it for me. He may find an unorthodox path to God, but in the end he is sincere and means well by his actions."

We both smiled, shook hands, and I left.

All the way to the steamer dock with my bag, and on the first steamer leg of the journey, in the carriage past the rapids where the soldiers toiled to build a military canal to bypass the roiling waters, and on the second steamer to Bytown I felt very out of spirits. Ever since I had left Montreal, I had felt false, as a man wearing another man's coat, with the pockets in the wrong spot and another man's trinkets to be found. I was sad not to have taken proper leave of the Algonquin. Whether they were representative of their people or not, I found them to be straightforward and honest, and their way of living attracted me.

When I arrived at Bytown, I stepped on to a dock just to one side of the locks there just being built. Much work had progressed, and they would come into use within the year. The grade was extremely steep.

I walked the path up toward an unmistakable Engineers building of some three stories. The door was open, and within bustled several men, both in uniform and without. A man in deerskin raiment, like the one packed carefully in my bag, but with very different hair came past me in the doorway. I smiled tentatively at him, but he only looked past me with a face of granite.

As soon as traffic permitted, I entered the building and asked a man in a major's uniform where I could find Lieutenant Colonel By. He scanned my uniform in distaste and pointed through a doorway toward the back of the building.

As I entered the room, I thought for sure I had come to the wrong place. The man before me was shorter than I by some inches. He was pale but with broken veins running through his cheeks and nose. He wore the uniform of the Lieutenant Colonel, but had more the look of a clerk. Could this truly be Lieutenant Colonel John By? By his reputation and the awe with which he was spoken in England, I had expected someone taller. Perhaps wearing the garb of an adventurer.

He turned to look at me, a pair of spectacles sat on his nose, over which he surveyed me with bemusement.

"Well Lieutenant, what the devil happened to your uniform? According to the paperwork I received, you graduated top of your class. And here you are a week late and your uniform shrunk and misshapen. "

"I got wet sir, on the river" I said, handing him the letter from the Auxiliary Bishop.

After reading it, he said "You have friends in high places young man. Now what could you possibly have got up to on behalf of the Papist church in Montreal? No, just a minute".

He went to the door and called to someone named Mactaggart for tea. Then closing the door, he offered me a chair and took one himself.

"Now young man, I need to know the whole story, and don't leave anything out. I will not be angry, even if you were lost in a brothel for a week- "I blushed-"and hearing your story will give me a measure of you. Then I can decide how I can use you best. Our relationship won't work if we aren't honest with one another".

There was so much relief in letting the whole story pour out of me, after feeling so sad and disappointed since I had left Montreal. The tea, when it came, was the best black tea imported from England, and it was so good. Something in this man made me want to talk, and talk, and talk. He simply let me go on, prodding me with questions now and again. He would nod, and say "hmmm". When my story was over and I finished with arriving at the front door of this building and hour ago, we both fell silent.

He reread the letter.

"So the Bishop, or the almost bishop, as the case may be, was afraid you would be penalized for caring for and helping some savages. It's clear he was trying to be kind. And while I would not penalize you for this behaviour, others would I am sure. "

He shifted approaches. "I must tell you young man that Bytown is a wild place. It's a lumber town. The spring cuts will be coming down stream shortly. There are no constables here, no rule of law. One of the greatest responsibilities for the King's Troops here is to keep the peace. It is circumstance very different than those in England, Ireland, or that matter, anywhere else that I am familiar with. I have met and had relationships with many savages here, and they have often earned my respect. It is in this atmosphere that we in the Royal Engineers are trying to build a facility suitable for His Majesty's ships. The funding is constantly changing, as is the estimate of the final cost for the Rideau Canal. I hope to finish in good time and to take my wife and children home to England. And that's where you can help me. And you can't do that if you can't stick to your duties as I assign them to you."

I felt so much better at the mention of a role for me, even phrased as it was in terms that would benefit him. I wanted to help him. I wanted him to get home to England. It was extraordinary that he would make me feel this way, but there you have it. This little man with the spectacles on his nose was a leader of men. Huh.

"Lieutenant, I would advise you to put on the skins your savage friends gave you, and take your uniform to the laundry of sorts near my house, yonder." He was pointing up on the hill to the rear of the building we were in. "They will fix it, re-block[21] and re-hem it. It will take a few days, but

---

[21] Wool fabric in the nineteenth century was steamed and "blocked" into shape before being turned into garments. If the garment got too wet, it would shrink out of shape and need to be "re-blocked" or simply "blocked" back into its original condition.

the cost is reasonable, and you'll thank me for the suggestion.

"Then I want you to return here and we will assign you some tasks until you are ready to take up a post at Chaffee's Mills. By then I will have some paperwork ready for you and your uniform will be ready. I believe Mr. Sherrif will be travelling down at the same time. Agreed?"

I nodded energetically, and took my leave. I had absolutely no idea who Mr. Sherrif was, and I wasn't sure how we got from "seeing what we could use me for" to Chaffee's Mills, which I knew to be the location of a planned lock, but I was willing to go along with anything By said. I liked him immensely.

The next week passed in a blur, with By and McTaggart teaching me how the canal was designed and how to carry out By's wishes. I studied charts and maps with the assistance of Mactaggart who turned out to be Clerk of the works, drafting diagrams and written reports about the characters involved at Chaffee's Mills. The owner of the various mills at the small rapids there had died last year of a fever that apparently struck in the summer months. His wife, as his sole heir, had taken title to the mills and some property in the area. However, he had owed money to his brother, now a businessman in a nearby town, and the brother felt he owned the property in payment of the debt. My first task was to work as an intermediary to settle the dispute as By's agent. He would finalize my arrangements. By gave me a great talk to build my courage.

The day came to proceed south. I had my uniform, newly cleaned and blocked back into shape. By suggested I remain in my skins, and take the uniform in special leather bag to keep it protected until I reached my destination. As soldiers we were never supposed to pop in and out of uniform as I was doing (remember the rule), but I suspected that By knew what he was talking about and did as I was told. Mr. Sherrif was one of two men, partners, who had contracted to build the lock at Chaffee's Mills. His partner was also partner with another man to build Davis lock, two locks away from Chaffee. He had also helped build the Welland Canal at the southernmost end of Lake Ontario. I was to manage this relationship in its entirety so I thought travelling together might set the foundation for a friendship. Or ruin it.

Sherrif arrived promptly the morning we were to depart. Despite his position managing 4 score men and commanding such a large part of a huge contract, he did not dress in the clothes of a gentleman, but instead wore the clothes of a workman. Probably a good thing for the journey we were undertaking. He had been in Upper Canada for eight years, having come from Scotland.

Sherrif indicated that although some preferred to canoe, he felt the best way to travel the canal while it was still under construction was on horseback. A track of sorts had been worn along the east side. There was a livery stable (a new expression for me, I thought livery was what servants wore) right on Barracks Hill, so it was extremely convenient.

When we entered the barn, we found about thirty horse bums in their standing stalls. The place was silent except for the sound of their chewing and farting. I became sentimental remembering our barn at home. I suppose I had taken it very much for granted, and now remembered it more fondly for having been without a horse for so long. I remembered now that there is nothing as soothing and wonderful as the sound of chewing and farting.

I wandered down the aisle, watching them all. A grey started nervously when I passed. A black shire rotated his ears around at the sound of my footfalls. He surely stood 19 hands (about 6.5 feet) and must have weighed 150 stone (over 2000 lbs). I bet that fellow could have pulled a right heavy load. I stroked his rump, but passed him by. He had a nobler calling than bearing my meagre weight.

Surely half of the horses in the barn appeared to be of the breed of black horse I had been seeing since my arrival in the colony. They all seemed to be quiet and somewhat placid. Their ears spun to follow the sound of my footfalls, but their chewing never slowed, and they showed no real reaction other than to shift their weight from one back foot to another. Their rumps were well muscled, better than a standard riding horse. They were black, but the high places on their bodies that had been exposed to the sun had bleached brown. I slid into the stall of a larger male. A quick check under his belly confirmed that he had been gelded[22]. His

---

[22] Gelding is the process whereby the testicles of a stallion are removed or the vase deferens is destroyed. Geldings make

body was solid muscle – this was no pasture puff. I worked my way past his shoulder and his big brown eye rolled around at me. The eye was in a very pretty face, not long and roman nosed like a draft horse, but with a petite nose like a far eastern Arab horse. The mane had been roached (cut off), but bits growing back showed an ample and wavy blanket that would be invaluable in the Canadian winters I had heard so much about. The ears were short and of a pleasing shape. I lifted all four hooves and they were clean, sturdy and well cared for, shod with good quality and well-fitting shoes.

Presently I heard male voices coming down the aisle, one of them Sherrif's voice saying "I saw him wander down this way". I emerged from the stall in time to meet Sherriff and a shorter man with the hands of a farrier, rough and powerful from building horse shoes and metal implements. He was half as wide as he was tall, with arms like tree trunks. Dark hair poked out from under his hat, and the face wore a carefully groomed full beard.

I introduced myself and offered my hand, but he was distracted by the deer skins I wore. I smiled and said "A gift from a very kind group of Algonquin". He nodded hesitantly and took my hand, glancing at Sherrif. Sherrif smiled too, openly and with pleasure.

"Sir, I am not familiar with this breed of horse. It very much appeals to me. Can you acquaint me

---

gentle and much more easier going companions and work mates, where stallions can be unpredictable around mares.

220

with its characteristics?" I tried to be just a little ingratiating, to make the poor man more at ease.

The man nodded and began to speak, in the broadest Scottish brogue I had heard in a long time. "Aye, they're actually called Canadian horses, as they were bred here in the colony nigh on 200 years ago. The original stock came from France, shipped over here by King Louis what's his name, to enable settlers here to farm the land and transport themselves as necessary. The weak ones died off, and so the breed now is all of horses that can withstand the winter here. They require very little in provisions and they are almost as strong as that Shire over there. Do you like this one?"

I said, "I'm sorry I didn't get your name?"

"Ooh aye, ma name is Seamus McDonnell. Pardon my rudeness, I was a little distracted by your.....outfit".

I laughed and shook his hand again. "Well Mr. McDonnell, I would like very much to buy this fellow. Are you willing to sell him? What would your price be?"

Within a short time I had possession of that lovely horse and a saddle to fit him that would accommodate my kit and my rifle. It was a much heavier saddle than I had ever seen before, bigger even than a cavalry saddle. Sherrif already had a horse, named Whisper, stabled at this very establishment each time he came to By town. Its location on Barracks Hill kept the horses safe in the event of unruly lumbermen or other civil unrest, which I had been told was not terribly unusual.

As we mounted and were ready to say good-bye, McDonnell asked "So, do ya like those clothes then?"

I assured him that they were the most comfortable things I had ever worn.

The journey to Chaffee's Mills was about five days on horseback, depending on conditions. If it was dry and the horses were able to trot from time to time, it might be less. If it rained, Sherrif avowed it could take ten days, and could be treacherous. As we rode I looked up at the clear June sky. I prayed silently that there be no rain.

As we rode, I asked Sherrif to tell me about himself, to pass the time. He rode ahead of me and as he spoke I watched the brown hair that curled out from under the brim of his hat. At our meeting, I had been impressed with how handsome he was. He was the sort of man that all men really want to be: confident, charming, but with an abundance of common sense.

He told me he had walked for two weeks to get to the port of Leith, and there he had bought passage in steerage on a Brig named Skum. He said he chose it because it meant the foam of the sea, and he liked that. He said he arrived in Quebec City on May 18, 1820. I laughed and told him I had arrived on nearly the same date but in 1828.

He disembarked at Quebec, and started working odd jobs, sometimes two or three at a time. He was a horse groom for a wealthy Frenchman, he cleaned latrines, and he cut down trees. But then he happened on a job with a stonemason. There he learned the mason's trade. He proved a quick study and when the old man died, he worked his way west and to Kingston. There he met Haggart, his partner who hailed from Perth. For my enlightenment, he explained that Perth was on a river system that fed back up from the Rideau River.

His story told me a great deal about him. He was ambitious, in the way that people believe ambition is a virtue and an aim in itself. It was clear to me that he was honorable, but only as honorable as would fit between the narrow confines of his values. Anyone who did not share those values simply did not merit consideration. He reminded me of someone, but I couldn't identify who. Perhaps it was someone from home.

As we rode through the day, we passed four work sites for the canal. The fourth, where we planned to camp at the end of the first day, was called Black Rapids. This sounded rather ominous to me, implying fast dark water. There were three little sets of rapids, looking rather minor, but I knew that such rapids could tear a ship apart in seconds. I was from an island nation after all.

Sherrif expressed a wish not to go into the work camp. He said sometimes he grew weary of canal talk in these camps, as he had plenty to worry about with his own construction activities. I told him I understood completely.

When we stopped just before dusk, Sherrif set up a tarp he had between four trees, with the downward corner matching the downward slope of the land. He explained that it was so any rain water would drain away from us. I collected as much firewood as I could find, deadfall mostly. I amassed an impressive pile, enough to last us all night.

Someone else had camped in this same spot, probably several someones, as there was a makeshift fire pit already, ashes left behind from other fires, and even a few sticks of firewood. So much so that I was surprised to have found so much.   Sherrif found a flat thin rock and used it like a shovel to get rid of the ashes. I built a triangular structure and filled it with dried plant matter and Sherrif lit it with a flint. We ate rations of dried meat and bread in front of the fire. And then I found something I had forgotten I had. Reaching under for my bible, my hand touched something hard and round. It was the pickled beans I bought in Plymouth the day I sailed. By some miracle through all my travels it had arrived here intact. Sherrif and I each had some, and they were a welcome treat. We kept the rest for another time. I wrapped the jar carefully in some of my clothing and packed it away again.

After being tied to trees a little further away while we set up camp and ate, the horses were moved to the trees that held up our tarp. Sherrif explained that people often simply hobbled the horses and let them graze. But he had once had a wolf pack attack a horse that had strayed away from its mates. He wanted to make sure that never happened again. I looked around with some trepidation.

There was no graze around us, it having been eaten by other horses that came before. Sherrif gave them each a generous helping of oats, and we lay down for the night.

Once during the night I woke to the sound of light rain hitting the tarp. I sat up and examined every shadow for the shape of a wolf. I threw some wood on the fire, to find the horses sleeping standing up. Their comfort was enough to convince me that I need not worry. I went back to sleep.

I woke up at dawn, and before I opened my eyes I lay there, and realized that I felt something heavy against the back of my legs, and I was laying on my side. After a minute or two, my brain realized that the thing against my legs was a very large something indeed. I pushed myself up onto my elbow, and looked to see my horse curled up behind my legs and sleeping, his head balanced on his nose on the ground. Seeing my motion, he lifted his head and looked at me. The gentlest, quietest of nickers emitted from his body. And then he stood, to join his fellow standing just there.

I wouldn't have believed it had I not seen it myself. I looked over at Sherrif and found him awake and that he had been watching also. "Have you ever seen a horse do that" I asked. "Only with another horse" he answered.

We chuckled over my gelding's predilection for human physical contact. We took bets on whether he would ever do it again. We were still talking about it when we cleaned up camp and it was time to remount and continue on our way.

As we rode on day two we spent the morning looking for the perfect name for this horse of mine

225

that loved people, or at least, loved me. We made our way through Greek and Roman Gods, which I knew and he did not, Scottish and Irish mythology, and then we started on every day English, and then we circled around again. But around noon, we finally settled on Piper. And so Piper he was.

On day two we passed two more locks being constructed, and stayed in an inn that night.

The morning of day three was still an hour from dawning when I was woken by a fist on my door. It was Sherrif. "It's raining" he said simply before turning away.

I hauled myself out of bed, and dressed with a heavy heart. I didn't relish riding in the rain and mud. And there was no fire to make the breakfast. The landlady gave us apples, bread and cheese to take with us.

As we set out I patted Piper's neck. "Sorry boy, this one won't be nice". Horses will toss their heads in positive response sometimes, and I swear that's what Piper did. I chuckled at the idea that Piper could understand me and respond.

Despite the weather, we made it to Kemptville that day, where the canal ran through the town without the need of locks. On the fourth day, still in the rain, we made it to Mirik's Mills. The town of Mirik's Mills was established at the end of the 18th century by one William Mirik, a Welshman by origin who had left the new American country in favour of the colony of Canada where there was a political system that was more stable and familiar, and in search of the land grants not available in the new United States.

The work camp was large, part of it perched on the land to one side of where the canal was being dry dug out of the rock. The sappers and their wares were camped on the island being created by the canal channel. The ground for a block house had been marked out, but appeared to have been abandoned until more important tasks, namely the building of the locks, were complete.

The reason for the dry dug channel could be plainly seen and heard throughout the area. On both sides of the river were mills, here and there perched on the edge of the water. I could see the smokestack of a foundry on the far side. I could hear the unmistakable sound of a saw mill. I could hear a grist mill, its rocks grinding together in a guttural rhythm. Any attempt to dig a channel through the centre of the river at this point would have brought the mills to a halt, and the economy of the little town that supported them would have halted along with them. Once the channel was complete, the river could simply be allowed to run through it without slowing the waters that powered the mills very much at all. It seemed an elegant solution.

Sherrif and I had been given the task of delivering a packet of documents to the proprietor of all of the industry we saw, William Mirik. But first we spent a pleasant evening in the company of the Commandant of the camp and his troops. We were given cots in a tent of the Royal Engineers. I felt very much at home in that expertly assembled shelter, and the cot was considerably more comfortable than the ground. Sherrif seemed able to make himself comfortable wherever and with whomever he was, and bunked in the same tent.

The horses were stabled with the rest of the military horses, and before bed were wiped down, curried and fed well.

The morning dawned clear and fresh. I put my uniform on, since we were to go on official business. We rode across the wooden bridge enjoying the fresh air and sunshine.   Before we left the main road we noted the presence of a small tavern on the far side. Sherrif told me that this was owned by one of Mirik's adult sons. Given its proximity to the mills, it would have done a brisk trade at the end of the day.

The distance to Mirik's house from the main road was considerable, being an eighth of a mile or more. There were Negro workers on the property engaged in all manner of tasks. I made a note to find out if they were slaves, which although legal in many places, seemed to be at least generally disapproved of in the colonies.

A large vegetable garden was just beginning to escape its confines. Tomato plants, corn, carrots, cucumbers, potatoes and squash all seemed barely controlled within their assigned area although there were no blossoms yet. Grapes grew up a trellis against a stone wall although they would not bear fruit until the end of the summer. Flower gardens grew likewise in beds arranged in front of the house. Many I recognized as being useful as herbs.

The house itself was an elegant and quite new two story affair. It was large enough to house a large family and the servants needed to accommodate it. Even in By town I had not seen such a fine home since I had left England. I raised an eyebrow to Sherrif as we rode up the pathway, his response being a tight lipped smile of suppressed humour and a shrug.

A man stepped onto the front porch as we reigned in our horses. He was about my height and held a beautiful wooden pipe between his teeth, except when he spoke. Which he did now.

"Good morning! Do I have an emissary of the good Colonel By? Sherrif, how are you? Nice to see you again. Welcome to you both". He ushered us to a generous grouping of chairs on the porch, over which a very temporary manner of roof had been erected as the construction of a permanent roof over the porch area had not yet begun. Not until we had made ourselves comfortable and coffee was on its way would he allow me to speak.

I gave him my name and explained that I was the new commander of the troops at the lock being built at Chaffey's Mills. I expected him to make comment but he was very attentive. He listened and occasionally nodded. When I handed him the papers I had brought for his attention, he snorted through his nose, and opened the packet.

After he had flipped through the documents, he put them down on a small table beside him.

The coffee arrived and he began to speak. "You know, this canal building is all very well, and I understand the military need for it, I do. But you know, I settled here more than twenty years ago, and I have worked my heart out to establish this town and a livelihood for everyone in it. I'm getting old, and I was ready to settle down and enjoy the fruits of my labour and encourage the labours of my sons, when John Bloody By emerged from the swamplands and usurped my river for the king."

"But Sir, I see a great accommodation has been made to allow your mills to continue operation!" In my peripheral vision, Sherrif had his hand over his face, and was nodding no. Should I have said nothing?

Mirik replied "You are right of course young man. But I have been a miller my whole life. If you split a river in this way, surely the flow of that river on either side is diminished? My mills require flow in order to work. I see Sherrif smirking over there, as he has heard me go on about this before. Perhaps we will table the matter for another time". He smiled ruefully. "It could be asserted that my real concern is that the town will no longer have been built in my image, the image I worked for so many years to create. It is called Mirik's Mills after all. "He made another wry smile.

And then I asked "Sir, I can't help but notice that your gardeners and your servants here in your home, are all Negroes. Are they slaves? "

Sherrif seemed amused by my question. Perhaps he had heard it asked here before.

But Mirik's cheeks had coloured, and his eyes seemed to have taken on an extra sparkle. "No young man, they are not. They are freed men, every single one of them. They work here of their own accord for monetary reward. There are a few working in the mills also. How they come to be here I cannot tell you for fear of exposing their history, but I am glad to have them. The Canadian Colony does have its own dark history of slavery you know. Take that aristocrat fellow in Nova Scotia. He left permanently for the home country and left his poor slaves to starve. I have a cousin out there who says that last winter the local people took it on themselves to feed them, get them land grants, and teach them to support themselves. What a barbaric thing for that chap to do. They are not dogs, simply to be let loose to fend for themselves. Slavery is going out of style you know. Any time soon it will be outlawed throughout the Empire by Parliament.[23]"

He sighed and then said "Never mind. If you head to Chaffee's, you will be heading into the swamp. Tis a foul journey that, stick to the road! And I will have my housekeeper give you some of the compound we use to keep the bugs at bay. Use it on your horses too, mind. They can be driven mad by the big ones."

He did that and more. I was given a chance to change into my deerskins, once he heard I had them. We were given bread and butter to add to our store of food, as well as some meat wrapped in wax paper that we could cook over a fire. He asked

---

[23] The first act for the abolition of slavery was passed in 1807, but final abolition did not pass until 1833. Shortly after the conversation related here.

after the route we would take and nodded approval.

The more time we spent with William Mirik, the more I became comfortable with him. There was something about him. He was dressed in quality clothing but it did not have the austentation of some wealthy men. His paternalistic approach was the product of a sincere kindness intrinsic to his personality. His pride in his home, his achievements, I felt was warranted, earned. He patted a large dog at his side regularly, and the dog responded by laying its head in his lap. A man who loves his dog is generally a good man I find.

While we visited, Mirik had our horses attended to, to prevent the loss of a shoe on the road. As he shook our hands and wished us well, I watched him carefully. His grey hair had fallen out so that what remained ringed his head almost in the way of a monk's tonsure. And finally, he gave us the gift of a really fine dog to protect the camp from bears and to protect us in our travels. This was a man who felt he had not the power to affect the world, but by God he would protect those he could. He really was a fatherly soul.

As we rode off, I was sincerely sorry to be leaving him. Our new dog curled up in front of me across Piper's neck. Neither she nor he was the least bit perturbed.

"By gum, he sure did like you!" said Sherrif.

"Really? I don't know why. I thought he was just a kind older man accustomed to being in control".

"He doesn't usually like soldiers. You're right, he is a kind man, always willing to provide for the needs of others. I think that is what his wealth has created for him. But I've never seen him warm to anyone quite like you. You're about the age of his sons. Perhaps that was it. I'm grateful for the dog though. Isn't she a pretty little thing?"

The dog was about forty pounds in weight, short haired, with the mustache and beard of a terrier. She was grey in colour, and her coat was wiry to the touch. She was an attractive little thing.

After some debate, we named her Willow.

The further we rode from Mirikville, the more the trees closed in around the road. They were aspens, poplars, cedars, and a sort of scrubby hazelnut. Periodically the aspect would open up to show miles of shrubs and evergreen trees ringing swamps and small lakes.

As we rode along the river, I looked on the far side and saw fine stone houses along a riverside road. They were relatively new and the trees had been cut down around them. I saw what looked like a graveyard just up and to the left of one of the houses.

"What graveyard is that? There is no church close by?"

"Aye, when building started here last year and the first sick season came, there was no church and no graveyard in which to lay the bodies. The farmer there, McGuigan, he offered to have the graveyard on the hill there. It was a generous offer, one the commander here gratefully accepted. The settler families have begun to use it as well." Sherrif was matter of fact.

"McGuigan, that's a name from home. Something about that farm and the graveyard begs my attention."

"Perhaps you will go and meet the man himself someday."

I shook off the odd feeling I had and rode on.

The first bugs hit us not far along the road. Mosquitoes, blackflies, and other much larger bugs that Sherrif said were horse flies. They came in a variety of colours and sizes and they took a significant bite. They were numerous enough in number that we were usually fighting off several at a time. They literally drove us to madness. I allowed Little Willow to hide under the blanket I had wrapped around me to protect from the bugs. We sweated, but it helped.

We snacked on the bread and butter as we rode and I shared with Willow. It was excellent, the bread having been baked that morning. We stopped to set up camp before the bugs multiplied their number after dark. Sherrif showed me how to light a fire that smoked, and how to keep it smoking. It gave me a headache but it was better than the bugs. We cooked our portion of meat over the fire, and it was excellent. I gave Willow a small portion which she happily took from my fingers. But we didn't sleep much.

The next morning, Sherrif advised that we piss on the horses. He thought it might drive some of the bugs away. Poor Piper sidestepped my stream, and it occurred to me he might be right. Think about the latrine, full of flies feeding on what was to be found there. As we got ready to mount I stood slapping and killing the big flies that landed on Piper's shoulders, back, haunches and flank – in short, everywhere. I found so many bites on his sheath that it bled freely. Willow's ears bled too.

Sherrif knew that there was a dryer part of the trail ahead and suggested we let the horses set the pace as long as the ground was even. And with that we relaxed our hands on the reigns and gave a gentle nudge into the flanks. We didn't have to tell them twice. Piper broke into an easy lope, more controlled than I would have expected due to conditions. I realized as we went along that he was blocking Whisper from breaking into a panicked gallop. Huh.

Alternating between a canter and a trot for over an hour, we finally arrived in a place where the forest seemed friendlier. Although there was no water near the path we rode, the spruce trees and cedars towered to the sky. The place felt as old as God himself. We had stopped to let the horses rest, to eat some bread and dried fruit, and to drink from our skins. There were mosquitoes here, but their whining in our ears was much less maddening than the horse flies that took whole chunks of flesh.

Presently Sherrif heard something, or thought he did. I listened to the absolute silence as I looked around at the trees. Until a man stepped out from between them.

"Pierre!" I recognized him immediately. Alona appeared shortly after. She looked tired, but some of her sadness had lifted. I wanted to hug her, but didn't want to impinge on her dignity. She smiled at me. Ahanu and Jean were also there, as well as several people I recognized as having been at their camp on the Ottawa River.

Pierre looked at our horses. "What are you doing to these animals White Boy?" Sherrif, who showed no reluctance to interact with the Algonquin, smirked and looked away when he heard their nickname for me.

Pierre examined both horses, wincing when he saw the blood on Piper's sheath. Before we knew it, both our horses were subject to the ministrations of the Algonquin, and soon were covered with a sort of lotion that stayed on the skin. I recognized it as being very similar to the compound Mirik had given us and that we had not used. It smelled of evergreen trees and the horses showed relief as soon as it was smeared on. Alona smeared it on Willow, on her ears, and on her belly, admonishing her not to lick it off. Sherrif looked at me with a sheepish look. We were idiots.

Pierre said "We have a summer camp a short way away, with fresh water and trees for shelter. Lieutenant Colonel By said you are headed to Chaffee's Mills. This would be on your way. Why don't we camp together tonight?"

Pierre had been reluctant to talk to the auxiliary bishop, but spoke of Colonel By as if they were old friends, or at least, friendly acquaintances. I thought about the things the bishop had said, and Pierre's attitude made more sense. I also thought about the things Lieutenant Colonel By had said, and it made still more sense.

Some but not all of the group rode horses, and Pierre was one of them. I was intrigued but not surprised that it was a hardy black, like my Piper. I asked the horse's name, and Pierre said "he doesn't need a name. He knows who he is". He smiled at me. "What's the dog's name" he asked, and I felt a bit silly when I told him.

We rode for about three hours at a slow walk and pulled up at the side of a small lake. The water was fresh and clear, though not very deep, and the trees were everything Pierre had promised. All of the horses were taken to the water to drink for as long as they wanted. We set up a tether line for them in a grassy area so they could graze a little as they stood tied to the line. Jean and Ahanu unfolded what I could only describe as leather buckets and put one down near each horse. I was absolutely certain Piper was in excellent hands. Willow ran straight to the water when I let her down, and drank deeply. But she came back to me right away and stayed at my heel.

Alona and two other women set about laying out dried meat, nuts and fruit on a cloth. They also had ale and water to drink. It was an excellent meal, and we all sat down to enjoy it. It was convivial with much talking and gesturing, storytelling and laughter. The story of how the White Boy took them to the bishop was told, although the ending where I abandoned them was not discussed. My eyes met with Pierre's and each knew what the other was thinking, but there seemed to be no rancour. The Algonquin talked of heading to the St Lawrence River (I don't remember their name for it) to fish and rest for a few weeks. I asked if they were not worried about being exposed to the American gunners, and they laughed and assured me any Americans would be far from where they intended to camp.

The summer sun had completely gone down when all the members of the party rolled out their beds in the area around the fire. There was some quiet talk, and I made my way over to Alona. I had to ask her how she was. I had to know how the situation in Montreal had resolved.

We sat together on her blanket and I mentioned that she did not look as sad, but that she seemed tired. I asked if anything I had done had contributed to either condition. She smiled a gentle smile.

"We knew where you went, and why. We knew you would be sent away because of helping us. We have experience with Priests. But we did not blame you. You had already gained our regard by involving yourself in my affairs to begin with. I thank you for what you did." She said.

"Was it worth it? Were you able to be with him? Did he recover, or did you sit with him at the end? " I asked, as gently as I could.

Her eyes misted over. "No, he died "she said as the tears filled her eyes. "I was with him at the end. His legs and his "– she gestured with her hands over her belly, and I said "Torso?". "-his torso swelled up.

The nun who stayed with me told me that because the liver no longer was working, these fluids were backing up to other places. He could not take water or food. I held a cloth and a bowl of cold water so he could suck on the cloth. It seemed to help. He had a lot of pain from the swelling. He held my hand so tight that sometimes it hurt. He begged my forgiveness. " Tears rolled down her cheeks, and I'm not ashamed to say, mine too.

I said "I'm so very sorry" It was all I had to say.

"Death is a part of life White Boy. It is a sadness we must all go through."

"Are you glad you were there", I asked when the tears stopped.

"Not glad" she said. "But as the one person who knew him best, it comforted him to have me there. So yes, it was worth it."

We sat talking quietly for a while. Then I crept off to my bed beside Sherrif, curled up and pretended to sleep. Willow had not left my blanket, and curled up next to me to keep warm. Her loyalty to me so early in our relationship was touching, if a little surprising.

In the early morning, the sun rose over the packing up of our belongings, watering the horses, and putting out of camp fires.

"White Boy, you are an easy day's ride from Chaffee's Mills. We won't accompany you. We don't want the soldiers there to think they are under attack when we ride into camp. One or two would be one thing, but a whole tribe might be too many" He grinned. "But look for us when we come back this way at the end of the summer. Good luck. Use the compound we gave you to keep the bugs off."

And with that they were gone, off into the trees.

"I didn't know you had run into Pierre before" Sherrif said as we began to ride on. So I told him the whole story, from start to finish.

When I was done, he said "You know, there is a foolish attitude on the part of many of the English military commanders. You know," he adopted a funny face and looked down his nose "These SAVAGES just don't know how lucky they are to have us come in and steal their land. This land all belongs to the KING and they are lucky we give them reserves to live on". I was laughing at his plum in the mouth imitation of an upper crust officer with a purchased commission. But he was absolutely right.

"I think that is part of the reason Mirik feels so put upon" he said. "He gets a land grant many years ago that includes a river, and now some British Colonel has sailed in and told him how lucky he is that we are going to take over his river and build a canal. "

I thought for a moment, and said "Colonel By doesn't strike me as that kind of officer though. I found him reasonable and broad minded. Do you think he really took that attitude with Mirik?"

"I doubt he was full on the upper crust officer for whom God, the King and the aristocracy are the same thing. But what matters is how Mirik perceived him. I do think that you should maintain a positive relationship with Mirik. He clearly liked you, and a man like that can be a tremendous ally."

We rode on through the day at a walk. There were a few scattered raindrops, but nothing miserable. And thanks to the evergreen compound given us first by Mirik and then by the Algonquin we only endured the occasional mosquito buzzing around our ears. Willow slept against Piper's neck.

True to Pierre's prediction, we trotted into the camp right about supper time. There were camp fires a plenty, many with stew pots simmering over them. There were lines of shanties built along one side of the river and up high closer to the ridge. Further down the bank and starting at the river's edge and extending up the gentle slope were more shanties, enough to house at least fifty men. Construction had begun well up away from the mills, which were at the bottom of the little valley on one side of the river. Sherrif and I parted company, he to the part of camp used by contractors and workers, and I toward the thirty or so troops under my command.

I was surprised by their reaction to me. Some looked at me with open indignation, as if I had no right to approach them. Damn. I had forgotten I had my deer skins on.

I dismounted, and asked the first man available where his Sergeant Major was. He didn't at first answer me, until I identified myself, loudly. The Sergeant Major, by the name of Harris, came forward. I gave the order for him to form up the men.

He did so, but not without a look of surprise and a begrudging obedience. As he gave the order, the men groaned at having to abandon their suppers. I normally would wait for his command to attention, but I was now annoyed. I stood on a rock and yelled "TEN-SHUN!!!" I gambled that they would do it for this tanned young man dressed in deer skins with a little dog at his heel. They did, so quickly I thought they would snap their spines. To a civilian watching an enlisted man snap to attention is like watching him have a seizure. But I wasn't noticing.

After I identified myself as their new commander, I pointed out that I didn't expect ever to be treated in this way again. "I don't care if I come into this camp wearing no clothes at all, when I approach you all snap to attention! It is obvious that discipline has slipped here, so we will work together to correct the situation". Here I let my eyes glare and my nostrils flare, just for good measure.

"Who is on watch?" Two men at the end of the second row raised their hands. "Warrant, what watch posts have you established?" Harris pointed to two points at the rear of the camp. I nodded approval. "Have you established patrols?" The man nodded no, and I added that to the list of improvements forming in my head.

"Where are my quarters?" Harris now pointed to a small shanty just off to the side of the camp. I nodded and left him to dismiss the men. Two privates took Piper to the area that was obviously designated as a stable.

"Warrant!" Harris responded "Sir!" "With me" I said as I strolled toward my quarters. "Have my horse unburdened and my things delivered to my hut. And I can smell that stable area from here. I want it spotless before taps is sounded this evening. We do have a bugler?" He nodded. "Fine. Get these things accomplished and the rest we will discuss in the morning after reveille. How often do you rotate the watch?" Harris responded "Eight hours sir". "Make it six. Dismissed. "

I didn't relax until I was inside. I was shaking. It wouldn't do for them to know that I was nervous. I was also powerfully hungry. I changed into my white pants and red tunic, and wandered out into the camp with little Willow trotting along beside me.

I went in search of Sherrif and his partner, John Haggart. They were sitting around a camp fire under a tarpaulin tied to two of the only trees left and a decent cabin, clearly their lodging. Chaffee had secured a contract to clear the land before he died, which explained the lack of trees in the area. There were logs around the fire for sitting on, and a little area for preparing food. It was all very comfortable.

The man who could only be Haggart sat by the fire with a bowl of stew in his hands. When he looked up and saw me, he put the bowl on the ground and came forward to shake my hand.

"And here we are! Our new officer. I'm glad to see you, they've been a bit casual up until now" Haggart said, and Sherrif laughed.

I smiled and assured him that "I have not yet begun to fight, to quote a naval commander from the American war". They invited me to sit, and Sherrif handed me a piping hot bowl of stew. I was very glad to have it as I had not eaten since morning. He also gave Willow a bowl and made sure there was meat in it.

"The Lieutenant is from the North of Ireland" offered Sherrif.

"Ahh, you can see Scotland from the coast" responded Haggart.

"Almost from my home. In past years there was much coming and going you know? Clan McDonnell took possession of Dunluce Castle from the McGuigan Clan, a castle that hangs over the sea. They became rather mercenary, hiring armies for whatever chieftains paid. All went swimmingly until the castle kitchen tumbled into the sea during a large dinner". It pleased me to tell this story of my home. I had a small pang of home sickness.

"So what brought you away?" asked Haggart, putting his spoon down and listening intently to me.

"I suppose there wasn't a lot there for me. I felt I must make my own way in the world, as I suppose did you both".

The three of us chatted while I finished my meal, and the other two men fussed over Willow, rubbing her belly and scratching the base of her tail.

I watched Haggart as he watched me. He had light brown hair bleached blond by the summer sun. His face was round, with a full beard cropped close. His mouth was wide, and I could see a charming gap between his two front teeth. Like Sherrif, he wore a simple cotton shirt, wool trousers and suspenders. And like Sherrif, his hands had the look of a mason's hands, calloused and gnarled. As I watched, he stood up and leaned against a nearby tree, with his hands in the small of his back and his right foot braced back against the tree. This was clearly a position of increased concentration for him.

"So we were just talking about Mrs. Chaffee and her brother in law. Not to poke our noses where they don't belong, but Colonel By and I had a discussion about her before I left Bytown. He intimated his intention to apply for a pension for her from the crown, but that would be a separate issue. Did he discuss with you what he felt the limit would be to the price of the land and mills?" I didn't feel that Sherrif was prying or interfering. These men were my allies, and I felt that we would work better as a team.

"Yes, we did speak of it, and I agree he is quite sympathetic to her plight. He indicated, however, that the dispute between her and the brother in law should be adjudicated by the Crown. We can't let a familial dispute interfere with the project we are undertaking." I avoided the matter of the value of her land.

"What's his story anyway?" asked Haggart.

"Well apparently he is a business man of sorts near Elizabeth Town. He started out as a miller but has gained other interests.   A bit too close to the frontier for the taste of most, but perhaps he is like the Algonquin, who feel quite safe. A few years back he spent time in a debtor's prison south of the border. In any case, there were a few bad years, and as brothers do, there were loans from one to the other and those remain outstanding. I suppose he felt that the mills should naturally come to him, given the debt. I suppose he doubts the legal standing of a woman to inherit. Ownership of the mills would be desirable to him and I suppose he felt certain that we would pay a premium given our plan to build a lock here."

"Well how much do the mills owe him" asked Sherrif?

"A thousand pounds" I answered.

"Damnit all, these mills are worth triple that! What monster takes advantage of his brother's wife in such a way? Do you know the old bastard has been threatening her, lighting fires and the like?" Exclaimed Haggart.

"That was By's feeling, and I did know about the threats and harassment. So we will negotiate accordingly. By said he would come in the third week of August to confirm the deal. We won't begin demolishing the mills until construction demands it. "

"You'll start talking to her tomorrow then?" asked Sherrif.

"Yes, right after I have a meeting with Harris to outline my concerns. So tonight I have to figure out what those concerns are. I rather think there are at least a few. Please do share with me if you have concerns of your own." Immediately each man handed me a piece of paper with writing on it. I laughed, thanked them for the food and bid them goodnight.

I sat outside my little cabin where there was a little table and a chair someone had built of sticks and wrote out my list with a stubby little pencil. Everything from the state of the latrines to emptying of food waste into the latrine trench. The stables I had already asked about. According to Haggart and Sherrif there had been much heavy drinking a carousing before my arrival. How were they supposed to defend the men building the canal if they were drunk? The Americans were not fifty miles to the south of us, and theoretically they could arrive any day. They had certainly proved in the 1812 war that they could do so. And where was the alcohol coming from? I would investigate very quietly in the morning before the rest of the camp were up.

As I sat, I looked at the men who were to build the engineering marvel in the plans By had given me. They had precious little in the way of possessions. Some were dressed in nothing more than rags. Many had skin conditions that I could even see from a distance.

I rose, and approached a few men clustered around a fire. I saw no evidence of food. They were responsible to feed themselves on the wages they were paid.

"Good evening men. May I ask you a few questions?"

One of them said "Are you the new guvnor then?"

I looked at the speaker and saw the pinched features and small stature of the young boys that lived along the docklands in Plymouth, and I supposed, other cities as well. But this was no boy.

"I suppose I am if it come to that. Were you all raised here in the colony, or are you from away?"

They were Irish, a few English and Scottish – the poorest of the poor, given passage in exchange for agreeing to stay until the canal was built. Though they were sly and suspicious of me, my heart broke for them. They barely owned the clothes on their backs. And they eyed Willow in an unpleasant way.

I thanked them for the visit and went off to inspect the stable area. It was at the top of the ridge, to keep it as dry as possible. There I found Piper, and Sherrif's grey Whisper, and a few others there belonging to Sherrif and Haggart. Their feet had been picked clean, and bedding had been provided in the form of leaves and pine needles. There was fodder for them, enough but no extra. There was a private there, anxiously wringing his hands that I should find all well.

"Where do we get our fodder Private?" I asked.

He told me that it was bought from some local farmers.

"By whom?"

"Harris, Sir."

"I see. Carry on".

Willow had been nipping around the feet of the horses. Once, a big draft lifted his shaggy foot, and she knew to make a hasty getaway. I thanked the young private and called her to follow me back down the hill.

As we walked, I looked around to get a proper view of the area. The mills were on the southeast side of the water, Mrs. Chaffee's home built into the hill on the opposite side. There were a few cabins at the riverside for the employees of the mill. Mrs. Chaffee had managed to keep the mills running while the situation dragged on. The noise from them continued even now, at dusk. I was to meet with this lady in the morning, and I mentally prepared myself for an agile mind and a determined spirit.

The rest of the camp spread across land along the river, which was truly nothing more than a flow of water from one lake to another. There were various groups of men, soldiers on the right, workers to the left, camped around small fires, very small in the summer heat. Water was fetched from the river in buckets. The cook had his mess at the bottom of the hill away from the mills. And to my delight, near the water, were five birch bark canoes. I would have to inspect them when I was less tired.

Willow and I retired to my shanty, my home for the next few years, and slept well in spite of the noise from the mills.

Before I did anything else the next day, I met very early with a small group of soldiers, and then I met with Harris. I wanted to know why the troops were thin, why the few workers already on site were starving, and why the horses were on poor quality fodder. His first reaction was offended pride, and he stated that he felt he had done well without the supportive leadership of an officer. He was mocking me. I held my tongue for a few moments. And then:

"Harris, you were given an allotment you were meant to use to feed the livestock and the men, and to provide whichever miscellany might be required. From my practiced eye, you have spent barely half of what you should have spent to date. Would you care to enlighten me about where you have put the rest of the money?" I already knew of course.

After a moment's pause, there followed a combination of protesting, insisting on his honesty, impugning my character and dismissing my authority because (he assumed) I had bought my commission. I flicked a finger, and two soldiers came forward and restrained him. Sherrif and Haggart were there also, drawn by the noise, and stood in support against Harris. They offered a small storage facility built from widely spaced logs as a gaol of sorts, where he could be kept until Lieutenant Colonel By's next visit or until he could be taken there by a detail of soldiers.

Before I had him led away, I looked at him and said "Just in case there be any confusion to anyone in this camp, I did not buy my commission. I first studied and worked in business, and then I volunteered for the engineers. My commission is based on merit. These things do happen you know. Regardless, any officer in His Majesty's army is accorded respect under any circumstance. Any man not prepared to accept this requirement may be given his discharge at a moment's notice." In a strange country, and with no resources, and they all knew it. And with that I waved Harris away and dismissed the others.

Once the crowd dispersed, Haggart slapped me on the back and said "I'm quite certain we like you!"

I retired to the shelter over their fire for a delicious cup of coffee (strong and smoky) and a scone made by Haggart. It was absolutely fabulous and melted in my mouth. Extraordinary, given it was cooked with lard from deer meat and baked in the fire. Haggart was truly a renaissance man. I wondered what he couldn't do.

As we sat, I asked "Why are your men so thin? What is their arrangement for their food?"

Sherrif spoke." Most of them were very thin when they arrived. They were 'recruited" in Ireland, and some in England and Scotland. They were starving, they had nothing to lose."

Haggart took over "You see, we haven't actually been paid. So we can't pay them."

I looked at them both levelly. "Alright, look, I will feed them until we can get this sorted. They obviously don't have the wherewithal to hunt or fish. Do we have fishing rods?" Nods no. "Right, let's see if we can rectify that. What's the fishing like in the lakes?" A wrinkled nose, a hand waggled back and forth. "Well it's better than starving. I will have a few of mine teach a few of yours. And does anyone hunt?" Haggart smiled.

We chatted more about solutions for a while, drinking our coffee.

Precisely at nine o'clock, we canoed down to the saw mill to meet with Mrs. Chaffee. There were two carts drawn by oxen waiting for lumber to be milled from timbers cut on farms further up the ridge. The big animals shook their big heads against the mosquitoes and black flies that preyed on their ears and their faces, where the skin was thinner. Poor things. I stroked their faces on the way by. The farmers smiled at me and patted the animals' heads.

We were welcomed into the mill by Mrs. Chaffee. She was a strong looking woman, wearing a man's breeches, with her hair tied up on her head. Her hands were work worn, and she wore a plain cotton shirt, not terribly different than the ones Sherrif and Haggart wore. She was young – maybe 18, and quite pretty. I had never met a woman like her. Apparently women were very different in the colonies.

She took us into a room in the corner of the mill. When she closed the door, the sound from the water and the saw was dimmed considerably. I asked her with what the room was insulated to make it such a sane corner in such a noisy environment.

She smiled at me and said "Samuel couldn't stand noise. He fought in the war against the Americans, said he never got over the guns. The walls are actually stuffed with wool. I thought it was a waste of good wool, but he was steadfast. I'm glad he was now." She pointed.

In a corner of the room was a bassinette where a baby slept. She must have been pregnant when her husband died. Sometimes fate was deeply unfair. And yet she looked strong and in control.

There was a knock at the door. A man came in, presumably Benjamin Chaffee, the brother of the deceased Samuel. Although he and Samuel hailed from England, I couldn't see anything typical of England about him, except his soft Somerset accent when he spoke.

"Exactly what authority do you have sir, or are you just a lackey of John By" he asked immediately after we had introduced ourselves. This belligerence was the reason for Sherrif and Haggart being present. Chaffee had been aggressive around the mills, and I didn't want troops there because I didn't want anyone knowing Mrs. Chaffee's affairs.

"Right, let's sit down shall we?" I said. Then taking out my papers and notes, I began. "Right, so you Madam, are the widow Mary Anne Poole Chaffee, and your husband was the late Samuel Chaffee, proprietor of the mill complex here at Chaffee's Mills. Is that correct?"

She nodded, but her brother in law immediately began to argue. "Now wait a minute, he was not the sole proprietor here! We shared all our business ventures we did. This is what I have been trying to tell you lot!"

"All right Mr. Chaffee, let's address the substance of that declaration. I see by Lieutenant Colonel By's notes and from letters you have sent him that you are the proprietor of two other mill locations, is that correct?"

He stammered a bit and said, "Well that has nothing to do with this!"

"Ah but sir it does. It establishes a prior pattern of action. So, my understanding from these letters is that the two of you established a mill in South Crosby shortly after arriving in the Canadian colony. Is that correct?"

He nodded a bit miserably. "Right, and the two of you shared the income from that enterprise?"

Benjamin Chaffee nodded yes, but Mrs. Chaffee exclaimed "No you did not! Every penny that came from that mill, Samuel had to sign a promissory note for!"

The man was beginning to look a bit uncomfortable.

I drove on. "Right, and then between 1820 and an indeterminate date, you were in the United States. Is that correct?" Chaffee nodded again. "So in your absence Samuel struck out on his own and settled here, married and built the complex you see here independently of you."

"Bloody hell I financed him!" he exclaimed, jumping up from his seat and beginning to pace about the room.

I continued toward the objective I saw in sight' "Yes of course, you loaned him the capital to begin

254

operations. That's very clear. Do you have the promissory notes with you Mr. Chaffee?"

He stopped pacing and handed over four somewhat worn documents, written in simple English. They all began thus: "I Samuel Chaffee do acknowledge that I owe my brother Benjamin Chaffee the sum of..." All four notes were for amounts in the hundreds of pounds sterling, totalling 1,043.00. I knew this in advance of course.

"Mrs. Chaffee, did your husband inform you of the income of this complex of mills?" I asked.

"Well it varies sir, sometimes it's ten pound a week, and sometimes it's a hundred. You understand, it's about who shows up." I knew the income of the mills to be considerably more than that. She was hedging a bit.

Benjamin once more lept up and declared "She lies! Or she's stupid. What would a woman know about a milling complex this size? This is the biggest milling complex in Eastern Ontario. "   He snorted in disgust.

I looked at the sawdust on her sleeves and a smudge of dirt on her face. "Mrs. Chaffee have you brought your records for the year of 1827?" I asked, as if Chaffee had not acted out.

"Yes, I have them. That is, the month of my husband's death is a bit incomplete." She handed over a battered book. Its outside did not match the inside. The columns were neat and legible and correctly totalled on each page. Even with Samuel's death, the mills had made a thousand pounds sterling in the last year. That's why the old bastard wanted it so badly. The more it showed a history of being lucrative, the more the crown would be willing to pay, or so he thought. And he could have any income between now and when the mills were torn down.

"Very well, Mr. Chaffee, I would like to address the concern you had when you walked in the door, that being whether I had any authority or whether I was – what was it?- a lackey.

"As you can see I have been well prepared. I have all of the correspondence between you and Lieutenant Colonel By, as well as copies of documents registered with other authorities including banks. Given the dispute here being addressed, I also have in my possession various references as to the people involved and their business reputations. Including a record from the debtor's prison in, just a minute, Ohio?

"I am authorized, based on all these materials here in my possession to adjudicate this particular dispute. The value of Chaffee's Mills will be determined at a later date. As Messrs. Sherrif and Haggart are only beginning work now, we estimate that we will not need to take down the mills until next summer unless the progress of construction necessitates demolition. If Mrs. Chaffee does not wish to continue, we can demolish as soon as ever is convenient for Mr. Sherrif and Mr. Haggart.

"Mr. Chaffee, I understand that you are owed a substantial sum. In my experience in my Family's business, I know that it is customary that interest be paid to a creditor with repayment of the debt.

Based on what I see here in the books" with a finger on the page "you have been receiving one hundred pounds sterling per month, is that correct?"

I got a muttered response for my trouble.

"Right then, the debt will be paid off in less than a year even taking interest into account. I suggest the operations continue until the debt is paid. Mrs. Chaffee will have made a modest profit, and I believe that should be satisfactory for everyone.

"And one last detail. Mr. Chaffee it has come to my attention that there have been attacks on the mills, and Mrs. Chaffee as well.   Some attempts to burn down the mills, that sort of thing. This kind of terrorizing is criminal. As such, if there is any more of it, I will come to arrest you with a detail of armed soldiers at my back. Do I make myself clear? And do remember that there are armed soldiers just over there to provide security not only for the work camp, but also for these mills."

I stood up, and made to escort Benjamin Chaffee from the room. He shook off my attentions and left, slamming the door.

Mary Anne Chaffee stood with her hands over her face, her body slightly bent forward. Sobs shook her body. I was utterly surprised as she seemed to strong. The three of us looked at the ground in embarrassment. Societal rules at the time did not allow us any recourse to comfort a woman to whom we were not married. She stood up then, wiping her tears from her face with her hands.

"I'm so sorry" she said. "It has just been such a terrible time. "

The three of us all shook her hand then before taking our leave. She really was a remarkable woman. As a woman succeeding on her own in the bush was hard enough, but she had also fought against a family member who should have protected her, not attacked. And she had done it through birth and with a new baby. We promised to be looking in on her from time to time.

Walking back to camp, Sherrif and Haggart teased me about Mary Anne Chaffee. I wasn't interested, but rather than say so, I said "She is more woman than I could ever handle."

They laughed, and made off for their tasks for the day.

In the early hours of that morning, two men and I had thoroughly searched Harris' bedroll. We had found money and bottles of rum. Apparently he had been purchasing alcohol with the allotment and then selling it to the men and also the workers at a significant profit. That was another reason why some of the workers could not afford food. He had played on their weakness. We had documented our findings and signed them. My next task was to address this booty and account for how it was to be spent.

I went to the cook and asked for a list of fruit, vegetables and meat that were required. I asked him if we had a garden and we did not. He had some nasty looking potatoes so I suggested he plant them and see if they would grow. It was too late in the season to plant a fuller garden, but we talked of collecting seeds for next spring.

Next I took a Sargent and the two draft horses from the construction work, a wagon, and a teamster. There was a fairly decent road that ran up the hill and away from the water, and I was led to expect that there were three or four farms there.

At the top of the ridge we found them, cattle farms mainly, but one market gardener who sold corn, carrots, and a variety of other vegetables. All three farmers were surprised when I asked for a better grade of fodder and advised them that I would pay appropriately. I also obtained a barrel of apples that were not quite edible for people, but the horses would love them.

The farmers asked about Mary Anne Chaffee, and their concern was genuine. I assured them that I had heard the case between her and Benjamin Chaffee and believed it had been brought to a resolution. I hoped I was right. I made a note to put a watch on the mills when I got back.

When we arrived back at camp, cook began making a wonderful stew with meat and corn and apples (good ones) in it. It was absolutely delicious with such surprising ingredients.

Life for the soldiers in camp was soon returned to a solid routine. Although all of them were qualified in masonry and explosives, most of the work was to be done by the contract men. Some of them chose to moonlight as contract when they were at leisure, and I chose to ignore this activity as long as their military duties were performed well and completely. It was strictly against military policy elsewhere, but I felt it was in our interests to help construction along where we could. (Another military rule: "snap!")

I busied my troops, and myself with improving the camp. One thing we had a lot of was soap, so we created a laundry using water from the river. We put up a washing line, and almost right away the men began to use it. As the day had been very hot, our cotton shirts and briefs dried quickly in the sun. In the civilian part of the camp, the workers followed our example, and though they didn't have as much soap, an immediate improvement was made among them as well.

There were drills, and work details. All of the campfire areas were tidied up and firewood properly stacked so it was no longer in haphazard piles. Bed rolls were pulled out of the shanties and aired out daily unless it was raining. Metal dishes were washed every night and returned to their storage place. Uniforms were worn at all times and in good condition. There were regular patrols through the surrounding area, which I would often accompany on horseback.   Nothing was rotten any longer in the State of Denmark.

Sherrif came to me after supper one evening. "You've definitely made an improvement since you got here" he said. "It benefits us too, thank you. I have to go back to Bytown tomorrow. I will probably pass By coming the other way, but I need to see McTaggart, so off I go. Do you have any letters or documents you need to send? "

I gave him some letters to send home to Ireland, if he so pleased. He smiled. "I'm going by canoe, so have your fellows look after Whisper" he said, grinning. And he was gone.

The stone for the weir and the lock came from the quarry down the same road we had travelled to see the farmers. It ran up past the farms and across the main path to Kingston, such as it was. The blocks were rough-hewn there and brought down to our work site by oxen. Masons then refined the shape of the blocks. The big Shire horse lifted the block using a block and tackle, and the block was laid in its place in the wall being constructed. At the moment, that construction was focused on the construction of the weir, which had just begun and would take the better part of a year and a half.

The weir was an overflow channel to run to on one side of the lock. In the spring, the lock might be overrun by ice and flotsam, and so the weir was provided to lower the level behind the lock when necessary. It would be completed first to accommodate the flow of water while the lock itself was being built.

On the day after Sherrif left, I was in camp rather than out on patrol so I saw my first delivery of blocks by oxen pulling a big heavy wagon. Oxen were used because they were more powerful than and not as valuable as horses. There were fifteen or twenty small and five large blocks on the wagon, and they were lifted off with the help of the big gelding. For him this was easy work, but it was an invaluable aid to the men who were moving the stones. Small ones they could do on their own, but some of the large stones were two feet wide and high by three deep. These were the head stones that buttressed the oncoming water where it would split between the weir and the lock. I helped with the unloading and setting the stones to be fine milled. By the end of the day, I was exhausted.

Over coffee the next morning, Willow and I were devouring another excellent scone and Haggart sat looking pensive. "Have you ever thought of getting married?" he said.

I looked at him in surprise and said "I was very nearly engaged once, but it didn't work out. You?"

"Aye, there is a girl I like the looks of. She's bonny for sure. She's clever too, and sensible. A good seamstress. And she has a real green thumb. She is very young, but I don't think that's an impediment."

"Are you looking for a bride or hiring a housekeeper!" I responded.

"Well I think it's important to be detached from these things. I want to build the best foundation, you know. I want children and a productive life. I want to build those things with someone who shares my outlook."

I looked at him. "I suppose, if you are building a dynasty." I thought of my own parents when I said this. I was sometimes surprised they had ever managed to produce children, so distanced were they from one another.

In the evening it was still terribly hot. I took Willow to the laundry with me, where I washed my shirt and gave her a cool bath as well. Out of the dusk came a man on horseback. I stood there with my naked chest and looked at him in surprise.

"I'm looking for Mr. Haggart sir." His face was sweaty, and although he should have been red in the face from the warmth, he was white as a sheet. As I stood there looking at him, he fell from his horse.

I shouted and three soldiers ran to my aid. We freed one of the shanties and turned it into an infirmary, since the man was obviously ill. Haggart having been summoned was there quickly. He touched the man on the shoulder and asked "You have a message for me?"

The man rolled his eyes in Haggart's direction and said "It's Sherrif sir."

"What about Sherrif?"

"He's dead sir." And with that the man became unconscious. He died three days later.

Haggart was utterly thunderstruck. Why Sherrif had been taken so quickly was a mystery, but there were prior stories about men merely canoeing through certain lakes and becoming deathly ill. It didn't matter to Haggart. He settled into a dark mood that lasted for weeks.

And so began our first "sickly season".[24] Men began almost to drop in their tracks. They suffered aches and pains and fever, feeling cold and sometimes shaking. But that is where the similarity ended. If a man had any pre-existing illness, a cold, a toothache, any kind of infection, the fever made it worse. Most recovered, but some did not. We

---

[24] http://www.rideau-info.com/canal/history/hist-canal.html

tried to bury them as fast as we could, because we did not know how the malaise was spread. There was a small burying ground up the hill where Chaffee and a small group of others were buried. We used pieces of stone from the works to serve as head and foot stones, and we buried several in one grave.

 We placed wooden crosses with the names of those buried. There are those who have come after who assert that we simply dumped them in the ground and did nothing to mark their passing. They are wrong. It's just that the wooden crosses, like the people whose lives they commemorated, eventually wasted away and became dust.

At the worst of it, there were only three or four men well enough to care for the sick. Mrs. Chaffee cared for the sick as well, stopping only to be sick herself for four days, and to recover her strength for a week. Her baby, fortunately, did not get sick.

 Haggart, at a loss as he was with the death of his friend and partner, barely functioned for a few days and then became sick himself. I feared he might not rally, but then I was finally able to feed him a thin soup. Within a week he was up and visiting the sick, administering water and soup. Fortunately we had not much rain during the month of August, and the ill could be moved outside to enjoy the fresh air while they recovered.

I was very lucky. Whether because of my relative youth, my fitness or my strength, although I did get sick, I recovered within three days, and regained my strength rapidly afterwards.

By the end of August, the men were back to work and Haggart and I were able to take stock of our supplies and the men we had left to feed.

Haggart's men dug the trenches where the water would flow with pickaxes and shovels. The stone and slag they dug up was carried away in a wooden wheelbarrow and emptied into a stone boat hitched to the horses. When it was full the load would be towed away and emptied onto a part of the bank being built up for docks. This was backbreaking work, and Haggart exhorted his men to ever greater heights of productivity with his own enthusiasm, and with occasional treats he cooked on his fire and in a makeshift oven as reward. His talent for efficiency and enthusiasm were known throughout the canal works, until Chaffee's was simply referred to as "Haggart's Job".[25]

In September, By arrived at long last, a month late. Several large canoes arrived at the end of one sunny September day. The air smelled of the freshness of fall, the freshness that makes one want to begin again, to start new projects, and to accomplish what summer's laziness has put aside.

I greeted my superior with respect but also with delight. We had come through such a terrible August, and survived, and I was happy to see someone from the outside world.

But By was pale and seemed weak. He had lost weight and his face was sallow. When I expressed concern I found that he was recovering from the

---

[25] http://www.rideau-info.com/canal/history/locks/h37-chaffeys.html

same miasma that we all were, and that he had truly not recovered his strength. It was his illness that had caused the long delay of his visit.

The men with By unloaded two hundred blankets to be shared among the contractors and my soldiers. By also told me that some friends of mine would be bringing furs a little later in the fall and I was to use part of my allotment to purchase as many as I needed. And finally, there was a generous provision of root vegetables and dried meat. It was a little bit like Christmas.

By spent three days at Chaffee's, learning about all that had gone on, and allowing me to ask questions and share our accomplishments with him. We met again with Mary Anne Chaffee, and seeing her complex of mills again, By was certain they had been much undervalued. He undertook to suggest a much higher price to the Ordinance department and had a man sketch out the entire site for a new survey. He visited with Haggart, who only stopped working long enough for the visit.

The best thing by far that came to Chaffee's from By's visit was a large pouch of very excellent black tea. It tasted a little different made with our water from the lake, but it was delicious all the same. We resolved to keep it aside for very urgent cases. Everyone knows that tea has remarkable restorative properties.

In my time alone with Lieutenant Colonel By during that visit, it was clear that he noticed where I had eased the rules for the troops under my command, allowing them to moonlight for Haggart and sometimes allowing them to remove their uniforms while off duty during the heat.

"There is something you really need to learn about being in command of a group of men" he said as I sheepishly returned his gaze. "A system of rules is to provide structure. But where those rules cause hardship, and possibly dissent, it is wise to bend them if necessary. This applies to your deerskin breeches" he said, smiling at me indulgently.

Haggart dearly loved to cook and his hospitality toward travellers of all stripes knew no bounds. During By's visit, the entire group of eight men were fed richly, including his excellent scones which I was learning I could not do without. There was a stew richly flavoured from a pouch of herbs which he hid somewhere in his living area. And there was always excellent quality rum. [26]

Early on the morning of the fourth day, the canoes were portaged the short distance from one side of the mills to the other, put in the water, and the group pushed off toward Davis Lock and Jones Falls. Haggart went with them, as he was also the contractor for Davis and was due a visit.

Haggart left a young man named Stuart in charge of the workers when he left. He seemed confident and knowledgeable. In two days, he got a load of stone from the quarry and the workers made significant progress with their shovels and pickaxes and wheelbarrows. I never tired of watching them. This business of digging a canal was a business of

---

[26] Ibid

muscle and sinew. I had not learned that in my training to be an engineer.

On the third day, large blocks finished by the masons were being moved into place on the wall. The stone masonry was so precise, so perfect, that a man couldn't slide a piece of paper between the stones when they were set in place.

The finished blocks were sitting on the wagon beside the work area. There were chocks behind all four wheels to keep it from moving. For safety, the draft mare was harnessed to it. The draft gelding was harnessed to a block and tackle that was used to move the stones.

While each stone was still on the wagon, metal rods were used to pry up the block, in order to slide rope under it. Once the rope was tied to the block, the horse moved one step to lift the block just far enough for the men around it to check that the ropes were even and strong. The block and tackle was on a boom that could then be rotated outward toward the work area. The block was swung over its intended location, the horse backed up slowly, and the block was laid in place by knowledgeable hands.

I watched it so many times, and it would never cease to impress me. One particular time, on that warm September day, there were four men, one of whom was young Stuart. Rather than standing back and letting the experienced men lay the stone in place, Stuart insisted on getting involved. He dearly wanted to be seen by the men to be working as hard as they were. When the stone was lowered to just above its final position, there was a flurry of activity and a misunderstanding occurred between the men and the teamster and the horse. One minute all was well and the next there was a bloodcurdling scream and a great deal of yelling "Up! Up dammit!"

The horse stepped forward and the stone hung ominously over the heads of the men, and there was young Stuart with his hand flattened where the stone should be. I and two other soldiers lept forward immediately.

Just moving Stuart's arm and poor mangled hand caused him agony. We fetched him cold water, to soak, and laudanum, to ease the pain, and we moved him into the infirmary. Sherrif's lovely grey was still in the stable, so I sent a man to ride for the travelling doctor. This was well beyond my skill with battle dressings.

I also had a man canoe to Davis for Haggart.

It took my man the better part of a day to find the doctor, and he did not bring him back to Chaffee's until lunch time the next day. Stuart was almost delirious with the pain, and I was terrified to give him too much laudanum. Upon returning, Haggart focused his attention on the young man, while I dismissed all of the men for the time being.

The doctor took a look at poor Stuart and shook his head. The hand must come off, or it would become infected and kill him. It was no use to him anyway, not as it was. I looked at this young man, not more than 22, who had been trying so hard to do all the right things, trying to show the men that he was useful and not afraid to get his hands dirty.

I found my best man with a sabre, and made sure the weapon was as sharp as could be. The doctor felt amputation in this way would be faster, neater. And so with one stroke, fast and deadly, the hand came off. Every man there was silent. Except Stuart. I am sure his scream could be heard all the way to Davis.

It was the oddest thing that as soon as the source of the pain was removed, the patient improved and began to recover almost immediately. Within days the doctor removed the laudanum entirely, and Stuart was on the mend. It only was left to change the bandages regularly and keep the wound clean.

Two weeks after the original injury, with his arm in a sling, Stuart resumed his supervisory duties. His men respected him mightily for it, and Haggart consented to keep him on as long as his health continued to improve and he was able to continue with his duties. There was no prejudice, no feeling that a man with a disfiguring injury was not worth having. Stuart had learned a valuable lesson, a lesson he would share with every man he knew for the rest of his life. That sharing had value to Haggart as an employer.

At the very end of October, Haggart invited me to take out a canoe with him to some of the islands in the lake. He felt there were deer on at least one of them, and we could use the meat for winter. I was delighted at the opportunity to use a paddle again, and so we packed a lunch and prepared to make a day of it. I left a good man in charge, left Willow with Mary Ann and embarked with pleasure.

We paddled out on the lake just after dawn and the water sparkled in the sun. The air was crisp. It was a perfect day. I thought I saw something moving on Berlin Island as we moved away from the canal channel. In the back of the Canoe, Haggart steered us to the far side of the island where there was a little bay and we could pull the canoe up on the bank.

Taking our rifles, we walked very quietly up what looked like a wildlife trail. At about the midpoint of the island, we found evidence that the deer had been resting here during the daytime. With some variation, deer graze at night and rest in the woods in the daytime. On the trees we saw rub marks and bits of velvet rubbed off. Taggart told me in a few weeks the breeding rut would have begun and it would be too dangerous for us to be in the vicinity of the deer until deep winter. [27]

We whispered to one another that we might have scared the deer off, or maybe they were resting in another spot. We had a choice. We could dig into a place where the wind would carry our scent away or we could keep looking. We found a spot with a large rock that we could crouch behind and have the west wind carry our smell away to the east. We settled in to wait.

This was a learning experience for me. I had never hunted anything, except a large helping from the buffet at candle lit dinners. I had watched cows and pigs be butchered at home and I appreciated that

---

[27] https://www.hww.ca/en/wildlife/mammals/white-tailed-deer.html

somehow they had to get from the field to my plate. But I had never done it.

As we sat very still, we listened to the forest around us. First all we heard was the wind in the leaves, but the longer we sat, the more we heard. I identified a few different birds that Haggart, Sherrif and the men had taught me about. Crows. A bird that was called a robin, but that was nothing like a robin at home. Haggart and I listened to a sort of screeching sound, after which there was the splash of a hunting bird. "Eagle" he mouthed at me. Finally I saw motion out of one eye, and turned very slowly to look. The deer were back.

One buck, two does, and three fawns, still with a few very faint spots. Haggart moved his lips. "We want the buck" he mouthed. With my military training I was to do the shooting. Haggart thought I would be the more accurate shot. I nodded and put my rifle to my shoulder, balanced the other end on the rock and put the spot between the buck's eyes in my sights. I held my breath, followed him as he browsed a bit. Pulled the trigger.

The buck died instantly, and the other deer ran off at the report of the weapon. I managed to keep any misgivings I had about killing him out of my mind. This was food, and now we had to field dress him, and then carry him back to the canoe and get him home. Then we had to hang him somewhere to age for a few weeks.

When we were finished gutting the buck, we found a stick large enough and tied his feet together and then hung him from it. I chuckled that it looked like a picture I had seen in a children's book about Robin Hood. Now I knew what that picture meant.

Standing up and getting ready to shoulder my part of the burden, my eyes landed on something in the bush. I froze.

"Haggart!" I whispered as loudly as I could.

He looked at me casually, with a very slight frown and said "Huh?"

I nodded at what I saw. There were two big animals, which I took to be wolves. Either that or they were the biggest dogs I had ever seen. They had fluffy coats, and yellow eyes. One was grey and the other was black. More childhood books flashed through my head and I think I had never been so terrified up to that point in my life.

"Now don't make any sudden moves" whispered Haggart, walking slowly over to the guts of the buck we had left on the ground. We should have buried them of course, but I guess my expert partner had overlooked that.

Haggart bent down slowly, not taking his eyes off the wolves. He managed to look so relaxed, when I didn't think I could move. Picking up the intestines of the deer, he stood up and tossed them in the direction of the wolves, so they landed just a few feet in front of them.

"Now, let's go" he said "and do not bloody run. Walk nice and easy".

Sure enough, when I looked back (to see if I was about to die) the wolves were eating our offering, and were paying us no further heed. We didn't slow down, however until we and the buck were all safely in the canoe and paddling away.

When we were a few good strokes out into the lake, Haggart stopped paddling and turned around to face me.

"That was fun wasn't it?"

If I had hit him with the paddle I probably would have killed him, so out of anger, relief and frustration, I used it to send up huge sheets of water in his direction until he finally called out "I'm sorry, I'm sorry! Bloody Irishman. No sense of humour".

Our arrival back in camp was greeted with cheers. The entire group stood around the buck, deciding how we were going to hang him out.

"Why, from a tree of course." Said one.

"Bears climb trees" said another.

"Is anybody here from this godforsaken place?"

"Ha, wait until winter, then you'll see godforsaken".

Haggart put his hands up. "I need a block and tackle and a tree with a branch large enough to hold a deer but not large enough to hold a bear. I am sure the Lieutenant here can find me a block and tackle, and you lot go find me three good candidates for the tree."

In the end, the deer was hung almost three feet out from the trunk of a tree, and a good ten feet up. The tree it was on was well out of camp, as it was sure to attract bears getting ready to hibernate, even if they couldn't reach it.

And then everyone was sent back to work with a wave of Haggart's hands, including my soldiers.

Haggart and I repaired to his fireplace shelter. We each took a few contemplative swigs of rum before either of us spoke.

"See there really is no such thing as the big bad wolf" began Haggart. "They are animals, period, and they have their own rules of conduct. They will attack humans, if they are threatened or starving. But mostly they stay away from humans altogether. We're too noisy and we smell bad."

"Speak for yourself you daft Scot. And speaking of smell bad, do you suppose our water is clean enough for me to bathe? I've been out here a long time."

Haggart shrugged. "I use a basin of warm water myself."

I opened my mouth but nothing came out, so I took another swig of rum.

We sat in silence for a while and I asked "What's her name?"

He looked at me. "Who?"

"The lucky domestic servant you're planning on marrying?"

"Isabella. I was thinking of inviting her to visit here sometime. "

"Where would she stay? Not in one of our shanties?"

"I could ask Mary Anne to put her up. You know, they're women."

That plan actually had merit. But it was October. To ask a woman to travel here when it could snow soon, that was questionable. But Haggart didn't think so.

Presently Haggart got up to meet with our cook to plan a common meal for the whole camp, as was becoming increasingly normal, and I went off to meet with some of my men about our preparations for winter.

That night in the very wee hours I woke to the noises a bear makes when it is frustrated. Sort of a cross between a grunt and a squeal. I didn't know that's what it was until Willow and I came out of my shanty to find several others including Haggart. Everyone was watching the place where we had hung the deer. Two bears, which Haggart identified as male, were dancing around under the deer carcass. Bear don't eat meat as much as they stick to berries, nuts, and fruits. But they *will* eat meat, especially when it is hanging over their heads and easily reached. Or not so easily reached, as in this case. I had to calm Willow and insist she settle. While I understood that her job was to bark at wildlife around the camp, I thought we already knew in this case.

As we stood planning our next steps we saw something that was more serious than the bears. In the shadows, just out of the reach of our torches, were dark shadows that flitted back and forth, moving smoothly like skaters on the winter ice. Wolves.

"There you go you Irish bastard, we don't smell bad enough to drive them away because you bathed" Haggart declared.

There was a chuckle through the group of men around us.

"The wolves will wait until the bears determine how to get the deer to the ground. The bears will climb the tree with the deer in it and put all their weight on the branch. It will take a while but they will break the branch and the deer will fall. Then the wolves will chase away the bears and eat the deer. Either way, we lose the deer."

"It was your idea to hang the deer from a branch too weak to hold a bear. So what do we do?" I asked quietly.

He looked at me for a minute. "We shoot them all. We won't need any more meat for some time."

I turned to the sergeant beside me, and instructed him to bring two men who were deadly accurate shots and two rifles. It turned out the two men of his choice were already with us, and had their rifles at hand against precisely this eventuality. Haggart retrieved his rifle and the three of them slid into the shadows using hand signals to coordinate their movements. I lost sight of them almost immediately.

After two or three minutes, there were three loud cracks that rang through the woods almost simultaneously. The two bears dropped and were still. The wolves had darted away at the sound of gunfire, but already they were slinking back toward the bears. The smell of blood was too much.

Shots rang out again and the wolves dropped to the ground.

As soon as all the shooting was done, I instructed the soldiers to build us a small building that would be impregnable to wildlife. No more nonsense. In a trice, trees were cut down, hand saws came out, and work began there in the middle of the night in the lantern light. With two men standing watch over the four animals, the rest of us pitched in and the building was done and sunk into the ground by the distance of a man's hand. All four carcasses were moved into the new butchery and hung. There is a rich satisfaction in working with a group of men who can accomplish such high quality work in such short order.

I thought of what Alona had said about not abusing the wild animals in the wood of the Algonquin. I hoped we had not. I knew we could eat all of the meat. I hoped that was enough.

I sent the men back to bed for a few hours, but for myself, I could not have slept. After all the excitement Haggart was awake as well, so we stirred up the fire, and made some coffee. Mary Ann Chaffee and her sleeping baby also joined us, she having observed all the activity. She nodded at the new building and accepted a cup of coffee. We three talked companionably about the events of the night, and other things. Willow took turns in each of our laps as we gently accused her of failing to keep the predators at bay. The sun came up over our little Salon under the tarp and the atmosphere scented as it was by pine and cedar trees, was convivial and more pleasing than any more civilized setting in London.

Isabella arrived at Chaffee's Lock with the first dusting of snow. She had been brought down the waterway by canoe, and came with her brother as chaperone. Mary Ann Chaffee had agreed to provide lodging for them in her home across the water from the mills.

For a week, there was much cooking. Excellent coffee, tea brought from Perth, meat prepared in excellent and surprising ways. And all out of doors under the tarp. These two really were made for each other.

I liked her. She was attractive, clever, well read and sensible.

On the day they left, camp was a very sombre place. Isabella had injected much comfort and happiness into our camp, and she brought out much good in Haggart. She was very young, about 16 to Haggart's late thirties. But I had no objection to that.

Pierre and Alona came in November bearing furs, as foretold by Lieutenant Colonel By. They weren't the best or most valuable, but there were enough of them to ensure that we could all remain warm through the coldest part of winter.

We told them the story about the deer, the bears and the wolves. I had a feeling that we had mishandled the situation, so I asked what we could have done differently.

"Don't attract wolves and bears" was Pierre's response. When I rolled my eyes, he told me that we had done everything in the wrong order. Start with building the butchery, then go hunting. Of course. Bloody common sense.

Alona looked better than the last time I had seen her. Her skin was better, and she smiled more. I told her so, and she hugged me. "We will speak more next time White Boy".

They were gone long before I was ready for them to leave. Haggart and I and the groups of men we cared for, and worked with, settled down to survive the winter.

I have been asked more times than I can count how it felt to go through that first Canadian winter. It was brutal, it was cold, and there were times when the frigid air blew through my body and I knew that if I strayed from shelter I would die. But the biggest irritant was the attitudes of Haggart and others of our acquaintance who were long-time residents.

In response to my complaints about the cold one afternoon, Haggart said the same infuriating thing Canadians have been saying ever since. "Oh that's nothing! You haven't seen cold until………" followed by endless litanies of near death experiences and stories about frostbite and hypothermia.

It irritated me because it was a denial of how I felt. As if I wasn't cold. As if I hadn't lost sensation from my toes. I learned to acknowledge the cold, but not to complain about it, in order to avoid being treated in this way.

Work continued throughout the winter on all but the very coldest of days. The furs and blankets that had come from By and the Algonquin were a godsend. We had spent a December afternoon making mitts from some of the furs with Haggart instructing the group. Some even wore fur boots over their feet. On brutally cold January afternoons, the sound of the pickaxe and the shovel against frozen rock rang through the little valley. When spring came, we had not lost one man, but only a couple of fingers due to frostbite.

By the end of May 1829, the weir was more than half finished. The work was first class. By came to visit again and nodded his approval. The men were all now experienced with their pickaxes, their shovels and their wheelbarrows. We had begun to make great progress and enjoyed he spring sun on our skin.

By had a project for us on that visit. He had been advised that the degree of illness of the previous year was due to a lack of air circulation. He wanted all of the trees in camp or near it to be cut down. That meant the canvas over our shared campfire in front of Haggart's cabin had to be taken down at least in the short term.

I organized a work detail and in three days my men had not only cut down several trees, they had cut them up into green firewood and had begun to tear out stumps with the help of Haggart's draft horses. The result was considerably less pretty. A week's rain didn't enhance the effect. And with the removal of the trees we noticed more puddles as the trees themselves were not there to consume the water. And when the stumps were all removed, there was more water standing throughout the camp and the work site.

About three weeks after the tree cutting, we noticed a preponderance of mosquitoes. The damned things were everywhere, buzzing in our ears and the ears of the animals. We used up all of the home-made bug repellant we had left. I sent a man by canoe to By to inform him of these developments, and that the puddles all seemed to be breeding places for some kind of insect. Given the mosquito population, I suspected they might be the culprits.

My messenger came back with large quantities of the home-made repellent, with a variety of labels and dates on the jars. By the time he arrived, we had filled in all the low spots with soil and had the horses tamp them down using a plank for them to step on.

Our landscaping efforts did seem to pay off, at least some. The incessant buzzing seemed to drop. The mosquito population returned to a dull roar.

That spring, we noticed that Mary Ann was visited by a gentlemen fairly regularly. He arrived by canoe, tied up outside her house, and sat with her on the porch during his visits. He was extremely well dressed and treated her well that we could see, bringing gifts and laughing a hearty laugh with her. We teased her about it occasionally, but secretly we hoped his attentions would be returned. The mills were due to come down soon, and we feared for her future. We knew she was resourceful and would land on her feet, but this nice looking gentlemen would perhaps give her the ease she had lacked since Samuel's death.

Mary Ann's baby was now 2, a boy named Benjamin. He tottered around on that porch, so close to the water. I begged her to restrict him more. I had nightmares about something happening to him. In my dreams I saw a toddler of like age to Benjamin, smiling and waving, but then the dream would end and I would be sitting upright crying with Willow in my lap and licking my face. My entreaties did convince Mary Ann to put Benjamin on a sort of leash affair to keep him on the porch and away from the water. As she did so, the dreams went away.

By the end of July, the weir was almost finished, and Mary Ann announced that she and the gentleman, a Mr. Scott, were to be married almost right away and she and Benjamin would move to his home away from Chaffee's Mills. They were married in Newboro and she moved away without fanfare. When she came to say Good bye and introduced us to her husband, he seemed extremely fine and with the means to give her the life she deserved. [28]

Life was definitely a little sadder after they left. I had my men tear down her house, and we found a few small things that had been overlooked in her

---

[28] Mary Ann's second husband, John Scott, died in a drowning accident shortly after she bore him a child. She spent the rest of her life keeping house for her bachelor brother in Newboro, Ontario.

departure. I put them aside. One day I would send them to her.

 The mills came down quickly, including the wool lined meeting room. Samuel's brother came and paid fair price for the mill stones and various pieces of equipment. He exhibited a strange combination of sheepishness and sullenness as he came to pick them all up.

The banks on either side looked naked. We had left the cabins where workers had lived, as they were high enough not to flood. But everything else was gone. We began to regard our little neighbourhood differently. It was less friendly.

In August we were ready to divert the river through the weir. But then the fever season hit. This year we were better prepared. We had laudanum, we had salt to mix with water to get cold compresses to bring the fever down. Haggart and the cooks slaved to keep broth coming to feed the sick and keep their strength up. We both got sick again, but we recovered. We buried 11 men that season, men with lives, mothers, fathers, and some of them wives and children. Families got sick too, and the saddest day was the one where we buried the three children that died. One of them was just a toddler. It was unmanly the way I sobbed like a baby and tried to hide it. I couldn't stop myself. I wasn't the only one, but the nightmares about the baby came back for a while.

And then just like last year, there came a day when no one was sick anymore, and the men were working to divert the water to the weir. As the water channel became exposed we beheld the rocky and uneven bottom of what was to be our lock.

I heard Haggart draw breath. "Aye, it's a touch rockier than I remember".

I had never heard him sound anything but confident before. I looked at him for a long minute. "Would more labour help?"

"Och Aye, but I can't do that for what I am being paid for this job. I don't think so anyway."

I realized that Sherrif would have helped him find a solution, but Sherrif was gone, and that was his main obstacle.

"I have a solution".

He looked at me.

"I have thirty men here, all with masonry and sapper skills, and they are already being paid."

I saw the light dawn in his eye. There was the man I knew.

It took thirty minutes to devise a plan and less time to put the men to work. Less than half of the soldiers were engaged with the work at any given time, as they did already have security to provide, and work for the good of the camp to carry out. But it was enough.

The smaller stones were moved out by hand, using various lifting devices to pull them out as the men in the riverbed handed them up. Three weeks later, the riverbed was clear, the largest rocks had been blown up and removed, and Haggart was ready to use explosives to clear the bedrock and to construct the lock.

A week later we went hunting leaving the man he called "Young Stuart" in charge. Stuart had so well recovered from his injury that he was a confident and talented organizer of work. He carried a book with him to write down messages, thoughts and questions with his good hand, using his stump to keep control of the book as he wrote. The men respected his personal and physical strength and he was a tremendous success.

As we hopped into the canoe and began to paddle, I asked where we were going.

"I don't know" he replied. "But we could go to the headland to the north of the island we were at last time. I've not been there, have you?"

"Do they allow Bloody Irishmen there?"

I could see his shoulders shake as he chuckled, and so off we went.

We pulled the canoe out of the water and pulled it across behind two trees so it wouldn't float away. We climbed the bank, which was not terribly steep. At the top we found an open forest of mostly young trees with the odd very large rock. We walked for a while, looking for sign of deer or bear, or rabbit for that matter. As we approached a large rock taller and wider than a stagecoach or even a train car, we had found nothing, so we elected to rest for a bit. We sat down in a bed of leaves beside the rock.

The forest was very quiet, just the fluttering noise of the leaves in the breeze. Then I thought I saw something strange where one tree had fallen against another. The tree bark seemed to blink. I touched Haggart's arm. We both watched and the image resolved into that of an owl resting there for the day. It was fascinating how well it blended into its surroundings. And even though we remained quiet and meant no harm, it finally spread its huge wings and flew away low over the forest floor.

"How beautiful" I said aloud, and Haggart nodded.

In that second something whizzed above our heads and lodged in the tree vacated by the owl with some apparent power. It was an arrow, and when I pulled it out, it had been imbedded in the tree to a depth of more than two inches. We looked for its source.

"Bloody hell Pierre, do you ever make anything but a dramatic entrance?!" Haggart yelled.

Pierre was standing about twenty feet away under some trees. He was laughing, but we couldn't hear it. We moved toward him a little, and he simply disappeared.

I felt the blood run out of my face, through my body to where my feet were supposed to be, if only I could have felt them. What felt like hours later, I looked at Haggart to my left, and his face was ghostly white. We hadn't seen Pierre or the rest of his little band since last November and I had thought it odd that we hadn't seen them so far this year.

We turned, and ran for the canoe. Notwithstanding that neither of us really wanted to remain in that forest by that big rock, I think we both knew that what we had seen meant something was very wrong. We had the canoe in the water and the paddles in our hands and dipping in the water in extreme haste.

We got back to the camp and ran toward Haggart's cabin, and to mine. And there she was. Alona sat in the dark in the shanty, holding Willow who snuggled into her neck.

She was dirty, very weak, and had bruises and scrapes but no serious injuries that we could see. One of the workmen who had a wife in camp asked her to come and she helped us by washing Alona carefully and dressing her in a borrowed chemise. The woman emerged from the shanty and told us in a very quiet voice and with great suppressed anger that it was clear Alona had been hurt "down there". We thanked her, and I gave her some coins to buy herself something nice. She bobbed her head at me, and went back to the cabin she shared with her husband.

When I looked at Haggart, he was crying.

We carried Alona over to Haggart's camp fire so we could watch her together. With blankets and boards and logs we made her a comfortable bed. When she woke a little bit we gave her broth. We gave her fresh clear water and raspberries picked just outside camp, the last of the season. One of my men knew where there were some wild strawberries still, and he picked some and gave them to her in a little wooden dish. We gave her food we thought she would like because we didn't know how to do anything else. We were men. We were of the same gender that had done this to her.

Overnight, sleeping there near her in case she needed help, I had a dream. Alona and Pierre were in a battle against people who had clubs and spears. But they weren't Alona and Pierre, they were white people. They were thin and hungry looking. And they were naked, with blue on their bodies. And that's all I saw.

A few days later, Jean and another Algonquin man who called himself Charles (he pronounced it in French, Charl) also appeared. They had clearly been in a fight of some kind. They had blood on them, burnt patches in their hair and on their clothes. Jean had a broken arm, which we set and splinted for him. We gave them tea. It was the only thing we knew, besides laudanum, which could reduce pain of the heart. And of course, there was Willow. She wriggled in close to them, put her head on their laps.

And then Alona started to talk.

"We were camping at the camp on the trail back up to our winter grounds where you stayed with us the first summer. There were not more than twenty of us. Pierre, me, Ahanu and Jean, as well as several others. We watered the horses, and put them to graze. We had three small children with us, and they played and laughed. We were getting ready to sleep. A group of men came out of the woods. They had a wagon. They said the land was theirs and we couldn't be there. They said we were trespassers and we should be on a reserve somewhere. We said we had lived in this way for thousands of years and that we meant no harm. We said we would be gone in the morning. We promised to leave no trace of our passing. Then more men and wagons arrived. There were two or three of them moving amongst the others, yelling at them that we were not really people, we were monsters, and we would steal everything they hoped to create. Suddenly everyone was angry. They had guns, and clubs, and knives. They knew Pierre was the leader. So they hit him in the head with clubs. I saw the insides of his head come out. Then they saw me, and forced me on the ground. They took turns. I smelled their whiskey breath. I smelled their dirty bodies. When I fought they hit me. Some took me two or three times. I bit one, and he called me a dirty bitch and kicked me over and over. Is this how they would treat their own women? When it was over they left. I don't remember how long after, I woke and knew that if I could get here you would help me. There were others lying dead. Several were simply missing, having run away. I know they have created new life in me. I don't know what to do. I don't know what to do ". She trailed off.

Nobody spoke. The other Algonquin stared at the ground. There were tears running down my face, for my friends, for Alona, and for the desecration of that beautiful place.

I put together a small group of men to go to the place where the events Alona described had taken place. They came back and told of a large cairn on the shore of the lake. When they opened it they found remains of men in Algonquin clothing, and only two or three in the clothing of settlers. They restored the cairn. But worse than that, a huge swath of the cedar trees had been cut down and the forest laid waste.

I sent a messenger to By explaining what had happened and what we had found. I also asked for a doctor to come see Alona to determine something better about her state than that she had been hurt "down there" It was highly unusual for the military to trouble itself over civilians, and more, natives, in this way, but Alona's family had been very valuable suppliers and allies, and I knew he would want to help.

While these things progressed, so too did the construction of the lock that was still progressing. Haggart hired on Jean and Charles when they were ready. He felt that work might help to heal their minds of what had happened. They proved adept at the work, Jean being of the right spirit for masonry work, and Charles preferring the heavier work of clearing stone and placing the blocks.

When Alona was a little stronger, I told her about seeing Pierre in the woods, and the arrow that flew over our heads. One tear trickled down her cheek, and she held my hand for a moment.

When the worst of her injuries had healed, she began to work around the camp. She found roots and fall berries to add to our stews and soups. She knew how to butcher meat and prepare the skins for use. From the skin of a deer she made pairs of mitts for the men to wear in the winter. In time she made herself indispensable.

And so the Algonquin became a valuable part of our family of men and soldiers. But they never recovered, not really. They had lost everything, families and a way of life. And it was not as if they could easily find another Algonquin group. How do you insert yourself into another family? Better to start from scratch with a family of strangers, like ours.

I don't mean to portray the Algonquin as heroes, the noble natives in the early Canadian story. No one in early Canada was all good or all bad, and that includes the Algonquin. Jean would roll his eyes and purse his lips when he disapproved of something. Charles tended to react with disgust when any of the white members of our camp got too close. And Alona didn't talk much. I didn't know how to help any of them really, except to provide them with a place they would be accepted, and to treat them with the basic respect each man deserves.

One evening when most of the men in camp were collected around their fires, a canoe landed close to where the old mills had been. Upon hailing them, it was three men, Lieutenant Colonel By, a corporal, and a man in civilian clothing. Once introductions had been made, the man was identified as Doctor Gabriel Tremblay. He had come from Montreal to Bytown on other business, and by coincidence By was able to convince him to come to Chaffee's Mills, or Chaffee's Lock as I suppose it should now be known.

And before anyone among you asserts that By was far too valuable to remove himself from the business of building a canal, I insist that you are wrong. Throughout the story I am about to tell you, messengers came and went constantly and he spent many hours keeping up with his correspondence. I should wonder if the men in any other of the camps even knew he was not in Bytown.

I brought Alona over and introduced her to the doctor. She really was very reluctant to have anything to do with him, so I suggested something a little out of the norm. I asked if Doctor Tremblay could work with a medicine man, would that help. With tears in her eyes shining in the firelight, she agreed that such an agreement would make her feel much better. I begged Doctor Tremblay to indulge me and not to take her reluctance personally. He was a man and he was a white man, and she had been badly traumatized.

Jean said he knew where there would be another group of Algonquin at this time of year, and they had a medicine woman. He thought he could convince her to come to see Alona. "Now working with a white doctor, we will have to see what she thinks. Our people tend to think they are pretty primitive." And with that he and one of my men departed together to find the medicine woman. I was glad Tremblay hadn't heard his comments.

It was an awkward three days until they came back. Accompanying them was a second canoe, not as large as Pierre's, but with three Algonquin men and a woman.

We all met around Haggart's fire while Alona was resting and she could not hear the discussion. Tremblay was offended that he had been asked to wait for and was now being asked to work with a "savage" and a woman at that; the woman, whose name was Nokomis, said Tremblay was a savage and a butcher. By and I both prevailed on them to work together for Alona's sake. I told them what had happened to her, what the local woman had said about her injuries, and the fact that she was now with child. The discussion went on until the wee hours of the morning, until we could get agreement.

The two healers spent the morning together. Nokomis wanted to give Alona a sedative made from plants and mosses in the woods. Tremblay was leery, but agreed that a sedative might make the whole experience easier for the patient. Tremblay was concerned if the damage was too bad, they might have to terminate the pregnancy. Nokomis didn't like that and felt they should find a better way. Neither one of them had looked between her legs yet.

Haggart and By and I tried to facilitate their discussions with tea, and the ever so wonderful scones.

Finally they were ready to see Alona, to determine how to help her. She asked for me to be with her, so we hung a curtain across her midsection. Tremblay almost balked at having a man with the patient, until I pointed out that we were in the bush, not in Montreal. Things are a little different when you are far removed from civilisation. I heard myself say this and wondered with some humour who I had become.

The very best light was by the afternoon sun shining in the door to the shanty. Men were posted to keep everyone away. Alona tasted the paste Nokomis offered, and laid down. Within minutes she was sleepy but not asleep, and the examination began.

I won't tell you how it went, the poking and prodding, and how even with the sedative Alona was frightened and some of the pushing hurt. She squeezed my hand and I talked to her.

All I know is that afterward, these two healers once enemies but now partners in crime, sat down together again and discussed what they could do for Alona. Haggart fed them. By busied himself around the camp. And I stayed with Alona, drinking tea and teaching her how to play cards.

And then they were ready. I offered to have everyone leave with they discussed it with Alona, but she preferred to have Haggart and myself there. We sat on either side of her with the two healers talked.

They said that there was clear evidence of a knife having been used, but the cuts were not deep and the healing was good. The birth canal could accommodate a birth. They thought. There was a concern that the birth canal was thinner where the knife had cut and it had healed. They also confirmed the pregnancy. In discussing it with Alona, they expected the baby was due in early June.

Nokomis thought the presence of a healer would be helpful for the birth, just in case the birth canal was not strong enough. She and Tremblay had discussed at length what to do should there be a problem. She would come at the end of May and stay with us until the baby came.

The entire camp seemed to flood with relief. While we still grieved for our friends, at least we had been assured that Alona was safe.

The next morning all of our company left. They had to go before the lakes froze and the canoes could not float home. We waved them off and then turned to the business of preparing for winter.

There is a thing women do when one of them is pregnant. Some of the men in camp had married over the year and a half we had all worked together. A few of these women were now pregnant. They went out of their way to bond with Alona as her pregnancy began to show. They gave her salves to treat stretch marks. They would ask about "practice contractions", conversations Haggart and I overheard with discomfort. They would pat her belly and their own and talk about sleep disturbances and how often she had to make water.

Now this was a new thing Haggart and I immediately agreed on. Neither of us had ever wondered how a pregnant woman made water or where her stretch marks were, or even what stretch marks were. Never. At all. We loved Alona, so we tolerated it, but there we times when these conversations made us downright queasy. So much for the mysteries of a woman's body.

One day after one of these such conversations, one that made my eyes water, and my stomach heave, and the woman who had taken part left, there was a momentary silence. And then a miracle happened. Alona saw our faces, and she laughed. She laughed as I had never heard her laugh. Her laugh was free and clear and beautiful. I held her, Haggart held her, and we all laughed together.

The new year of 1830 dawned clear and cold. Food was plentiful, the workers and the soldiers were in good health and bore the cold well. Game was plentiful and a good store of potatoes and other root vegetables had been laid away.

Spring came early and there were sunny afternoons in March where we could remove an outer layer and enjoy the warm breeze. And all the while, the canal walls crept higher. The floor of the lock was smoother and chinked with lime scale from the kiln up the hill. And Alona got bigger.

At the end of May, we planted a larger garden than we had in the previous year. We had precious seeds for cucumbers and tomatoes, and we planted squash and potatoes. When it was done, we stood looking at it, willing it to grow before our eyes.

Nokomis arrived in the third week of May as promised. She had wonderful lotions and salves for sore feet and stretch marks (there they were again!). She enlisted the help of one of the women of the camp for when the time came. After all there would be water to be boiled.

I asked Haggart one morning why boiled water was always called for. He answered without looking up from the papers he was reading "washing". I looked at him in surprise and he answered "I have several siblings".

Alona had never vacated my shanty, and I really didn't mind. She didn't snore, although she did talk in her sleep, sometimes having very animated conversations with someone I couldn't see. Now the shanty was swept clean and laid with some of the forage for the horses. Ten candles were laid by with a piece of wood to which they would be affixed with melted wax. The women of the camp contributed blankets and cloth in which to wrap the babe when it came. A cradle and a papoose had been procured from somewhere. All was ready.

It was the 13th of June when Alona dropped her metal cup of tea in surprise one morning. She hadn't slept well. And in her summer skins, we could see fluid running down her leg.

Nakamo (Sing) was born at 3:15 in the afternoon. She was a beautiful little girl so like her mother that we imagined Alona must have been just like her as a child. There were a few complications, but Nokomis was equal to the task. Alona was to lay down for two weeks to allow herself to heal. Nokomis assured her that all she would really want to do was to suckle the baby and sleep.

And that's what she did. As the pickaxes and the hammers swung, as the stones were dropped down by block and tackle, Alona rested quietly and fed her baby. We had been worried that she might not be able to bond with the little one, but it seemed our fears were unfounded. We found as many berries as we could find in the bush. Nokomis had taken Haggart through the woods and shown him which berries. She urged him to feed them not just to Alona but to put them in the stews and soups that were fed to the men of the camp.

Nokomis stayed as long as she felt she could, and then she took her small canoe and returned to her people. We all thanked her and watched her paddle out of view.

Our garden was a thriving success that summer, producing bumper crops of cucumber, tomatoes, and we were glad we had made enough room for squash and potatoes. Had the squash not been planted a little way off from the other foods, it would have suffocated all, it grew so rampantly.

When the sickly season approached, we fretted and worried about how to protect Alona and the baby. Alona pointed out that she had never had the sickness, and that she did not remember any Algonquin suffering from it. I felt that false confidence was a mistake. Nakamo was not full blood Algonquin. We discussed taking them both away to somewhere not affected by the sickness.

"White Boy" she addressed me using my old nickname "I am a grown woman. I will take whatever steps to protect me and Nakamo that I think are necessary. Even if I feel no steps are necessary".

That August was desperately warm. The bugs seemed to retreat to the cool of the forest. The first case of the sickness happened in the third week of the month. The patient was the young wife of one of the workers. We had our treatment plan down to a fine science, but she did not suffer to the same degree as others had in the past. By the time Sickly Season was over, we had lost three workers and one woman. While we were sad to lose any, we were grateful to have lost so few and we could only attribute it to the extreme heat. And neither Alona nor Nakamo had gotten sick.

On September 22 that year, a small group of Algonquin came into our camp. I recognized some of them. Ahanu, a woman I knew to be his wife, and six more of their original tribal group. It was merry around the camp fire under the tarp that night.

In the dark around us and around the smaller fires, eyes reflected back at us as we talked and told stories. It was the first time I had been aware that the ease between Haggart and myself and the Algonquin could be a cause of consternation. I made a choice.

I stepped into the darkness and brought all thirty of my men into the firelight and asked them to sit down with our group. They all reacted with surprise but did as I asked. A few of the contract men followed. Ahanu immediately understood and a large leather pouch full of bear meat jerky was passed around. The Algonquin looked at the men with expectant eyes, and the men reacted in a variety of ways, but none that could have been construed as rude. Within a while the story telling now included these men from the British Empire, who had no relationship with the land before now. I wished Pierre had been there. And maybe these men would react with understanding when they came into contact with the Algonquin in future.

I awoke the next morning to find all of the Algonquin had departed. And Alona and Nakamo were gone too. I had suspected that she would wish to depart with the other Algonquin, but I had forgotten their penchant for coming and going without ceremony.

I suppose I was a bit glum, because Haggart suggested we go hunting. We took our rifles and one of the canoes and paddled into the early morning sunlight. We were a little too cowardly to go out on the point where we had seen Pierre. So we paddled across the bay to the wooded shore on the far side. Pulling the canoe up onto the shore, we entered the woods.

There we a lot of hardwood trees and the floor of the forest was a carpet of many years of dead leaves. We proceeded as quietly as we could. Occasionally a pheasant started. But we saw nothing. We found a place to sit and wait for game.

We talked in whispers, first about the lack of game, then about camp and the progress of the lock. In the spring we would be able to hang the lock doors. The wood to build them had already arrived.

And then we started talking about Alona and how she left, and how I felt. I kept explaining that I was not having relations with her, that we were not lovers.

"Everybody knows you weren't keeping her around because she had anything to give you in that way. Everyone in that camp loves you and respects you for caring for her so carefully. Everyone knows you're made differently, with honour. I suppose what we all would like to know after all is who you are involved with. That way. If you will". He struggled at the end. Like he was trying to say something to me that perhaps I wouldn't like.

We sat in silence for a few more minutes and then I realized what it was he was trying to say.

I looked at him and said "Are you asking me if I prefer....."

"Men" He said. And then he simply sat and looked at me. He was waiting for an answer.

I felt a tingling all over. That tingling that sometimes happens when you realize you are experiencing something that could change your life.

"Well....." I began. "I might have wondered. But I've never done it. It's a sin. I've read all the bible passages that mention it. It's not good." I looked away from him as I was speaking.

"Oh dear God. Alright, the first thing I have to teach you is that you will not be struck by lightning."

Oh my God, he was telling me........

And suddenly Haggart was kissing me, his tongue sliding over all of my teeth, his hands undoing the thongs on my breeches. To my surprise I had a huge erection. He sucked on it but then flipped me over. He stuck a finger in my anus and whispered "Relax, relax, I can't drill into a brick wall" so I took deep breaths and forced myself to relax. And then he was right up inside me from behind, moving slowly and rhythmically and reaching around stroking my penis with his hand. I put my hand on his and together we pulled and stroked until I felt like I was exploding from the inside out. It started from my anus, ran through my balls and shot out my penis as I came. Haggart came right after me, clenching his teeth and moaning.

We lay together on the leaves, resting while our breathing slowed down.

"So, does this change anything? I mean, your friendship is probably the most important of my life, even more than Alona. Does this mean that will change?" I asked. This was all new to me.

"It means, you stupid Irishman, that sometimes we fuck, and sometimes we don't. "

"But what about Isabella, your engagement ...children..." I faltered.

"I am of the opinion that the two things are not connected, as they do not have the same purpose." He said shrugging.

"Yes but can you *make* children? I mean, can you get it up? Can you fuck a woman? Because I can't. I tried once and it was a disaster. I couldn't have a normal life, I'm positive."

"That's interesting, because for me the two things are unrelated. I have no problem getting aroused with a woman, enjoying her tits and bringing the whole thing to its logical conclusion. "

"So what we just did, are you, well do you have a problem cheating on her like this?" I asked.

"No you silly young Irishman. There is a kind of sex I have with her, to make babies and to keep her happy. And there is a kind of sex I have with a male and that is to feel mind-blowingly good. No cheating. Not the same thing."

I wasn't convinced, but I had discovered sex. Hitherto, sex had only rarely been a part of my life, and here was a way I could have it and have it be, in Haggart's words, mind-blowingly good. I felt like I had finally found a huge piece of the puzzle that was me and I liked it.

Not that either one of us were under the impression that we could ever share our sex life with anyone else. We were both painfully aware that were it to come out, we could be beaten to death, or worse, ways a man could be tortured before he died that would make him long for death.

After we had done that lovely thing again once more, we decided to actually hunt before we were missed. And we could not come back to camp empty-handed.

We finally came into camp just at sunset with a doe and hung her in the butchery and retiring. I was so tired I simply had a Haggart scone and a mug of tea and went to bed.

Over the next week or so I did a lot of thinking. On the one hand I felt happier than I ever had. It was like I carried a special secret in my heart. I didn't say the word Love to myself. That was something our society taught men to say to women. I loved Alona. I loved Josephine. But neither of them created a passion in me the way this experience had.

In the England of my time, the penalty for sodomy was public execution. In fact, in 1828 the Buggery Act, enacted by Henry VIII was repealed and replaced with something called "The Offences Against the Person Act 1828" wherein the penalty for sodomy was still death.[29]

Military law also held the penalty for sodomy to be death, per the Articles of War last updated in 1749. As an officer of the crown, I could be required to preside over a case of sodomy and pronounce this sentence, which I now realized was despicable. There was an alternative. Assault with intent to commit sodomy covered anything else that two men could do to one another that didn't actually involve penetration. Penalties varied widely from being on the pillory to beatings (that often got out of hand) to jail terms.[30]

And then there was the church. Any church and all churches approached sodomy in the same way. Up until my first experience with Haggart, sermons on Leviticus truly went right over my head. [31] I have read those verses many times since, and now I see them as the expression of a culture surely more primitive than our own. Not the words of God, but

---

[29] Cocks, H.G. (2003) *Nameless Offences: Homosexual Desire in the 19th Century.* I.B. Tauris, p.30 ISBN1860648908
[30] Frances H. I. Henry (2019) *Love, Sex and the Noose: The Emotions of Sodomy in 18th Century England.* Western University Doctoral Thesis Program. Electronic Thesis and Dissertation Repository. 6736 https://ir.lib.uwo.ca/etd/6736
[31] The Bible, Leviticus 18:22 and 20:13

the words of men desperately trying to control all aspects of a world they did not understand.

In 1830 clerics of all stripes were still preaching sermons on that exact same theme, having advanced not at all.

In the meantime, I defined myself in a million other ways. I was a member of a family, originating in a place, a military officer, a friend to many people. I was the same me I had been before, the same man. And in this way I made this experience not a deep dark secret, but a cherished and private memory whose magic I did not have to share. And I was deeply satisfied because rather than wondering why I could not satisfy a woman, I realized that my sexual purpose was to satisfy a man. I felt like I had come home.

Just before Christmas of 1830 two teams of dogs pulling sleds arrived at Chaffee's. Willow was ecstatic. Lieutenant Colonel By rolled himself out of one of the sleds, along with McTaggart, and a group of soldiers wrapped in layers of furs on top of their uniforms. It surprised me to see them arrive this way, for they had never done so before. And usually By and McTaggart did not travel together.

Once we had all sat around Haggart's fire with our furs around us, Haggart gave us tea with sugar to warm us and buns, rather than scones this time. The food made us warm and relaxed.

"So I have a few matters of business to discuss" By began. "The first concerns both of you for certain. I have received this letter" – McTaggart handed an envelope to me "and we are going to have to deal with it. Please read it."

I took the letter out of the envelope and unfolded the paper. It read:

Attention Lieutenant Colonel By, Chief of the Works, Rideau Canal, Upper Canada.

Dear Sir;

I hold a land grant near Chaffee's Mills, Chaffee's Lock I suppose it must now be called. I unfortunately must tell you that this past August I was witness to a most awful sight.

I was in the woods near to Chaffee's around ten pm and saw two men engaging in an activity so lewd and awful that I have not yet managed to shake off the feeling of being soiled by it. I am certain what I saw was buggery between these men, and one of them was in a red coat. His partner was dressed as a mason would be, in a cotton shirt and wool trousers. Mind, neither man actually had his trousers on.

I knew immediately that I should report this to you, as I know this offense carries a death penalty and you will want to pursue it, lest it contaminate such a fine group of men as you have at that station.

I presume also that there will be a generous reward for this information.

Sincerely

Benjamin Smith
Brockville

At first reading I felt my bowels turn to water although I was careful to simply furrow my brow as if I was taking the subject matter very seriously, which I was. But then I read it a second time.

"It's utter falsehood" I said, handing it to Haggart.

"What makes you say so?" Asked By.

"Well the writer asserts that he saw this event at ten pm. The sun sets at nine in the evening here in August. And yet he describes the nature of their clothing, including the red of the coat. As described, the thing is impossible. He might as well have seen two dogs rutting as two men. And I note the name. Benjamin Chaffee now resides in Brockville or so I have been told. Both the request of a GENEROUS reward and the Christian name also would indicate Benjamin Chaffee, a man with an axe to grind if ever there was one."

By now was laughing freely. "I agree with you! Although I had not made the connection with Benjamin Chaffee.   I think I shall simply record our findings and file this away. There is no point in stirring up more bad feeling between us and Mr. Chaffee if it's not necessary. If he is composing falsehoods in order to demand more money from the King, I suspect he is in dire enough straits. "

Haggart and McTaggart and I all responded with mutterings of "Very wise sir, very wise".

Later, in a quiet moment, Haggart asked "Are you sure we weren't seen?"

I looked at him and said simply "It was October, not August when we were hunting."

We enjoyed bear stew that night, which By seemed to enjoy greatly. After supper and while enjoying some brandy which he had brought, he turned to subject to business once more.

"Haggart, your lock appears to be complete. Are you ready to let the water flow through it?"

"Ah yes Sir, the doors are currently frozen in place, and not completely finished. The men are carrying out small finishing jobs until March, at which time, the water will have warmed enough to remove the blockage yonder."

"Well then we are right on schedule. I wish to open the canal officially in April. Thought I might sail a steamer to Kingston and back. There will still be time to finish cosmetic work after that if necessary" answered By. As I looked at him I realized that my superior had been an excellent supervisor in all respects that concerned us.

"As such", By continued," I have brought a Christmas present for each of you. A generous bonus to each of you for such a problem free, well run operation" McTaggart handed each of us a bundle of notes with a string around it. "And one more thing. Lieutenant you will be no more. I am granting you a field promotion to Captain. You have earned it" he said as he removed one pip from my coat and placed two pips there instead. I was too surprised to speak as Haggart, McTaggart and By all shook my hand.

After we had all settled down around the fire with our furs and our rum and our coffee, I sought an opportunity to talk to Lieutenant Colonel By aside from the others.

"Sir, I am very proud of the promotion, but I think I should let you know that I am intending to resign my commission when my duties here are concluded. I feel I have been given an open door to a future through which I do not intend to travel. I feel it would be dishonest to accept, however grateful I am for your generosity."

"Why do you feel you do not wish to stay?" His question felt loaded.

"Because Sir, I have fallen in love with the Canadian colonies, the aboriginal peoples here, and the friends I have made. I don't want to get posted to the next canal by the King. I want to stay near the one I have built. I don't even mind the cold. Much" I answered, and my answer was absolutely truthful.

By laughed. "I am proud of you. You have become so much more than the young man in the shrunken uniform who appeared in my office three years ago. You knew then how to think with your heart, but not how to translate the murmurings of your heart into a language the world could understand. And now here you sit, having managed a busy group of men, having wrung from them much better performance than they knew they were capable of. And here you sit with your superior two ranks more senior speaking with confidence and assertion. Well done young man. Never mind, there is much work left to do before we are finished here". He gazed out over the landscape around us, where sat piles of rubble and rock. "But you keep the rank. You have earned it, and you are not stealing it from me now. When the time comes, I will ensure that you get all of the monies owing to you and all the well wishes of King and Company."

We returned to the fire to enjoy a little more rum before bed. I was much more comfortable now.

That spring the grand opening was prepared for, our landscaping now much closer to finishing. The wilderness around the works was tamed. We were proud, military man and civilian alike of what we had accomplished. The day before we were to expect By, a lone soldier in sapper's uniform passed through in canoe.

"Hallo! " Haggart shouted at the man. "What news?"

"Not good news!" Said the man, slowing to enter the open lock. "No Grand Opening at the moment any road".

Haggart and I looked at one another, expecting very bad news indeed. "Something prevents the grand day?" I asked.

"Oh aye Sir, bloody Mirik, that's what. He's dammed up the waterway!"

In unison our mouths dropped open.

"Tis true Sirs, dammed it to a trickle and asserts his right to do repairs on his mills. I must continue on my way. Passing the word. I have been canoeing since breakfast having come from the Narrows and aiming to reach Kingston by dark."

Haggart and I looked at one another in surprise.

"By must be apoplectic." I said.

You know how sometimes a thing is such a shock that you become giddy in response? We laughed for several minutes before settling, and each going off to inform our respective groups of men of the change of plan.

The lock and its massive doors were completely done in the summer of 1831. Even the landscaping was done.

A small group of infantry troops came to live at the lock, to protect it from any marauding persons. But in three years the only marauders we knew of were those who had killed Pierre and attacked Alona.

A blockhouse was planned for but not built until some twenty years later.

Haggart and I left on the same day and took the same path. By made us promise that we would come back for the real grand opening in 1832, and we agreed.

We actually travelled with a group of Haggart's men, no longer skinny and hungry, but well-muscled and fit. We moved the Shire horses with us, as well Sherrif's grey, Whisper, Piper and a Canadian Horse that Haggart had bought recently. As usual, Willow rode with me on Piper's neck. We had lots of insect repellent compound, and had a wagon full of some of the summer's proceeds from the garden.

We made it to Perth in five days.

Much of what is left is on the historic record. Haggart bought a large packet of land with one mill on it already, and he built several more. On that same land there was room for a stately home for the family he wanted even more as he aged.

We did return to Chaffey's next year, and I wore an excellent quality suit of clothes. I bade Lieutenant Colonel By a fond farewell. I congratulated him on such a huge accomplishment. None of us suspected that the Rideau Waterway would be the death of John By. The repeated bouts of malaria and the strain of victimization at the hands of politicians in England killed him before the decade was out. [32]

The day of the grand opening, a small steamer came in sight and docked just before the lock. It was one where passage had been booked to Bytown by a small number of individuals. I woman dressed in black appeared on deck, and made to climb out onto the dock. To my surprise it was Elizabeth Elliot.

As I helped her onto the dock, she recognized me and I asked after her health and that of her family. She was still very beautiful, but she had aged greatly and wisps of grey had crept into her dark hair. I remembered her silliness ship board. There was no silliness around her now.

When I expressed concern she told me the saddest story I had ever heard. She had lost one child to a bear almost as soon as they arrived in Kingston. They had built a cabin, but didn't have enough furs,

---

[32] Deachman, Bruce: Ottawa Citizen, August 5, 2019: "The Capital Builders: Lt. Col. John By, Spending Scapegoat"

and their first winter was brutally cold. They lost a daughter to the swamp sickness. Her husband had tried desperately hard to clear their land and was gaining some success until wolves killed his horse. He had finally died of the sickness last summer, and she had determined to go home to England as soon as ever she was able. She stayed with friends over the winter and had quit their home only this morning.

It was the most awful story I had ever heard. I had been shaking her hand when she began to speak, and now I could not let go. I kept telling her I was sorry, over and over again. Haggart freed my hand to allow her to escape from me. I have never forgotten her and her family.

After the opening of the canal and saying goodbye to John By, my perspective really started to change. The town of Perth provided me with ample work as a masonry contractor and engineer, so I could settle there if I wished. My friendship with John Haggart, with his hospitality and knack for entertaining ensured I would always have social opportunity. And I had come to love the town. I was there to see Haggart finally marry Isabella in 1836. I was there for the birth of their first child, John Graham Haggart. And every fall, we found more and more secluded places to hunt together, and were sure to come home with game so none could question our activities away from the eyes of others.

But Haggart's attentions more and more focused on the mills and the building of the wonderful house, his gift to Isabella. His young son, already a remarkably intelligent and gifted little man, was his pride and joy. I was still important, but the practicalities of making time for me were ever more difficult.

I simply got tired of waiting for the attention of an important man. My social circle was predominantly one he had given me. I needed to strike out on my own.

I left in September of 1839. Piper was gone, dead of colic on a cold December night. I missed him terribly. Willow too had died, of old age, and was buried out behind the house on Haggart's estate. I sold most of what I owned, and struck out on the canal, boarding a steamer for Mirikville.

William Mirik, now an old man, greeted me with joy. I wasn't sure if he would remember me, but he did. And as he had before, he treated me like a son. I wondered why it never occurred to him that I had been part of the military that stole his river. But it just didn't seem to matter.

Mirik had heard tell of a place called Shipman's Mills some ways due north of Smith's Falls. It was a little settlement growing around mills on a river, and he knew the original miller, Daniel Shipman. He felt it might be a great place for an engineer and a mason. With homes and buildings just begging to be built. As before, his advice made perfect sense.

A week after arriving, I left with a new horse, a big mare named Suzy, and a pack horse, a grey named Silver. Mirik ensured I had adequate bedding, a tarp, and food for the two week trip through the wilderness. And insect repellent compound.

I was sorry to leave the old man, and hugged him warmly and sincerely. As a gift for all his kindness, I gave him one of my Captain's pips. I never saw him again, and he died in 1844. One of his sons returned the pip to me.

I made it to Shipman's Mills in good time, having secured a land grant in while I was in Smith's Falls. It was a very small plot and it sat on a main trail between Shipman's Mills and another settlement to the south. There was ample stone, so I hired a small crew and went to work. I built a house in the military style, and attached a barn for the horses at the back. Finally, the men and I cut down enough trees to have firewood for about two years.

And so by Christmas, I was safe in my own home, furnished by my own hand, warmed by wood from my own trees.

Just after dark on Christmas Eve, there was knock on the door. The house was close to the trail, so visitors were not out of the question. But I was wary of 'arrivals in the dark. I lit a torch from the fire and opened the door.

It was Alona, three men and an adolescent girl, as well as a huge dog that was similar to large wolf hunting hounds I had known in Ireland so long ago. Where they got it I will never know.

The girl approached me, and I looked at Alona with tears in my eyes. "Nakamo, this is the White Boy I told you about." I suppose I had become a little lonely. Or perhaps I thought they were dead and was relieved. Or these were the people I was meant to be with all along. I grabbed both of them to me and cried, openly.

One of the men, who turned out to be Jean, said "Hey White Boy, your hospitality is slipping. Didn't Haggart teach you how to make scones?"

The Extraordinary Capacity of a Horse

All evening my hat had been slipping. You know, the kind that were sort of built on a slab, with layers and layers of fabric, and decorative fabric flowers. I loved it because it was the most beautiful blue, to match my dress, and it had taken me weeks to make. But it was slipping, pulling the pile of hair down off my head, and it distracted me as I walked down the sidewalk. I hated the way hat pins often stuck into my head, and when I resituated my hat, the pins drew blood.

The distance along Westmorland Street from the opera hall (in the upstairs of an old livery stable) to the corner of Westmorland and Brunswick Streets wasn't far at all. It wasn't the best lodging in town, but it was ours and we loved it.

Patricia said "Did you not think the story of the maiden was so affecting?" She drew out the "so" and the "affecting" with a drawl that made me smirk.

I gave up, and pulled a six inch hat pin out from my bleeding head and carried my hat under my arm.

There was some noise coming from an alley ahead, but Patricia was busy telling me that walking on the street without my hat was disgraceful and I was protesting.

Wham!! Something hit me from my left, and a man's voice was yelling at someone named "Paddy" and I was trying to extract myself out from underneath the body of a grown man with light brown hair. His head was bleeding. His tormentors were kicking at his legs and his torso even as I was pulling away.

You know, I had just had it. I leapt up, dropping my crushed hat and brandishing my hat pin. I held it like a sword.

"That's enough!" I yelled. And then I realized who I was yelling at. Why that was Harry Spare. He had been courting me and we sang together in the Anglican Cathedral Choir. The other two I recognized as friends of his.

"You get away Harry Spare. You get away or I'll tell your mother what you've been doing. And don't you think you'll get another chance to try to grope me at the pictures. I despise this kind of thuggery. Maybe I will tell your mother after all."

 "Aren't you afraid what people will think of you coddling a damned Paddy?" Harry said.

I snapped back. "Aren't you afraid what your friends at the Cathedral will think of you ambushing an unarmed man in an alley? Perhaps the constables would be interested."

There was a general grumbling and the three men moved off. "Won't your parents like to know that you're consorting with Paddys?" said a high pitched voice as they moved off.

I turned to Patricia, and she had things well in hand. She could be silly but when she settled down to work, by goodness she meant business. The man was sitting up now, but was definitely woozy. Patricia had torn a piece of her petticoat and was holding it to his head to staunch the bleeding.

"Hello. Sir? What's your name? Where do you live? We should take you home."

Stale beer breath wafted up at me. "Name's Jack. So sorry to be a bother".

Just then two other men approached and before I could brace myself for more of the foregoing, one of them stuck his hand out to shake mine.

"Well you ladies seem to have been heaven sent" the man smiled.

And then I realized that these two men and Jack were brothers. Same blue eyes, same light brown hair, or was it blond, the arch of the heavy brow exactly the same.

"I'm Clem McGuigan, and this is my younger brother Fred. And of course, you've met Jack."

Patricia was suddenly looking at Clem McGuigan very intensely. Very intensely. And then she said "by McGuigan, would you be related to John McGuigan, who was involved..."

Clem answered hurriedly as if to get her to stop speaking. "Err, yes, that would be my Father. We weren't born yet. Know nothing about it. And frankly neither should you." He grinned to take the sting out of his words.

I frowned in confusion as the McGuigans picked up their brother and helped him home, thanking us and doffing their caps.

Patricia was holding my hat. "I think it's ruined she said. Got Jack McGuigan's blood on it. "

"Your petticoat is ruined too, I said pointing at the tear up to the knee.

We picked one another up and walked the remaining block to the rooming house. As we went, I had Patricia explain about John McGuigan.

"Well, John McGuigan was part of the Fenian uprising of 1865. The Fenians thought they would claim Canada for Ireland. I can't imagine they ever thought it would come to much. But of course, the friends and neighbours of those involved felt very betrayed."

"Is Mr. McGuigan still alive" I asked.

"Oh yes," replied Patricia. "He does cartage for lots of people in town. Quite well respected for it too. If it wasn't--"

"For the Fenian thing" I answered.

The next morning, being Sunday, Patricia and I were up and out early to make the walk to the Anglican Cathedral for church. It was a beautiful old church, even if it hadn't quite recovered from the fire a few years ago. It was situated in a small park just a few steps from the Saint John River.

When we entered the church, the whisperings and pointing that usually occupy a congregation waiting for the service to begin stopped dead. A few even turned to stare at us. My eyes went up and down the pews. And there, with his mother in her full brimmed Sunday hat with the plume, was Harry Spare.

"Would you like to know what happened" I spoke levelly, but loud enough for everyone to hear. "Harry Spare and two of his thug friends were beating a man and were prepared to continue until they beat him to death. They were still kicking him when I was extricating myself out from where he had fallen. They were very brave. I stopped them by threatening to stab them with my hat pin and threatening to tell his mother. There was nothing untoward about *my* behaviour".

When I looked up, the Dean of the Cathedral was standing at the end of the centre aisle looking at me.

"Yes Father, after services in your study." I wasn't trying to be flippant. My tendency to rise to the occasion had gotten me a stern talking to. Once or twice.

"Yes Miss. And then you Mr. Spare".

 As it turned out, the Dean really just wanted to scold me for speaking out inside the cathedral. I didn't see how it was alright for me to be gossiped about in the church in such a way, but it wasn't all right for me to defend myself in the church.

"I'm going to address that right now young lady. Have a lovely Sunday afternoon."

I passed Harry Spare in the hallway as I was leaving. His mother was with him. Oh dear.

Patricia had a date with a man, whom she had met at the library, that Sunday, so I wandered onto the Green by the river and sat on the grass to read a book. It was <u>The Prussian Officer and Other Stories</u> by DH Lawrence. I was just getting to the part of the first story where the orderly takes revenge on his selfish officer when.........

"Good afternoon Miss. May I join you for a moment?"

It was Jack McGuigan in a three piece Sunday suit and hat. The fabric of his suit was slightly shiny, like fabric when it has been ironed too hot. His tie was of the Windsor knot variety, tied expertly and evenly. His shirt was crisp and immaculate white cotton. His hat shaded his face except for hints of skin when he turned his head here or there.

"Of course Mr. McGuigan. How are you feeling? That was quite a knock on the head you took."

He sat down beside me gingerly and smiled shyly avoiding my gaze. "I'm feeling much better thank you Miss. I'm here to tell you that my Mother wishes to invite you and your friend to dinner today, by way of thanks. I told her you would say no, but I wish to issue the invitation all the same."

As he spoke, I saw that like his brothers he had dimples in his cheeks. But his shyness kept their display to a minimum.

"I don't know why you thought I would say no Mr. McGuigan. I would be delighted. Patricia, Um Miss Gallant, has another appointment. Will I do?" I asked.

"Yes, I think you will do Miss, since it was you that so bravely defended me with your hat pin. " He grinned, and nodding at my book "What are you reading Miss?"

I told him that it was a book of stories, and explained that the one I was reading was about the futility of jealousy. He asked me to read it to him. So I turned back to the first page and began to read. I finished with the officer and the orderly dying together in the woods in spite of each other. While I read he pulled out a tobacco pouch that smelled of apple and rolled a cigarette, lighting it with a wooden match against his shoe.

He had sat quietly as I read and when the story was done he said "That's terribly sad. And it was all for nothing." He levelled his blue eyes at me and I had the feeling that he was quite clever and yet a very sensitive soul.

"What do you like to read Mr. McGuigan?" I asked.

"Oh Miss, I don't have much time to read. I paint houses for a living and when I don't have houses to paint I work for my Father or my brother Clem, whom you met. They both do cartage, which you no doubt know. I come home at night and I fall exhausted into bed. Then I wake up the next morning and do it all over. An indulgent Saturday night is all the leisure I can afford.

"I'm pretty sure a fine lady such as yourself doesn't have to work from dawn until dusk. Do you enjoy reading often?"

"Oh no, I don't have as much time as I like to read either. I attend the ladies business college on

Queen Street. I am learning to account for the finances of a business operation, and how to type and do shorthand."

He turned his head just slightly toward me, and with a slight smile asked "And do you like that Miss?"

"Yes, I do. I like it because it makes me feel that I am good for more than just living in the shadow of a man and having babies."

He sat up and looked right at me, his blue eyes dancing. "You're a suffragette Miss! I do take your meaning though. My Mother is one of the bravest people I know. Father thinks he makes her life possible, but she is what holds our family together. When we were little ones she had a lively smile. But the older we get the more her mouth turns down out of habit. As if the weight of our family pulls the corner of her mouth and will not let it rise. I had a brother, Harry, who died of brain fever[33] when he was twelve. I suppose that's when her mouth first began to turn down. I wonder what her life had been had she married a gentleman, had she more time to devote to the things that interested her."

"I'm so sorry. Was he much older than you?" It was a neutral question but I was crying inside. My mother used to say that when poor people had babies and they died, it was because the people were negligent and didn't feed them properly. I could never understand how she would possibly know, being neither poor nor responsible for the feeding of a child.

---

[33] Probably meningitis

"Yes he would have been three years older. I was nine when he died. It was the only time I have ever seen my father cry. But I suppose there were more of us to feed and they had to move on."

He looked at me again then.

"Oh no Miss, I didn't mean to make you cry!" An immaculate white handkerchief emerged and he handed it to me. It was the softest Irish Linen. I dried my eyes and handed it back. The hands that took it had nails bitten to the quick. To me it indicated a focus inward and worry about what he found there. How interesting.

"How many brothers and sisters do you have?" I asked.

He smiled, as if prepared to amuse me. "Well, let's see. I have an elder sister Eveline, and she is married to Harry Black and lives in Saint John. Nene, she still lives at home and helps Mother. The nieces and nephews love her. She may never marry, I don't think. Clem is two years younger than I. Fred is four years younger than I. He has always been sickly. But he works with Father as he is able. Frank is nine years younger than I, and he works with his own horse and sloven. He's a bit of a character is Frank, but I will let you work his character out on your own. And finally there is Allie, just fourteen. Allie is the only one of us to go to high school. She's the best of us I guess. So how many is that?" Again with the twinkling blue eyes and just the hint of a smile, the little dimple.

"It's seven, Mr. McGuigan, not counting your brother Harry. Your mother had eight babies."

"How many brothers and sisters do you have Miss? " He asked.

"Oh, I am one of only three children. I think there came a time when my Mother simply refused to go through birth again. She said it was demeaning". I didn't talk about the chill in our house, how my mother really just didn't seem interested in her children unless the world turned its gaze on them.

"I beg your pardon Miss, but if one is determined not to go through birth, does one also not have to stop from what gives rise to the birth? That seems to me to be far sadder than what my mother has borne. "

His eyes were very serious now, and looking at me steadily.

"Mr. McGuigan, are you suggesting something that would be improper between two people who have only just met?" My attempt at steering him away from the subject didn't work.

He stood up and leaned against the tree, placing his right foot against the bark. "No Miss, I am not. For I believe in people taking their lives very seriously and doing the right thing. I am merely saying that a life without that love between two people, without that connection, that shared joy, is a sad thing.

"Come Miss, if you are still willing, it is time to walk to Westmorland Street."

He was like nothing in my experience. He was from the wrong kind of people. But he was wonderful and gentle and he analyzed things in a way foreign to my own experience. No man with similar background to my own could have talked about childbirth or infant mortality in that way. I could never have refused.

Sunday dinner at the McGuigan house, to my inexperienced senses, was like a ride on a runaway wagon and several times as noisy. There were huge platters of food – potatoes, carrots, peas, fried tomatoes, and a roast of beef. Around the table were all of the siblings Jack had talked about, except the absent Eveline. Clem's young wife, Eva, and their little girls Stella, Muriel, Marion and Phyllis were there also. The cacophony of all of those people talking and passing food, the clank of forks and knives on the plates was more noise than happened in my parents' home in a year.

My parents' home in Moncton was a large two story home on a prosperous street. My father, a businessman, and my mother, a socialite from a time when Moncton didn't know what a socialite was. Thank goodness for the servants or we would never have eaten and we would have wallowed in our own filth. The self-sufficiency and personal power of a woman like Mrs. John McGuigan would have been utterly lost on my mother.

The more I sat quietly and watched, the more I realized that it was indeed Mrs. McGuigan who ran not just the household but the entire family. All of those rowdy boys were under a subtle control of hers. A withering glance was all that was required in response to their boisterousness. When she wanted Allie to get up from the table and clear the plates, Allie did so without a word of complaint, even though she appeared to still be in step with the lively discourse at the table. Nene, the older sister, quietly produced dessert plates, while Mrs. McGuigan produced two blueberry pies still warm from the oven.

Beside the pies, Allie put two jugs of cream and an "Ooooh!" Went up around the table. Frank, the youngest brother said "Oh Jack, you bring your girlfriends home any time!" and I blushed.

"Well Mother may have laid on the cream to impress Miss, but she really is not my girlfriend. Well, unless she wants to be." He smiled that gentle little smile again, and this time, I returned the humour.

"Actually," I looked around, "McGuigan family, I think today I have fallen in love with you all." And smiling brightly I added "Do you think I could be your home child[34]?"

When the McGuigans laughed, it was a full throaty laugh, shared by all. It was a mutual appreciation of the joke and the joy of life. And I was included.

The final course of the meal was tea, made much stronger than I was used to. The tea leaves were refreshed with hot water several times. There were no bone china tea cups. The beverage came in a motley selection of chipped cups, mugs and a vessel

---

[34] In Fredericton, the Home Children were mostly brought to Canada by the Middlemore homes. They were widely believed to be living better lives than they had in the British Isles, but there is much anecdotal evidence from the children themselves that they were often badly mistreated and used as slaves and servants. This from personal interviews and private family information.

I took to be a beer mug. Judging by the tea stains on it I didn't think it had ever been used for its original purpose. Every mug of tea was accompanied with a hand rolled cigarette, and Mrs. McGuigan scolded those who dropped ashes on the floor or the table cloth.

The family dispersed somewhat with their tea, Allie upstairs to study for a school examination, Frank and Clem out to tend to the horses for the evening. That left Jack, Nene, Eva with little Phyllis, and Fred to sit with Mr. and Mrs. McGuigan and I in the parlour at the front of the house.

"Well Miss" began Mr. McGuigan, filling a long stemmed pipe with tobacco. "Why don't you tell us a bit about yourself? We would like to know you." His hands were larger than they would surely have been in his youth, the muscles in the fingers enlarged by a lifetime of working. The pipe was clay, and very plain. Like his sons, he wore Sunday clothes, consisting of a brilliantly white shirt and black pants. His vest and suit jacket had been discarded earlier in the day.

So I told them a little of my upbringing in Moncton, and how, against my parents' wishes, I had elected to come to Fredericton to go to the Business College and make a life for myself with a small inheritance from my grandmother. I told them how I had rebelled at having my life made for me.

Mrs. McGuigan smiled. "You may come to regret that choice Miss. That life you turned your back on is one many would envy."

Mr. McGuigan looked at her and quietly asked "Do you regret your choice?"

Before a silence could develop, Fred, who I now saw was not as robust as the others, and who was gentle and quiet, like Jack, spoke up.

"Miss, what do you think is important? What is it that makes you face the day?" Everyone else in the room nodded.

"Well.......I am devoted to my studies at the moment, and completing them motivates me." I looked around, and I knew there was something more they were driving at. "Well look, my brother Simon is young but he's already married. I don't like his wife. They are silly people, who think appearances are important, like they are oblivious to what life is really about. But my problem is that while I think they are wrong, I'm not sure I have figured out what is right. And I guess by making a life for myself, being independent, I am trying to get to that rightness."

The room was quiet and they all seemed to be considering what I had said.

Mr. McGuigan spoke into the silence. "But Miss, independence is all very well, but to make it through this life, to survive, a person needs help. A certain amount of work needs to be done, whether you are rich or poor. Widows and bachelors and spinsters often have the hardest, loneliest time, or at least we think they do. The best way to get that work done is to have a partner to split it with. Women run the home and men earn a living from the outside. My point Miss, is that sooner or later, unless you inherit your father's money, which is not something you can count on, sooner or later you will have to marry. And all your independence will go for naught." As he spoke, his right hand gestured up and down, the index finger pointing to nowhere.

I sat for a minute and I looked at him. "It's not that I don't want to marry. It's that I would have the warmth and joy your family has rather the ice cold atmosphere of my parents' home. Stupid parties with all the right people. Having the right friends, friends who do all the wrong things. It's not even about a love match, but about marrying someone who shares my faith and my morals so that we can attack the world together and not wasting energy on fighting each other."

I might have said too much. They had only just met me after all. And maybe they thought my ideas about marriage were just so much luxury they could never afford. But their faces didn't look that way. I think they agreed with me, and didn't understand why my ideas were something I would have to fight for.

"Well Miss, I will never marry. I could never support a woman of any quality, and I could never ask a woman to live here and be supported by my family. I accepted it a long time ago "said Jack. Eva was watching him carefully as baby Phyllis suckled. There were complexities here.

As he had said this, Clem and Frank and Allie had all re-entered the room and the whole family were staring at him. (Fred had fallen asleep in his chair) I was looking at him, trying to gauge the seriousness of what he had said. He sat in a small parlour chair with one leg crossed over at the knee. He had taken his jacket off when we came in, and he wore a crisp white shirt with his vest, and a simple watch and fob hung across his belly. Not gold, and not even silver. Maybe brass. He was looking at his work worn hands, examining the cuticles. And his face wore a sad expression.

I reached up and touched his hands and said "Well Mr. McGuigan, I am certain then that we shall have to be the best of friends as marriage is lost to both of us."

"Perhaps we shall" he said, smiling just a little at me in response.

Jack walked me home, but it was really only a block and a half. There were no marauders that night. And I sat on the step with him at the boarding house. It was a gorgeous evening, not quite the harvest moon. He looked really nice in the moonlight.

I asked him if he was painting a house at the moment, and he replied that his ribs were still too sore for climbing up and down a ladder. In the morning he would go with his father to the railway station and wait for freight. It was interesting as I had seen those sloven[35] when I had travelled to Moncton and back. I never thought about the lives of those men before.

---

[35] A Sloven was a wagon developed in Saint John for unloading freight from ships. The cargo deck sat lower than the axles to make the wagon more stable and the loading and unloading easier.

I asked him what time they would leave for the station. Apparently the first train would arrive at 7:00 AM, so they would leave at 6:30 to ensure they got there on time. I made a note to set my alarm clock, as I could see the McGuigans gate from my window. I had just never watched before.

Jack shook my hand before he left, a choice of greeting no doubt chosen at least partially based on the twitching of the front door curtains behind me.

The next morning I was awake early enough to be dressed and ready for breakfast in time to watch the McGuigans set out for the day. Patricia was still asleep. Three slovens emerged from the gates, a wagon type with a low cargo deck. This style had originated on the docks in Saint John, but had spread all over New Brunswick as loading freight was so much easier with the low deck. I grew up with the sight of slovens at the back door of every commercial establishment I came across.

As I watched from my window I saw Mr. McGuigan open the gate and stand beside it. The first sloven emerged with one horse and Frank's unmistakeable silhouette on the driver's seat. The horse was a large muscular grey, with a beautiful gait. The second sloven was pulled by a team, and by the style of cap he wore, the driver was Clem, with Fred beside him. His horses were much younger than Frank's, almost black in colour but clearly greying out as they aged. The last sloven was drawn by a chestnut. Jack was driving and pulled out into the road and waited while his father closed the gate and hopped up beside his son, giving him a hand signal to drive on.

While the first two slovens had proceeded up King Street to York, one of them, the last one, drove up Westmorland and turned on Brunswick right past where I sat looking out the window. Both Jack and Mr. McGuigan doffed their caps at me as they passed. They knew I was watching the whole time.

By noon that day, I was fighting sleep, but it had been worth it. Quite apart from the McGuigans themselves, their horses fascinated me. I adored horses, but as a well-bred young woman, had never been allowed in the barn or even the carriage house at home. It infuriated me to be kept away. I felt like I could hear their voices talking to me as they trotted by. My girth is too tight. The bit hurts. I have a sore foot. And sometimes: I feel wonderful today! I can run like the wind! My owner loves me, I would do anything for him! And once: My lifelong partner died today, and I didn't get to say goodbye.

It was nothing I had ever told anyone, and it was so subtle that I wondered if I imagined it sometimes. But then it would happen again, and I would think "no, no, it's really there". I felt no need to share with anyone. I just became one of those silly people always asking to approach other people's horses.

I had to contrive to meet the McGuigan's horses.

When Patricia and I finally arrived home at the same time on Monday evening, we had a lot to discuss.

"How did you like Mr. Myshral yesterday?" I asked her.

"Not much really. He's nice enough I suppose, but he is rather dreamy. I think I might prefer him to be a little more confident, perhaps have more leadership ability. Be a little less insipid. " She wrinkled her nose.

I asked what his occupation was.

"He's a poet, if you believe it. He let me read some of his stuff. It's quite excellent and he has already been published. It's just I wish he was a little more.....firm. " She kept making apologies for not liking him.

She asked about my day. "I expected you would sit on the Green until dark reading, but then I saw you come home last night with Mr. McGuigan. He looked rather nice in his Sunday clothes. "

"Oh that was you twitching the curtains. I was asked to dinner as thanks for helping him the other night. You were asked too, but you were with Mr. Myshral. It was a delightful evening with his family and he walked me home."

"Oh really. Did you meet the infamous Mr. McGuigan senior? What was he like?" Patricia asked.

"They were none of them anything like what I thought." I responded, and turned over on my side to go to sleep. I wasn't trying to be peevish. It's just that I had a lot to think about and I wasn't sure I could come up with a short answer.

I heard Patricia turn over and sigh. We would talk again.

As the week went on, I noticed the McGuigan slovens a few times. On Tuesday, I saw Frank on Queen Street, with his lovely grey horse at a trot. "It's a beautiful day!" the horse sang as he trotted by. I saw Clem and Fred with the team, having picked up a block of alum at the railway station, and taking it down Smyth Street to the water purification plant. They moved at a solid, steady walk. They felt the weight but did not doubt their own strength. For them this was normal work. I saw Jack and Mr. McGuigan twice. Once they had a load of trunks and a list of addresses. The chestnut radiated good humour and contentment.

On Friday, I had left the Business College on Queen and was adjusting my book bag on my shoulder and I heard "Miss!" Turning around I saw the pretty chestnut dozing with his back foot up, while Jack sat up on the driver's seat all alone.

"Can I give you a ride home Miss? You look right tired. And where is your friend?"

"Oh you mean Patricia? She's training at the Victoria Hospital to be a nurse. I'm sure she is just starting her walk home."

He grinned and said "Aw, can't have that!"

He helped me climb up to join him from the cargo floor in the sloven. It was quite easy really. I was careful not to sit too close, for everyone we passed could see me clearly.

Jack and his lovely chestnut turned up a side street and took King Street until it became the Woodstock Road. We were rolling along at healthy trot when we saw Patricia coming along at the side of the road in the distance. The horse, Caesar, whose name I had learned on the way, pulled up short on the side of the road. When Patricia came close, Jack helped her climb up in the same way I had. Now the three of us sat up there, while Caesar trotted us home, singing "I was a valiant steed to my Laird".

"So, Miss Gallant, I understand you are to be a nurse" said Jack to Patricia, across me.

"Yes Mr. McGuigan, I will be finished by March." Patricia was looking at him with the peripheral vision of her left eye.   Her hands were folded primly in her lap, except when the right one strayed to hold on to the side of the seat.

"And will you work in the hospital here in Fredericton until you get married?" asked Jack. I had never even asked her that.

"Actually I hadn't intended to Mr. McGuigan. It is my intention to become an army nurse and work overseas. Since the start of the war, the army has been crying out for nurses. "

Jack and I both stared at Patricia as we rounded the corner onto Westmorland Street. I had no idea this was her intention. She looked back at me and said "What?"

"Mr. McGuigan, would it be alright for you to take us into your stable yard? I would like very much to see the horses, if it would be all right with your father. "   I was tabling this issue of Patricia becoming an army nurse.

"I don't see why not" Jack said, with that hint of a smile and subtle dimples I was getting used to.

When we drew up to 135 Westmorland Street, the gates swung open and Caesar took us into the yard. The other two slovens and the horses that pulled them were standing at rest in the yard. They were cooling down before they went into the barn in the back corner for the evening. Chickens clucked around the horses' feet and there was a chicken coop at the side of the house where a summer kitchen bridged the gap between the main house and the barn. I could see at least two cats, and a lovely black spaniel roaming about.

Frank came to help Patricia and myself down from the sloven. Jack was tending to Caesar. I watched him remove the bit from Caesar's mouth and hang it on a protrusive part of the sloven after wiping it down. As I came beside him to watch, he stroked Caesar's beautiful neck.

Jack looked at me and said "Every horse has his own self. Caesar here will do anything I ask him, as long as I am respectful and kind. If I were demanding and I treated him like I had a right for him to do as I tell him, he would buck the sloven and me with it. "

"Yes, I rather got that feeling from him" I said smiling.

"Good afternoon Miss" came Mr. McGuigan's voice from behind me. "Your friend has gone into the house with Mrs. McGuigan. Would you like some tea?"

"Good afternoon Mr. McGuigan. It's a pleasure to see you again. Jack was just telling me about Caesar here. By the way I think there is something brewing in this hoof, right here."

"Eh?" He answered skeptically, with the pride of someone who takes great care of his horses. They were indeed immaculate. I could just feel something vague, and so I began to slide my hand slowly down his leg.

"Oh Miss I think you had better let me do that!" said Mr. McGuigan as he rushed forward and removed my hand.

I pointed. "Something right here, not sharp, but vague, like a bruise. I don't know what it is, I just know it's there."

Mr. McGuigan positioned his hip into the big horse's shoulder, slid his hands down and picked up the hoof. It was fully the size of a dinner plate. Caesar seemed a little reluctant to have Mr. McGuigan examine it, putting gentle pressure all around and underneath the hoof. When he pressed on the spot I had indicated, Caesar tried to pull his foot away. A knife with a hook at the tip came out and peeled small amounts of hoof away, a little at a time. Shortly a small hole opened under the knife, and a little bit of pink fluid emptied out.

Jack was there with a bucket of warm water and Epsom salts almost as soon as we stood up. Mr. McGuigan looked at me with a thoughtful frown as Jack lowered Caesar's big foot into the bucket. As soon as the hoof hit the water, Caesar emitted a groan and I felt tension leave his body through my hand that I had resting on his flank.

"Well, Miss, I wonder if you would look at my other horses. The barn is absolutely no place for a woman, but if we stayed here in the yard, would you look at the others? That is, we are all experienced horsemen here, we all know how to touch and sense a problem. But all five of us missed that." I think he was a bit shaken. It was so far out of his experience to have a woman come near a horse, let alone be clever with them.

"It was a coincidence Mr. McGuigan, I am sure. But I would very much love to examine your other horses." The last thing I wanted was to offend him. He was the kind of man his children were slightly afraid of I and knew that he wouldn't hesitate to discipline them with the back of his hand. But I sensed deep emotion in him, and pride in the way he cared for his children, his horses and his family to the best of his ability. I hoped he liked me.

With a tilt of his head and a wry smile, we examined the other three horses. I talked as I moved. One of Clem's horses was a little afraid on the road, which was why the comfortable one worked on the outside facing traffic. Each trusted his partner and felt safe with Clem. I patted the skittish mare on the nose. Their names were Samson and Delilah, and I loved the trust between them, and they love they radiated toward Clem. And finally, Frank's horse, the big grey whose name was Goliath, told me about a few of the aches and pains of old age that Frank would put lineament on. In fact, he stank of lineament. He had a wonderful philosophical approach to life. He knew that one day he wouldn't work on the streets anymore, but he loved this life all the same.

At one point, Mr. McGuigan said softly to Jack "there's culch there Jack" and pointed at a pile of fresh manure behind old Goliath. Huh. I had never heard manure called culch before and I presumed it was a word from the Irish language, occasionally heard at the Farmer's market and other places around Fredericton.

Mr. McGuigan walked me into the house for that delayed cup of tea. I found Patricia sitting in the parlour talking to Allie about being a nurse. As I sat down to my cup of tea, a big tabby cat came and cuddled up in my lap. His purring and the warmth of him in my lap were delicious. I could have stayed in that parlour all evening, dozing in my chair and listening to the others talk.

We were brought to the table where each of us were served a plate of fresh bread with butter and molasses.

And then from the yard came the sound of a brass horn. I didn't recognize the tune, but the sound was beautiful. Mrs. McGuigan said "Clem and the band have a job tonight. I believe they are playing at the Bicycle and Boat Club. Will you ladies be going to the dance?"

I had not been to any social occasions since I came to Fredericton. Not if you didn't count church and IODE[36] meetings. A dance sounded lovely. But before I had formulated a vocal response, Patricia spoke.

"Oh yes, my beau, Mr. Myshral is taking me. I am to meet him at the boarding house at eight. When I stared at her and raised an eyebrow in surprise she said "What?" in a slightly defensive tone.

---

[36] Imperial Order Daughters of the Empire – A protestant women's club of the Victorian Era which persisted in Fredericton long after it had died out elsewhere.

Jack, sitting on the steps to the kitchen door, said "I would like to take you Miss, if you would like to go." He was looking down at his hands again, and a rolled cigarette hung loosely from his fingers.

"Mr. McGuigan I was feeling very warm and sleepy just now but hearing of a dance does put me in mind of some exercise. I would be delighted. Thank you."

Mr. McGuigan's surrey wagon was pulled out for the occasion and another horse which had been grazing in a vacant lot behind the McGuigans' was brought out. He was a beautiful black named Ned. He was much finer boned than the horses that pulled the slovens. He had a few faded brown spots from grazing in the sun, but he had beautiful long legs, and a shapely neck. He nickered at me, pleased to make my acquaintance. I felt the brooding wisdom of the Canadian wilderness from him, his hardiness, and his intelligence and happy good nature.

When we set out, we were a party of six in the surrey. Patricia came with us and we picked up Mr. Myshral on the way past the boarding house. Allie came, with Nene as her chaperone. ("When did I cease to be the one to be chaperoned and become the chaperone?") Mrs. McGuigan had insisted I sit in the back with the others, and not beside Jack. She was certain my parents would get wind of my behaviour and interfere in the life I was making for myself. I simply couldn't understand how my parents had any power over me any longer. How little I understood.

I was delighted to meet Mr. Myshral and to put his character in perspective. He was in his mid-thirties, and wore a decent quality brown tweed suit. He wore good quality shoes, but they hadn't been polished. His brown felt hat looked a bit like it had been folded a few times. His hands were fine, with long lithe fingers, the kind you might see on a pianist. His build matched his hands, tall and slender. He was modest and reserved in his manner. His care of Patricia was wonderful, and he clearly thought very much of her.

I had forgotten how well a dance can be enjoyed. Jack danced with me, but he also danced with Nene and Allie, teaching Allie steps and rhythms. It struck me that she was very lucky to have such a group of brothers to care for her. Nene danced with a few different gentlemen as well as her brothers, and she was in great demand.

Frank and his girl Rachel Bailey (Rae, he called her) arrived a little later into the dance. One thing I noticed about Frank, not only was he handsome with the same dimples and light hair of his brothers, but his dress and deportment were impeccable, more so even than Jack. When I had seen him driving his sloven, he wore grey coveralls and a bow tie. For an evening such as the dance, he wore the classic McGuigan glaring white shirt with a bow tie and arm bands and his Sunday suit. I noticed that his watch fob was not brass either and from it hung a gold cross.

Frank's girl Rae was beautiful. She had wonderful peaches and cream skin, with dark brown hair pinned up under her boater hat. She wore a white blouse, almost as white as Frank's, and a flattering brown skirt. But there was something about her that didn't quite twig. And then I had it. I would estimate she was ten years his senior. It was interesting but I wasn't sure what I thought of it. But she was positive and smiling and had eyes for no one but Frank. But that wasn't true. She didn't cast her gaze to anyone else. But she didn't look directly at Frank either, while he stared constantly at her. There was trouble in paradise.

It was almost eleven when the band retired for the evening. Our party approached the edge of the stage to thank Clem and the other players. To my surprise, Eva was there with little Phyllis, and for the first time I noticed that Eva was showing pregnant.

I greeted her, I hoped with warmth. I wanted to know her. She had a gentleness to her, and I had found out from Jack that she and the children lived out near Morrison's Mills, while Clem went back and forth to work with his family and to take band jobs that added to the family income. The journey took the horses about an hour each way at a trot. The hope was that eventually they would move into town and have home and a yard for the horses.

When I spoke to her she teared up a bit. "Oh no Eva! Are you all right?" I tried to speak in a way that conveyed my sympathy but that did not make obvious to anyone else that she was upset.

Eva looked down at the baby sleeping in a small packing crate, which I though was ingenious. Before the conversation got much further, Jack approached. He put his arm around Eva's shoulders and gave a little squeeze. He also gave her a small cloth pouch that clinked.

"It'll be all right you know", he said looking at her. "We will always look after you".

Eva turned her face into his shoulder and stayed there for a few moments.

Clem approached with his instrument in a case, looking back and forth between Jack and Eva. Jack raised his eyebrow. Clem looked at the ground and then up at Eva.

"Honey, you know I will look after you. Let's get Phyllis home and out of the cold". He handed the instrument case to Eva and picked up the baby in her box. As they walked away, Clem hollered to Frank to come along with Rae if they wanted a ride.

"I didn't mean to open up a sore wound" I said looking at Jack. "I obviously upset her. I feel very bad."

Jack smiled his just a little bit smile. "Oh Miss, that wouldn't be your fault. Clem is trying very hard to support four of Eva's siblings, as well as she and their own children. He has been doing it ever since they married six years ago. When I can, I slip her some money to buy things for the children that Clem can't afford. Never mind, let's collect the others and wake Ned up so he can take us home."

The weeks flew by, with my schooling, occasional dinners with the McGuigans, dances and walks by the river.   I entered into examinations just before Christmas, and my parents were expecting me to home for the holiday. I didn't want to go, as I expected a lot of dull parties with people I didn't like and ideas I didn't appreciate. I was so happy in Fredericton and I had to admit the McGuigan family and their kindness to me was certainly a part of it.

In inverse relationship to my happiness, I noticed a colder reception from the other parishioners at the cathedral and my acquaintances at the IODE meetings. I presumed their chilliness was due to my choice of the McGuigan family for company, a perception which made me feel impatient and annoyed.

On the day I was to take the train, Jack took me to the station, as he was taking Caesar there anyway. He was hoping for trunks and goods to arrive with the train.

When I entered the ticketing office, the ticket agent advised me that my ticket had already been purchased. My mother had it forwarded to me. It was one way. I thought seriously about turning around and going home without ever boarding the train, but I didn't. With some last vestige of duty I found my seat and waved to Jack as the train pulled out of the station.

As I had suspected, the entire holiday consisted of opportunities to meet eligible men. They all shook my hand and called me by my Christian name. One or two were surprised when I asked them to please be more formal. It was obvious that my mother had given them to understand that I was known to be more casual with the men of my acquaintance. Perhaps she thought if my behaviour was a little looser than was proper, I would be hastily married and once again in the family fold. I was disgusted. It was like she was putting me up for sale.

I left early in the morning on Boxing Day, making sure to thank the servants for the care they had taken of me. My youngest brother, Charlie, took me in the trap.

Before I walked into the station, he said "They are having you watched. They receive regular reports. They know everything you do."

I looked at him for a moment, considering. "Thanks Charlie. I appreciate the warning."

When I got home I didn't unpack, I simply pulled a book and a box of chocolates out of my bag and curled up on my bed. This was my way of letting the back of my mind process the information I received, while comforting the front of my mind about having received it at all. My book was about a coup attempt on the English crown in the 1490's. One of the men involved who really should have been beheaded for his involvement got off scot free and in the end became a great favourite of the King. There was something about this story that bugged me and that attracted me too. This man was called Maurice Fitz Thomas FitzGerald, the 9th Earl of Desmond. There was a drawing of him in the book. In it he had long dark hair to his shoulders and pale skin. He was a warrior, depicted in his armor. I wished I could talk to him somehow, as if we would have much to say. And the depiction of his hair worn in the style of the times bothered me. Somehow I expected it to be tied behind his head.

Thus I passed three hours amusing myself and daydreaming that I knew this character from a book. I ate so many chocolates that I felt a little sick. Unfortunately I didn't feel any less angry or betrayed. They were watching me. Why should I care? But I was beginning to understand that my family had the money and the power to make my life pretty uncomfortable. And no matter where I went they had the means to continue to meddle in my affairs.

I had to wait until Monday to act, but early Monday morning I set out in my winter boots to walk to the University. It wasn't a terribly long walk but it was snowing and there was a wind. I wrapped my scarf around my face. It would have been impossible to recognize me under the layers of wool. Or so I thought.

"Miss! Miss! Get up and we'll give you a ride!" It was unmistakeably Clem. Fred wasn't with him that day, perhaps because of the weather. I climbed up onto the driver's seat and thanked him so much for the offer. I didn't want to take him out of the way however, so if he just took me a little up Regent Street, it would be a great help.

The slush made a swishing noise around the wheels as we rolled along. The horses' feet had a rhythm as they walked, and the snow was building up on their backs, as their thick winter coats kept any warmth from escaping and melting the snow.

"Did you have a nice time with your family Miss?" Clem finally asked to break the silence.

I looked at him a minute and I couldn't help it. The tears came, and I found myself telling him the whole story. How I loved his family, how I felt so welcome with them. I told him I really liked Jack, with his shy ways and his simple wisdom. I told him about my parents trying to auction me off to every eligible bachelor in Moncton. And then I told him about Charlie's dire warning about my parents having me watched.

He listened and then after a minute he asked "how did you spend the last 24 hours?"

I looked at him in surprise. "What do you mean?"

"Miss, I want you to think about everything you did and then I want you to imagine Jack doing that very same thing. Would Jack read a book? Would he write a letter? I understand that he is a man and you are a woman and some of your activities will never be the same. But right now, while you really have a chance, and before the hornet's nest in Moncton gets really stirred up I want you to think exactly what it is about my brother that you like. Is it worth severing ties to your family? Is it worth ruining Jack's reputation? Because they will make sure he is publicly smeared for his involvement with you.

"Don't get me wrong Miss, I like you, I know Jack likes you, and I can see how comfortable you are with my family. But how long will it be before you feel slighted when we talk in Erse[37] and you don't understand? You know that my Father runs our family, but have you ever seen him angry? Do you

---

[37] Irish Gaelic

350

know how angry he will be when your people threaten us, our livelihood, our reputation, such as it is?

"I want you to think of these things before you take legal action against your parents, because that's what you're doing here Miss. I will take you right to the Law building Miss. But please, know what you're doing."

He squeezed my hand before I got down. I thanked him profusely and assured him I was just seeking an opinion.

The gentleman I met was the father of a friend. He did not know me or my family before our meeting that day of the snow storm. And as a member of the faculty of law I trusted in his experience and knowledge. He advised me to stay low key, avoid making a public spectacle of myself, and try to avoid being seen by the other citizens of Fredericton to be living outside of my own sphere. He advised very much as Clem as done, that I should be very, very careful and considerate of the other people in my life. It made me quiet and sad.

I walked home in the snow, and finding no one at home, settled down in the bath to warm myself. As I did I thought about Clem's advice. Would a member of the McGuigan family ever have time to do this? Mrs. McGuigan would make pies for supper. Nene would stir the soup and add salt to taste. Allie would come home from school and study until bed time. I knew from listening to them talk that baths were for Sunday.

Feeling ashamed of my leisure, I got out of the bath, dressed, and undertook to scrub the room that Patricia and I shared. Neither of us were great housekeepers, and the large room hid dirty corners, spider webs and dust. I was almost finished when I heard someone come in the front door, come up the stairs, and there was Patricia, weighed down by bags and the man in layers of winter clothing carrying her trunk up the stairs was.....Jack.

I hugged Patricia tight and took her bags and set them down. When Jack had set the trunk down, I addressed him.

"Hello Mr. McGuigan, what a delight to see you. I hope you passed a pleasant holiday?"

His dimples made an appearance as he said "Oh yes Miss, but we missed you at the table. Mother cooked a goose. It was delicious."

"I had nothing so fine, I am sorry to say. I missed you all" I said smiling at him.

"Will you both be joining us for the New Year Ladies?" He asked.

I looked back at Patricia and she was nodding positively so I did too. "I wouldn't miss it. Can we bring something?" I had never done that before, and so I wasn't sure how it would be taken.

"That would be lovely Miss. I must get on, I'm melting" he grinned as snow from his coat melted onto my clean floor.

After he was gone Patricia began unpacking and we chatted about our families.

"I won't be seeing Mr. Myshral anymore" she said very matter of factly.

Distressed, but cautious of my response, I asked "Why ever not! He is a lovely man, and I am sure he is fond of you".

"My course will end on March 31, and then I will join the army and depart for Europe. There is no point in encouraging him" she said.

"But is there no value in just spending a lovely time with someone you like?" I answered.

"It will only hurt him more when I leave" she stated flatly. I was somewhat deflated. I liked Mr. Myshral, and I loved watching his deference and kindness to Patricia. But I supposed it couldn't be helped.

I told her about my dreadful time at home and how I had come away early. I also told her about Charles' warning, and Clem's advice, as well as the legal advice I had received.

Patricia sat quietly mulling over what I was saying. She nodded her head at Clem's advice.

"But there is one thing I do not think you have told him" she said quietly, looking at me very levelly.

When I cocked my head, she answered "You could marry Jack McGuigan right now, and you have enough money to keep you both clean and fed. You haven't told me but I know you do. I have seen the way you go to the bank for money, almost like you're afraid to be caught. And I see the manner in which you pay your rent here. All matching bills, arranged in a brown envelope. And the way you talk about your family, I know it didn't come from there. "

"Jack McGuigan does not want to marry me. He has made that clear. "

"You silly girl! Did you not see him look at you just now? He was delighted with every word out of your mouth, and you with your hair a mess from scrubbing the floor. Tell him. See how he reacts. And then you will know his true feelings. "

I considered Patricia's advice for several days. But I held off, partially because I was not sure the McGuigans in general and Jack in particular would not hold it against me. I liked my relationship with the McGuigans. They were the family I had never had. I didn't want it to change.

I also was unsure how I felt about Jack. A few dances, Sunday dinners and a wounded head were really not enough to tell me much about his character. I learned more watching him roll his cigarettes from loose tobacco and seeing that slow partial smile of his. He was always thinking, always considering. But I wasn't going to put any McGuigans at risk until I knew I could control the rest of my life, to keep my parents from eating me, and anyone with me, alive.

Fredericton has always been a city of wooden buildings. It is a place where the lumber trade produced a world of its own, and wooden homes were its by-product. Cities made of wood are subject to frequent fires, and Fredericton had a volunteer fire brigade that lasted for more than a hundred years. It was comprised mostly of the Irish working poor, with a few other ethnicities thrown in. Rich men could have sport and culture, but poor men could be part of something bigger than themselves and prove their worth to the whole City.

The fire brigade would mark significant occasions with torchlight parades. Fire fighters would march on foot carrying torches, with their horses and equipment.

Mr. McGuigan was a member of a hook and ladder company, and had been since before most of his children were born. Regardless of politics or social class, he and his colleagues had earned honour and respect many times over saving lives and homes and businesses.

When New Year's came, there was a Firemen's Procession with lit lanterns down Queen Street and then back up King. The lights were so pretty, some with different colours.   Jack, Frank and Clem walked in the parade with Mr. McGuigan, but Fred was at home. We returned home for warm drinks and sweets. When the countdown to midnight came, and the hour struck, Jack leaned over and kissed me. His lips tasted of tobacco and a touch of rum, and he smelled of the apple in his tobacco pouch.

There were dances in the winter, but not at the Bicycle and Boat club because of the cold. There were other dances, in the opera hall, and a few other places. All of the dancing people and their body heat kept the hall warm, and allowed us to stay late, dancing to encore after encore. Sometimes there was a full band, with Clem nodding and smiling from the stage. Sometimes it was just a small dance band, and there he still was. Sometimes Eva was there, sometimes she wasn't. I hoped the little extra he made by playing in a band was enough to make the commute from his family worthwhile. But then I realized that it wasn't just about what he made. It was about how much he loved to play in the band, with fellows he knew, and for people who admired him because of it.

By the end of January I was a Sunday dinner fixture at 135 Westmorland Street. Now every time I went I took a dish that I cooked myself in the old wood stove at the boarding house. It was tricky, regulating heat in that old thing, but over time I figured it out and was proud of myself. Nobody taught me how to cook, I had to intuit the nuances for myself. And with some thanks to my landlady, that's exactly what I did.

In February Eva had her fifth baby, a girl she named Leona. Leona had brown hair and dark eyes, but the intensity of her gaze was all McGuigan. I didn't see Eva much, as winter time was not opportune for driving back and forth to Morrison's Mills. I hoped that she was all right, and I fervently wished that Clem would put together enough money to move them all into town.

As March drew near I watched Patricia begin to pack her trunks. Things she would not need before she left but would want later went into one trunk. Old books, and other keepsakes that would be stored she put in another trunk. I helped her wash all of her clothes, regardless of which trunk they were destined for.

She had stubbornly stuck to her goal of nursing overseas, no matter how many times I had tried to talk her out of it. She was bound and determined that this experience would give meaning to her life: it was what she was supposed to do.

She gave me a few of her things: a dress I had always been fond of; a book she had read and loved. And she had bought me a gift, a pretty little silver bracelet. I loved it of course. I had bought her a pretty silver necklace with a little pewter charm in the shape of a shamrock.

On March 17 there was a huge winter storm, almost two feet of snow in temperatures just under freezing. It was right on schedule. Most Frederictonians look for a big storm in the last two weeks in March. This big dump of snow in turn contributes to ice dams on the Saint John River in April, and the resulting floods on the river are legendary.

The McGuigans had been active plowing snow all winter. Their big horses easily pulled the plows that were stored all summer with the City of Fredericton. After the big storm they were more needed than ever, and I didn't see any of them for two weeks, except from the path worn in the snow over the sidewalk as they worked. Eventually those were cleared too, as much from warming temperatures as from any plowing.

On the day it was time to take Patricia to the train, Mr. McGuigan brought the surrey wagon specially, with Ned in front. Mr. Myshral met us at the boarding house in conflict with her insistence that she wasn't seeing him anymore. Jack was there and put her trunks in the back and then sat up front so that Mr. Myshral and I could sit with her for the short journey to the station. We were great chums and I was very sorry to see her go. I was very proud of her. I couldn't imagine the courage it took to make such a choice. Her family would collect her at the station in Saint John, and tomorrow she would go into the recruiting centre in Saint John and present her graduation certificate.

I stood beside the train and held the hand she put out the window. The last thing I said as the train pulled away was "Be careful. Just please be careful".

When the McGuigans dropped me at home, I thanked them profusely for their kindness, but I declined the offer of a visit to their house where I wouldn't have to be alone. I really wanted to be alone, to cry with no one there, and to indulge myself until I felt better.

Mr. Myshral accepted the offer of a ride home to St. John Street, and I waved as they drove away. Jack was in the back of the Surrey rolling a cigarette, but he stopped to wave back at me.

The first two weeks of April were taken up with final exams. I passed with high enough marks that I was satisfied, and began to seek a position that would allow me to earn a living and to learn all that my schooling had not taught me.

On the Saturday after my exams were complete, I cleaned my room and organized my things. Patricia had left a trunk to be stored in the McGuigans' barn, if they were willing, and I set it out on the landing.

All of the McGuigans, and frankly, all of the town, were out sandbagging along the river at the most vulnerable points. The Miramichi River was reported to be high and packed with ice, and various docks and landings along its length were being torn out by the ice. The ice and logs would pass into the Saint John, increasing the size of the ice pack.

I put on my new blue hat and a blue dress and walked down the length of Westmorland Street to the bridge at the end. All along the river bank, there were people strolling, and just standing and watching the water. It was mesmerizing, as the speed of the water was much higher than usual. The odd large chunk of ice floated by but the water under the bridge which was just low enough to let it pass.

Presently a hand slid through my arm. I looked up and to my delight, it was Jack. Since it was Friday, I was most surprised to see him, and on foot.

"I am so happy to see you Jack. Why, you're wearing your Sunday suit."

"Yes Miss, a day off of sorts. I've been looking for a chance to talk to you, but spring is always such a busy time. Shall we walk?"

He gestured along the river, although the Green was partially submerged.

"I would like that very much" I replied with a smile.

"Miss, there is something I would very much like to tell you. I have waited a long time, because I have been afraid what you would think. But I think you need to know."

I looked at him for a minute, trying to measure his demeanor, and what he might say.

"All right then, Mr. McGuigan, I am ready to listen."

As we walked casually along the flooding river, he told me of a woman he had known actually not that long before he met me. Her name was Annette, and she had been a member of the Salvation Army Church. He met her at a dance. Like me she was from Moncton, from a fairly well-to-do family. She had come to Fredericton to live with her sister. Theirs was a whirlwind romance, and Jack asked her to marry him early on, and again at least once more. And then she fell pregnant. The family tried to have him charged with seduction, to send him to jail, but in court he was able to testify that he had proposed, twice, and at least once before she was pregnant. In the end she had to admit that this was true and the charges were dropped. However, he had to promise never to contact Annette again and never to seek any contact with the child.

When he spoke of the loss of his child, I actually saw him brush away a tear, fearful that I might see it.

When he finished speaking, I was speechless. We walked in silence for a few minutes and then turned back and walked in the other direction. We stopped for a moment to watch two men in a canoe trying to rescue a dog from a block of ice in the river. They actually succeeded and managed to steer the canoe back to shore, but it was some distance down due to the current.

"Mr. McGuigan, since we are telling secrets, there is one I need to tell you. I have been considering it for some time, but I haven't known how. My grandmother believed that young women should not be at the mercy of the men in their lives. She felt that marriage was a partnership, that each have their roles, but that a man should not be able to control a woman's choices. So you see, I am not the suffragette after all, it was she all along. When she died, her will bypassed my father altogether, and settled her estate on me. He has tried to challenge it in probate court, but as long as I only spend the interest it generates, the matter sits in a stalemate. That small income is what has allowed me to come here, to further my education and to learn something that would make me useful.

"In the last year my parents have repeatedly introduced me to suitors of who they approve, whom my father feels he could control in the use of my money. They are all repugnant to me and do not share my values. I feel that my parents, having been poor role models themselves, have betrayed me by continuing to attempt to control me in this way. I know that a good young woman should listen to her father and bow to his wishes. I suppose then that I am not a good young woman.

"The warmth of your family and their willingness to include me has been a boon to me. I expected to be very lonely here, but thanks to the McGuigans and Patricia I have been very happy."

When I stopped talking we had reached the highway bridge at Carleton Street again. We continued to walk, but were unable to stay by the river due to the military grounds, and so we went around by Queen Street.

It was a beautiful spring day, warm with a drying breeze to clean up the muddy streets. There were a few puddles on the sidewalk, but he offered me his hand, and using his balance I could navigate around them without dragging the hem of my skirt.

"If they want you to marry, could you not then marry the man of your choice? Surely the issue would be settled then?" We were stopped now and he was facing me. His words were heavy with implications.

"Only if I knowingly married a man my father could manipulate. Otherwise I suppose the validity of the marriage would be questioned" I responded.

We resumed walking.

After a moment I said "What was the objection of Annette's parents?" But I knew. I had gone to her wedding shower, her wedding and her baby shower, paid her a call after the baby's birth. The whole thing had been tidily handled, sparing the appearance of her virtue. I just didn't know if he knew.

"My father was a Fenian, and I spent my days pushing horse shit, sniffing paint fumes, drinking and fighting. None of it was a lie. And you might think I would be happy to get rid of a child I did not plan for, that I did not want. I wanted him. I felt he was part of me. But I had to put it behind me. There was nothing I could do."

So he did know. And his feelings were so different than what I thought they would be. And he knew the sex of the child. That didn't surprise me. The McGuigans knew people all over the province. Dear Jack. He really was a decent man, no matter his politics, religion or fighting habits.

There was a pause. "Once at the dinner table Frank was bitterly complaining that we Irish are treated poorly here in town. We are considered less than human, or we are just people who quietly deliver things, fix things and mow the grass. My father looked up and said 'Well at least you're not black'. That's our life Miss. "

 "So I suppose, Miss, that we really are destined never to be anything but friends." I wasn't sure I understood the connection, but I let it be.

We had come to Westmorland Street again. He stopped again and faced me. "It's just a terrible shame" he said. I didn't answer.

Turning to walk up Westmorland, he said "There is one other thing. See that fellow over there?"

He didn't point, just looked. I followed his gaze and saw a man in a dark brown suit, with a cigarette in his hand, standing sideways so that it was impossible to tell if he was looking at us or at the river or down Queen Street. Seeing us look at him, he dropped his cigarette and put it out with his foot and began to walk away.

I had seen him too. He seemed to turn up in the background when I was out in public. I had never really remarked on him until now. He was the sort of person that you didn't question why he was there, he just was.

As we stood watching the man walking away, Clem and Fred happened to be driving by. Jack doffed his hat and nodded at the man in the brown suit walking away. Clem doffed his hat back, and also nodded at the man.

"What are you doing?" I asked Jack, concerned there was something amiss here.

He smiled at me and responded "We would never do anything that Father Bernard would disapprove of Miss. But we will for sure find out what's going on here. There is something creepy about that fellow, and I have my suspicions of what he is up to".

Friday supper in the McGuigan kitchen provided us with our answers. We arrived in time for Jack to help care for the horses. I went to each of them and paid my respects. Goliath seemed quiet, but nothing was amiss that I could tell. He was his loving wonderful self. I stroked his face and gave him and extra hug.

When the last bucket of water was set down, we turned and entered the kitchen door. And there in chair at the table, with a large slice of fresh bread smeared with butter and molasses, and a large cup of tea, was the man in the brown suit. Mr. McGuigan and the others sat with him, Fred and Clem with self-satisfied grins.

We took our places and accepted our portions. I really was beginning to love the bread and molasses suppers, and Mr. McGuigan would smile at me and tell me it was a poor man's supper, that I must have poor folk roots. I would grin at him and take a sip of my tea.

But there were no smiles this evening, at least not between Mr. McGuigan and me. Clem smiled at the visitor, with a glance at Jack, and then back at the man.

"Miss, Jack, I would like to introduce you to Mr. Monahan. Mr. William Monahan was it sir?" A flick of the eyes at Monahan, who nodded. "Freddie and me found him walking down Woodstock Road. We could see he was a stranger, since we didn't know him, so we invited him home here for some food and a cup of tea. Hospitality, you know?"

I couldn't really tell, but I got the definite feeling that Mr. Monahan was beginning to feel slightly uncomfortable. After all, while none of the McGuigans were big, there were five men with rough hands and bodies accustomed to the strength of horses surrounding him. They seemed mild enough, but then maybe not.

Clem put his elbows on his knees, and looked down at his hands. "So, Mr. Monahan, you know we have been seeing you around town quite a bit. Are you here on business of some sort?" Monahan nodded. "Well, see, that's really strange because for a fine gentleman such as yourself, you're spending a lot of time out of doors. What is your business, if you don't mind my asking?"

Monahan swallowed, and said "Oil. I work for an oil company out of Saint John. I'm here scouting locations for the new filling stations. For the new motor cars."

"Motor cars?" Clem now sat back in his chair. "I can't say as I've seen many of them here in town, although I'm sure we have read about them in the papers. Not enough for a filling station anyway. Why would you have filling stations when there are no motor cars?" It was a genuine question.

"Well you see, Mr. McGuigan, it is our strategy to have the stations in place by the time there are cars on the road. While our competitors are waiting for the Fredericton residents to buy cars and then meet the need, our company will have stations already operating. By the time the other companies are ready we will have stations already dispensing fuel and customer loyalty already in hand. It's quite a clever strategy really." Monahan had momentarily forgotten his unease and had warmed enthusiastically to his subject.

Now Mr. McGuigan spoke. "That's an interesting business to be sure. And how will they get the fuel to the stations?"

"It will come to Fredericton by rail, in cars specifically built to carry it. I confess we haven't yet made the link between the railway station and the filling stations yet. But I am sure we will".

Mrs. McGuigan fished out a grubby calling card from a cupboard. She handed it to Mr. Monahan.

Mr. McGuigan said "I would be delighted to help your company in whatever way I can. What did you say your boss' name is?"

"His name is Grover Keith sir, and the company is Canadian Independent Oil. I will be happy to pass your information on to him. Thank you."

He rose from his chair, and Allie brought him his hat. I seized my opportunity and stood up.

"Mr. Monahan, you may know my father, as he does some work with the oil companies in Moncton. "

I told him my father's name, and he stared at me for a moment, as if deciding how to answer the question.

"Indeed" – stammering ever so slightly "He advises that as soon as you are finished your course here in Fredericton that you will be looking to get married. You are a lucky lady to have such an interested and protective family."

"I know of no such plan Mr. Monahan. I have no intention of marrying. I have means of my own and therefore I will wait until I am good and ready. Perhaps my family are just anticipating my choice. Do give my regards to my father when next you see him. And please reassure him that I do not require his protection. As you see I have friends aplenty".

Monahan practically fell out the door. He could not get away fast enough. Frank followed him and opened the gate for him. No one pointed out that he could have simply climbed the front stairs to the parlour and exited to the street.

Mr. McGuigan looked at me and said "We *were* going for the subtle approach. Oh now crying never helped anyone Miss."

Jack caught me and walked with me to the parlour. He smelled of apples and tobacco and soap. I had never had my cheek against him before. He sat me on the settee and he found a gold and white quilt, beautifully made, and tucked it around me. I laid down and rested my head on the red velvet. I could hear Jack telling me to rest, but I really just wanted to cry.

I woke up a little later and by the light in the window I could tell it was about eight o'clock. I sat up, and Jack's voice said "I'm here." He was sitting in his customary chair in the corner, the ember of his cigarette glowing in the dark.

"How do you feel?" he asked.

"Not much different" I said, "but I think I have to drink a bunch of water so I can produce more tears".

A low chuckle.

"Jack?"

"Yes?"

"You always smell like apples. I've been close to you a couple of times, and you always smell like apples".

Another chuckle "I always put a piece of apple in my pouch of tobacco, to keep it fresh. I think that's what you smell. "

"Yes I know".

A large intake of breath.

"I think we have to say everything that needs to be said. And then we have to stop seeing each other, for the sake of both our families. And for your sake. Either that or I will marry you. I would marry you in a moment if I didn't think everyone would suffer for it, including me. I have been trying all this time to do the right thing. I thought your friendship with my family would keep our friendship limited to the right things. But the truth is I love you. Loved you since the first moment I saw you brandishing your hat pin at Harry Spare. You're beautiful, you're brave, and you won't take the culch[38] from anybody. Imagine the courage it has taken you to defy your family. And when you bend your neck to look at the ground I ache to kiss it.

"Marrying you would be a horrible mistake, but I would do it, for love of you I would do it. Even though I could never earn the kind of living you could provide, I could never share in your class or your church. I would do it, because you make me feel manly, the manliest I could be. I feel like I would be able to do so much more with my life spent by your side.

"But it's all a lie. Soon I would resent your class, your book learning, and your money. I would feel small. And you would tire of me because I am just a simple man, who didn't go to university, and doesn't come from money like you. I can never understand what that's like. You would tire of the

---

[38] Erse (Irish Gaelic) for shit

fact that we McGuigan boys like to drink and to fight. It's beneath you."

I was crying again, sobbing out loud. My family's utter betrayal, the loss of Jack and the McGuigans. It was too much.

Presently he moved to sit beside me and pulled me up close beside him. I nuzzled my nose into his neck. He stood, and taking my hand, climbed the stairs up and then down again into the kitchen. Through the back kitchen door to a small room. There was another door at the rear that led out to the barn. But this room had a bed with spotless white bedding. He said that when this house had been an inn, the room had been for storage of beer and ale.

I asked where everyone was. Mr. and Mrs. McGuigan had gone out, to allow him to have this conversation with me. Everyone else was at the dance. We were alone.

"Will you let me?" he asked.

"Oh please……….."

Jack was a modest man, and he believed some things were just private, so there are some things I won't tell you here. He wouldn't like it.

But I will tell you this. In the heat of passion, I said over and over "My name is Charlotte! My name is Charlotte!"

I left before anyone came home, and went to my room and crawled into bed. I stayed there for two days, before the headache brought on by hunger drove me out in search of food.

On the morning of the third day, my landlady knocked on my door. She handed me two letters from Patricia, and told me Mr. McGuigan was in the parlour.

My heart skipped a beat. Jack! Maybe he had changed his mind! Maybe he had come back for me! I dressed hurriedly, leaving my hair down and wrapping a shawl around my shoulders. I practically ran down the stairs. Patricia would cluck if she could see me.

I bounded into the parlour and stopped dead. It was Frank.

"I'm sorry to disappoint you Miss" he said with a wry Frank smile.

"Not at all Mr. McGuigan, I'm happy to see you! I hope everything is all right?"

"Well, it's just I thought you might like to know Miss. Goliath died last night. I let him rest yesterday, he seemed off his feed. But this morning I found him, laying down and looking like he was sleeping peacefully. I know you liked him Miss. I thought you might like to know."

He spoke awkwardly and as if he was afraid to cry.

"I'm so sorry. Goliath was such a lovely horse, so gentle and so wise. I know how much he loved you. And you took such good care of him."

"Father already called the meat man to come and get him." Here he sobbed and put his hands over his face.

I sighed. "Frank, I know that Goliath wouldn't have cared. He cared about living, and he cared about you. And he loved that you took such good care of him. Please don't be grieved. Will you get another horse?"

"There's an auction in Maugerville tomorrow night. Clem has offered to take me. We will go this afternoon, as there is a dance there tonight. I can't say I feel much like dancing, but I suppose it might take my mind off things. "

He rose to go and I saw him to the door. I thanked him for coming to tell me. I told him I looked forward to meeting his new horse. I waved as he walked away, down the street toward home.

I felt terribly for Frank. He was cheeky, but he really was quite sweet under it all. And he had loved that horse. Like the other boys, he had attended school until he was needed to drive horses, about ten years since. I think Goliath was the only horse he had until that point.

I returned to my room to read my letters from Patricia.

April 15, 1915

Dear Charlotte;

Here I am in Halifax at the medical training camp! While our enterprise is very serious and will require strength of character, I can't help but be excited.

There are some five hundred nurses in camp, from all over Canada. Some are newly qualified, like me, and some have been nursing for years.

We have been running through drills. How to put gas masks on, that sort of thing. Oh yes, and lectures on venereal disease! Some were downright offended by those, but the instructors have informed us that various types have been more a problem with Canadians than soldiers of other countries.

Must dash. My love to Jack and all of the McGuigans. They are a delightful family, although I wouldn't want to make Sr. angry, would you?

I will write when I know when I leave for "over there" as the song says.

Sincerely

Patricia.

April 17 1915

Char:

Just short. Have just discovered that a cousin of yours is in camp with me. Her name is Penny, and she says your parents are widely regarded by family as silly and unpleasant. Not sure if that comforts or offends you; I hope the former. She says to tell you that your whole extended family is rooting for you.

Patricia

I sighed and sought out a stylus, some ink, and some stationery. But the pen stayed motionless in my hand. Maybe later. I just could not bear to tell her what had happened.

Have you ever known someone, or maybe you have felt it yourself, who knew the instant she was pregnant that there was life stirring inside her? It is probably a sensibility that reaches back to our most primitive roots, but in some women it allows them to know before there is any obvious change in their physiology.

I had known before I had left the room behind the kitchen in the McGuigan house that night. I knew I was carrying Jack's child. I went through agonies trying to decide what to do. It wasn't the "what to do" that plagues a modern woman. I had the option of approaching a woman on the other side of the river, whose name I knew but whom I had never met. Her reputation was both only whispered and somewhat dubious. But the thought never really entered my mind.

No, my problem was whether to tell Jack, whether to stir in him the age old desire to love and protect the woman carrying his child. That was exactly what I would stir in him. He was a decent man, a kind man, and a man embittered by the loss of his first child. He would insist on marrying me, and in so doing would plunge himself into the very dilemma we discussed on that last night. Would he lose respect for me?   Would I try to make him over into a polished gentleman who could never more indulge his family's love of horses and the feel of the reins in his hands? That love of horses and the part of himself who drove the carriage would leave him eventually wondering what he had ever known about horses and perhaps knowing the shame of being unable to provide for his own family and relying on his wife's money for his livelihood.

The moral implications of not telling Jack, of depriving him of choice in how to act, was at least as onerous as the burden of telling him. I saw how badly Annette and her family had hurt him with their society machinations, insisting that he remain forever away from his son. But then, what role could he have truly played in that world where children enjoyed lavish toys, feather beds turned and cleaned by servants? Would Annette have ever allowed him to teach his son to drive a horse or paint a house, the only skills he truly had to offer?

If I didn't tell Jack, I would have to make arrangements for my child, our child, to live a safe and comfortable life. In Fredericton society in 1915, there were children born without fathers, but they lived their whole lives with the stigma that their fathers had not been there to teach them simple skills like how to use a sling shot, and to fix a broken toy wagon.

It wasn't just stigma, it was shame. The mother and her child could not attend church, and the child would be bullied and shamed at school. No, there had to be a husband. I had to get married, for the sake of my child.

My other option was to take the child and move somewhere we were not known and to play the part of a widow. That would be a lonely existence for us both.

After a few more days of wallowing in my misery, I did finally write to Patricia and tell her all of my thoughts. She was so practical and able to set aside her prejudices, I knew she would have something useful to say.

I didn't know mail between Fredericton and Halifax could pass so swiftly. Two weeks flat. Perhaps it was the war that was making the post more efficient.

Dear Charlotte

I am so sorry for this turn of events! I honestly thought that you and Jack would marry!

Nevertheless it is your pregnancy that worries me most. What a disaster in the battle you are waging with your family. There must be a way to still find you victory.

I have thought of two.

First, you can end the pregnancy. Don't look so shocked, I know you know this possibility exists although I would never admit it to anyone of the male sex. That way the situation simply goes away. No pain or confusion for Jack, no guilt for anyone, and no opportunity for you to be ridiculed or shamed. I have included the name and address of a woman on the north side. She is reputable, if such a profession can be called so, and most of all she is safe.

The second possibility might be more palatable for you. I have a cousin who would like to get married. He is nice looking, honourable, and wealthy enough

*to keep people from wagging their tongues. He
would not bother you in that way, and I will let him
explain the rest. I think you should meet him. I am
sending him a letter also, so that he may contact
you. This might be your best option, given how I am
sure you feel about option number one.*

Good luck and tell me what you decide.

*By the way, I leave for Jolly Old England at the end
of May. Not sure where I go after that. I guess I find
out when I get there.*

Love

Patricia

Frankly neither option sounded very good.
Disposing of the baby in such a cold way turned my
stomach, like repudiating all my feelings for Jack.
And as for the marriage, it sounded a very odd
marriage opportunity indeed, and why would a man
want such a thing? I thought of Jack telling me that
my parent's cold alliance made him feel sad.

I went about my business. I borrowed the kitchen
downstairs to bake a pie and burnt it to a crisp,
much to my landlady's disapproval. I thought about
applying for positions to begin using my education,
but I couldn't bring myself to do it. I felt so sad. I
took long walks. It rained and I read books.

One afternoon when I was walking down Queen
Street Mr. McGuigan passed me with Caesar and
the sloven. He slowed down a bit to accommodate
other vehicles, and I asked where Jack was. Why
was he not helping?

"Signed onto a painting crew Miss, in Saint John". He looked at me kindly. "You will be all right Miss. A gentleman will come along and sweep you off your feet. Such a fine lady you are."

Tears reached my eyes without warning, and I pulled my handkerchief out, turning away and waving back at him. Perhaps I should simply tell Jack. But no, that would be unfair, I was sure of it. If only my stomach didn't hurt.

As I walked down the sidewalk with my handkerchief to my face, I suppose I wasn't looking where I was going. I collided with a gentleman and almost knocked him off his feet.

Amid profuse apologies and him helping me up and readjusting my hat – stupid hat- I finally stood up and looked at him.

His eyes were brown, his skin very fair and his hair very dark. He wore a very nice brown tweed suit, with the extraordinary addition of a deep red vest. He was definitely handsome, almost too handsome to be real. The shape of his shoulders and chest under his clothing hinted at the physique of someone who enjoyed sport, or exercise of some other kind. I even noticed that the shoes on his feet were immaculately polished, and of recent style.

Something about him was familiar, as if I had met him somewhere in passing, at a dance or a concert. Fredericton wasn't a big place, so it wouldn't surprise me.

He held out his hand to shake mine. "Thomas Fitzgerald de Burgh, at your service. Are you all right Miss?"

I shook his hand and assured him that I was all right, although he had already noted the handkerchief in my hand and my watery eyes.

"I'm sorry, I don't want to presume, but, are you Charlotte Driscoll?"

I looked at him in confusion for a moment.

"I believe your friend Patricia mentioned to you that I might contact you. I was going to write, but, well, here we are."

My mouth dropped open in sudden recognition. "Oooh! You're her cousin! How did you know I was the woman you were looking for?"

He smiled. "Patricia described you as having beautiful auburn hair and a constant struggle with hats." When I smiled he continued "and that you love to wear blue dresses, you are close to the carter agents of the McGuigan family, and there I saw you talking to Mr. John McGuigan. He and his family moved my belongings into my new home over on Church Street last week. I must say they struck me as honourable and knowledgeable of their work. They did a smashing job of moving a brand new piano in."

My facial expression must have betrayed me, because he stopped smiling and continued "Look, I would like very much if we could hear one another's stories. Then we can decide if a – partnership- between us would meet both our needs. I don't mean to be presumptuous. If nothing else we can listen to one another's sad tales and seek solace. I have reserved a carriage just down the way here, from Barker house. Please accompany me. I assure you no harm will ever come to you in my company"

Whatever else I thought, I believed absolutely that no harm would come to me. And so though I had been told all my life never to go anywhere with strange men, I agreed to go with Mr. de Burgh. I decided that if someone saw me go into his house with him alone, well, it couldn't be any worse than being and unmarried pregnant woman in a small maritime town before women even had the vote.

The ride in the carriage was mercifully short, and uncomfortably quiet.

We arrived at 97 Church Street shortly. It was a large home, and had once been the home of an Anglican Bishop. I knew of him by reputation even though he had died some time ago. After several families resident there since, the house had again fallen vacant. Mr. de Burgh told me that the verandah and the tower-like shape at the right had been newly added. There were flower boxes along the railing of the deck above the verandah, and marigolds were flowering there. It was truly beautiful, exactly in the style that made me love Fredericton.

Mr. de Burgh held my hand as I walked up the steps onto the verandah. A closer look at the windows revealed beautiful stained glass along the top of each of their panes. He produced a key and unlocked the front door.

There was precious little furniture in the house, besides a beautiful grand piano and a few small pieces here and there. Mr. de Burgh had been educated in England, at a series of the best schools and universities, but he actually hailed from Ireland, from Dublin. Some of the pieces bore more history than I had ever seen.

I was drawn to a chair that he said was of medieval vintage, from his mother's family. I ran my fingers along the arms, touched the carved wood of the back. With his permission, I sat in it. It was as if I could almost hear the noise of a great party, if I could just reach the memory I would remember – no, it was gone.

We walked to the kitchen, which was large and beautifully appointed. He sat me at a small table there and made us both a cup of tea. It impressed me that he knew how. Most men of means would have someone else to do kitchen tasks such as tea. It was a point in his favour.

He looked at me across the kitchen table for a minute, and then he said "you look like you need to tell your story first."

And so I did. I was surprised how easy it was to trust him with my secrets. But I needed a way out, and what he offered was seeming less and less preposterous. I told him about my family and their dreadful treatment of me, their attempts to control everything in my life and how I was ill suited to tolerate it. I told him about the inheritance from my grandmother and how she had bypassed my father. I had come to wish in a way that she hadn't. Being ignored by my parents would have been easier than being manipulated, followed and judged.

"I think I can help you with that, regardless of our relationship. More and more cases granting women control over their lives and their money are passing through the courts, although still not as many as there should be. In any case, go on."

I told him how I had met Jack, and how we had spent almost a year going to dances and for walks. I told him how the McGuigans had welcomed me to their family and loved me at a time in my life when I was very lonely but unable to admit it. I told him at length how I loved Jack's gentleness, his kindness, and I respected his ethics and his view of the world around him. I started to break down when I told him how I believed that Jack and I could have made a good marriage and how I thought we could have surmounted our differences and the problem of my inheritance. But that Jack could not sacrifice his own lifestyle and values to my money, my upbringing.

I told him how I knew I was pregnant right away, and I had been struggling since not to cheat Jack, to force him to give up his position toward our relationship, by blackmailing him with the pregnancy.

And finally I told him that I had completed my course at the business college, and that I was able to work for a living if I had to.

Silence. He sat in his chair, leaning back, with his legs fully outstretched. His fingers were matched against each other to form a small finger cathedral. He examined it like it were Notre Dame.

I was starting to panic because he had been quiet so long, when he began to speak.

"I am so impressed with how hard you have tried to allow him the freedom to remain true to himself." My stomach started to unclench. "However…" Uh oh. "However, I think what you are doing is also terribly unfair. The baby you have there is his baby too. It's your right to decide what to do with it, but it's his right to be allowed to attempt to change your mind. The courts believe babies belong to mothers only, but this is one of very few places that I think the courts might be wrong".

My jaw had dropped. His view was diametrically opposed to the views of the average Frederictonian. The churches, and just everyone believed that if a girl got pregnant, it was her fault and she was shunned. If a man got a girl pregnant, well, that was shameful, but not the end of the world. After all, he didn't have to raise it. Mr. de Burgh was expressing values that were revolutionary and well ahead of his time.

"All right" I said, "Now you."

He blew out a sigh. "Indeed. Fair's fair."

The story he told me was long, but I will summarize it here.

He was born of the Irish Aristocracy, what was left of it with the changes happening in Ireland. His parents sent him to be educated in all the best schools, a series of remote institutions which included Eton and Oxford. So he became somewhat more British than Irish. He studied the law and was accepted to the bar in London. His relationship with his parents had drifted so far that he honestly felt he didn't know them anymore, or they him. They had fallen out over a variety of situations, specifics not forthcoming, and in the end they offered to pay out his share of their estate if he would leave the British Isles. And here he was, preparing to practice law in Fredericton and in need of a wife to validate his position in Fredericton society. The fact that I was pregnant pleased him, in a detached way. A readymade family to provide a good back drop for his career.

The chilliness of his plan seemed repugnant to me. And what kind of people did that to their own son? What could possibly have been so bad?

Before I could fully decide what my reaction was, however, he was talking terms.

I was to keep my inheritance to finance my own interests, and he would help me to prevent my parents from harassing me any further.

He would own my child as his own and provide all necessary expenditures for its care and wellbeing.

He would be delighted if I could do some law-clerking for him. That way I could maintain my skills.

I would hire a housekeeper and whatever other staff I deemed necessary to keep the house and grounds in good condition.

I countered.

If Jack chose to see his child and have an influence on it, we would find a way that would not subject him or us to censure.

I wanted a horse. I wanted to train him and have a gig or small carriage.

I insisted that he take an active role with myself and the child. He was to be a father to it, not an absent source of funds.

I had another month before I started to show, but maybe only another two weeks before the due date of the baby would make people count on their fingers. I wanted a couple of weeks to get to know him.

There were a few small items added – silly things like no toothbrush left on the sink. But essentially we were done. It was preposterous. I couldn't believe we were even discussing it. But I was considering it.

We agreed that breaking the agreement could be unilateral.

He then offered to take me home, and let me think about it all.

At supper time I got out some ink and a pen, and some paper. After several tries, I ended up with this:

Dearest Jack:

While I will always love you and will always feel you are the man for me, I respect your decision that you could not be happy in a life with me.

I have something to discuss with you that requires privacy. Could you please make some time for me in the next few days?

Sincerely

Charlotte

Since 135 Westmorland was so close, I simply put the letter in an envelope and walked down, dropping it in the letter slot in the front door. I turned away and was halfway back to the corner of Westmorland and Brunswick I heard a shout behind me.

"Charlotte!!" I turned to find Jack running up the street after me. After everything, after all my tears and loneliness when he reached me I came to a screeching halt in front of him. He had hurt me. I wasn't going to fall into his arms. But I was so happy to see him that I stood trembling. Whatever God made him run to me like this, I was deeply thankful.

After a moment he steered me back to his house. The big gate was slightly ajar and he walked me through it. He let go of me long enough to close the gate behind us. Caesar was there resting but he was alone and not harnessed. He nickered at me, and I went to touch him for a moment. He was well, although tired, and convinced as usual that he was the most glorious horse ever. I hugged him again and said goodbye.

Jack and I went into the house, and he invited me to sit with him in the parlour. I sat on the settee and he sat on his usual chair and lit a cigarette.

"Where is everyone?" I asked.

"Nene is out knitting socks for the war effort before Father comes home and finds out she has been there. Allie is with her and doesn't care if Father finds out. Mother is nursing a neighbour who is sick with the flu. Frank, Father and Clem are all working. We don't have long."

Now that the time had come to say the things I needed to say, I wasn't sure where to start. How do you tell someone you love them and are pregnant with their child? Especially when they have said unequivocally that they don't want you? And do you tell them there is someone else in the wings prepared to take over if the answer is no?

"I thought you were in Saint John" I said tentatively.

"I just got home."

He was looking at me expectantly, the blue eyes peering out from under the heavy brows.

I dove in.

"I'm pregnant. It couldn't belong to anyone but you, as I have only ever been with you. I long for us to be a family but I don't want to blackmail you into it. If you were to do it, it would have to be because you want it, not because you have to.

"I can look after it, I can move somewhere where no one knows us and pretend to be a widow. I can find someone else to marry me. You don't have to do anything, but it's right that I tell you, you have a right to know."

"I have been trying so hard to let you go, to let you be yourself. I have suffered so, but I didn't want you to enter into something that would make it hard for you to simply be Jack, and not the husband of a rich wife."

The words tumbled out of me in a jumble. And now that I had said them, there was silence.

And then he lept up out of his chair and began pacing the room, stopping by turns as if he meant to speak. Then he came to me and pulled me off the settee. He pulled me in tight and sobbed at length. I put my arms under his and rested my hands on his back. We stood there like that for some minutes. And then he waved his hand at the settee, inviting me to sit again.

"I thought you would come back. I thought you would come back sooner. I thought I might change my mind, but I wasn't sure. Now I understand that you loved me that much. I'm so sorry.

"I have to tell you. No one knows this but Clem and you. I have made a commitment and I am certain I am doing what is right. I feel it is something I was meant to do, that I can do. I can't back out."

A commitment??!! To whom? What on earth was he saying?

"Clem and I are going to Sussex tomorrow. We're going to sign up. We have both been thinking it for a long time. We never said anything because of Father. He will be furious over it. But we're going. "

I didn't expect this. I don't know why, but maybe because most of the young men under thirty had already gone. Maybe because Mr. McGuigan was so against any war waged by the British Crown. Maybe just because he had never spoken of it.

Of course I had been reading the papers daily and following all the reports. Harry Spare had gone overseas. While I thought he was a bully and a truly unpleasant person, I worried for him. There were casualty reports in the Gleaner regularly and daily I expected to see his name. The battle reports indicated that our casualties were light but the casualty lists kept getting longer. These things were all true, but they were things that did not easily touch my life. I did not think of them happening to me.

He was looking at me, watching me and listening so intently the way he always had. I was trying to think what I should say, how I should feel. He was mine, truly mine, if I wanted him. But he was going to make me a widow.

"I will marry you now, right now before I go. You will be my wife. No one will question about the baby. We will go to whichever church you want. I don't care. Just marry me. I've been a fool."

I started to cry again but I stopped. "I can get legitimacy on my own. I don't need you to marry me for that. I want you, with all my heart. But you are going to go away and all I will truly have of you are the letters you will send home. I want the letters, I sincerely do, no matter what we say here today. And if you die, I will stand at your grave and defy anyone who tells me I have no right. And if you come home, and you still love me, then I will love you back. But a child needs a father Jack. A child can't get that from a bunch of letters. "

"You threw me over for the sake of your male pride. And now you want to marry for the sake of your male pride, so that no other man may have me, or my child. Jack McGuigan, I think I have found your flaw."

He was smoking furiously at this point, and running his free hand through his hair. I had hurt him, his eyes told me so. But I would gain nothing if I was dishonest.

"You are the one throwing me over. You won't let me care for my own child. Is this out of some sort of snobbery? Is it out of selfishness? Other women, women with small children, have their men overseas".

"Yes but Jack, could you not wait to go away, even a few weeks? After Christmas? Why do you have to go now?" I asked.

"Because it's important to me to go, and if Father finds out, it will be like the Book of Revelations. The four horsemen mean nothing compared to John McGuigan."

He looked at me for a second. "And because I am terrified I will lose my nerve."

"Without you, there will always be other women. But none will ever be you. For all my life I will see you from afar, living with another husband and my child, and wish I could have said something differently. But I can never be anyone different than who I am. I'm so sorry Charlotte." His eyes were welling with tears as he said this. It was all I could do not to throw my arms around him and say I was sorry, I was wrong. I would have done it, but for the baby.

"Will you write to me, Dear Jack?"

"I'm not much of a letter writer, but how could I not? I have no idea what I will say, but I will write." He pulled me to him again, held me so tight I almost couldn't breathe.

Presently we heard the back door open and close, and Nene and Allie entered the house. I turned quietly and slipped out the front door, and walked away, feeling I had lost everything.

Late that night Clem and Jack snuck out of their father's home, against his wishes and his politics, and took the midnight train to Sussex. Why Sussex? Because it was the largest recruiting centre in the province. Because in Fredericton or Saint John, the recruiting agents would know their father, and his Fenian leanings, and they would have been barred from recruitment. Fenians were enemies of the King. The recruiting men in Sussex had no such knowledge of Mr. McGuigan and his participation in the Fenian uprising and so had no such compunction.

Clem returned the next day. He had been rejected because he had four daughters and a pregnant wife. Had he had sons, they would have accepted him. I felt very sorry for Eva, that he apparently valued her so little. But perhaps she didn't feel that way.

Jack did not return.

By now I was very, very ill in the mornings. I would have dry toast and tea for breakfast, and then vomit until lunch time. At lunch time I would be famished. I would eat everything I could find, and then feel fine until supper. I knew absolutely if the Good Lord allowed me to survive morning sickness, I could survive the birth with strength and grace.

A week passed since Jack left, and all Hell broke loose. Apparently Mrs. McGuigan received an envelope containing a notice of pay assignment from Jack. As a Private in the army, he would earn $33.00 per month, almost twice what he made as a house painter, and more still than he made as a carter agent. $15.00 per month was assigned to his mother, to put toward housekeeping and the costs of giving Allie whatever education she wanted. I know this because Mr. McGuigan arrived at seven in the morning and banged on the front door calling my name.

My Landlady was not impressed.

I met him in the parlour shortly. I was dressed, but not feeling well at all. There were two paper bags discreetly tucked into the arm of the couch with the words "just in case" written on them. Indeed this whole situation was getting out of hand. I thought I had been more secretive than that.

Mr. McGuigan merely paced the room in answer to my greeting, rubbing his balding head much in the way his son had done just a few days ago.

Finally he said "Is this your doing?"

It had to be a male thing, to jump to such a ridiculous conclusion.

"I assume you are talking about Jack and Clem, running away to enlist. And I have to tell you that yes, absolutely, this makes my life completely perfect. The only man I have ever wanted to marry has now thrown me over twice, once out of pride, and once for the army and almost certain death. Yes, I am thrilled Mr. McGuigan."

Upon which I picked up one of the paper bags and vomited several days' worth of food into it. My landlady tiptoed into the room with a warm rag and traded it for the bag. God Bless her, but surely that meant she was listening at the keyhole.

He looked at me levelly. "My dear young woman", he began, "Lottie and I have had eight babies, and that's just the ones who lived. I know a pregnant woman when I see one." He thought he understood and it was palpable in the room.

He waited while I threw up again. I wiped my mouth.

"Mr. McGuigan, Jack did offer to marry me. The night before he left. In any church I wanted. But he was still leaving the next day. Many young men of my acquaintance have gone, only to appear on the casualty lists. I wanted us to be a family. I didn't want to be a widow at least for a short while. My own childhood was very lonely as you know. I don't want that for my child."

He was surprised. No, my attitude was beyond his understanding. He sat looking at me as if I had answered in Russian and he was struggling to master the grammar.

Finally he asked "What will you do?"

"There is a man who has offered to marry me, and I am thinking I might accept".

That statement settled on the room, punctuated only by my retching.

"Will you ever tell the child?"

"Yes, when the time is right. But I would like it very much if you and Mrs. McGuigan would support me all the same, see the child from time to time. You have been my family through a time when I really needed you. Can you forgive me? Can you forgive Jack?"

I was asking him to be much farther down the emotional road than he was ready to travel just yet. He was still angry, but after a moment he nodded, put his arm around me and kissed my head. That took courage given how I smelled.

He left me then, and I crept back upstairs to crawl back under the covers and die quietly.

No sooner had I fallen asleep than there was movement in the room. I opened my eyes when I felt Mrs. McGuigan sit on the edge of my bed.

I began to sit up. "Mrs. McGuigan!"

"Now sit down girl, and let me look after you and my grandson."

She smiled. "Now all this being sick isn't good for you my girl. You need to drink more fluids. I've brought some crushed ice from the last little bit we have from last winter. Now there, you drink it only as fast as it melts. If you don't you will only feel sicker. I have brought you some mint leaves to chew and settle your stomach. That's it, now you rest a bit. I won't be far. "

I was too astonished to fall asleep quickly, but I felt safe and cared for. I suppose my own mother would normally be expected to do this, but my mother was a million miles away, both in mind and spirit.

I woke later feeling ravenously hungry again, and she was there. She gave me fresh baked bread thick with butter and molasses. Then she cut up apples and put a little cream on them so they weren't too acid. I felt much better than I had in days. I suppose you don't realize how sick you are until you aren't any more.

My room was spotlessly clean, the discarded clothes of several days off the floor and the furniture and clean in the clothes press. The floor was swept, the room tidy. Fresh clothes were laid out on the foot of my bed.

While I dressed, Mrs. McGuigan stripped my bed and arranged with my landlady to have the sheets sent out for washing. Then she sat me on the bed.

"Now, since your own mother doesn't have the sense God gave a goose, I will be the one to give you a little motherly wisdom" she said.

She sat on a chair and began to talk. "My grandmother was a full blood Mi'kmaq Indian, did you know that?" I nodded no, but now I looked at her face, I realized that must be where her square jaw and the shape of her eyes had come from.

"She married my grandfather for love, but she didn't hold with the way white women bow to their men, and the way white men treat their women. She taught me that women love and honour their men, but that women had to think for themselves and do what was best for themselves and their children. And that's what you're going to do. Do what's best for you and the baby, and everything will fall into place. So tell me."

She had always struck me as the silent power in the McGuigan house, even with her husband's unorthodox politics and his legendary temper. I was feeling that power full force.

I told her everything, what Jack had said to me the day he threw me over, and how we both cried and he took me to his bed. I told her how I knew I was pregnant right away, but with the things Jack had said I didn't feel it was fair to blackmail him into marrying me. I told her about the weeks of misery, and how Patricia had put me in touch with her cousin and his very businesslike proposal. I told her that Mr. de Burgh had convinced me to tell Jack, that Jack had a right to know. And I told her about that last day, and that I could not accept that Jack would marry me and then go to war and how I felt I had pushed him away when if I had married him that night, he might have stayed at least for a few days. And then the nausea had become so bad that I just couldn't get any further forward.

She was looking at her hands as I talked, and then looking up at me, and then back at her hands. Her nails were bitten to the quick like Jack's. She was simply but beautifully dressed, in clothes that were conservatively fashionable but easily washed. Her hair had been dark but was now mostly grey and pulled back behind her head. And her brown eyes examined me, probing me for any sense of falsehood, and I knew it.

Finally, she spoke. "I think you should marry Mr. de Burgh. One way or another, Jack has failed in his responsibility to you by living up to his responsibility to the King, and I don't think you can marry him and simply wait around until he comes home, no matter what other women are prepared to tolerate. We would support you of course, whatever your choice. But you need to make a home, your own home, for your child. And I think I know why Mr. de Burgh's proposal is so businesslike. But I would like your permission to interview him, if that's all right. There is something he is not telling you, and you need to know what that is before you make a final choice. "

I loved her more than ever. Good, sensible, unbiased advice. Unjudgemental support. Yes, she was a very good mother.

I wrote a brief note to Mr. de Burgh and asked him to expect Mrs. McGuigan at four pm and to please be accepting of her questions, as she was acting in my interests.

She left me with instructions to rest and drink mint tea, and to eat as much bread and apples as I wished. I hugged her tight and thanked her, and she looked awkward, like it wasn't something she got very often.

Obediently, I pulled out a book about Scottish History, about the Lords of the Isles. I was fascinated by the people and the choices they made. I loved the story of the Laird Alasdair Carrack McDonnell, with his pockmarked face, and who pioneered a new clan dynasty, a clan that lasted until the Jacobite uprising. He didn't always get it right, once razing a monastery, but the sheer force of the personality it would take to accomplish what he did pleased me.

I had read for an hour, when there was a tap on my door. My landlady stuck her head in and told me Mr. Clem McGuigan was downstairs.

Clem confused me. He was charming, charismatic, always working those McGuigan dimples to best advantage. He often dismissed and sometimes disrespected women, but he was respectful of me and kind to his mother. He had an active sense of humour, and he seemed to be well liked, almost in spite of his father.

When I walked into the parlour he was standing with his hat in his hands, chin down, looking up at me.

"I should have come sooner Miss, I'm sorry. I need to tell you some things, about going to Sussex. I've been trying to explain it all to my Father. It's not working."

I invited him to sit.

"First, I want you to know that Jack talked about you the whole way. I had no idea he feels so strongly about you. And he talked about Harry Spare."

My eyes must have widened in surprise.

"You may well be surprised Miss. But you know they knew one another quite well. They were both house painters and worked on a lot of the same crews. They didn't like each other much, as Jack is Catholic and Harry was Anglican, and Father, well, you know about Father. Harry would call him Paddy all the time. As you know Miss, Harry only came here from England a few years ago with his Mother. Not sure why they came. But they did.

"Well a while ago Jack found out that not only did you save him by shaming Harry and bravely brandishing your hat pin, and I hear shaming him in church" - here he smirked and his eyes twinkled at me - "But that you had been going with Harry and threw him over for Jack. All of this served to endear you to Jack and to confirm his opinion of Harry. Don't get me wrong Miss, sure Harry wasn't a bad fellow, besides his aggravation toward Jack. But then Harry went overseas, one of the first here in town. Jack has always felt that if a bully like Harry could go overseas and show bravery, getting promoted, and now rescuing wounded men[39], well then why was he, Jack, resisting and staying at home?

"It was partly about how he appeared in your eyes Miss, but it was more how he appeared in his own. He thought Harry was a toad, but Harry was proving otherwise. Do you understand?" He was looking at me with his brows furrowed.

"Why didn't he tell me this?"

"I think he only worked it all out on the way to join up. Up until then it was driving him, but he hadn't made sense of it. And then, with your news, it all came to a head for him, and he felt he had to go

_____

37 Service Record Harry Spare

more than ever. He would have married you, to save your name, but other men with children are going, to save face in front of those very children. How could he do differently?"

I sat for a moment, digesting.

"Is that why you were going to leave your wife and five daughters to go to war?"

The question hung in the air for a moment, before he looked down and then began to speak.

"I suppose that was part of it. But newly signed up troops make more than thirty dollars a month. That's more than I make in two. [40] If I could buy a truck, I could do twice as many loads in a day. Make more money. Get my family away from Morrison's Mills, and in to town. But I guess that won't happen now."

My mouth hung open for a minute. I had never known poverty like what the McGuigans lived with. I loved them, and I wasn't blind to their situation. Nor would I ever have dared to help them, as they would have been deeply offended. But what Clem had been willing to do to rise his family out of their situation – it gave me a pain in my throat. The recruiting agents had been right to send him home. But I felt his crushing disappointment, his despair. He was an honest man.

"Stay here for a moment would you please?" I said to him.

---

[40] Service Record, Jack Toner.

When I returned, I had a cheque book in my hand, a pen, and some ink.

"No Miss, please don't shame me in such a way!"

"I'm not shaming you Clem. I am issuing you a loan. No one will know unless you tell them. Consider it an investment in keeping you away from the recruiting office. Consider it a testament of my esteem for your wife. Now, how much does a truck cost?"

His face had twisted up and he looked a little panicked, like he was going to cry, but I raised my eyebrows at him, and sat with my pen hovering over the surface of the chequebook.

"I would say about $400 Miss." He was looking down at the hands that were crushing the cap in his hands.

I wrote out the cheque to Clem McGuigan for $450, and handed it over. "I expect to be the first to ride in it. ". I hugged him. Hard.

Mrs. McGuigan arrived hard on the heels of her son's departure, right after I had returned the cheque book and ink to their rightful places. We retired to my room, and she looked me over carefully.

"I told you to rest young woman" she said. She made me some tea, not mint now, but chamomile. "Back into your bed you go. I will have Nene bring you some supper. Liver and onions. Apple crisp for dessert, how's that. It will help you make it through the liver. "

On the threshold to my room she paused. "Was that Clem I saw leaving?"

"Yes Ma'am, he came to tell me some things that Jack had said before he left. He thought it might ease my hurt feelings over my…..predicament".

She smiled. "And am I right to suppose that you chastened him for trying to leave his wife and family in such a stupid way?"

I nodded, smiling.

"How is Mr. McGuigan?" I asked. "He must be heartbroken."

"Fit to be tied Miss, and not fit to be with. But I will tell you when I come back and we will talk about Mr. de Burgh as well. Right now I have a family to feed." She closed the door and her footsteps went down the stairs until I heard the front door close.

I sat up and returned to my book and continued reading until shortly I heard footsteps coming up the stairs again. With a knock on the door, Nene entered with a plate covered with a dishtowel, and a bowl also dressed.

"I was told I have to watch you eat every bite" she smiled at me.

Fortunately I don't have the violent antipathy toward liver and onions that some people have. I ate every bite, as instructed and then passed the plate back in exchange for the bowl. The apple crisp was wonderful beyond compare and I savoured each piece of apple.

Nene was smiling at my enjoyment of the food. "You were hungry!" she said, and I suppose she was right.

We sat chatting for a few minutes, talking about minor things. And then" "Father is terrible just now. He can't imagine Jack and Clem betraying him in such a way. I wonder if he knows that we all have things in our lives that have nothing to do with him."

She was soft spoken, wiry hair pulled back in a bun, and pretty, with the same McGuigan blue eyes. She didn't say any more about Mr. McGuigan but changed the subject quickly to something that couldn't be construed as disloyalty to her father. When Mrs. McGuigan came in Nene picked up the dishes and left, winking at me as she went out the door.

"Well, I met your Mr. de Burgh. Would you like to know what I thought?"

I nodded enthusiastically. It would be nice to have an alternate perception.

"Well, as I think you know, he hasn't told you everything, and I don't think he will. There is wisdom there, and gentleness, but pain as well. His story about his family, what on earth could he have done to anger them so? I think the explanation is in his reluctance to have a normal marriage with a woman."

"You think there is something wrong with him, that he.........can't?" I asked.

She raised an eyebrow at me for a moment. "Let me tell you a story. When I was a child, we knew a family where there were very few children. The father was kind, and the mother was confident and clever. They were nice people, good neighbours. One summer night, my brother and I were sent to our woodpile to bring in wood for the stove in the morning. When we got to the stacked rows of wood, several rows, as tall as a man some of them, we heard a noise, and when we pursued it, we found the neighbour man standing and leaning against the wood, and another man on the ground before him with the neighbour's organ in his mouth. We were silent so they didn't see us, and we ran. When we arrived back at the house with no wood we were scolded, but we didn't tell our parents. The only person I ever told, before you, was my grandmother. She said that in every country, every tribe, there are one or two men who cannot be satisfied by women. It is not their fault. Perhaps God punishes them, but men like this see the world in a very different way. They are special, and we should leave them alone with their secrets, and keep those secrets away from normal men."

I sat staring at her. The back of my neck tingled, my scalp felt like it would creep off my skull. The only place I had heard anything like this before was in church, always condemned in veiled terms, so that I never quite understood what was being said. But now I did. And now I understood exactly what Thomas Fitzgerald de Burgh was asking me to do. He wanted me to help him hide it. And to turn a blind eye..........

Men didn't talk about these things in front of women, but I was vaguely aware these things happened. Indeed there was something familiar about it, the need for forgiveness, and for honest love in secret.

I looked at Mrs. McGuigan. "I need to think about this tonight. Thank you so much for seeing him for me. It explains so much. It explains that niggling feeling I had, that there was something very serious that he did not tell me. I think I will go see him tomorrow, if you think it advisable."

"Well you don't seem to be able to get much rest here at home!" She was smiling at me.

I hugged her and thanked her once again for her help. She made sure there was water within reach of the bed, and left saying good night.

The next morning, Nene brought me a fresh loaf of bread and some cherry preserves. Once I had tea I felt much better. I hoped that meant the morning sickness was passing.

I walked to the house on Church Street and was there by nine. When I rang the bell, Mr. de Burgh came to the door in pyjamas and a housecoat. His hair was tousled, but he was obviously wide awake.

"Miss Driscoll! What a pleasant surprise! Please come in! Please make yourself comfortable in the parlour. I will be with you in just a moment."

While I waited I wandered around the house a bit. There were dirty dishes in the kitchen, but otherwise it was as I had seen it. A new Chesterfield had appeared in the parlour, antique if

405

I wasn't mistaken. It desperately needed recovering.

In about fifteen minutes he reappeared, freshly shaven, dressed in elegant gentleman's clothes. After we were comfortable at the kitchen table, I began to speak.

"Mr. de Burgh "-at which time he insisted I call him Thomas – "Thomas, I have been seriously reluctant to accept your offer, and the reason is that I know you have withheld a great deal of your story from me. This withholding has both worried and offended me. I am not stupid, nor am I accustomed to a lack of honesty in my friends. If friend is what you wish to be, then I believe you have a great deal to tell me. I laid awake for a long time last night, considering what to say to you, and what I need to hear. I am here to offer you the opportunity to right the wrong you have already done me, and we are not even married yet. I don't have to accept you. You are not my last chance. I can yet go to Saint John and marry Jack, the father of my baby, and will be able to do so as long as he is there training. Please choose your words carefully."

I sat for a moment, saying nothing.

He looked at his watch. "I have to prepare for court. That's what I was doing when you got here, I have to see the judge at 11".

"Then I suppose, Mr. de Burgh, you had better speak quickly, as we both have things to do. I believe there is a train to Saint John at 11 as well."

He looked at me in distress for a moment. And then he muttered, "Damn-it-all. And what if I tell you my secrets and then you decide I am too abominable to reside with, as well you might? Will you then tell others and expose me to censure?"

"I will sign whatever form of legal document you want, but I simply cannot enter into any arrangement with you unless I know the full reason that you are in need of a superficial wife."

His cheeks were bright red against his pale skin, and he sat forward on his chair and leaned on both elbows, hands pulling on his dark hair. He looked familiar when he did that, but I had no idea why.

"Mr. de Burgh, it's a word I cannot even say, and in some parts of the world, you would be executed for it. But I know that when I arrived here there was someone else in this house. While I waited for you I heard the back door creak open and closed. Turning around and looking out the parlour window, I saw a man come from the right hand side of this house, just there. He checked to ensure no one was watching as he walked to the sidewalk, but he did not see me watching. If I go upstairs will I find yours is the only bed disturbed in this house? And am I right in presuming that you want a wife in order to disguise that this is your" – nighttime activity?" My voice was becoming shrill. I was feeling sick again.

He was looking at me, tears rolling down his cheeks. "You drive a hard bargain Charlotte. I have never openly spoken of this, never. Not even with the men I....I disgust myself, when I think about it. But it is the only way I feel any joy. I was made this way, made by God as sure as you were. For this my parents have banished me, sent me away, so that word of my licentious activities should never reach them again. But like any man, I wish for children, a family, and a home where I am not alone. This empty house begins to wear on me. I wish for a woman who is my friend, and who will forgive me for what I am. This is what I truly ask of you. "

I considered. What were the disadvantages to this arrangement? A great deal could go wrong. Someone could find out despite all precaution, and what then? How would it reflect on me? Mrs. McGuigan and I both felt he was a decent man, if man he could be described with his flaws. And there was something else, that feeling of familiarity, the feeling that I already knew him. I still couldn't put my finger on it.

"All right Mr. de Burgh – Thomas. I will marry you, against my better judgement. On one condition. None of your men, for social purposes or – those purposes, will ever darken the door of this house again. You must swear it. I don't care where you go with them, or what you do with them, but that part of your life must not ever touch this house".

He put out his hand and said "Done".

And then I threw up in the sink.

He went to court in time for his appearance, leaving me to rest in the house. There was only one bed, the one recently shared, so I could not lie down there. The chesterfield in the parlour had springs showing, so it was out of the question. In desperation I sat in the medieval chair I had admired on my last visit, pushed it to the wall, and leaned my head against the panelling. I dozed for the better part of an hour, and had strange dreams. In my dreams I was at a great celebration, a wedding I thought, and I sat in a chair very like the one I was actually in.

Mrs. McGuigan arrived with Clem and Mr. McGuigan. They brought a brand new brass bedstead and mattress in the front door. The bedroom that Thomas was using was larger, but the one next to it had a cheater door to his and a birthing room, a small room at the back specifically designed for bearing children. They claimed that room for me and set the bed up in it. Mrs. McGuigan had brought soup and fresh bread. I was fed and escorted to bed.

I could hear whispering in the hall, Mr. McGuigan telling the others that I should marry Jack, and Mrs. McGuigan insisting that Jack had already made his choice. There was some talk about why on earth Jack was going overseas anyway. Then there was shushing and they went downstairs.

Thomas took me home as soon as he arrived back from chambers, concerned that I needed rest in my own bed for the rest of the day. He asked that I be ready for him to pick me up at one tomorrow afternoon. We had shopping to do.

That night I dreamt again of the wedding. I couldn't see the bride, but Thomas was there, with dark hair long to his shoulders and dressed in scarlet clothes that were from some ancient period. Oddly, Jack was there too, looking almost exactly as he had the last time he hugged me, except for his clothing. And then the dream was gone again, and I remembered nothing more.

Mrs. McGuigan insisted I lie in bed all the next morning, although I actually felt better than I had since before I was pregnant. I didn't have the heart to tell her that the vomiting the previous day probably had more to do with fear and enormity than it had with being pregnant. But I loved the way she cared for me.

We talked about what I should wear for the wedding, and she went through all of my dresses. I had to admit they were starting to be just a smidge snug through the hips. She looked at my best dress, a navy serge suit, and then decided against it. The tightness showed too much.

"Leave it with me" she said, and left.

She came back an hour later with a gorgeous piece of fine wool, light blue. She also had soup for me. As I ate, she measured every single part of my body, including my ankles. And then, as it was almost one o'clock, she left.

When the hackney arrived at exactly one o'clock, Thomas wasn't in it. The driver indicated that he had been instructed to drive me first to S. F. Shute's jewellery store, and that I was to meet Thomas there.

A pink diamond solitaire and two wedding bands were procured at Shute's. I was surprised at Thomas' enthusiasm. I decided to simply accept it and go along with him.

Then we went to Lemont's and ordered crockery, nursery furniture, another bed for the birthing room, bedding, etc. At Edgecomb's we arranged for a man to come and recover the chesterfield in the living room. We had ordered two new chairs in a similar style at Lemont's, so some care was taken to match upholstery fabrics. We also ordered a small phaeton for me, and chose upholstery for that.

At the end of the day, we were at 135 Westmoreland Street, just as the slovens were coming in from the day. Caesar whinnied at me, and Frank had the new mare he bought at the auction. She was a pretty brown mare, and I later learned he called her Betty. Clem was nowhere to be seen, but his grey Percherons were in the yard.

As Thomas dismissed the carriage, I went into the yard and visited with all of the horses. With each of them, I felt for their sore spots and talked with them about how they felt. Caesar had a fall on some ice in the previous week, despite winter shoes. He was still a little sensitive about his right shoulder, but his work did not bother him and he was in good spirits. Betty, the new girl, was sweet and placid, simply putting her head close to me. Her hair coat wasn't great, but Frank was addressing that with rubs and good food. And Clem's greys, standing off to the side, were subdued. They told me that they might be going to a new home, but they didn't know where. Petting them I looked quizzically at Mr. McGuigan and he shrugged.

Just then we heard the most God awful noise, and Frank opened the big gate. And there was the explanation for Clem's absence, the sadness of his horses. Clem had brought home his truck and sounded the horn at the gate. It was a great big black thing, not fitting into the yard while the horses were there. It excreted smelly exhaust. It was made by the Ford Motor Company, and I was indeed the first person to sit in it besides Clem.

When I got out of the truck, I looked back at the Percherons. They were lovely, very experienced, and in excellent condition. And I loved them.

"Clem, I understand you are going to sell these horses."

"Well Miss, I don't want to but work horses have to work, or they will be miserable. I just haven't been able to bring myself to put in ad in the paper."

I looked at him for a moment. "How much do you want?" He gave me a price and then I offered him a generous amount more, on the condition that he bring them to me trained to go single or double, and that they be kept at Westmoreland Street until my carriage was ready.

I looked at Thomas and said "Not a small Phaeton. I will go back tomorrow and work it out."

He answered gently "They won't do anything for you unless your Fiancé is there."

All of the McGuigans quickly averted their eyes and found something else to do.

"They will if they want to get paid."

A few chuckles were suppressed around the room.

It turned out that Thomas had provided the makings of a lovely supper, with a leg of ham and all of the trappings to go with it. Of course, Mrs. McGuigan and Nene had cooked it all, but they would never have had such a meal on a weeknight otherwise, so it was appreciated by all.

As we left for the walk to my rooming house, I thanked Thomas for the day sincerely. But I also pointed out that I did not appreciate plans being made for my time and activities without my express involvement. He looked at me in surprise for a moment, and then nodded.

The next day I went back to Edgecomb's[41] with my cheque book and instructed them to build me a carriage suitable for either one or two Percherons. The proprietor asked if I thought I could drive such powerful horses. Then he asked if Thomas knew what I was doing. And then he asked if he didn't think I should hire a driver.

"Mr. Edgecomb do you want my business or not? I brought my chequebook to appropriately increase your deposit, but if you feel the need to undermine my authority to make this order or to comment further on what you think are my skills, I would be happy to take my business elsewhere."

He looked at me steadily for a moment. Then he told me how the cheque should be. And immediately after I left, he called Thomas to ask permission. To his credit, Thomas said that the

---

[41] Edgecomb's made carriages and other kinds of vehicles, but they also did furniture upholstery in the same way that they upholstered the inside of their vehicles.

order came from me and as such he had no requirement to be involved.

Thomas and I were married on November 15, 1915. The dress was an empire waist, in the beautiful fine delicate blue wool Mrs. McGuigan had shown me. I was married from Westmoreland Street and Caesar took me to my wedding pulling the surrey. If anybody found any of the details odd, they said nothing. A reception party was held at 97 Church Street. And I was no more a Driscoll, not a McGuigan but a de Burgh, of a great old noble family.

It was a remarkable party, attended as it was by all facets of Fredericton society. One of Thomas' lawyer friends did ask if the McGuigans were clients, thankfully out of their earshot.

"Honest and dear friends of my wife's" he answered with a twinkle in his eye, almost daring the man to put his foot farther into the pile he had stepped in.

I was asked more than once who made my beautiful dress. I pointed at Mrs. McGuigan across the room and smiled. She smiled back, every time.

We took a brief honeymoon to Boston about which I remember almost nothing. A lot of walking along the shore and visiting sites important to American history. But it was amiable and companionable, and that I will always remember.

When we returned we fell into a rhythm at home. Mrs. McGuigan found me a woman to help with running the household and doing the cooking, a Mrs. McGinn. We also hired someone to do the scrubbing and cleaning. Thomas and I spent part of every day together, whether it be reading to one another, playing a board game or playing and singing at the beautiful piano that the McGuigans had put in the parlour. In this way we did become friends, or at least happy roommates.

Christmas of 1915 was saddened by war, by yet more casualty lists. But the true highlight, the real highlight, is that Jack went absent without leave and came home from Christmas. I didn't know until on Boxing Day the bell rang for the front door. I opened it to see him standing on the porch in uniform, his hat off and under his arm. He looked better than I could ever have imagined.

As I stood in the doorway staring at him, Thomas came from behind, offering Jack his hand. Clearly Thomas was expecting him.

"Jack! Please come in, please. Would you like a drink? Please, do come in!"

He stood to one side, gently moving me over, as Jack entered our house. We all moved in to the parlour, Thomas steering me to one of the new chairs, allowing Jack to take the settee, newly back from reupholstering. His eyes roamed around the room, taking in the furniture, the piano. They rested briefly on the medieval chair.

"So how goes the training Jack?" asked Thomas, to fill the space in the room.

Jack's eyes flicked toward me, and then back to Thomas. "Well Sir, we have spent so much time marching I think there is some strategy to beat the Huns by simply marching us all over them. Depending how things go overseas, the brass says that we will probably ship out by late summer ". His eyes came back to me as he said this last.

There was another pause until finally Thomas spoke again. His voice was calmer this time, without the forced jollity. "Look, this is a decidedly awkward situation. There probably isn't another like it anywhere on earth. If we are all going to make it work, we need to get some things out in the open." Nodding at me, "Charlotte taught me that. So let me say a few things and get it out of the way.

"We all know that baby Charlotte is carrying is your child Jack. And I know without a shadow of doubt how much love is in this room. I'm deeply sorry I'm not part of it. Just let me say that it is my intention never to come between the child and its father. I don't know how the two of you, and to a lesser extent, myself, are going to handle all this. But we will. Jack I wish you to have no hesitation about coming here, ever. "

He sat for a second, looking back and forth. "Look I will leave the two of you alone. I am sure you have much to say."

Jack stood up and shook Thomas' hand, nodding as he did so. When Thomas had left the room, he turned to me, pulled me from my chair. I cried as I stood there before him. I had missed him so much, thought of him every second. He wiped the tears from my face and I noticed a bandage on his thumb.

"Caught it in my rifle" he said with a smile.

"Is that what you train for besides marching?"

"Well the rifle we are training with is not the one we will be using. Overseas we will be issued with the Ross rifle that the Brits are using. All the same, we drill to take it apart, put it together, load and shoot. It's noisy." A smile.

"Would you show me your lovely new home?" he asked.

I took him on a tour, paying special attention to the nursery and to my room. I was decorating both in yellow, just in case. I showed him the birthing room, and how my windows overlooked the new stable. I took him downstairs, through the kitchen and out the back door. We visited Samson and Delilah.

He approved of the stable, the new carriage fitted for winter with runners. As I saw him out the back gate, it started to snow, big fat, fluffy, flakes.

"I could never give this to you. (A wave of his hand encompassing the house and stable). And I would feel useless and unmanly if you gave it to yourself. But I am very glad Thomas is being so generous. I'm so happy for you. And relieved. I know I let you down, we let each other down, but I think you will be happy here. I see what you mean about him being good and kind. Give him my thanks."

He walked out into the snow, turned left and headed for Queen Street, for home on the other side of town.

A letter came from Patricia later in the week. They came often and they were always interesting, interested and supportive. I missed her tremendously but her letters helped.

December 24 1915

Dear Charlotte;

I hope that you and Thomas have had a lovely Christmas, as it will be by the time you read this. I have finally left England, and am "Somewhere in France". I am sure the Huns know where all our major field hospitals are as they fly over us with their biplanes often, but we are not supposed to disclose our location. .

I see men from the Fighting 26th New Brunswick Battalion from time to time. The injuries that come through here break my heart, not that I could ever admit it to anyone here. Gun shot and shrapnel wounds (caused by bombs that shatter) are the most common. If I survive this, I will be able to stomach anything.

You must be getting pretty big and showing by now. I hope you have begun seeing Doctor Bridges. He is older, but he knows how to care for a pregnant woman. Our mothers would never have seen a doctor during pregnancy, and it is an extra expense, but it's a modern world dear Charlotte, and your baby deserves every chance.

There are plenty of handsome fellows here, some doctors, some patients and medics. No one I would set my cap for, but it sure is lovely to be surrounded by them.

Oh, and you will never guess who I ran into. Harry Spare has transferred from 26th to the Field

Ambulance brigade. He has changed a lot, not the brash fellow you once knew. He was driving an ambulance when I saw him, but he said he is actually a stretcher bearer, going out in the action to find injured men. A God Awful job if you ask me. Keep him in your prayers if you can.

Take care Charlotte. If I can find someone with a Brownie camera I might make use of it.

Love always

Patricia.

We stood with the McGuigans and beside Jack for the New Year's parade. Each man carried a candle, and wore black arm bands in memory of the men overseas. We had our own candles to be lit in response to those marching by. When the time came, Jack produced one of those strike anywhere matches that he always had with him and struck it on his shoe before lighting our three candles, with the little skirts on them to keep the wax from dripping on our hands. As he marched by, I thought Mr. McGuigan looked exhausted and sadder than the occasion called for. He didn't look at Jack.

After the parade we retired to Westmoreland Street for hot chocolate. The atmosphere was convivial enough and there was much singing – such beautiful voices that family had – and we stayed to count in the New Year.

Jack came to take his leave, explaining he was going back the next day. I hugged him tight, and every eye in the house turned to see. Then he shook Thomas' hand, and went off to bed. His father hadn't said a word to him.

Before we left, I approached Mr. McGuigan, out of earshot of the others.

"Mr. McGuigan it hurts me to see you so sad. If I am in any way responsible for your misery, please let me atone".

His eyes welled with tears as he looked at me. "No Miss, Lottie has apprised me of the entire situation, and I think I agree that you have made a workable choice. I would prefer that you married the father of your child, but I understand why you did not. It's a new and strange world my girl. Perhaps it has passed me by and now I've lost my son, my oldest son. I don't even know what to say to him."

I was pretty sure Mrs. McGuigan hadn't told him everything, and for no money on earth would I disabuse him of his notion of events. I had no need to hurt him further.

"May I make a suggestion?"

He lifted his head in my direction.

"Please go say goodnight to your son. Let him talk to you. Forgive him if you can. I truly don't believe you have lost him. I think it is good and right that he have opinions of his own. He is aching for you to speak to him."

"I just don't know that I can forgive him Miss. I don't know that I can talk to him without losing my temper." The muscles in his jaw flexed and tightened.

"Try". I touched his cheek before I walked away.

I don't know if it worked. The next day Jack was gone back to Saint John and I didn't see Mr. McGuigan for a few days, by which time it was out of mind. But Mrs. McGuigan did ask what I had said him, and nodded pensively when I told her.

104 Reserve Bttn

Saint John

January 9, 1916

Dearest Charlotte;

It was so lovely to see you at Christmas. You look wonderful, with that blush in your cheeks that expectant women sometimes have.

I know you did what you had to do, and it seems that Thomas really is the nice fellow you told me he would be. What a shame that he is unable to be the real husband a woman should have.

It is a very strange arrangement the two of you have, and I am not very comfortable with it. You could probably tell that. But you are a married woman now, whatever your arrangement is, and so

I can only ever be your friend. I hope you understand that.

I am trying so hard to do the right thing, in the face of the mistake I made in the summer. If I hadn't disappointed you and sent you away, everything would be different now. For this I will have to pay for the rest of my life.

Whatever happens when I go overseas, know that I will never know another like you.

With love

Jack

Hearing me crying, Thomas came running through the house. He picked me up, put me on my bed, and lay with me until the sobbing had subsided. I handed him the letter.

After reading it, he said over and over, "I'm so sorry Charlotte, I'm sorry."

When I was finally quiet, he said "Men like me learn to live outside the rules of polite society, because it is the only way we can seek happiness. We forget that the rest of the world does not share our acceptance of odd arrangements."

Throughout January, Clem would come in the evenings and teach me to drive the horses he loved so much, the horses that were now mine. We started by driving one horse at a time with the carriage hitched behind. Both horses excelled, as I knew they would. It was a revelation to me the way

I could touch the reins and feel the mood and the intent of the horse. I had always known that horses and their drivers had a special relationship, but now I knew that the good drivers, the really good ones, like the McGuigans, were in an almost telepathic relationship with their equine partners.

We drove all over Fredericton, up and down Queen Street and King, up the hill on the Regent Street and back down again. We went over to Smythe, to the Railway Station and up and down Westmoreland.

When the day came to hitch the team, I knew every nuance of harnessing, getting the britchin in the right spot, seating the collar properly over the collar bones, making sure the hames sit correctly in the notch and are even. A well-made and correctly fitted harness is a miracle of engineering, designed to maximize the horse's comfort and safety so that he can be successful in the job he performs for the driver. I knew how to use saddle soap and water, how to oil and polish. I wanted to learn, and there is nothing as wonderful as the smell of harness leather, saturated with the smells of horse and oils, polish and soap.

Harnessing a team is increased in complexity by adding the yoke, which connects the two horses and lets them feel each other's movements and keeps them working together. Each horse is connected to the load, in this case the carriage, by a separate system, called Whipple trees. The weight of the load travels up the traces to the collar, placing it squarely on the horse's shoulders. This allows for the most natural movement of the horse, pulling against the load with the shoulders, aided by the haunches.

Clem drove the team to the fairgrounds, over by the race track. The parking lot was a big empty space which allowed for a few errors, and Clem was there with me.

Teams work together in more than just the bearing of a load. They work together psychologically as well, reassuring and informing one another about everything from road conditions to a shift in the load as it glides along the ground. Horses are prey animals, and as such they are always assessing potential threats regardless of their current activity. This can be disastrous if they are confronted by things like cars, fire bells, barking dogs etc. with which they have never been acquainted. A great deal of effort goes into "bomb-proofing" so that the horse experiences very few surprises in the course of its work. It also becomes the driver's responsibility not just to assure the horses that they are safe, but to allow them to feel his own sense of calm and confidence through the reins.

Driving a team of horses is like being attached to a shooting star. The combined power of their two bodies can accomplish limitless tasks for mankind from pulling loads of lumber to moving train engines in the railyard. And they do it willingly for us, in exchange for a safe and comfortable existence.

There in the fairground, when I put my two hands on the reins (one for right, one for left) it was like there was an electric current running right up my arms. I started carefully, learning what it took to get them to transition from a stop to a walk, to a trot, and then back down again. We did wide turns and tight ones, and I did make a few mistakes. I learned humility, and joy, and euphoria. I had never felt anything like it.

We went to the fairground about four times, as I recall, before I felt confident enough to take them on the road. And then one evening, as the days were lengthening in February, I took them down the Woodstock Road along the river, at a trot, and for a short while, I let them canter. The weight of the carriage was light, and they were gleeful. I felt sorry when I asked them to slow down, but I still felt their gratitude wafting up at me.

Every time I took control of the team, there was the finest thread of absolute panic underscoring my joy. I loved them and I trusted them, but I did have both subconscious and conscious knowledge that if I ever let my attention wander, if I trusted them just too much, that there could be very, very serious consequences.

During this period, my dreams, always vivid, took a new twist. I dreamed of a team of beautiful greys, young, mares, being handled roughly, wrongly, by young men who did not know the consequences. The longer I worked with the team, the less often I had this dream until it finally went away.

Of course, I was getting a bit of a reputation in Fredericton. Many of the residents felt my husband should rein me in. A woman driving was bad enough, but a woman in the third trimester of pregnancy driving a team of Percherons all over town was absolutely unseemly. And there were still a few dark whispers about how I had been going with Jack McGuigan and then suddenly married the very rich Mr. de Burgh esq.

I certainly didn't care. I remember those months as some of the happiest in my life. I wrote to Patricia and Jack of the joy of it, and how I took to it as if it was all I had ever been meant to do. As if I had done it since the beginning of time and just didn't know it.

Of course, Thomas was regularly approached by well-meaning (and some not so well meaning) busy bodies, insisting that my activities should be curbed as they would damage his reputation as a lawyer.

I once over-heard one of these exchanges. I loved Thomas' response.

"Well madam, if my clients are more concerned with the conduct of my wife than they are with my ability as a lawyer, then I suspect there are larger problems than that she loves to drive our horses around the city at night. I assure you that she is in all other respects the ideal spouse and I am fiercely proud of her".

I spent my days running the household, planning the meals, etc., and working for Thomas as his clerk. I took dictation and typed his letters, made telephone calls on the brand new telephone in his office, and filing papers away in the cabinets. We had become fast friends.

I was the only one who knew all the details of all the cases Thomas was working on. I knew who he thought was guilty and who he thought was innocent, and I know it was a matter of ethic to him to defend both equally well. He fumed when he felt someone was being railroaded. I was proud to be a part of the work he was doing. It was an honest crusade.

By March, I was enormous. Mrs. McGuigan had let my maternity dresses out as far as they would go. Dr. Bridges said I was either carrying twins or a longshoreman from Saint John Harbour. My feet would swell if I stood up too long, and I took my rings off and stored them in the safe in the office. I was tired by about two in the afternoon and would have to take a nap.

Mrs. McGuigan was now helping with the household, and helping to prepare for the birth. The birthing room was stacked high with towels, the bed covered with layers of butcher's paper and then made with two layers of luminous white sheets. There were multiple pillows, one long and cylindrical. I knew she knew exactly as she was doing, so I simply gave her permission to proceed as she saw fit. Dr. Bridges, a midwife and Mrs. McGuigan would all be there for the birth. Every day I realized how my own mother should have behaved, and every day I thanked God fervently for this quiet, determined, and clever woman.

March 3, 2016

Dear Charlotte;

I have now been permanently assigned to No. 3 Canadian Stationary Hospital, well as permanently as things get in war time. We treat men coming from the front who have been wounded. Many of them we can simply treat here and send them back, but the worst wounded come here too. We stabilize them as best we can and then they are transferred to England, usually Liverpool, by hospital train and then hospital ship across the Channel.

This is deeply satisfying work. I don't know how I will ever go back to taking temperatures and treating rashes when I go home. The men have a haunted look about them when they arrive. Some talk about what they have seen, horrible, horrible things, but most do not. Instead they joke, smoke cigarettes and offer to marry me. If that's what they have to do to feel all right, then I will indulge it in perpetuity.

Is it bad if I say I don't really miss home? Oh yes, I miss Mother and Father, my brothers, and you. But that is different than missing home. This is a horrible place, and bad things are happening to these poor dear men. But here I am useful, and my skills and my intelligence are respected.

You will be ready to burst by now. If Dr. Bridges says you are going to have twins, he knows what he is talking about. It's very important now that you rest. And tell Mother McGuigan that I, too, am deeply grateful for her attentions.

With Love

Patricia

Rest. That is all I did for the last half of February
and into March. Mrs. McGuigan taught me to knit,
as something useful I could do that didn't involve
rising from a reclining position. It took me a while
to get the hang of it, but then I started knitting
socks with a pattern drafted out for me on paper.
Once I had done two pair of socks, beautiful soft
wool appeared in my basket, enough to make a
baby blanket – or two.

March 12 1916

Dear Charlotte;

*Mother has written to me that the doctor thinks
you will have twins, and that you will probably
deliver any time now. Do I have the right to be
excited, that a child or children I helped create is
coming into the world? I know I am not there, and a
father should be there, even one who is not your
husband. I suppose it's better that I don't blow your
cover, that no one knows your baby is mine. But
know that I am painfully aware of what you are
going through just now, and wish that I could lend
my support.*

Your dear friend

Jack

On March 16, Dr. Bridges advised that I move into the birthing room. It was an awkward place to sleep as the butcher's paper crinkled each time I moved. Pregnant women everywhere make jokes about being a beached whale. I am witness to the fact that it's not a joke – in fact I could have given most whales a run for their money. I had trouble turning over, couldn't sleep for longer than a few hours. And then I woke up convinced I had wet the bed.

I suppose Mrs. McGuigan heard me muttering at myself about peeing the bed at my age, and she came to see, turning on the overhead light.

What was in the bed was not urine. It was pale yellow on the white sheets and contained little bits of what I can only describe as – well, never mind.

The midwife arrived in less than a half an hour, summoned, I suppose, by a telephone call from downstairs. I stood up to allow the bed to be layered with towels. And then I felt not that my body was trying to expel a baby, but that I had eaten bad meat about three weeks prior, and was now suffering the cramps from a sort of delayed food poisoning. Bad food poisoning. I might be dying.

This is joyous? This is fulfillment?

The midwife, a Mrs. Kelly, had only been in Canada for a few short months. She checked very private parts of me every few minutes and reported back to Mrs. McGuigan, whose job was apparently to wipe my face and tell me stories about her children and her life, and her wonderful grandmother, so that I did not feel fear.

Dr. Bridges arrived just as I stopped feeling that I had food poisoning, and started to push.

Except that I wasn't pushing to Mrs. Kelly's satisfaction. The reason being that I was terrified of evacuating from the wrong place and soiling the bed again. This is absolutely unacceptable in Western Society. Don't poop your pants, don't poop the bed, don't poop anywhere but in appropriately designated places and in the deepest of privacy. So I pushed out with one hole and held in with the other.

Mrs. Kelly lost patience with me.

"Now you looket here!" She yelled, in her Irish brogue. "When I tell you to push, you're going to push, and you're going to feel like you're splittin' from your coont to your face! But I'll tell you something – it's not goin' back in!" The crudeness of her assertions seemed to surprise only me. I suppose childbirth is such a primal act that all pretences of civilization can be dropped without anyone taking notice. But step outside the door of the birthing room and civilization will reassert itself.

Mrs. McGuigan was now standing with a warm wet cloth just to one side of Mrs. Kelly. I surmised what her role was. At least a stranger wouldn't be doing the wiping.

You spend your whole life being told that certain parts of you are deeply private, that no one should ever see them, even the father of your children who supposedly procreates with his eyes closed. And then you have a baby. A group of people assembles in a little room to watch you and to stare and prod this very private part regularly and to assess its fitness to evacuate an object the size of a Christmas turkey. And then when said Christmas turkey begins to make an appearance, they cheer it on. And then they catch it.

A little boy was born shortly after I gave up trying to be delicate, his sister following him two minutes later. They were small, but healthy, with lusty big lungs. They both evacuated the contents of their bowels built up during gestation, smearing me on the way out of my body and into the arms of the helpers there in the room. This childbirth is a dirty business.

I was vaguely aware that there were suddenly raised voices and that Thomas was called but I was so tired that I remember very little past that point.

When next I opened my eyes, the daylight coming in the window revealed Jack's face as he dozed in the chair beside my bed. He was holding my hand.

He started and looked into my eyes for a moment before calling "Dr. Bridges! She's back!"

I was confused by wherever I might have been, but I loved that he was there beside me, holding my hand, face all concerned. An irritation in my arm alerted me to a needle inserted there, with a tube that led to a glass bottle hanging from a stand. The fluid in the bottle was clear.

"Well Mrs. De Burgh you gave us all quite a scare. How are you feeling?"

And then I remembered.

"My babies! Where are they? What have you done with my babies?" I cried out as I bolted up in the bed.

Jack caught my shoulders and gently pushed me back down to the bed. "Shh my girl, they are safe, they are safe. They are just down the hall. We had to get a wet nurse for a bit, but they are safe."

I looked at him, confused. A wet nurse? "Why?"

"Mrs. De Burgh you had a bit of a complication. You have been sleeping for three days. If it weren't for the fast thinking of Mrs. Kelly, we might have lost you. You had a uterine hemorrhage, bleeding that is, and Mrs. Kelly knew just where to apply pressure to get the bleeding to stop ". He nodded at the bottle. "Just a precaution. I find it helps the mother recover faster. New medicine. In a little while I will remove the needle, and if you continue to recover we will bring your babies to you." He left the room, left Jack with me.

"You came after all" I said, settling back into my pillow.

"I couldn't stay away." His blue eyes bored into mine.

"I was so frightened" he whispered. "Thomas and I have been taking turns here by your bed so that the others could sleep. Could you hear me talking to you?"

"I don't know. I dreamed. You were there. It was the oddest thing. You showed me how to make a fishing line out of a horse's tail hair. And then we were hiding in a wood, laying on our bellies in the

433

long grass. We had a little girl with us, a girl that was my daughter. And then we were in another wood, and there was an owl. And then you were older, sitting up on horseback, smiling down on me. It was all strange and tumbled together."

He looked at me steadily for a moment. "I have had that dream too, about the owl. Just a brief flash. It flew away and then there was an arrow."

"Jack I am tired again. Will you stay with me while I sleep?"

"Charlotte I have to go back soon. I have gone absent without leave again. If Christmas was any indication, I will be scrubbing floors for at least a week. I can't imagine why there is anything left of those floors what with the number of people scrubbing them." He grinned.

I must have fallen asleep then, and the next time I woke he was gone, and it was Thomas sitting beside me. He wore his spectacles on his nose and was reading what appeared to be a legal brief. He didn't see me watching him as his pencil scribbled here and there.

The next time I woke, I was ravenously hungry, and Mrs. McGuigan had come into the room with a small plate of food. It smelled so good my mouth watered. She tried to feed me, but I took the fork and fed myself.

My babies were brought to me four days after their birth. Mrs. Kelly taught me to nurse them and assured me that my milk would flow and I would be able to feed them quite normally. She was right of course, but it took a few days.

434

The days flew by after that, a round of eating, sleeping and feeding babies, into early April. We intended to baptize them on Easter Sunday. We agonized over names, like any new parents.

April 10, 1916

Dear Charlotte;

Thank goodness I finished floor scrubbing duty (officially "confined to barracks") about a week ago, and am back to the mind numbing routine of marching, shooting, sports, marching, and a bit more marching. We are basically ready and are just biding our time until it is time to go overseas.

As for name suggestions, I love the names Joan, Alice, Evelyn, and Eudora for a girl. Took a lot of thought that. For a boy, why not stay away from the names of father or grandfather etc. and start a new tradition? Let the boy grow to be his own man. I like Archibald, and Alastair. Not sure what I think of your suggestion of Maurice.

I am managing to keep my fingers out of my rifle bolt now. Hope that makes you smile.

I might try to come home for Easter. I am trying to spend as much time with family as I can before I go. Once we ship out I don't know when I will see you all again. The brass are letting us get off pretty lightly for it, because they know we are getting fed up with endless marching and drill.

Let me know what you decide about names.

Love

Jack

Thomas was in favour of the aristocratic habit of children having many names to reflect their heritage, right back to the days of William the Conqueror if necessary. We all have our family traditions. In the end, our daughter became Joan Ellis Charlotte Patricia de Burgh, the spelling of Alice being after a female ancestor of Thomas. Our son become Alistair John Maurice Thomas de Burgh. We joked that they had so many names that they would be worn out from carrying them by the time they were adults.

By the time the babies were two weeks old, the wet nurse was gone entirely, despatched with my sincere thanks and a generous payment. Mrs. McGuigan had a household of her own to run, and so a nurse was hired to come during the daytime to assist in the feeding and care of the children. I was still encouraged by Dr. Bridges to sleep as much as possible, so not to risk reopening the rupture that had caused the bleeding. Mrs. Kelly came one day a week to check on the babies and the healing of their umbilici and to ensure they were putting on weight. She would also examine me, and she disagreed with Dr. Bridges about my fitness for daily activities. In deference to him however she didn't encourage me to be up and around, but she did insist that I stretch gently each day to prevent blood clots.

My babies were an endless source of joy to me. Simple acts like holding them, feeding them, washing their little bodies, and kissing their cheeks filled me with happiness. I suppose every mother loves her babies in this way. But I also had the richness and kindness of an adopted extended family, and the devoted support of Thomas and Jack.

My life would be perfect, if only I could have driven the horses in that time. No one knew, but once the needle was out I would sometimes tiptoe out to the stable to see them. Clem and his friend Murray Head were exercising them regularly for me. I would kiss their noses and promise that we would be out again together soon.

When you leave people you knew in the past, they stay fixed in your mind, as if they will never change. I hadn't spoken to my family in more than a year, but something prompted me to write to them and advise them of my altered circumstances and the birth of their grandchildren. I received a response shortly thereafter.

April 5, 1916

Stormwell

Dear Mrs. De Burgh:

Thank you for your letter informing us of your marriage and the birth of your children. We did however already know of the change in your circumstances, as we received legal documents preventing us from ever accessing your inheritance, and served by one Mr. Thomas Fitzgerald de Burgh Esq. I presume he has now absorbed your small fortune into his own considerable estate (we are aware of the position of his family). I cannot imagine why he would be so greedy when your own father had more right to that money. Perhaps in later years your husband will see the error of his ways and return those funds to their rightful owner.

Regardless of your husband's failings, not to mention your own, I must express relief that you abandoned your rebellious connection with the papist street urchin and his thieving family. Why you chose to consort with such dirty people is beyond me. I can't imagine what you saw in them except an opportunity to cause grief to your family.

I also kindly inform you that you no longer have brothers. Charles and Simon both signed up, against our wishes, and fought overseas. I received a wire just a few days ago telling me that Charles was killed by a sniper on March 17, and Simon was bayoneted just a few days later. The military has seen fit to leave them where they fell. Why they would do such a ghastly thing rather than send them home to be buried with family members I cannot imagine.

Yours Truly

Mrs. Driscoll

It would take me years to recover from the spitefulness, narcissism and utter self-absorption of this dreadful letter. As always, contact with my Mother made me worry that I might have some common personality traits with her, that I might in some way reflect her. Fortunately I was raised by a long succession of nannies, country girls from outside Moncton, whose down to earth approach to life encouraged more practicality and kindness in me than my Mother would ever have intended. I hope.

The news about my brothers was a source of bitter sadness. While I really had no time for Simon, who was so like my Mother, I rather liked Charles. Their deaths, so close to one another in time, sparked feeling in me much deeper than I ever would have expected. My Mother's dismissal of their service, and the circumstances of their deaths infuriated me

I was still angry and sad by the time Jack arrived home again on April 16 in time to go to church with his family at Saint Dunstan's on Regent Street. He only had a few days, and although he had hoped to come home for Easter a week later, he was advised that staying that long would be unwise. Apparently absences without leave were increasingly being frowned on where they had not been before. When Jack had discussed with his sergeant about the birth of the babies and his need to see his mother as much as possible, the sergeant said "Go. Hurry back. And get your floor scrubbing fingers on."

On Monday, Mrs. McGuigan, Jack, Nene and Allie arrived on the verandah, and they came bearing gifts. There were layettes knitted by women from all over town it seemed, my favourite foods, and gifts for the children. Jack had a silver rattle, with names inscribed, for each of the babies.

Thomas was in court that afternoon, so he did not get to join in the party. I knew the case he was working on was a demanding one, so I refrained from asking him to postpone. He needed to be left alone with it just then.

Everyone took turns holding the babies. Allie held them each like they were made of glass. She had held Clem's children as babies, but because they lived a distance away, she didn't have the experience that being an older sibling would have given her.

Nene had held at least two of her siblings and helped to care for them. Her hands were confident but tender, and her face was ....wistful. I looked at her perfect skin, dark like her mother's, and her pretty face. I just could not imagine why she wasn't married long since to have the babies she obviously longed for.

Jack held his children as if he had been doing so all his life. He stroked their cheeks. He kissed their foreheads. He calmed them naturally when they fussed. Allie joked about how it was sad that Jack could not give birth – he was obviously a natural.

I watched these people, so beloved to me, watched them cuddling and loving my babies. I was overtaken by love, and tenderness for them, and something else. There was a mixture of sadness and foreboding. As if it were all of them about to go away for a long time. I couldn't shake it.

Mrs. McGuigan looked at me. "What's wrong?"

When I waved her off she insisted. "I know your face young Miss, I held you when we thought you were dying. What's wrong?"

I paused for a minute and then I said "I'm just cherishing the moment. You are some of my favourite people".

They insisted they could not stay for supper. They were just all headed out the front door when Thomas was coming in. He was polite as they left, but his face was ashen.

"How did court go today? Did you win?"

He was quiet for a minute, as if he was swirling around what he had to say in his mouth before he spat it out.

"He got off. The defense said it was her own fault, since she was pretty and she wore her hair done to emphasize it. She showed her ankles too much. She should have known if she smiled at him that he would attack her, rape her, and beat her to a pulp. The jury ate it up. They sucked it up like rats drinking blood when you kill a pig."

I simply sat quietly. I knew there was nothing I could say. The best I could do was listen to his words and try to understand.

"She's thirteen years old! And then they put her father on the stand, and he testified that her mother regularly tempts her father in this way, coquettishly, until he attacks her. This was supposed to be proof that a thirteen year old girl knew that she was asking for it and wanted to be beaten almost to death.

"I couldn't believe it. What could I say to her? How could I tell her that sometimes the world is just wrong?"

As he was speaking I followed him and he paced around the house. I hung up his coat and his hat, made it clear that I was listening to every single word he said. Tears welled up in my eyes, spilled down my cheeks. But I listened and I never made a sound.

"I'm sorry Charlotte. I shouldn't upset you so. But thank God you understand."

He hugged me, kissed my hair, and then turned and trudged up the stairs to his room and closed the door.

Knowing to leave well enough alone, I had a quiet supper with Mrs. McGinn and retired to my room. I lay down for a bit, knowing I would have to feed the babies around eleven.

I woke up at eleven and the house was very quiet. Thomas' room was soundless, but he could have been asleep. He could also have been sitting in his chair with a glass of bourbon. He could have been still upset.........I knocked on the door.

"Thomas? Are you there? Are you all right?"

Hearing still nothing at all, I tried the door. It was unlocked. I stepped into his room. I was immaculately tidy, and completely empty. The bed was still made, and nothing seemed disturbed. I thought back to the second time I had ever been in this house, the day I insisted that his private life never touch our home life. And I thought about the man sneaking down the back stairs and out the back door.

I felt sad and upset, but I told myself I had no right to be so. After all, he had accepted the McGuigans as his in-laws and Jack as a dear friend, in the same way he would if Jack had been a woman. He had accepted Jack's children as his own. What right did I have to complain?

I fed the babies when they woke. Midnight came. No Thomas. One o'clock. Still no Thomas.

At two I woke Mrs. McGinn and asked her to watch over the babies. I hitched up the horses to the carriage and headed out.

As I handled the leather, connected the yoke to the pole, slipped bits into mouths, I argued with myself. Maybe he was with a friend. Maybe he was somewhere I really didn't want to find him. I didn't want to see. Maybe he needed me to find him. Maybe he was hurt.

There was a place on Queen Street that had a bit of a reputation. Music, many men, scantily clad women. I started there. I pulled up across the street, by the wall of the regimental barracks (unoccupied by the military since the 1870's but still used). Out the door of the place came two familiar faces. Jack and Clem.

Their faces were florid, they were slurring their words, but when I told them Thomas had not come home, they became more serious.

"Oh stop being such a nervous hen Char" Clem said in a patronizing tone.

"Don't talk to me like that Clem McGuigan. I know the difference between what it would feel like to have him defy me and what it would feel like if something were wrong. This feels wrong."

Jack put his hand on Clem's arm and said "I'll go".

"I bet you will" said Clem with an unpleasant leer.

I would have hit him, really hit him then, but Jack was climbing up and got in the way.

He stood beside me and said quietly "It's alright. I know how it is when you have to go with your feelings. And I think I might know where he is."

And to Clem "Go home and sober up Clem, before you say something I will make you regret."

He directed me to drive on. We went up a side street and back down King. We went down past my house and out to Waterloo Row. The water of the river was lapping up over the banks, and there were ice chunks out in the current. I allowed myself to reflect for just a moment. What a difference a year makes.

We drove past the Lieutenant Governor of New Brunswick's mansion, where there were lights on. In front of the university we turned left and headed out the Lincoln Road. There was a place out there, right along the river, that had once been a very respectable home, but time and shifting fortunes had turned it into something considerably less desirable.

I pulled the horses up in front. Music was playing, and there was the same flow of drunk men in and out, but there was something different here. Ah yes. There were no women. Dear God, where had my life ended up.

Jack went in, attracting much attention from the partiers in his uniform. He gently repelled their advances, where a lesser man would have felt angry and threatened. I thought if I could ever get Jack to tell all his stories, how fascinating it might be.

He was inside for several minutes. Several men walked past the carriage, doffing their caps at me. A few asked if I was alright Miss, sitting there with my horses and carriage outside a bar full of homosexual men in the middle of the night. I asked a few if they knew Thomas de Burgh as he was missing from home and we were worried. They looked right at me and said No. They were lying. I could tell that they thought I didn't know, and they had to protect him from my wrath. I mean, a cheating husband is bad enough, but this kind of cheating? There was no way in HELL they were going to tell me, I was not a member of their little private world.

Jack came out and climbing up beside me said "Let's go?"

I urged Samson and Delilah on, and into a trot.

"Where are we going?"

"Along the Green."

"But we just passed there and we didn't see anything."

"We wouldn't have" he said.

I turned the horses around back toward town and Waterloo Row. The Lieutenant Governor's guests were finally leaving, a well-dressed group in tuxedos and evening gowns. Carriages were pulling up in front of the door, but there were a few of the new hand drive cars too.

Jack urged me onto the Green itself just past the tennis courts which were partly underwater.

"We aren't supposed to drive on the Green, it wrecks the turf. I could get a ticket for this!"

Putting his hand over mine and very serious, he said "Just trust me and do as I say."

It was pitch dark and the carriage lamps only gave so much relief. We went along not speaking, and even the horses did not make a snort or moan. Just the sound of their feet and the wheels crushing the grass as we went along.

We were almost coming up behind the cathedral and not far from our house when we heard something. We stopped, not hearing anything again for several minutes. And there it was, a moan in a voice hoarse with calling out for help, from despairing that help would ever come.

We both jumped down, but Jack said "Tie up the horses!" with a hand gesture that made it clear that I was not to follow him. Samson and Delilah followed his voice, watched him walk over to a large pine tree growing there. There was a dark shape behind the tree, its shadow protruding on either side of the trunk.

"It's not Thomas, but he's badly hurt. We need to get him help. Can you bring the carriage closer?"

I pulled the carriage as close as I dared.

"Do you have a blanket in the trunk?" he asked, nodding at the storage box on the back of the vehicle.

I hopped down, giving the horses the ground tie command. "Don't move".

There were a couple of large wool blankets and a quilt in the trunk. I sacrificed a wool blanket, which we then rolled the man into. Getting him into the carriage was tricky. Jack kept trying to lift and carry the man all by himself, and I ran around him trying to catch the bits that fell. It was like those moving pictures where the characters do preposterous things to make everyone laugh. But this wasn't funny. This was punctuated by the cries of a man in pain, where every move increased his suffering.

We laid him on the floor of the carriage. I stayed with him while Jack cantered the horses past the cathedral and pulled up in front of the house. The poor man moaned with every bump. I had never seen anyone suffer so much.

The verandah light was on, and Thomas and Mrs. McGinn came out the front door. I was surprised and angry to see Thomas because he had frightened me so. But there was no time to lose. Thomas and Jack brought the poor man into the house and laid him on the floor. Mrs. McGinn called Dr. Bridges, and I stayed with him, talking to him. He was crying on and off and occasionally softly calling a name.

"Thomas!"

I felt a sensation like all of my organs were plunging off a cliff. Could he be calling another Thomas? It was not an uncommon name. Maybe his own name was Thomas? But I knew. Neither of those things were true.

Thomas and Jack came down the stairs, having dismantled a bed from a spare room. They pushed the dining room table aside, and set up the bed on one side of the dining room. When they brought down the mattress, Mrs. McGinn was ready with the bedding. Then she disappeared for a few minutes, and came back with a large bowl of warm water from the tank on the side of the stove, and a wash cloth. I started the process of getting him cleaned up.

As I did so, Thomas was watching me. He looked miserable.

"Charlotte, your horses are still standing out front. Why don't you go put them away and I will take care of this."

"I'll do that" said Jack, heading out. Whatever was going on here, Jack knew, and so did Thomas, and I was the only one in the dark. But before I could ask, Dr. Bridges came in the front door.

"Good evening, or should I say good morning. Oh dear, poor chap has had a very bad night. All right, let's lift him carefully on the bed. One, two, and three..."

The poor man cried out at being moved again. We laid his body on the clean sheets, and Thomas and I continued to remove his clothes, so Dr. Bridges could assess all of his injuries. And at last, Dr. Bridges pulled morphine out of his bag to give the poor fellow some comfort.

"All right, let's just see who the poor fellow is. He must have a family worrying somewhere". He reached into the pocket of the man's jacket to find a pocket book in the breast pocket. It had a generous amount of money, a letter, and a few other slips of paper.

Before the papers could be examined any further, Thomas said "His name is Lawrence Bailey. HIs family lives out on the Hanwell Road, but he is not in communication with them. He is a law student up the hill. I know him. I recognize the ring he wears."

Dr. Bridges looked at Thomas for a long minute and then responded "Of course, you'll know him through your legal practice no doubt. "

"Yes, I just finished a terrible case, and he had done some work for me to prepare witnesses. This is — this is very distressing." It wasn't a lie, I knew it, but there was so much beneath the surface of his words.

"Indeed Mr. de Burgh. Perhaps then you would like to take control of his belongings" he said, handing over the pocketbook. As both of their hands were on the pocketbook, Dr. Bridges looked significantly at Thomas and then let go.

Just then the babies cried. It was six in the morning. How time flies when it feels like your world is crumbling around you.

After feeding the babies and resting for a couple of hours, I reappeared downstairs. Mr. Bailey's condition had not changed, but now there was a glass bottle and a tube feeding his body through a needle. Dr. Bridges had gone but said to expect him again in the evening. I asked Thomas if he would recover.

He sighed. "It's too soon to tell. He has taken so many blows to the head. We can actually see boot prints, just there. He has broken bones in his arms where he tried to defend himself. He has bruising all over his legs. There is so much damage between his legs that Dr. Bridges is afraid he might never be able to urinate normally again. He will have to go to Boston for surgery if he is to survive. But he might not live that long."

The seriousness of Mr. Bailey's condition made me speechless. I felt sick to my stomach. My chest hurt.

"What monsters would do such a thing? This is not Montreal or New York. This is Fredericton, where people know almost everyone else that lives here. The people who did this probably knew him. How could anyone hurt another human being like this? Did they intend for him to die?"

He looked back at me, clearly without sympathy.

"Charlotte, this is what people do to men like me. This was a group of three or four men, known to the constables for other attacks like this. You went out last night looking for me, no doubt various others heard Jack inquiring about me, heard someone answer where I had gone. A frantic wife looking for a husband with a secret life is not new in that quarter. I left Lawrence about an hour before you found him. And now Lawrence will die, and I am known to them. And the life that we have built, in part to protect me, is useless for that purpose."

I sat with my mouth open. How many times can one experience that trickling feeling throughout the body before the heart stops? But then the voice in the back of my head began to protest.

"Thomas you went out in the middle of the night without telling anyone you had gone. I feel like I have been drawn into a sweaty, sordid drama, and the whole town will know it. Yesterday we were a respectable, well liked little family, and now with the sun rising I and the children are tainted by your midnight activities. How could you do this to us?"

He stared at me with an expression I had never seen before. He rose from Lawrence's bedside and began to walk toward the stairs. Then he stopped, with his back to Lawrence and me, lifting his right foot, as if to climb the stairs, and then putting it down. Finally he turned to face us, both of us.

"It's all very well for you Charlotte, you and your Jack, and your wildly odd relationship with his family. I like them, I have accepted them, and never questioned how we look in the eyes of our fellow citizens. The talk about you driving the horses at night with Clem McGuigan, big and pregnant, and how shocking it was – it never bothered me, and I defended you every time with good humour and grace. Jack and Mrs. McGuigan were here for the birth of the babies, and I have defended that more than once too. I like the McGuigans very much. They are kind, hardworking and honest. But you have never thought even once about how they affect this household.

"And now in your night dress you have rescued a homosexual man from the Green in the middle of the night. Had you never left this house, Lawrence would have had this assignation with me, and then we would have simply gone to our respective homes. And no one would be the wiser. You should have minded your own business.

"And incidentally had you not demanded that my personal affairs be kept out of this house, none of this would have ever come to pass. I am sure you meant well, but your actions have such repercussions."

He turned and went up the stairs to his room, slamming the door behind him.

And there was Jack standing in front of the kitchen door. He ran to me and I crumpled. He helped me to a chair, a chair which just happened to be the medieval chair.

"Charlotte I have to go back. Thomas is angry, yes, but you will work it out between you. And you can tell him, I never used his name. The other thing you can tell him is that many a wife has gone looking for her wayward husband in the middle of the night. Even when that husband prefers women to men. And Dr. Bridges is obliged to silence. It will be all right my dear. It will be all right."

He kissed me on the forehead, and left.

For the Christening on Easter Sunday, the Cathedral was almost full. The Christening took place as part of the mass, and although many of the parishioners were simply there for Sunday observance, many were there to see, and meet, the twins. There were many of Thomas' clients, past and present. There were acquaintances of us both, and of the McGuigans. The McGuigans themselves were not present. They were attending mass at their own church, St. Dunstan's, over on Regent Street. I thought of them during the service, kneeling, praying and taking communion. I looked at my twins and prayed for their father's safety while Thomas took responsibility for those fatherly spiritual duties. And it didn't feel wrong to me.

Arriving home, there were several carriages lined up down the block, and there was Clem's unmistakeable Ford. As we arrived home a passel of children poured out of its doors. Some were clearly Eva's siblings, and of course Clem and Eva's girls bore resemblance to their parents. Stella, the eldest, ran to us.

"Hello Auntie Charlotte and Uncle Thomas. Can I see the babies?" Her approach drew a smile from Thomas for the first time since Lawrence's injuries.

It was a glorious afternoon, one we really needed. Lawrence had been moved upstairs, and to our surprise, a nurse tended him.

"I took the liberty of getting help for him. I hope you don't mind" said Mrs. McGuigan. I didn't even know she knew, but it shouldn't have surprised me.

The house was full of the laughter of children, the bubbling happy talk of adults, and the noise of babies being spoiled and loved. I didn't care that they would be too stimulated for sleep after. This was a special, wonderful day.

And if christening day was noisy and joyous, Easter Monday was deeply quiet. Thomas read Shakespeare to Lawrence, and Lawrence twitched his fingers and moaned in response. I sat knitting war socks and tended to the babies. And we had leftovers for supper. It was a good, gentle day.

The Tuesday morning paper shattered the peace of Fredericton, populated as it was largely by Irishmen and the parents of fallen soldiers.

EASTER RISING IN DUBLIN

The headline screamed at me from the newspaper laying on the verandah. And I knew what it meant. My heart sunk. There was only one place I wanted to be. I put the babies in their pram, put on a hat, and headed out.

By the time I had walked to Westmoreland Street, a small crowd had gathered outside the McGuigan house. I pushed my way through to the gate.

"Mrs. De Burgh, now that you are a fine lady, I am surprised you should allow yourself to be seen with rabble like the McGuigans" said a middle aged woman I recognized from the market.

I turned around and looked at them all. There were about fifteen people there, all familiar faces for some reason or other. Jeffery McFarland had a rock in his hand, as if he intended to throw it. Two of the Saunders boys were having great fun participating in the spectacle. Mrs. Parker stood with judgemental hands on judgemental hips.

"Scripture says, 'Let he who has not sinned cast the first stone'. Jerry McFarland, you should be ashamed of yourself. The gossip vine has it that just last week you took your daughter out to Doaktown to quietly have a baby and put it up for adoption. And yet you were going to throw a rock through the windows here for something you don't know the details of, and which you don't understand. Isabel Parker, your husband regularly cheats his customers on the price of carrots. Yet here you are harassing the family of a man you know to be deeply honest and kind. And you (pointing at the lady from the market), if it was fine for me to associate with rabble yesterday, then I would be a hypocrite if I did not associate with them today. This is my family.

"You people should be ashamed of yourselves. Go home, and tend to your own failings."

As I finished speaking, a constable arrived. He was prepared to move the crowd along, but they had started to drift away already.

The constable was beside me when the gate opened. He motioned for me to push the pram in ahead of him, but it was clear he was coming with me. Frank closed the door behind us both, locking out the sidewalk beyond.

Mr. McGuigan sat on a stool in the yard, smoking his clay pipe. "Oh great, now everyone's here" he said morosely.

I would have hugged him, but I knew I would be rudely waved away.

"Ah, good morning Mr. McGuigan" the constable began. "I've been asked to talk to you about your political, ah, affiliations." He looked around the yard at the family all assembled but trying to pretend they were there for other purposes. Fred was there, toting water to the horses. Allie was collecting eggs with an angry red face. Mrs. McGuigan was feeding chickens from a black vessel. Frank stood awkwardly beside his father, just out of arm's reach. I took a position with the pram just near the side of the summer kitchen. Caesar and Betty stood dozing in the back corner by the barn.

Just then, the big gate opened again, and in came Thomas, in his most casual suit, but carrying his satchel that he took to the court building. He smiled and nodded at each in turn, and then turned his attention to the constable.

"What seems to be the problem constable?" said with a smile on his face that indicated he was not really in a good mood.

"Well Mr. de Burgh, pleasure to see you sir. I've been asked to talk to Mr. McGuigan about certain funds he has been sending to Ireland."

Thomas raised one eyebrow, and waited. After a minute he looked at the constable and nodded his head, as if to ask a question.

"Ah, well you see sir, once a month for many years, Mr. McGuigan has sent an envelope to an organization in Ireland. The postal clerk, Mrs. Franklyn, attests to it. And Mr. Smith, at the bank, says he withdraws a money order each month, made out to the Dublin Theatre Company."

Thomas paused for a moment, digesting, and shifting tactics to accommodate what he had heard. The lawyer in action.

"So constable, you have two persons willing to divulge information from their occupations dealing with the private information of others, and all you can tell me is that Mr. McGuigan supports a theatre company in Ireland? For all you know, he may be a frustrated poet and actor.

"Constable, did you know that I am Irish? I don't sport the accent, as my education was all taken in England, but I have a great love for Dublin and its cultural activity. I have attended productions put on by that very theatre company, and it supports some of the greatest Irish playwrights of our day.

"No one is more grieved by what is happening in Ireland than I constable. Dublin is my home. And surely the perpetrators of the insurrection were naïve enough to believe they could do this thing peacefully and with honor. They simply neglected to consider that the King is at war, and there is no way he could ever tolerate such a thing sapping away energy and popular opinion from the war. He dealt with it the way I would have, with extreme prejudice, to end it immediately. Any other action on the part of the King would be weak, and would erode public support for the war in England. As it is, while there is sympathy for what the insurrectionists were trying to accomplish, their assumptions about what the King, and the peoples of the British Isles, would tolerate were entirely incorrect. "

There was silence. Thomas had defended Mr. McGuigan, but had chastened him too. The constable was entirely outmaneuvered and seemed to have given up.

"I see" he said. "Well then I shall report your comments to my superiors, and let them know that you are supporting Mr. McGuigan. Let us hope this shall be the end of it. Good day."

Frank let him out through the gate.

As the gate closed, it was like an oppression lifted from the group. Suddenly there was a bustling and a great earnestness to appear normal. Everyone went into the house for tea, and a delightful sort of flat bread that Mrs. McGuigan called bannock. There was home-made raspberry jam from last year.

I did find a few minutes to commune with Caesar and Betty. They were both in excellent form and seemed to have formed a comfortable bond with one another. I couldn't find any soreness or discomfort, but the tension of the last few hours had definitely made an impression on them.

There was a conspicuous silence between Thomas and Mr. McGuigan, but when the time came to leave, Mr. McGuigan came to the door and shook Thomas' hand. When he looked at me, he spoke.

"Now Miss, don't you give me any of your youthful words of wisdom, because you don't have any, and you can wipe that pity off your face."

I responded "Mr. McGuigan you are a curmudgeon, and I love you both in spite of it and because of it."

I hugged him tight, a hug he returned.

Lawrence Bailey had remained in our house, and was the beneficiary of full time nurses and the best care we could give him. The doctor came daily. Enough time had passed that Dr. Bridges was now certain that he could not heal from his injuries. Thomas sat with him daily, reading poetry out loud as well as the latest novels. Lawrence did suffer some agitation from time to time in his comatose state. Dr. Bridges felt that it was due to the brain injuries he had suffered. But when Thomas read to him, the agitation stopped. I was certain that Lawrence was still in there somewhere.

The Friday after Easter there was a knock at the front door. When I opened it to my surprised there stood Rae Bailey, dressed in her customary white blouse and skirt. She wore a simple and elegant hat, and her beauty was as perfect as ever.

"Why Miss Bailey, please come in! What a pleasure to see you!"

She came in, looking around her with partially disguised wonder at the loveliness of the house and its furnishings. She walked to the medieval chair and ran her fingers over the carvings, as if she had seen it before.

And finally "Mrs. De Burgh, thank you for seeing me without an appointment. I understand my brother is in your care."

I suppose my expression must have spoken volumes. And then: "Oh, Mr. Lawrence Bailey is your brother!"

She had an awkward look on her face. "He is estranged from the family, a situation I deeply regret. May I see him?" she asked.

I hesitated for a moment before saying "Your brother's condition is very grave Miss Bailey. I have no objection to you seeing him, but you must prepare yourself."

I led her upstairs and down the hall to where Lawrence lay. Thomas was reading to him.

That will be in warm September,

In the Stillness of the year

When the River Blue is deepest

And the other world is near.

When the apples burn their reddest

And the corn is in the sheaves

I shall stir and waken lightly

At a footfall in the leaves

It will be the Scarlett Hunter,

Come to tell me time is done;

On the idle hills for ever

There will stand the idle sun

There the wind will stay to whisper

Many wonders to the reeds

But I shall not fear to follow

Where my Scarlett Hunter Leads.[42]

As Thomas read, Lawrence's face moved ever so slightly in response to what he heard, either to the voice or the words it intoned. Not recognition per se, but perhaps the sound vibrations in the words stimulated the nerves in the face to move.

I looked at Rae, and the tears were streaming down her face, as if that person lying there who purported to be her brother was some sad imposter. Maybe the disaster that befell him was all a lie, and had befallen this poor creature who bore no resemblance to her brother Lawrence.

But no, this was Lawrence, attested by the hands on the counterpane, and the cleaned and repaired coat that hung in the room in preparation for the need of its owner that would never come. His suit too hung there, cleaned and repaired, as if he would step out of bed and wear it tomorrow. Rae knew these things, and knew right away that this man lying in bed would never sit up and dress again in those familiar things that belonged to her brother.

Thomas yielded his chair to her, and we both left the room, left her alone to make peace with Lawrence in her own way.

When Rae came down stairs, her eyes were red, and her hat was I her hand, a few wispy strands of dark hair having come loose against her neck. When

---

[42] The Grave Tree, Bliss Carman, 1898

461

passing the medieval chair, she touched it again thoughtfully.

She looked directly at me before she said "Have you remembered the wedding?" and then she crumpled to the floor.

And I could have sworn as we picked her up and carried her to the parlour that the delicate form I carried in my arms was that of a young teenage boy, not that of a 33 year old woman in Fredericton New Brunswick.

But then the feeling was gone and I attributed it to stress we were both under, certainly that Rae was under.

"Rae, would you like me to call Frank to come get you and take you home?" I asked her.

She looked confused for a minute, but then responded "Frank McGuigan and I haven't been going together for weeks. No, I will be fine, if I could just have another cup of tea and rest here for a moment, thank you."

I left Thomas with her, his gentlest side being aroused when there was someone in need. I hitched Delilah to the carriage, leaving Samson to enjoy her share of the morning's hay.

When Rae was ready, I took her home to where she lived with her mother and ran a small weaving studio that supported them both.

In the following weeks, Thomas made arrangements for Lawrence, and he included Rae in his thoughts, and together they imposed on her mother that he should be buried in the family plot, with honors.

And so when Lawrence finally died, he was buried beside his father and one older brother. His belongings, except for one small volume of poetry, were returned to his family. The poetry volume Thomas kept and read from sometimes when he wanted to remember his friend.

After Lawrence died, Thomas was different. He grieved his friend in silence, but his ready laugh and his open heart was just so much less so. I tried to take him out of himself. I insisted he teach me to play chess, and I would let him beat me, only occasionally rallying and crying "Mate!!" with joy. I knew he would get better, and I tried to be part of that recovery, but it was clear to me that a part of him had changed and would never come back.

June 30 1916

Somewhere in France

Dear Charlotte

I hope things are well with you all. Your letters about Lawrence and Rae Bailey have been so sad. I only met her at the one dance, but I remember her beauty. I am so sorry for this terrible thing that befell their family. And also I am sad for Thomas. You don't mention the nature of their friendship, but knowing him I can imagine how very low he feels just now.

The hospital is being moved again, to get us away from the front but also to make getting patients to us easier. It's a dreadful lot of work, upending patients and equipment every time. We should be settled again soon.

I did hear one rather sad rumour. Harry Spare was killed a couple of weeks ago. He was in an open trench with a group of others when a Bosch pilot dropped a great bomb on them all, killing the lot. It broke my heart. I never really liked him at home, but he really seemed to become a new man, a better man, over here.

I hope you are not too upset. But it really does just seem to keep taking the best of us doesn't it.

Take care

Patricia

July in Fredericton is often swelteringly hot, and 1916 was no different. The babies slept in only their diapers but they mewled in misery. Daily we bathed them in cool water to take away the heat. They began to teethe and their front teeth erupted. We gave them cold cloths to chew on.

We opened all of the windows in the house to catch to the breeze off the river. We took the babies to the bank and dabbled their toes in the cool water, making them laugh and gurgle. We ate sandwiches on the green and enjoyed the breeze.

In August the nights became cooler and the sleeping easier. Logs slid down the river toward the mills in Lincoln. We took picnics in the lumber cuts west of Fredericton and made a day of it. We sat high on the hillsides over the river and watched the world pass by our door.

Industrialization was sweeping away our lifestyle along the river. In the years to come, the trees and the mills that consumed them would be gone. But in the summer of 1916, we hadn't quite realized that yet, and the only scar on our collective skin was the casualty lists appearing regularly in the paper.

August 30, 1916
Saint John Training Ground

Dear Charlotte

I am glad to hear that the twins are taking break from the teething that made them so miserable earlier in the summer. If memory of my siblings serves me right, there will be another period when they turn about a year old. Sounds like you are doing all the right things, and Mother is never far away if you need help.

It sounds like the fuss at Easter has finally died down. Things at home seem easier and business is picking up again for Father. Allie had taken it very hard. She is at the age that popularity with the other girls is especially important. Hopefully she will forgive Father in time.

I finally have my orders and will be sailing to England later in September. I can't share the details with you, but am sure they will reach you by another way. I can't decide if I am frightened, proud, or confident. Some of each anyway. Leastways I can load, aim and shoot and march for days afterward. I can wrestle too, if my winnings against the other chaps in my unit are any indication. Not bad for an old man.

I am sure we will be in contact before I go. Please take care of Thomas and the babies. I trust him to care for you all without any problems.

Love

Jack

This letter from Jack explained the foreboding I had felt all summer. While he trained in Saint John, for me the war did not touch him. But now, knowing he was finally going, a reality opposed to the lists of casualties, gave me an icy pain in my stomach, one I shared with no one.

A group of us arranged to be at the gate to the training ground in Saint John on September 22. Mrs. McGuigan and I held hands. The twins sat up in their pram, elated by the crowd and the band. Nene looped her arm through Clem's. Thomas stood behind me with his arm around my waist, supporting me.

Finally, the band led the troops through the wooden palisade, turning right to march along toward the railway station. They were to travel to Halifax and board ship there. The men marched by us, heads rigidly faced forward, bodies resolutely toward their fate. When we saw Jack emerge from the archway, we saw just the barest hint of a smile and though his eye did not focus on us, its lids winked at us.

When the troops were gone and the marching band was echoing far away in another part of the city, we turned back to Clem's truck and climbed in for the ride home. There was no talk, but I continued to hold Mrs. McGuigan's hand.

Autumn in the Saint John River Valley passed as it usually did, with the glorious riot of colour it has become known for all over the world. A wide variety of deciduous trees poisoned their leaves, causing them to turn a full palette of reds, yellows, oranges, and purples throughout the valley. The best place to see the display was from the top of the hill, and from the University Campus, slowly expanding now from the Old Arts Building into a small collection of educational edifices.

A couple of times a group of McGuigans and de Burghs headed up the hill by horse carriage and Ford Truck to watch the leaves. We tucked bricks warmed in the wood stove and furs around our bodies to keep warm, and sat on the hill absorbing the beauty stretched below us. We carried thermos full of hot chocolate to drink, the logical accompaniment to the show.

When the snow came, we went sliding. We built snow men on the hill. We formed shooting parties and brought home rabbit for rabbit stew. We tramped through the woods on snowshoes and cross country skis with sealskin undersides so we could get up the hill. We cut trees for Christmas and decorated them with fragile glass ornaments and popcorn strings. We burned fires in our cast iron stoves and our fireplaces.

And Jack was gone for all of it. But he wasn't. With every slip of a ski, every step of a snowshoe, he was there in our thoughts, just to the right of our everyday reality. We talked of how he would have loved the stew, of how he always put the top on the Christmas tree. But even when we didn't talk of him, he was there just next to the feel of the cold on our cheeks and the feel of the flannel sheets on our beds at night.

On Christmas morning, there was a package from Jack for the children. It was full of beautiful and thoughtful toys for them. For Joanie, a wooden doll with a porcelain face, hand painted delicately right down to her eyelashes. For Alastair, there was also a doll, but it was a manly doll, dressed in a Canadian military uniform, complete with little ammunition pouches strung across his chest, just like the real thing. He had two hats, one the forage cap of the regular uniform, the other a little Brodie helmet to protect him in battle. They were so precious I knew they could not be played with. Fortunately also in the package were two sets of blocks that Jack had carved in his spare time. They were both perfect and imperfect and we loved them. While Jack's gifts had neither the polish nor the perfection of those that Thomas and I had provided for each other and the children, they were far and away the best of the bunch.

That year, the firefighters held their traditional New Year's Parade, and although Thomas and I attended with the children, Mr. and Mrs. McGuigan were not there, the very thought of where Jack was and was going making it too much for them to bear the memorial parade.

By the end of February, when the back of winter was truly broken and the heavy snows of March came around, the twins began to walk. A toddler is a busy little person when alone, but two made for constant exercise and vigilance on the part of the adults in their lives. They pulled on furniture, grabbed at cups of tea, and cried when they could not climb the newly installed central heating radiators in our house. Fortunately for every miscreant moment there was a delightful one, a smile, a laugh, an accomplishment of understanding.

But ever-present throughout those months of 1916 and into 1917 was the spectre of Jack having moved one step closer to the battlefields of Europe. Behind every thought, every peal of laughter and every quiet moment was Jack in his uniform and with his weapon held at the ready, about to embark for that place that produced the casualty lists that appeared in the paper every few days.

April 8, 1917

CEF Training Camp

Dear Charlotte;

Happy Easter! We all went to the local Cathedral for Easter Mass, not Catholic, but I am deciding that maybe it's not as important as all that.

My mates and I have been laughing over your stories about the twins and their escapades. The one about how Alastair reached the cookie jar on top of the ice box is a favourite. Everybody loves an underdog.

Mother will be so proud of me when I come home. I have become so good with a shovel I can dig a trench for seed potatoes twelve feet deep, and do it in a hurry. Some days I wish I could just go home now. I have travelled, seen how other people live, and learned a lot about what I want for the rest of my life. But I also have the opportunity to go further, to know more, and to benefit others as I go along. I am very proud of the things I have learned.

I wish I could be with you all on your family outings. They sound such fun. I am not surprised to hear that Frank has purchased a handgun and is such a shot at rabbits. I know a few English girls who would be very happy to meet him.

Pray for me in the months to come. As usual I won't be able to tell you where I am, but I can tell you some of the details. I am thinking of you all, all the time. Please give my extra love to the twins. Some days I just wish so hard I could hug you all.

Sincerely

Jack

If you have ever had a long distance relationship with someone, be it a lover, a friend, or a family member, you know the sad pain of living through someone who is not there. The wondering where that person is, what is happening to them, and what choices they are making occupies so much of your mind that the rest of you becomes only a shell of who you used to be. The only living left to be had is the waiting between letters and visits, the looking at the moon and knowing the object of your affections is looking at it too.

April 30, 1917

Dear Charlotte;

I am sorry I have not written for a while. It has been so very busy here what with the extra patients from the battle at Vimy Ridge (it's in the papers so I can write about it without some silly censor scolding me).

There have been so many men with facial injuries. Between the machine guns and the shells, these poor men have not much to look forward to with large parts of their faces blown away. There is talk about a New Zealander in England who is working with these terrible injuries. I would be fascinated to study with him.

Thank you for your wonderful letters. I love them, and I sometimes read them to my patients to make them laugh. I can't decide which of the twins is funnier, Joanie or Alastair. The fact that they work together to get what they want is a little frightening. Tell them one day Auntie Patricia will make cookies just for them.

I haven't seen Jack yet, which is a good thing. My understanding is that he and his friends will not join the party until some of the other guests have left. I am sure he will be fine, and that he knows how to protect himself and his friends.

Give my love to Thomas and the twins. I must admit that although I am dedicated to the work I do, I am starting to feel tired and a bit discouraged here. Send your prayers up for me.

Patricia

In May of 1917, the New Brunswick legislature passed prohibition of the sale of alcohol into law. It would stay that way for ten years. Prohibition provided the perfect opportunity for entrepreneurs who could outrun the authorities to provide rum brought in along the Fundy and Atlantic coasts, sunk and marked like lobster pots, picked up and transported to a series of remote and private sales locations throughout the province. Oddly, this change in law coincided with Clem paying me in full for the loan he had used to buy his first truck. It also coincided with the purchase of a second truck, to be driven by Fred. Nothing was ever said, especially around Thomas, who was an officer of the court, but this sudden prosperity did not go unnoticed.

On Victoria Day, the de Burghs and the McGuigans had a picnic on the Green by the river. The freshet had long since receded and the grass was dry and green. We sat on old quilts and blankets and the twins basked in the attention of all of the adults while they played. Each had a new outfit from Grammy McGuigan, outfits that were grass stained and food soiled almost as soon as they were put on.

In a quiet moment, Mrs. McGuigan slipped me an envelope with something rigid it. I withdrew two photographs affixed to display boards, both 5x7 in size. They were pictures of Jack in uniform, one of his face and head, and one of him sitting on a wall in full uniform, holding a crop. They were beautiful, and the photographer's art drew out the gentleness of Jack's temperament. Perhaps it was the way he held his mouth, or the gaze away from the camera. Oh perhaps it was a trick of the light that this man who was going away to kill others could appear so soft and gentle for the benefit of his family at home.

"Oh yes, "said Frank, "Artie Steeves says they sell you those to send your mother right before you go to the Front."

Behind him, Thomas looked down and put his hand to his forehead. Mr. McGuigan walked away down the Green. I put the photos gently back in the envelope and handed them back. The saddest thing about the absence of a loved one is that their absence becomes larger than the presence of all that is left. Every event and emotion becomes measured by the gaping hole once occupied by someone else. That day on the green a large number of family enjoyed the twins and their antics, but it was the fact that Jack was missing that day that we all remembered. What would Jack think of this? What would Jack think of that? Wouldn't Jack have thought that was funny?

And underlying all is the fear, the terror, that the absence will become permanent, that the loved one will never return and the hole will never be filled. Every casualty list in the paper, every idle report, every telegram stimulates the physical manifestation of the fear that this time, this time his name will be there, announcing in bald language that he is gone.

In early June, the McGuigans and the de Burghs rented an allotment for the summer and planted a large garden together. Cucumbers, squash, tomatoes, corn, beets, seed potatoes, peppers, radishes and bean seeds all were plugged into the ground and watered from large watering cans brought to the allotment by Samson and Delilah, by Caesar and Betty. It was a wonderful family weekend. But late on Sunday, when the planting was almost done I found Mrs. McGuigan sitting quietly with a packet of cucumber seeds in her hand.

"Jack doesn't like cucumbers" she said in a flat tone. "He says they make him peptic".

June 29, 1917

Somewhere in France

Dear Charlotte;

Do you like the location at the top of this page? That is what we are supposed to say when we write home to indicate we are on active duty. Anything else might lead to the Bosch knowing something he shouldn't.

I have been here for four days but haven't yet seen any action yet. Apparently we will move to the front soon. The fellows here who have been at the front lots tell some pretty interesting stories. They tell of the various type of bombs, and the nicknames of them, but by far the scariest threats are apparently lice and rats. Goodness, I could have faced those at home!

There are lots of fellows from New Brunswick here, some of whom I know. Harry Lynn, who lives on George Street, was with me in Saint John, but has transferred to the cavalry, brave fellow. It seems to me that a man on a horse makes a much better target than an infantryman in the mud.

Where we are now, there are various agencies from home (Red Cross etc.) who provide us with things to do, things to read, and things to provide comfort. The local French also do their best to cater to the troops. The odd thing is that we have come here and torn up their country and yet they seem so grateful to us.

I will write more as things go along. I know that you would find the people here and their ways of doing things very interesting, and so will try to pass some of that along in my letters.

We will be soon going to join the show, so I will not be able to mail letters until we come back from that. But rest assured I will be thinking of you all and keeping you all and the children in my heart. Regards to Thomas. He is truly a good man.

Sincerely

Jack

That summer, Frank's behaviour changed quite a bit from the sweet boy who had doted on Rae Bailey.

Somehow his parting from her had brought out a cynicism in him. And as his good looks matured he became the desired party goer of every girl in town. And of course, so many of the young men were away that there weren't many left. While other young men who did not join up were called slackers and cowards, Frank took on much of the painting, carting and handyman work that was left behind. He was happy to step into the shoes of every absent soldier and to comfort the lonely women left behind. In fact, the only woman he was truly in love with was his horse, Betty, who had blossomed under his care into a muscled, sleek black.

It turned out that Nene had taken up writing to Harry Lynn while he was in Saint John with Jack. She followed his fortunes as he trained with the cavalry and now while he was in and out of the front.

Thanks to Jack's extra wages, Allie had finished at the business college in the spring, and started in a local real estate office that summer. I would have thought she would be happy, but she radiated a complicated discontent. I suspected that it had still to do with her father's politics and personality, but since she had not discussed it with me, I could only surmise.

That is, until one rainy July morning when she arrived on the verandah. Like her mother, she was impeccably dressed in stylish but practical clothing. Her hair was swept up off the back of her neck in a roll, complimented by an understated but flattering hat that I was sure I had seen in a magazine the previous week. Unlike her mother, she was only about four feet tall, perhaps the result of an impoverished diet when she was a small child. Like her brothers, her face was a perfect oval, with dimples in her cheeks when she smiled or laughed. But she wasn't smiling or laughing at the moment.

Over tea and Mrs. McGinn's fluffy, buttery tea biscuits, she began to relax, to uncoil from the tension she had brought across the threshold.

"The truth is you know I really miss Jack. I think about him all the time, and I wish he was here. I feel so alone. The whole family pushed me to finish high school and to study secretarial skills, and yet now that I have done it, they call me a know-it-all and a busy body. They accuse me of looking down on them and thinking I'm better than them. Clem says a woman's place is cooking potatoes. Which is better than Frank. When Daddy or Mother are not around Frank says women are only good for being underneath a man. And Daddy will barely speak to me. Jack would understand. I have written to him but not heard back as of yet. I hope that doesn't mean he is in trouble"

This remarkable speech poured out of her seventeen year old mouth at high speed and in better language than any of her siblings would have used, but only subtly so.

Upon hearing Allie come in the front door, Thomas had come to join us for our visit. Allie was one of the few people who could make him smile any more. She was smart, she was brash, and she was opinionated, but she was usually right, and he found her delightful.

477

He tilted his head to the side and said "Allie, what is happening to your family is extremely common in families of lesser means who see the potential in their children and make it their most cherished ambition to vaunt their children to a better life than they have had. But then they find that they and their children do not understand each other anymore. The parents are afraid, sometimes rightly, that the children judge them for their poverty. The children feel punished for the very success their parents pushed them to achieve. "

She looked at him for a moment, processing what he said. "But what do I do?"

"Use your intelligence to try to reach out to them. What does your mother say about all this? She is a very wise woman."

Allie smirked. "She says it is a woman's lot to be smarter than the men around her."

Yes, that was what Mrs. McGuigan would say.

"Say, young woman, shouldn't you be at work?" Thomas asked.

Allie blushed. "I quit. The boss thought he was smarter than me."

Once the laughter had subsided, Thomas said "Do you know, I have a lawyer friend who is looking for a smart assistant. Would you like me to give him your name?"

She nodded enthusiastically, so Thomas went into the office and made a telephone call. When he emerged, he had a piece of paper with a name and an address on it. "You're to go around and see him

as soon as ever you are done with your visit here",
he said, smiling.

July 24, 1917

Somewhere in France

Dear Charlotte;

*So I have finally seen the front lines. All of my
training prepared me to sneak into the area
between Fritz's trenches and ours in the pitch black
of night with a pair of wire cutters and spend hours
with the rats cutting barbed wire intended to make
it hard for their troops and ours to cross the area.
There was a bit of a fuss two nights ago, when a
small group of Germans tried to attack. One of our
fellows stood up on the edge of the trench and fired
a gun from the hip and that was the end of those
Germans. There was some cheering I can tell you.*

*And here I am back at rest, having had a bath and a
hair wash even. Some of the English are going to
put on a play and we are all looking forward to it.*

*Please thank Thomas for providing Allie with a
referral. Apparently the gentleman was pleased with
her and so far they are getting on well. She is so
smart but she has trouble knowing when not to bite
the hand that feeds her. She will be a remarkable
woman, in time.*

*There are newspapers here published by troops for
the troops to read. There are comics and articles
and poems. One of them is called The Dead Horse*

Gazette! It's an awful name but we pass it around to one another and enjoy the stories.

We also have books available to us thanks to the Red Cross. I am reading a great deal, especially when we are in the reserve trench waiting to go to the front. I tried reading Charles Dickens, but I find him a little too hard going. I am a simple man, and he obviously is not.

I am glad the twins are growing so fast. They will be taller than their mother soon!

I miss you all at home. I will return to you as soon as ever I can. Keep me in your prayers

Yours Truly

Jack

When the twins molars started to come in and they were feeling quite grizzly about it, I started loading them up in the open carriage and taking them for a drive in the evenings. The rhythmic movement of the vehicle and the changing light in the sky, as well as the trotting of the horses' feet seemed to soothe them and send them off to sleep.

I loved these quiet times with the children while they were tucked in behind me in their quilts provided lovingly by Grammy McGuigan. Toys sent by "Uncle Jack" had become favourites, until the wear and tear on them had rendered them nothing more than scraps of cloth and fill. In short they were safe and comfortable with the sounds and smells, and usually fell asleep within the first few blocks.

Samson and Delilah too seemed to enjoy these excursions in the cool of the evening. From them I received not words but the reverberation of contentment and happiness at being with the children whom they also considered to belong to them.

Thomas never joined us on these excursions, always claiming work, or leisure or some other activity. He joined us in the carriage only when it was necessary for conveyance to a given location. I realized I had never seen him ride a horse either. To him the horses were not a joy but a necessity. And one perhaps not really to be trusted. I was certain he couldn't hear their thoughts the way I could. Otherwise he would have exhibited completely different behaviour.

Early in the summer, Joanie had snuck out the back door and I found her sleeping on the ground where the horses were dozing. She was within inches of Samson's feet but he was completely awake and aware of her presence. When I found her I praised him for protecting his little girl. And he assured me that was exactly what he had been doing.

After that Thomas installed a hook on the back door above the reach of the twins' little hands, so that they could not get out to the horses.

NOTHING – is to be written on this except the date and signature of the sender. Sentences not required may be erased. <u>If anything else is added the post card will be destroyed.</u>

I am quite well

~~*I have been admitted to hospital*~~

~~*{sick   } and am going on well*~~

~~*{wounded} and hope to be discharged soon*~~

I have received your { letter

{ ~~*telegram*~~

{ ~~*parcel*~~

Letter follows at first opportunity

~~*I have received no letter from you*~~

~~*{ lately*~~

~~*{ for a long time*~~

Signature only {   *Jack McGuigan*

Date *August 25, 1917*

43

---

[43] This is a Field Service Postcard, used by all British and Canadian expeditionary force members to ease the worries of family members and girlfriends at home, as well as the soldiers themselves. The idea was to expedite their transit by reducing the attention required from the censors.

The foregoing postcard appeared in the post at the beginning of September, and apparently Mrs. McGuigan had received one too. The casualty lists in the paper had been very long again and we knew that something big had taken place, despite the article on a battle at the town of Lens, in Belgium, where our casualties were said to be "light". [44]

On Labour Day weekend, we all assembled at the allotment and harvested the garden. Clem's trucks groaned with the weight of fresh vegetables and fruit. It was McGuigan tradition that the men sat and peeled and chopped while the women cooked, pickled and sauced. We harvested on Saturday, and by the end of Monday, all of the families involved had enough relish and sauce and pickles to last for two years. I had never been involved in a pickling bee before, and it was wonderful to belong in such a large family gathering, especially one that brought so much of summer's goodness to winter's table.

Thomas brightened considerably as part of the family group as well. The greatest benefit seemed to be that the McGuigans simply included him and accepted him for who he was, and it wasn't just the family lawyer that he had become.

October that year was dreary and dark. It rained a lot, and even the fall colours throughout the river valley couldn't raise our spirits. We burned wood in the fireplace despite the central heating, and we welcomed family and friends as often as we could

---

[44] The Daily Gleaner 1917-08-16 Hill no. 70 Not seriously Menaced – Canadian Casualties Considered Slight

to take the edge off. Fredericton locals spoke darkly of how the freshet next year would be more extreme because of the extra rain. Conversation was harder to keep going, smiles were fewer, and hearts were heavier, and except for the rain, no one could figure out why.

Until I opened the door on a rainy Tuesday early in November. Mrs. McGuigan was on the verandah, no hat, hair wet, and clothing clinging to a shaking body. She held an envelope that, although also wet, held a dry telegram.

I called for Mrs. McGinn, and we sprang into action. Quilts that Mrs. McGuigan herself had fashioned were wrapped around her wet and shivering body. We sat her in the kitchen where both the fire and the range were warm. We found her tea. I made sure she was warming up before I turned my attention to the envelope she still clutched in her hand.

By now Thomas was in the kitchen as well, and he talked softly to Mrs. McGuigan while coaxing the envelope from between her cold fingers. When he had succeeded, he handed it to me. I slid the telegram out from its hiding place, the hiding place of an electric eel between piles of rocks, and read what it said.

Mrs. John McGuigan

135 Westmoreland Street

Fredericton, New Brunswick

Canada

Your son Pte John Albert McGuigan seriously injured in battle November 6. Gunshot to right side of face. Currently with 1 Field Ambulance.

Adjutant General

There was silence. The kitchen clock ticked. I was determined not to succumb to my own distress in front of this woman who I loved and who had just received this dreadful news about her eldest son. But I couldn't speak. I couldn't move.

But Thomas was there, the same way that Thomas was always there, had always been there. He gently sat me down in a kitchen chair and Mrs. McGinn found me a cup of tea. Mrs. McGuigan and I sat together in front of the kitchen fireplace mutely holding our cups of tea, saying nothing, reacting to nothing.

Mr. McGuigan arrived shortly with Frank in tow. They had brought a sloven to bring her home, but Thomas convinced them that they should bide until she was calmer. Mr. McGuigan stepped into the kitchen and crouched at his wife's knee. He looked beseechingly into her face and waited. After a moment she took the unconsumed tea in her left hand and threw the contents in his face. Whoever else had forgotten the Easter Rising, she clearly had not.

Over the next two or three days our home became headquarters for information about what was happening to Jack.

November 9, 1917

3 General Field Hospital

Dear Charlotte

You will have heard by now through the adjutant's office, but Jack has been injured. He passed through here today on his way to England for further treatment.

All I can tell you is that he was hit either by machine gun fire or shrapnel – the stretcher carriers are not sure, nor is Jack himself. Apparently he was hit shortly after going over the top while he was in No Man's Land. He took refuge in a shell hole but he had trouble keeping himself from sliding down into the mire at the bottom where he would surely have drowned or been poisoned by the water. He held on to the side of the crater with his fingers. He dared not let go to keep the rats away from his face. He has no idea how long he was there before 1 Field Am found him, screaming to be heard and to try to scare away the rats.

By the time he writes to you he may not remember much of what I am telling you. It is common for their minds to protect them from the trauma they experience on the battlefield.

Of his injury I can tell you this: the wound extends from just below the right cheekbone down to the mandible joint, and down the jawbone about half way. The teeth are mostly shattered and there is no skin covering the injury area. The mandible joint is gone entirely. He is very lucky as both the carotid artery and jugular vein were missed. Had they not been, he would have died.

I know it is very hard to read this but you need to be prepared. He will be in hospital for many months. I asked my surgeon to put a note on his file asking that he be treated by the new surgery group that I told you about, and he did, but he says there is a great deal of healing required before something like that can be attempted.

I am so deeply sorry about this. Jack is a sweet, gentle man, and it breaks my heart to see him injured in this way. You will shortly hear from the hospital providing you with contact information. I encourage you to send him letters, photos etc. to distract him. He will need it.

Please pass along my love and condolences to the McGuigans.

With love

Patricia

The level of shock experienced by all of us who loved Jack cannot possibly be described. If a loved one dies, the family can commence the rituals of death and the recovery of the heart. If a loved one is injured near home that person can be visited in the hospital. Family members can support that person, tell funny stories and bring gifts of distraction.

But Jack was so far away that his presence there was almost not real. We could no more visit him than we could sprout wings and fly. The very idea that any of his family members could board a ship and travel to England in the middle of war time was preposterous. Ships were for the war effort. And besides, the time involved to travel to him was prohibitive. Mr. McGuigan had a whole family to support, and Thomas had ongoing legal cases to continue. And certainly the question of two women travelling by sea alone in that age would have been out of the question.

So we did what we could. Mrs. McGuigan and I went back to our regular routines. In preparation for communication from the hospital, we prepared a package for Jack. Thomas and I took the children to Harvey Studios and had our picture taken, with two small copies to include for him. I considered putting in the box my copy of The Prussian Officer and Other Stories by DH Lawrence, the book I had read to him that long ago day on the green. But I decided it might be considered seditious. Instead I sent Lady Rosamond's Secret: A Romance of Fredericton, by Rebecca Agatha Armour. It had been published as a serial in the Telegraph Journal in Saint John, and I had kept all of the installments carefully cut out for years. It wasn't a great book but it was full of references to places and people whom Jack would know. Thomas included two packages of Woodbines and two packages of Players, as he knew the Government Issue cigarettes were pretty awful.

The McGuigans prepared their own package, with hand knit mittens for the coming winter, a throw for his bed, more cigarettes, and pictures and letters.

November 20, 1915

1st Western General Hospital,
Fazakerly, Liverpool
England

Dear Mother;
I am so sorry that I have taken five days to write
to you, as the arrival of the telegram must have
frightened you greatly. I am all right, just a bit of
alteration to make my face prettier.
I can't write too long as I get a bit tired, but
Nurse will make sure this gets mailed straight
away, so you get it as soon as possible.

Love
Jack

Now having an address, we sent our packages, with the addition of many letters for him to read. It was a great relief to have something in Jack's own writing. I think maybe only Mrs. McGuigan and I caught his reference to being tired and his reliance on humour to downplay the seriousness of the injury. All the same, we read and re-read the letter over and again and cherished the fact that his hands had touched it.

Not a day passed where I did not think of Jack and what had happened to him. I worried about his injury. First I would worry that I would not be able to live with his disfigurement, and then I would feel guilt and demand even more attentiveness to his recovery. I sent letter after letter. I sent locks of the children's hair when no one was looking. My stomach hurt all the time but Dr. Bridges could find no real cause. He gave me a white liquid cure to drink that was worse than the disease.

What was making me so miserable? I suppose it was the fear that whatever disfigurement he had suffered would be too much for me and that I would not be able to bear it. What would that say about me? How superficial would that make me? It was about my failings, not his.

December 15, 1917
1st Western General Hospital,
Liverpool, England

Dearest Charlotte:

My poor girl, how much you are struggling. I read between the lines of your letters and I can see your fear that you will not be able to love a gargoyle.

What you do not understand is that you have never been under any obligation to love me. We are friends now, friends who share two children. You will never be obligated to look at me and love me the way you once did. You owe me nothing dearest. Please stop agonizing.

Thank you for the locks of the children's hair. You have no idea how much it means to me to have them. They both have hair the same colour that I did as a child. To know they are in the world, a small secret part of me, is a huge comfort in my current situation.

The hospital has stabilized my jaw. I wear a splint now and can eat small amounts. Mother sent some molasses cookies, my favourite, and I was able to eat some by sucking on them and swallowing. The other fellows in the ward were very grateful for those that I could not eat. It made me very sad to give them away.

I am mostly eating minced food since I cannot chew very well. But the taste is not bad. The other fellows here are mostly in the same way as me, and we jolly one another along quite well.

What the other fellows do have a problem with is that I have terrible nightmares. I don't remember them, but I wake up screaming and I can smell the odour of the battlefield when I wake. I won't describe the smell, but it fills me with horror. The nurses administer rum when this happens, and I am usually able to go back to sleep.

Please tell Thomas the cigarettes went over very big. The Government Issue ones taste like horse manure when you smoke them.

Dear Charlotte, please don't struggle any more. However you feel about me when I come home will be perfectly all right. I miss the ease with which we talk to one another. Look forward to that as I do.

With Love

Jack.

While all of the excitement was swirling around Jack in November and December of 1917, Thomas was his most kind and supportive self, more so than he had been since Lawrence died. I was surprised at the degree of his support until he announced that he would be taking a partner in his legal practice in the New Year. He brought Walter Estee home for dinner the week before Christmas to introduce him to me.

Mr. Estee had very gentle country manners. He was very tall, over six foot, but did not have the build of an athlete, rather that of a man who could pluck cherries from the top of the tree. He had the hands of a concert pianist and proved it by playing Beethoven for us on the piano in the parlour.

At dinner, I wanted to know about his family and his upbringing. In short I wanted him to tell me about himself.

"Well Mrs. De Burgh, I come from a little farming community up country. My people are God fearing Baptists who work the land and live very strictly by God's word. Accordingly I worked very hard in school and attained a scholarship to study law up the hill. And here we are."

The setup of the new practice took most of January. Many of the files in our office at home were moved into the new office on King Street. Mrs. McGinn and I scrubbed the walls and floors, and Thomas and Walter painted the office a nice light shade.

It turned out that the friend to whom Thomas had recommended Allie was Walter, so she came along to the new practice as well. I was delighted. She had matured into a clever, opinionated, and politically astute young woman. I continued to provide legal clerical work to Thomas, except when there was too much for me to keep up with the children.

Walter's gentle laugh and sharp intellect seemed to fit into our strange group very nicely and as a lawyer he was very serious and in earnest. You wouldn't think there would be much call for lawyers in a place like Fredericton, but business was steady right from the start. Mind you, both men had thriving practices to begin with.

March 2, 1918

3ʳᵈ Gen Field Hospital

Dear Charlotte;

I'm sorry I haven't written for a while. My work is exhausting. Either I am holding the hand of some poor young man as he dies, or I am lying to another that he will not lose a body part or that his girl will still love him when he goes home. I suppose I am not always lying, but it sure feels like it.

I am sorry to sound so negative, but I really am very sad and tired. I have seen enough young men die, just here in the hospital, to replace the male population of Fredericton. It is such a waste! How will we, as a Dominion, recover from such a terrible loss?

I am looking forward to going home now, to seeing you and my parents and my brothers. I can't wait to see the twins! There is talk of an armistice coming soon, and I am glad to hear it. Perhaps I will go home and be a childbirth nurse.

I enclose gifts for the twins second birthday. I had these lovely little blankets made by a local woman. You see little children carrying them all the time. Rather than pink and blue, I had her use green and yellow. Something different.

I look forward to coming home. Let's all pray for an end to this madness, and a future of happiness and sunshine.

With love

Patricia

Patricia was killed by a bomb thrown onto the hospital by a German pilot on May 3, 1918. When staff from the hospital demanded to know why he attacked a building with a prominent cross on the roof, he insisted he had not seen it. When pressed, he admitted that he had seen it, but given the light railroad track leading to it, he had been certain it was a munitions dump in disguise. The light railroad, he was informed, was the best and only way to get the wounded from the front to the hospital in time to save their lives, and often even that wasn't enough. These interrogations took place as he was given medical care after having crashed his plane shortly after dropping the bomb. He killed 11 patients in the surgical ward where the bomb hit, 16 patients throughout the rest of the hospital, four nurses including Patricia, and one surgeon.

Perhaps the tone of her last letter was so sad because it had been prescient? In her heart could she have known she would die in such a sad and futile way? Or was it futile? How many lives had she saved, had she enriched, had she comforted since her arrival in France in 1915? How rich and wise had she become in return? Was this simply the purpose of her life?

No amount of rationalization made the loss of my friend acceptable to me. The heaviness of it would weigh on me throughout the summer of 1918.

Ontario Military Hospital
Orpington, England

June 14, 1918

Dear Charlotte;

I have just heard about Patricia. I am so sorry.
She was a lovely girl, brave and charitable. I just
keep thinking back to how nursing in the war
was all she ever really wanted to do. I don't
know if that helps you or not, but it does comfort
me some.

Mother says you all planted a great garden this
year. Where did you get the watermelon seeds?
I asked one of the fellows here who knows these
things and he said to make sure the seeds have
lots of water.

My face has finally healed closed now. I saw the
doctor's notes yesterday, and even though I
can't chew much, his notes said "sinus closed".
That means I will go to Queen's Hospital to have
it all looked at next week. I am not sure why
they waited until it healed to possibly cut it open
again, but I am no doctor. They speak of Dr.
Gilles here as if he were God himself, so I am
curious to meet him.

You need to know about this thing that is
happening here. There is a new flu passing

around that can be pretty serious. Some folks are dying from it. The troops are bringing it home with them, so you will need to be careful with the twins.

I am sorry again about Patricia. We will miss her, but I would like to remember the honor with which she served. She really was an excellent nurse. I remember more than she thought about the time I passed through there, and how well she cared for me.

I will write again from Queen's Hospital.

Love

Jack.

July passed in heat and unrelenting sunshine, as if we were all under some kind of scrutiny in which blazing light would be of benefit. I felt like a beetle under a child's magnifying glass.

Queen's Hospital
Sidcup, England

July 24, 1918

Dear Charlotte;

I have much to tell you! I have already had my first surgery and will have another next week. They are very careful not to push healing too quickly. They took photos of me before they touched me, and then they started working on it.

After each surgery, there are photographs, so we can see progress.

There is so much more to the care here than just the medicine. Dr. Gilles has put blue benches outside the hospital just for us to sit on when we smoke, and that no one else can sit on but us. We are called gargoyles, and some are so very much worse off than me. Some of the chaps have formed a football team. They joke that when they play the local teams they can scare them into losing just by their faces.

There are also classes for learning how to do things. I am learning how to write poetry, something I have secretly wanted to do for years. I am also learning how to paint pictures, so now I can paint in more than one way!

I am sure you can tell that I finally have hope for the future. I will write again when there is more change. Or when I learn to play football.

Love

Jack

In late August we chose a bath night, and Clem brought home two watermelon from the garden. We all sat on our front verandah and ate the sweet juicy fruit, spitting the seeds across the grass and joking about watermelon growing the next year. Predictably the twins were a sticky happy mess. They squished seeds between their bare toes and flesh of the melon between their fingers. Allie was there with her brownie camera, now a fixture at all family gatherings, and the best moments were recorded for posterity. When we were done, the adults adjourned to the kitchen for tea and Mrs. McGinn and I swept the children up to the bath, only to have them reappear clean and cherub-like in their night dresses, ready for bed. By the time everyone had held them and kissed them goodnight, they were just sleepy enough to go back upstairs for sleep which came swiftly. Looking at them with their pink cheeks and long lashes, I thought they were absolutely perfect.

Spanish Influenza hit Fredericton in October of 1918, when it travelled home with the returning soldiers. The Province of New Brunswick's first Minister of health, Dr. William Roberts, outlawed the gathering of more than five people and closed schools and churches for five weeks to prevent the spread of the disease.[45] Not that anyone was safe from contracting it. It was an ugly disease, less likely to take the elderly or the weak but more likely to seize the young and vigorous, causing fever, aches, and severe cough, sometimes that brought up blood. In Fredericton the number of cases was 7.5%; one thousand people, or one per family. [46] Thirty people died in our town of 7,500.

---

[45] New Brunswick Tourism, Heritage and Culture website, In New Brunswick History, October 11, 1918.
[46] New Brunswick Media Co-op, "Shutting the Province Down: the 1918-1919 flu epidemic in New Brunswick.

While the adults in our home, including Mr. Estee who was only an occasional resident, escaped infection, the twins both contracted it. For those who were not infected, it was an all-out assault for the sake of those who were. Eva made soup for her neighbours out in Morrison's Mills. Mrs. McGuigan likewise made gallons of soup, the only food truly consumable by those abed. We washed the twins in rubbing alcohol baths to bring down their fevers and then spooned soup into them for the sake of the caloric support. We spent nights up singing to them, and trying not to hold them too tight lest we bring up the fever. We cried when they coughed so hard their little bodies spasmed. We cried to the heavens when our children recently so active and mischievous were unnaturally quiet.

Alastair started to turn around after two weeks, chewing steak that Grammy had already chewed for him, and grinning as he downed mashed potatoes. Joanie took longer, not really fully rallying until four weeks had passed. It wasn't until her fever dropped and didn't come back that the mood in our house brightened. I found Thomas watching over them a few nights later, openly crying to see them sleeping deeply and without sweating and thrashing.

November 11, 1918
Queen's Hospital
Sidcup, England

Dear Charlotte;

Armistice at last!! We can all go home. I have one more surgery and then I will be transferred to a recuperation camp so I can be demobed[47] home.

But never mind that, how are the children? When last you wrote Joanie was still a bit punky but on the mend. Has she completely recovered now? It was very frightening for me to be so far away and able to do nothing. It sounds like what you got at home was not nearly as bad as what we had in some of the military camps where there was a much higher death rate.

Not sure how long it will take to send all these lads home. It's easier for the English fellows, and the French. But the Anzac's and Yanks and we are in a bad way as there are only so many ships left.

Please write as soon as you can and tell me about Joanie and Alastair. And in return I will write as soon as I know when the ship will dock and where.

With love to all

Jack

---

[47] Demobilized.

Christmas that year was a merry affair. Rationing had been repealed and so there were foods we had not eaten since early in 1917. And the best gifts of all were the health of the twins and the joy that Jack would soon be home.

We had no idea that our Jack would never be the same. The spectre of Shell Shock had never raised its ugly head in our world. We did not know that the sound of a car backfiring, the terrifying dreams of the battlefield and the unprotected world outside the gates of 135 Westmorland Street would at times prove too much for Jack. The only coping mechanism he had at his disposal was a flask inside his vest pocket and a bottle in the drawer of the old tavern table beside his bed.

Twice weekly the troop trains would arrive from Halifax, from Quebec and Saint John. Twice weekly the entire town would congregate at the train station on York Street, waiting to see who would arrive. They would stand in the coal smoke, some sickened by its stench, and wait quietly for the train. It went on for months, and for months Mrs. McGuigan met every train, sometimes with Mr. McGuigan, sometimes with Thomas and me, and sometimes alone. Every train left her disappointed until the third week of March, when finally there he was. Still in uniform, thin, overwhelmed by the crowd, and a bit disoriented, but it was surely Jack, the man who had gone away almost four years ago.

His scars were obvious but not grotesque. The earlobe missing, the right side of the face slightly misshapen, as if something was wrong but you couldn't put your finger on it. We tried not to stare but we had to look, we had to see how bad it was. Could we live with it? Could we stand to see what the weapons had done?

Thomas and I were both there, and I had the children with us. He knelt down to see them, touching their faces and holding them in his arms. Thomas was their father but they were his babies, and he held them.

And then, just there, not far from where we were standing, a car backfired. It was a nothing really, just a small bang. Alastair was in his arms, and Jack wrapped both arms around him, held him tight and cowered away from the noise. There was silence for a minute, and Alastair was crying "Unca Jack, let me go!"

I took Alastair and Mrs. McGuigan put her hands on either side of Jack's face. He didn't want to look at her, but she made him do it. She saw the right side of his face, the missing ear lobe, the scar under his jaw. But what she was looking for, really looking for, was her son deep in the blue eyes under the heavy brows. He was there, but like me, she saw that Jack was broken.

We took him home in the surrey, back to his home, and his own room behind the kitchen at 135 Westmorland Street. He was very thin, so we fed him, fed him his favourites. Mustard pickle from last year's garden, raspberry jam, made with honey instead of sugar. Mrs. McGuigan's home-made bread.

He spent hours with the children at 97 Church Street, teaching Alastair how to make a small parachute and talking to Joanie about her doll. We sat by the river, him and me, and watched the freshet of 1919. He couldn't bear to help with sandbags that year. Trenches had been reinforced with sandbags.

We soothed him, we comforted him, but we could not heal him. We would never be able to.

To portray Jack as only a broken man would be grossly unfair. History looks at him that way and it's wrong. He said many times that he was just an ordinary man, and he was. He read the paper daily and took a keen interest in current events and provincial and national politics. He liked Mr. Borden, but felt conscription had been a mistake. He and Thomas had animated but friendly discussions about politics, and Jack would sometimes attend court to watch Thomas work.

The things he had learned at Queen's Hospital stood him in good stead. On good days, he would take a cedar shake and paint a landscape scene on it with the same oil paints that he had saved from painting houses. He wrote beautiful poetry about his experiences and tucked them in a book he often carried.

He had taken to reading. He read voraciously, sometimes popular fiction, sometimes poetry, and sometimes classic fiction. He read War and Peace, Jane Austen, and Rupert Brooke. He had no scruples about what men should read or what women should read. He read it all and discussed it with others regularly. Well, mostly me.

Within a month of being home, Jack signed on to painting crews again. He was somewhat agoraphobic as a result of his experiences, but he was determined and was able to control his fears with the help of the little flask in his breast pocket. On one awkward occasion he fell from a scaffold and broke his arm. To say he had whiskey on his breath would have been true of every man on the work site. Notwithstanding, he worked regularly as a painter until the early 1940's.

The bad times were extremely bad. The agoraphobia assuaged by alcohol, he would wander around Fredericton, occasionally stumbling, touching every corner of the home town he loved but could no longer relate to. He would doff his cap to ladies and they would move to avoid him. He would trip over winter cracks in the sidewalk, and well-meaning acquaintances would pick him up and patronizingly put his cap back on his head and send him on his way.

Being drunk does not necessarily mean being unaware. A drunk who is not insensible still perceives the reactions of those around him, and what he saw filled him with self-loathing and sent him on a downward spiral. Paintings and poetry would be burned in disgust at his own presumption. And if he came home too drunk, Mrs. McGuigan would lock him out of the house in a well-meaning urge to teach him a lesson.

Finding himself locked out, he would sleep at Clem's or at 97 Church. The morning would come and he would be fed. Sometimes the change of scenery would be enough to put him back on an even keel, but sometimes not.

The Canadian Government did a very poor job of welcoming its victorious sons home. The prosperity of wartime gone, jobs taken by others in their absence were gone, they went home to the towns they had come from and tried to figure out what to do. There were some small programs to repatriate them, but the vast majority were left to acclimatize on their own. Away from the sounds and smells of the battlefield, bearing visible and invisible scars, the generation of the Great War were rapidly forgotten in thanks for their sacrifices.

In 1920, Thomas and I jointly bought a farm in Greater Norton, a village just at the base of the isthmus sometimes referred by Saint John Residents as The Peninsula. The idea was to buy a farm that could no longer be afforded because of crashing produce prices after the war, and pay the seller to continue to run it with the aid of labour provided by returning war vets. The idea was to break even. Some years it did, some years it didn't. But we built a second house on the property and it became a summer home. When Samson and Delilah became elderly they were retired here, rather than to the rendering plant or the horse meat man. Mr. McGuigan thought I was crazy to feed horses that couldn't earn their keep, but to do otherwise seemed wrong to me, after everything they had done for us. Soon other teamsters retiring their drayage horses in favour of trucks began to quietly inquire if they too might consign their old friends to the fields of grass at our farm.

Nene married in 1919, to her beau Harry Lynn, to whom she had started writing even while he was still training in Saint John. He became a member of Canada's cavalry, and was injured in 1917. A bullet broke the radius and ulna of his left arm, doing nerve damage that could never be repaired, and he was sent home. By 1921, Nene and her baby girl Patricia were home again. Patricia later remembered that she and her mother shared the same bed until she married some 25 years later. Nene spent the rest of her adult years running the household at 135 Westmoreland.

By 1921 Clem owned five trucks, at a time when with the returning soldiers and a downturn in the economy had plunged the Maritimes into the Depression ten years before the rest of the country. After the birth of Leona, Eva had been advised not to have any more children. Save for a miscarriage in 1922, She was successful in avoiding pregnancy, largely because Clem avoided being home. However it happened, abstinence failed in 1924, when she died of a cerebral hemorrhage brought on by what is on the death certificate as premature labour.

Eva's funeral was small and understated, both because Clem had not the heart for it and because his activities with his trucks all over New Brunswick, but mostly in coastal towns, demanded his constant attention to keep ahead of the RCMP and Maine Law Enforcement. Eva was buried in the Anglican cemetery at the top of Forest Hill with no grave marker.

Clem had long since taken the deed of the Blizzard family home as his own, having financially supported Eva as she raised the last of her siblings at home as well as his own children. He sold the house after she died and moved into town, taking up residence on King Street near the fire station and the dairy. He was finally close enough to the fire station to fulfill what he felt was his obligation to be a volunteer fireman, like his father before him. He and his children remained at this address for several years.

With the repeal of prohibition for the province in 1927 and the United States in 1933, the less legitimate part of Clem's business dried up and he had to sell his trucks. He reverted to single horse drayage for the next ten years. The horse's name was Tom, who once opened the back gate and found his way to the Green to graze on the sweet grass. Tom also took an uninvited part in the King Billy parade one year, an activity accepted in Fredericton with less approval as he was a Catholic horse.

Fredericton was the last town in North America to rely on horses for transport to and from fires. When at last they elected to sell the horses, Frank bought the mare, named Doll, for his own activities. She was pretty and pliable and he was delighted with his purchase.

Not long after the union of Frank and Doll, Frank was to pick up coffins at the railway station on York and transport them to McAdam Funeral home just a block south, not far from the Fire Station. There were too many for one load, but not enough for two, so Frank piled them high on the sloven and proceeded with them overloaded, thus saving himself the second trip. Just as he was nearing his destination, the fire bell rang one block away on King Street. Doll, whose entire life had been to react the bell before she met Frank, sprang into action and galloped the length of York Street down to Queen, leaving precisely one smashed coffin every few feet on the way.

In 1925, Fred, the McGuigan brother who had never been strong, died in his sleep. Mr. and Mrs. McGuigan had been preparing themselves for his death for many years, but it didn't make it any easier. The entire family, including Eveline and her husband Harry Black, turned out for the funeral. For the first time since Harry's death, the close family felt the loss of one of their own.

One morning when the twins would have been about ten, the telephone at the office rang while Thomas was giving dictation. I was having trouble keeping up as it was an important case, and his inner warrior had been activated.

Allie came into the room with a knock, and said the school was on the line. There had been some kind of incident and the constable had been called. Both of the twins were involved but Joanie had been hit by another child.

It took less than ten minutes by car to get to the school, and we both went. Thomas wouldn't have ordinarily, but there was something urgent in Allie's tone that made him want to be there.

When we arrived, the principal's office was humming with energy, and we found the source when the door opened to admit us. In the office were Joanie, Alastair, a boy I didn't know, their teacher Mrs. Dibblee, the principal Mr. Dykeman, the constable and Jack. It was awfully crowded, so we all moved to an empty classroom.

"Well look, I think things have been blown out of proportion here" said Dykeman. "I don't know that we really need a lawyer to sort it all out". He smiled at us. He was young, handsome and confident, and I had seen before that he had a gift with people. When he spoke he could often be heard in the next room. I suspected a hearing deficit.

"We were together when we took the call Mr. Dykeman. I hope you don't mind" I responded.

"Not at all, not at all" he said, "might be helpful".

"Now, who is going to start explaining this mess?" He looked back and forth between the three children. Nobody spoke.

"How about if I start?" said Jack.

"How about if you do Mr. McGuigan, because Mrs. Dibblee seems to think you're the one responsible for the ruckus and that you interfered with the children in some way that was ...inappropriate. But I know you to be a fine man of good character. So please do, yes." Mr. Dykeman was letting just a bit of his exasperation creep into his voice.

"Well, I was walking down the street past the school. The children were out for recess. Alastair saw me and came running over to the fence. I thought he was saying hello, but he was crying. He told me that Joanie was in trouble and I should come. There was a knot of children in the play yard, and when I stepped in, this boy was on top of Joanie, and I thought he seemed to be hitting her. So I took him by the ear and pulled him away. Just then this woman grabbed my arm and started screaming that I was hurting the children." There was just a hint of a slur to his words as he spoke.

"The man is drunk" said Mrs. Dibblee. "The temperance union..."

"The temperance union is not in this room Mrs. Dibblee, and there are still doctors in this town who prescribe alcohol for various conditions. It's illegal to sell it, not to use it." Thomas allowed just a tiny touch of acid into his voice.

"So far, we have Alastair running to Mr. McGuigan for help, Mr. McGuigan taking Don Smythe here by the ear, and Mrs. Dibblee misunderstanding and calling the constable because Mr. McGuigan had alcohol on his breath. Am I missing anything?" Seeing only nods, Mr. Dykeman pressed on. "All right young Don, tell me what happened to you."

But before the boy could speak, his parents arrived. And if alcohol was suspected to be an issue in Jack's case, Mr. Smythe wafted the smell before he had even entered the room. Mrs. Smythe had the look that some women do, like mice, waiting for the shoe to hit them on the head, never sure where it would come from. Mr. Smythe was dressed in workman's clothes, clean enough but disheveled. The Smythes are not a caricature, couples like them can be found everywhere, in every social class and culture.

Thomas stood up and approached them, holding out his hand. "Don! What a pleasure to see you again, sorry about the circumstances. We were just about to hear your son's side of the story." The handshake was firm, the smile genuine, and the approach respectful. I knew the couple too, although not as well. And the diversion prevented an outburst or a confrontation. I vacated my seat and sat on the other side of Joanie from Mrs. Dibblee, to allow Mr. Smythe to take a seat beside Thomas. Thus they were allies.

After the Smythes were seated, Mr. Dykeman looked to their boy. "All right son, tell us your side of the story" but the boy looked like he had lockjaw and could not open his mouth. He shot pleading glances at his father, asking to be released from his position.

With a nod to Mr. Dykeman, Mr. Smythe and the constable, Thomas pulled his chair opposite the boy. He stuck out his hand for a shake which the boy reluctantly took.

"I'm pleased to meet you, Don, is it? My name is Mr. de Burgh, and I'm a friend of your dad's." The boy rolled his eyes a little in his father's direction, as if in disbelief. "Yes, we worked together on an important matter some time ago, didn't we eh?" Senior nodded grudgingly. "So young Don, I think it would be all right with everyone here if you told the story just to me, and then I could share it with them. Would that be all right?" Emphatic nodding.

Thomas and the boy retreated to the back of the room, and there was murmuring, talking, gesticulating, and some crying, the story was told in a matter of five minutes or less. The rest of us sat awkwardly while this took place.

When they came back, Thomas began. "So Don here tells me that Joanie told him he was stupid, ugly, and that he looked like a toad. This hurt his feelings a great deal as he is really rather sweet on Joanie because she is usually pretty and nice." He waited for the boy's approval before he continued. "He chased her, to make her take it back, as I suppose boys sometimes do. But when he caught up to her, she turned around and hit him. And he might have pushed her, tearing her dress." More approval from young Don. "And the next thing he knew, punches were flying in every direction, and he was defending himself."

"No Daddy, that's not right!" Alastair shouted.

"Okay son, but we all get a turn to talk, and once everyone has spoken, the truth is in the middle. Isn't that what I have taught you? So, it's Joanie's turn. Come here sweetheart".

Joanie came and sat on a chair placed beside Thomas by Mr. Dykeman and prepared to testify. There was no doubt they were a lawyer's children. I glanced up at Jack and saw that he was so proud, so approving, that his eyes were shining.

"He tried to kiss me!" exclaimed Joanie, starting with a bang. "I didn't want him to, and I told him to go away – "

"And that he was a toad –"interjected Thomas,

"And he wouldn't listen and he grabbed me and tore my dress and I ran away and I tripped and he was hitting me and then everybody was hitting him and then Uncle Jack and Mrs. Dibblee were there". Run on sentences were Joanie's preferred method of communication.

Alastair's version included a few punches thrown of his own, and then seeing Uncle Jack coming down the sidewalk at just the right moment.

When all the stories were told, Mr. Dykeman spoke. "Well. Well. As Mr. de Burgh said, the truth is in the middle. Now we need to talk about what went wrong". Any parent has sat in on a number of conferences with school officials and knows what happened next.

When the discussion was over, young Don apologized quite sincerely, and admitted that the way to approach a girl was with words, not lips and not fists. Joanie apologized for calling him a toad. Alastair was praised for going for help. The constable was sent on his way. Jack climbed in the car with us in the back seat with Joanie and Alastair, and Thomas stayed to have a quiet word with Mr. Dykeman and Mrs.

Dibblee, I suspected about characterizing Jack unfairly and finding fault where there was none.

And you know, I worried about the Smythe boy for the longest time.

All children involved in a scuffle with their peers, whether bordering on sexual assault, like Joanie or a fistfight, as Alastair had a few times in his young life, will have bruises. But Joanie had bruises that didn't get better. And they were odd, made up of thousands of little pinprick bruises forming the whole. She started having odd illnesses, with mild fever and tiredness that came and went.

Any parent who has ever had a child with this disease recognizes the symptoms. Leukemia.

There was a new doctor in Fredericton, taking over from the rapidly aging Dr. Bridges. His name was Dr. Everett Chalmers, and he was making a reputation for himself. He was indefatigable, working long hours and being everywhere at once. With his matter of fact delivery and his knowledge of all the newest methods and diseases, he was very popular.

Dr. Chalmers examined Joanie carefully and with humour, made her laugh, and tired her out with his visit. He echoed Dr. Bridges diagnosis. She would struggle and rally in turns. She would be sick and be better and be sick again. Sooner or later she would begin to have bleeds and begin to have swollen and bruised joints. Nose bleeds.

Bleeding where there was no cut, but simply the blood would seep through the skin. And sooner or later, she would die.

We asked about Alastair, after all they were twins. He nodded his head no. There was no rhyme or reason about which child got Leukemia and which escaped it. But given the statistics, Alastair would be unlikely to contract the disease as well as his sister.

Once more, a hospital bed and nurses occupied our home. I left her side only to sleep. I read her stories, helped her do a little school work to keep her occupied. We read Gulliver's Travels a few pages at a time, but she would get too tired to pay attention. And when she slept, I sat beside her and knitted. Ever since the war and my pregnancy when I had learned to knit socks, knitting had become something I could do with my hands when my mind was occupied. I knit so much the blankets on her bed had both come from my hands.

Thomas sat with Joanie a few hours each evening when he came home from the office. Mr. Estee brought her gifts and told her funny stories. Grammy and Nene and Allie made stew and tea and washed bedding. Mr. McGuigan sat awkwardly with Thomas, talking of the weather or the price of wheat, to distract from the trauma of the moment. But it was Jack who often would sit by her bed through the night, sleeping in the chair and holding her hand in case she had bad dreams. Jack knew what it was like to be near death.

A few days before she died, I was sitting beside the bed, knitting furiously when she woke up and looked at me.

"Hi Mummy."

I smiled at her. "Hi Joanie, how are you feeling now?"

"Not too bad Mummy. Know what?"

"What is it my little one?"

"I'm going to be an angel."

"Well I have it on good authority that you already are, but what makes you say such a wonderful thing?"

"God told me. And know what else?"

"What else Joanie?"

"At least I won't get run over this time."

It's a trite thing that people say that no parent should ever have to bury a child, but they say it because it is absolutely true. To do so means to bury a whole lifetime of hopes and dreams, for your child and the life they would have lived, and for all the hopes and your dreams you have held for them. The loss of achievement, loss of life, loss of happiness and the loss of where life leads.

Clem drove Samson and Delilah for the last time that day before we took them to the farm. McAdam Funeral Home provided the hearse and the black blankets and plumes for the horses. And bless them, the horses knew. I suppose they can smell their cargo, but whatever the case, they were subdued and laid their faces against mine when I stood with them.

After all these years, I still have difficulty talking about how I feel about Joanie and her death. Only if I force myself can I do it, and only if I seal away the rawness of it and pretend I am talking about someone I never knew.

I could have allowed myself to crumble, to cease to function, but Alastair was still a growing boy, still needed me, and still had his own reactions to his sister's death. We would go for long walks, holding hands, talking about her and what it had been like to still have her in our family. Alastair did most of the talking, but I would encourage him, listen to him.

Thomas became a sort of walking spectre, much as he had when Lawrence died. He did what he had to do, went where he had to go, spoke in court with his usual passion and accuracy. But the only people he really talked to were Walter Estee and me.

The day we finally took Samson and Delilah to the farm was another blow for me. Not nearly the same as the loss of a child, but rather the proportion of icing on a cake, a bittersweet confirmation of sadness and loss. They were old horses by then, Delilah's broad mare's pelvis and hips protruding. Samson had protruding hips and shoulders, not those of a starving horse but of an elderly man. I sadly agreed that we could afford to deprive them the dignity of walking to Norton, something they would have loved. But we took them in a truck and brought them to their final home in the same day. They had their own paddock rich with grass and grains growing as if just for them.

I stayed with them in the paddock for hours. They had taught me so much, about them and about myself. I barely had to indicate to them what I wanted, and they obeyed. They had rushed Lawrence Bailey to our house for help. They had taken the twins for a million rides to calm them when they were babies, taken me for night time rides around Fredericton in the cold night air when I was learning. They had taken us to garden plots and drayed home the fruit of our labours. They were afraid of nothing. I had snuck out to them in the middle of the night when I needed their warm beating hearts for comfort. They had carried my baby Joanie to her grave. I could not imagine living without them.

Long before I was ready for it but long after I needed it, Mrs. McGuigan arranged a quilting bee in my living room. The quilt in question was a wedding quilt for a young couple, in the Wedding Rings Pattern. I had never done any quilting before, although I had certainly slept under enough of them. The ladies taught me how to rock the needle with the thimble on my finger, my hand under the quilt to meet it.

And the conversation was second to none.

"Oh Mrs. McFadden, you must be so pleased your son is to marry!"

"Oh yes, Mrs. McAdam, we are most pleased to have such a lovely daughter in law."

"Oh my Mrs. McFadden, I thought you weren't much keen on her, owing as to she's Presbyterian and all".

"Well Mrs. O'Neill, I suppose I don't have much choice but to become keen on her now do I?"

"Oh. When's your grandchild due then?"

Had I felt even just a little better, I would have found the rich humour in these groups of ladies. But I did enjoy learning to quilt. They even taught me to piece the tops so that I could present my own top for quilting.

"Oh Mrs. De Burgh, what a lovely fan quilt, and in such lovely colours. What room will you put it in then?"

"I'll be putting it in my daughter's room, in memory of her". The fussing and threading of needles stopped utterly.

After a minute "Well there is nothing better for a broken heart than a busy needle, I always say. Isn't that right Mrs. McGuigan?"

"Oh yes Mrs. McFadden, I always say that too", and a little squeeze of my hand under the table.

I didn't see Jack for some time after the funeral, as much as six months. No one commented on it, but he simply disappeared. I wasn't worried about him, as no one else in the family seemed to be. But I missed him terribly, missed turning around in a group to find his blue eyes under his heavy brown watching me approvingly and in support of all I did or thought.

When he finally reappeared, several pounds lighter, and a shade or two paler, I hugged him tight and asked him where he had been.

Oh, I was visiting a friend in Saint John." He was lying of course.

"You were at the veteran's hospital? I would never judge."

Tears sprang to his eyes. "I got the DT's this time. I didn't know I was that bad. I'm dry now, but how long until a car backfires, or there's a smell that sets it off. What then?"

"Was it Joanie? Did Joanie set you off this time?"

"Bless her, it's not her fault. But it broke my heart and I was already almost there."

"Jack it grieves me that you suffer so. I wish I could take away your pain. "

"Well Char, maybe I had it so easy that now I have to have it hard, do you suppose? Never mind. Let's enjoy today. May I be invited for supper?"

That summer, Jack and I and Thomas and Mr. Estee took to playing cards in the evening on the weekend. Jack told us all about playing cards in the reserve trenches and the rest camps during the war. The Canadians and the Australians loved to gamble, but the English really weren't for it.

I have advice for you. If you ever find yourself playing cards opposite a McGuigan, be careful! They will wrap your hand of cards around your ankles and trip you with it. You won't even know what hit you.

Playing cards was something the four of us, grieving as we were, could do to distract us from our own sadness. We would send Alastair to bed and then sit down and deal a hand. Jack almost always won, and each of us was determined to see him fail at least once each evening.

There wasn't a day that went by that I didn't think of Joanie and wish she was still with me. I still do.

In 1928, Thomas announced that he would like to take a trip to England and Ireland. Walter was to stay and take care of their legal practice, but he wanted me to go with him. There were places he wanted to show me.

We took Alastair with us, hoping he would forget the misery at home and emerge from where he had crawled after Joanie's death. We all needed to emerge out into the sun.

We sailed to London where we bought a car, and Thomas showed us where he had trained as a lawyer (or a barrister as it was in England). The Temple district where the best legal offices were fascinated us, as did the Temple Church itself with the effigies of crusaders set in the floor. We attended church there and found the very different tone of the service to be surprising and interesting.

From London we drove west, to Wales. When it seemed we could push no further without falling into the sea, Saint David's rose in the middle of the town of Saint Davids, rising from the tiny valley where it sits. I was dismayed and saddened to see that the monastery had been demolished by King Henry the eighth, and Oliver Cromwell later on. But there were still (or again) a cadre of religious men who cared for the cathedral and rang the bells on the hill to summon worshipers. The little hotel at the centre of town catered to our every need and the big fireplaces in the pub downstairs were never permitted to go without coal. It was a magical visit, warming us in our hearts.

From Wales we sailed across to Ireland, stowing the car in the cargo hold of the steamer. Ireland in 1928 was an odd sort of place. After 1922 the pendulum of power swung over to the Republican cause, and the Roman Catholic Church, which now dictated much religious dogma as civil law. We were careful to identify ourselves as Canadian, lest we be mistaken for English. And Thomas' long lost Irish accent made a reappearance, and Alastair giggled to hear his father speaking so strangely.

We travelled through Wexford and Waterford, visiting local merchants and staying in local inns. We stayed in one in Waterford that was very much as it would have been in the medieval time when it was built. It still boasted a stable yard in the back where horses and wagons were stabled. Our motor car was parked on a side street. The fireplace in the public room downstairs was burning merrily to ward off the seaside chill. The mantel was an obvious modern replacement, the need for which was attested by the scorch marks on the stone beneath it.

The innkeeper suggested that we drive further west before driving north to Dublin, to the town of Lismore. He said there was a grand old castle that had once been owned by Sir Walter Raleigh. It dated way back to early medieval times, although it had been updated several times. He thought we would particularly enjoy it and the gardens that were maintained around it.

The trip to Lismore took the better part of a morning. We could have done it faster but we kept stopping to look at the scenery. With the low lying mountains to the north, and the ocean off in the distance to the south, it was a stunning drive.

We came at the town from the south, and so the castle was mostly obscured by the buildings of the village. We checked in at the inn, parked the car and walked to Castle Lane on the directions of the innkeeper.

Before us as we walked was a large stone gatehouse, surely bigger than our house in Fredericton. In an arch at the base was a wrought iron gate. An elderly gate keeper emerged as we approached.

"The Duke is not at home" he said, in an Irish accent deep and thick.

"Who is the Duke?" asked Thomas. "Is it he who owns Lismore now?"

The man eyed us cautiously. "The Castle has belonged to the Cavendish family since 1753. The Duke of Devonshire resides here, but is not at home" the old man repeated.

Somehow I felt let down. The Cavendish family was not who I expected to hear about somehow. Thomas' face showed he felt the same. I was confused why I should feel as if someone else should be there.

Thomas took pity on the man and explained that he used to live Dublin, but had moved to Canada and that we were his family. We had been told that the gardens were very special and had travelled to see them.

Still eyeing Thomas suspiciously, the old man swung the gate wider and stood to the side to let us in. We smiled and thanked him, stepping into the castle yard beyond the gate. He informed us that the gardens existed mostly to the left, and went on for some ways.

The castle itself stood in front of us some 300 feet away. Although much of the stone work needed repair, it was still imposing. There were obviously later additions to it, differing in style from the original Norman castle. But the original could still be discerned. I stood staring. I almost felt I could see people in the windows.

"Char? Charlotte!" Thomas tugged at my arm. He and Alastair were ready to explore. We walked off down the path that had been indicated by the gate keeper.

We wandered through lawns and flower beds. It seemed the gardens had every kind of plant we could think of. Alastair ran on the lawns, areas so austere that we felt the need to beg him to be quieter. But it was good for him to be out of the car, so we didn't scold much.

Always the castle was off to the north, dark and brooding but somehow it felt like home, as if children of mine had played in its shadow many times. I was always conscious of it there, as if it called my name.

The sound of Alastair's play finally attracted the attention of a man in a gardener's apron, with tools hanging from loops and pockets.

"May I help you?" The voice was English, not Irish, the face lined with weather but not old. The gardener then.

We smiled, talked, and explained ourselves. We reigned Alastair in at least for a moment, but the man waved him off. "Let the boy play" he said.

He explained the structure of the gardens, and instructed us as to the location of the oldest parts. There were walnut trees there, he said, that had been planted by the ninth Earl of

Desmond, before the coup attempt that nearly lost him his lands and title.

Thomas and I stared at him. He smiled, and proceeded to give us a lesson on the history of the ownership of the castle. He told us all about the Fitzgerald family and their one time dominance of Ireland. The Earls of Desmond had the southern part of the Fitzgerald demesne. Sadly the last Earl had died in 1583, and the lands and title had passed to others, among them Sir Walter Raleigh and Sir Robert Boyle.

"How did the Desmonds die out?" I asked. I remembered suddenly, the book I had read long ago about the 9th Earl of Desmond and his insurrection against the King, and yet he retained his lands and title and even gained a few more.

He smiled gently. "Oh, the way most of these things go, picked the wrong side or other. Many a year ago now. Now there used to be a large tree on that lawn, but it died and was cut down, about fifty years ago now. The former Mrs. Cavendish had the stump left, and now there grow flowers and vines. Very pretty, it is."

He took us and showed us the stump, big enough and cut close enough to the ground that a wrought iron decorative chair sat on it. It was very pretty, but before I knew it I was crying, and trying to be surreptitious about it. The stump was large enough that the tree would have been at least four hundred or four hundred and fifty years old.

The next day we left Lismore and headed for Dublin, stopping along the way in small towns at local inns. Sometimes the locals eyed us suspiciously and scowled at our Canadian accents. But mostly the people we met were friendly and hospitable.

Nevertheless we made a joint decision not to head into the Province of Ulster, now remaining part of Great Britain, and not part of Ireland. It was a shame. We would love to have seen the McGuigan's home of Limavady, but there were still lingering pockets of violence there and we were travelling with Alastair.   Instead, after a few days shopping and sightseeing in Dublin we arranged to head to Scotland by boat.

We travelled by steamer, shipping the automobile again as cargo, to Glasgow. It was a highly industrial city then, and did not bear much interest for tourists, but we found tea rooms and shops, some of them designed by the great Scottish architect C.R. Mackintosh. There were plentiful trams around the city, and we were able to see the medieval cathedral while Thomas visited the University of Glasgow, the fourth oldest English speaking University in the World.

With a series of maps laid out on our hotel room floor, Thomas and Alastair plotted us a route that would allow us to see a lot of Scotland within the time we had left. The route swung east to Edinburgh, passing through the historic battlefield of Falkirk on the way. After a few days in Edinburgh, we would travel north through the hills, double back west to the coast, and then south again to Glasgow. Our innkeeper oversaw our planning so that we would not end up in anyplace untoward. We thought very seriously of travelling to Orkney, the northernmost islands of Scotland save for Shetland, and we were very disappointed that time did not allow it.

We spent a few days shopping and exploring Edinburgh castle as much as we could – the castle has been a military installation throughout its long history – and then we set out early one morning. We drove on through the rain, stopping at little towns along the way. The scenery was stunning, the locals polite if reticent. They regarded us as some strange beings from another world, which of course we were. By the end of the day, we had made the left turn to go south east to Fort William. We were tired, and losing out sense of humour. The late evening sun came out just as we entered the tiny town of Roy Bridge.

We unfolded ourselves out of the car, and entered the local pub.

Do you ever get the feeling that people describe as déjà vu? When we entered that pub and all conversation stopped as the local farmers stared at us, I knew with certainty that I had been there, in that exact spot, being stared at, before. I felt it intensely for a split second – and then it was gone.

Once we were introduced to the publican, and then to the rest of the house, we were welcomed warmly, and we soon became the centre of attention. We were asked to tell of our home and our travels, and we obliged.

"Aye, we 'ave our very own tourist attraction, don't we Mac?" said a deep voiced man crowned with a knitted hat.

"Stop it Carew" responded the man named Mac.

Another voice piped up "Aye, it's a castle, or it used to be. It was torn down after the Keppoch murders. Foundations are still there, on Mac's farm they are, aren't they Mac".

Mac was looking decidedly discomfited. "Aye, it's true, but it's not an interesting place now, nothing left but a few stones".

"I would very much like to see it, if you wouldn't mind, Mr. – Mac. Would you show it to me?"

And thus it was in spite of his discomfort, the product of a modest farmer interacting with strangers, he agreed to show us the spot in the morning.

We walked down the farm track from the village just after nine the next morning. Mac, or

MacDonnell, as he introduced himself on this occasion, was watching for us when we came near the gate of his farm. He took us on a track along the river, until the land rose to our right. A rough path ran up the bank.

We found ourselves standing in the foundations of a stone structure wider at one end than the other, almost pie shaped. It sat at the confluence of the Spean and Roy Rivers, with two large mounds to the south of the main structure. I saw, in my mind's eye, the footbridges from there to each of the mounds. I smelled, oddly, dog faeces, and checked my shoes. To the west was a large area, now a farmer's field that had once produced crops and where Mr. Mc Donnell grazed horses and cattle. The feeling of déjà vu returned, but again not long enough for me to recognize whence it came.

As we walked back to his farmhouse, McDonnell told us a story of Alasdair Carrack McDonnell, his ancestor, who had built the castle and started the clan of Keppoch. The castle was torn down after the murder of the 12th Laird of Keppoch and his son. After Culloden, that great marker of highland Scots defeat, control of Keppoch was lost, but his family had managed to hold onto the original farm.

We thanked him sincerely, for the tour and for the story, before we set off again for the rest of our tour of central Scotland.

As we passed through Fort William, I couldn't stop thinking about Roy Bridge, and the remains of the ancient castle. How was it that I felt familiarity of the area, that feeling of déjà vu? And for that matter, how was it that Lismore had seemed so familiar to me?

From Glasgow, after selling the car, we hired berths in a Steamer back to Montreal. Saint John would have been preferable but there were none available. Throughout the crossing as I slept, I dreamt of places that I was certain I had been but that I couldn't quite remember. People I loved were there too, Thomas, Jack, Clem, and a few others.

The thing about vacations is that you are not exerting less. What makes them feel restful is that you are exerting differently. On the way home we were physically exhausted, especially Thomas. But he didn't sleep, not as much as I expected. He complained of a mild ache in his stomach that came and went but wrote it off as too much rich food and ale on our trip.

We had encouraged Alastair to keep a diary of our trip, and much of his trip home was spent in drawing pictures of the things we had seen. Scottish mountains, flocks of sheep, and ruined castles. He often included Thomas and me in his pictures, usually to one side to frame the main subject. His drawings were excellent, touching even, and we talked quietly of paying someone to tutor him.

We arrived in Montreal and watched trees and evergreens out the window of the train home. I arranged overnight berths in the sleeper car for us. We could have had seats in first class, but Thomas just seemed so tired.

When we arrived home, Mrs. McGuigan and Jack and Clem were waiting for us at the railway station with Tom and the sloven. We had a wonderful trip, but I hadn't realized how much I missed them all.

A few days later, we had a party at our home to tell everyone about our trip and to show them the photos we took with our camera. We had gifts for everyone. Fine linen, beautiful woolens, crystal from Waterford, and lovely books and sweets. Jack stayed afterward while Mrs. McGuigan and Mrs. McGinn and I washed up all the dishes and tidied the house of torn wrappers and ribbons.

"So did it work?" asked Jack. "Do you feel better? Have you forgotten her?" His tone was level, not accusatory.

"I can never forget her. Every time I close my eyes she is there with me, telling me a story in a run on sentence and that she would become an angel. But I do feel a little better. I feel like my feet are not heavy, not held to the ground and hard to move anymore."

He nodded and lit a hand rolled cigarette. Then he winced a little. I looked at him enquiringly.

"I get stabbing pains in my fingers sometimes. It comes and goes. Dr. Chalmers doesn't know what is causing it. He says he has written to someone in Saint John." He shrugged. Mrs. McGuigan said nothing as she put the platter away in the far cupboard. I noticed a subtle shake to her hand. I had never seen her do that before.

Thomas went to bed early again that evening, the same as he had been doing since we left Scotland. We assumed it was just fatigue from travelling. I checked on him before I went to bed and found him curled up in a ball in the middle of the bed. I pulled up the blankets over him and retired to my own room next door.

Thomas went back to work two weeks after we got home. He felt badly that Walter was carrying the entire load of the practice. But even then he simply could not take on more than a part case load. Finally I spoke to him and insisted that he talk to Dr. Chalmers. Something was wrong.

That April, Mr. McGuigan found Mrs. McGuigan slumped over her sewing machine, dead suddenly of a heart attack. We were all devastated.

"Are you all right?" I asked him.

"What does that mean, all right?" After a pause, he continued "She's been my partner and my helpmate since I was 18 years old. I just feel as if my right arm is suddenly gone. I don't know what to do. No, I suppose I'm not all right."

I hugged him tight, and I was afraid he wouldn't let go. It was true. While the rest of us had been plunging into our affairs with abandon she had been steering the family, hers and mine, in silence and with care. How would we ever learn to internalize her role for ourselves?

The wake was held at 135 Westmorland Street. A dizzying array of Fredericton society paraded through the house. Everyone from the mayor, to contacts from the oil company Mr. McGuigan hauled for, to a broad array of customers and friends came to pay their respect. I thought wryly that her power as Mr. McGuigan's wife had rendered fenianism long forgiven, had wrought inclusion in Fredericton society, as long as everyone knew their role in that society.

I was at the wake throughout with the family, including Eveline arrived from Saint John with her five children, Allie, Jack, Clem, Nene and Frank, and many cousins, siblings, and friends. Thomas came and went, with the excuse that he had work to attend to, but I knew that he was exhausted and was going home to sleep at least some of the time.

All of the McGuigans were there for the funeral at Saint Dunstan's, even extended family from other parts of New Brunswick. The heating pipes overhead still creaked and groaned, as if to protest the cold April rain outside. The priest said mass in Latin, and Thomas and Alastair and I sat in the back of the church.

Charlotte Anne Porter McGuigan was buried in the Catholic Cemetery, beside her sons Fred and Harry. We all threw dirt in over the coffin, and Allie and I, Eveline and Nene threw in handfuls of flowers. Mr. McGuigan's face was the colour of the granite obelisk that marked the family plot. I saw Jack surreptitiously slip a flask back into his pocket. He saw me and smiled sadly.

But Jack's latest love affair with alcohol never really blossomed. He constantly drank, but he never seemed to attain the inebriation that he had before. It became a more subtle part of him, always there in the background, much as his mother had been.

Nene took over most of her mother's role in the McGuigan home. She cooked, cleaned and did laundry for Jack and Frank and Mr. McGuigan. Mr. McGuigan sold his horses and his sloven, and gave over to puttering around the house. He was, after all, in his eighties. But the light that had kept him working his horses despite his age went out.

Mr. McGuigan had a stroke one dark night coming back from the privy that still sat behind the barn. Nene found him in the morning, lying dead on the cobblestones with a look of serenity on his face.

Once more the wake was held in the family home, and once more we all attended to the stream of mourners. Not one person mentioned fenianism, although one or two mentioned Mr. McGuigan's temper with a wry smile. He was acknowledged by all to have been a deeply honest man, hardworking and motivated by a sense of integrity. This was the way he would want to be remembered.

We buried him beside his beloved wife and his two sons and now there were four in the plot beside the obelisk.

Alastair watched the family through this all, and it made its way into his drawings. He drew beautifully of the funerals of the only grandparents he had ever known. He showed his drawings to Thomas and me, but then he did something unexpected and showed them to Jack. Jack reciprocated by showing Alastair his own sketch book. They compared notes and methods with one another, and it was a new dimension to their relationship. Jack became even more of a mentor for Alastair, occasionally splurging for drawing paper and pencils that he would not buy for himself.

After the deaths of the McGuigans, I struggled to recover. These were the only real parents I had ever known, and I felt rudderless. My life was grey, even though the sun still shone and the rain still fell. Alastair and Thomas worked to comfort me and to distract me. Jack commiserated with me.

In June, Dr. Chalmers came to the house one evening. I poured us all tea, served cakes, and then we waited for him to speak.

"Well Thomas, you know I never gild the lily. The X-rays have come back and it's as I feared. The pains you are suffering are due to a tumor" he pointed "here".

"So it's"...

"Cancer" he finished my sentence. "This is a very fast moving one. Usually by the time you have pain like this, I'm afraid the prognosis is months, rather than years. "

Thomas hadn't reacted until now. "It's a shame. I had rather hoped to see my son into adulthood".

"Look Thomas" Chalmers said, "I would advise you to concentrate on enjoying him today rather than focus on the parts of his life you will miss. Treat every day as a gift. Enjoy the day on its own terms. Today I have pain, tomorrow I don't. On your death bed, you won't worry about the case you lost, but about the time you could have spent with your family and didn't. Go to your farm for the summer. Enjoy your son. Talk to your wife and your friends.

"I'm giving you a prescription for morphine. The pain will get worse. Don't worry about becoming dependent, but rely on it to maintain your ability to live your life. I'm also giving you some medicines for the vomiting and the"- a glance at me "other issues that will crop up. And later, it might be nice to have a nurse.

"As long as you are here in town, I am just a telephone call away. If you go to the farm, I can give you the name of a very good man for anything that might crop up."

There was a pause. The grandfather clock ticked. I thought, with every tick and tock, another second of Thomas' life ebbs away. I looked at his face. He didn't seem surprised. He had obviously been suspecting something like this. I knew that he had probably been spending time in the university library up the hill.

"Thank you Dr. Chalmers" said Thomas at last. "I appreciate the work you have done for me. And I'm grateful for the support you are offering." He took the prescriptions, and stood up.

Dr. Chalmers and I obeyed the social cue. The conversation was over, and in this case, it was appropriately Thomas who was in control of it. He shook Dr. Chalmers hand and saw him to the door.

"Anything you need, you just let me know" Chalmers said before walking out the door.

I looked at Thomas. "You knew."

He gazed down at me with a gentle smile. "I suspected, but I had rather hoped I was wrong. I think the doctor is right. I think the farm might be the very place. Alastair doesn't have to go back to school until September. We could spend the summer there."

Thomas insisted that he was well enough to drive to Norton, but he was exhausted by the time we got there.

Our farm manager, a rough and tumble man by the name of Bob Monteith, helped me to set up a bed for him on the front verandah of the farm house, so he could rest and see the activity on the farm around him. I made sure there were rocking chairs not far away, so there could be someone there for him to talk to if he chose. I had a nurse on hand within two days of our arrival. I hired a cook and made sure everything she cooked was a favourite. He couldn't eat much, so why waste time on food he didn't like? I managed everything, except what I could not control.

Two days after our arrival, we found a little white pony at our gate tied to a fence post. He was blind in one eye, sway backed, and sported the heavy belly of an old pony. [48]

---

[48] Ponies are often prone to Cushing's disease in old age, especially if they are allowed access to unlimited hay and rich spring grass. Cushings interferes with the body's ability to process sugars and fats and leads to weight gain, usually causing serious foot problems. Little feet were never meant to carry horse sized bodies.

"Mummy, can I keep him!" Alastair exclaimed as Monteith led him up the driveway.

"Now young master, you must understand that this pony is not long for the world" said Monteith, parting the pony's lips to look at his teeth. "He has paid his debts already in this life. You have to treat each day you have with him as a gift. One morning you will come out to find him gone, you understand me?"

Alastair nodded eagerly, accepting the rope and leading the little fellow away. "His name is Silver, because he shines in the sun like he's made of silver".

Silver gave us all a positive focus for the summer. He clearly doted on Alastair, and learned to step over low obstacles, to choose between piles of hay, and to lay with his head in Alastair's lap. He was a delight, with the wisdom of a little old man.

One evening in late July, after Thomas had gone to bed, Alastair and I sat on the verandah looking at his sketches for the day.

"Mummy, is Daddy dying?" He asked me.

I considered lying but then I realized that he would see through me. "Yes darling, I am afraid he is".

He considered for a moment or two. "So it's like what Mr. Monteith said about Silver. That we enjoy each day just for that day. That's how it is with Daddy."

"Yes I suppose it is. We are trying to give Daddy the best summer we can, enjoying each day for just that day."

"Are you sad Mummy?"

"Yes, but I don't want my being sad to ruin whatever good days Daddy has left. It's no fun for him if I mope."

He sat silent, considering and snuggled up to me.

The next day was a good day for Thomas. The pain was not as bad and he was able to eat a small breakfast. Alastair seized his opportunity.

"Daddy, do you know how to use a bow and arrow?"

Thomas looked surprised, but said "I used to. Why?"

"If I get Mr. Monteith to pick me up a bow and some arrows next time he goes to town, can you teach me?" He hesitated. "You could do it just by talking to me if you're not feeling well."

"I think that's a wonderful idea son. I will talk to Mr. Monteith today about what you will need." He looked at Alastair and said "How did you know to ask?"

"You said something about it when we were in Scotland. That you had practiced archery when you were a student. I thought it might be something you could teach me."

For the next two weeks, Thomas spent at least some time every day teaching Alastair archery skills. On good days he stood behind him, showing him where to hold the bow and how to pull the string. On bad days, he coached from a lounge chair behind Alastair, calm, gentle and consistent. And when Thomas stood with the bow himself, even though he was very ill and in a great deal of pain, the arrows landed in the smallest part of the target every time. He must at one time have been a very fine archer.

July 14, 1931

Dear Charlotte

Thank you so very much for the invitation to the farm. I would be delighted to come, as would Frank.

Frank says with your leave he will bring Helen with him. As you know they see a great deal of one another these days, and although I doubt he will ever marry her, they are certainly friends.

Clem is working very hard with poor old Tom. He is saving up for a new truck again, but as you know the girls are all quite big now, and big girls need dresses and shoes and other things that can be expensive.

I am going to be in Saint John at the VE hospital next week. Yes, they will have me give up drinking again, but I mostly want them to address the pains in my hands and feet. I am having trouble painting and am dropping brushes more and more often, and not from the drink, no matter what anyone would assume.

After they release me, I would love to come to the farm for a week or more. I would like to be of help to you all and I would like to spend some quiet time with Thomas if he feels well enough. Perhaps we could play a round of cards if Walter is there too.

I hope to be done at the hospital by the end of July. I wonder if Mr. Monteith could pick me up on one of his trips into town. I would be happy to help him with any loading necessary.

I will see you when I get there.

Yours Truly

Jack

The last two weeks of July were hot and humid. The horses huddled together under the trees at the edge of their pasture, nesting their faces into one another's flanks to escape the face flies. Their tails twitched and flew in irritation. We bathed them often, as often as one can bathe a whole herd of horses, one at a time, to cool them off and to ease the flies' attraction to the smell of their dirt and sweat.

Alastair bathed his little Silver pony regularly. The face flies were causing eye irritations, and the horse flies were merciless. When the water hit his body he would stiffen and then sigh. When it was done, he would go to the nearest mud puddle and roll in it. We wondered what he knew that we did not.

Jack arrived at the beginning of August, and to our surprise, so did Clem, bringing Frank and Helen with him. Most surprising of all, Clem brought a young woman. Her name was Frances, and she was just 18 to his 50 years. She was young, beautiful, and opinionated as many 18 year olds are, and beautifully dressed. She wore fashionable clothes in serviceable fabrics, as Mrs. McGuigan had done. She had been to the business school in Fredericton, as I had done, and had lots of ideas about how Clem should run "his business".

Frank thought she was putting on airs, but I suggested that she was young and just trying to feel of value in a group of older adults. Thomas smiled at her pretention. She reminded him of Allie, now living in Moncton with her husband. Jack was tolerant of most people, especially young people, and said she might be just what Clem needed.

That August was languid and almost perfect. We sat under the trees and read books, dozed, and played cards. Family members came and went, and Alastair played with Silver and practiced archery (not at the same time). We drank cool drinks and sat on a blanket on the grass.

Jack told stories of some of the men he had known in the war, men we had never met, and many of whom had died long ago.

Thomas told court stories. Walter came and went, came and went, talking to Thomas about current cases. He knew exactly how Thomas' clients should be handled, but he pretended Thomas' personal touch was required.

Clem came two or three times, once more bringing Frances. She worked at a restaurant in Fredericton, smiling at us as she said that she did the books and cut the pies. She wore pretty summer frocks, pursed her lips and crossed her ankles, as someone had told her that ladies did. She wasn't quite perfect, but she was a good enough facsimile.

"Mr. Estee", she asked one hazy afternoon, "why is it that you never married? You're a nice enough seeming fellow".

Conversation stopped. Thomas looked away. Jack's face froze, and Clem raised one eyebrow. Everyone waited.

"Well, I suppose I have just never been fit for marriage" Walter replied. "Not everyone is as lucky as your Mr. McGuigan." He smiled at her, a smile that said don't push it little lady, and she smiled back in agreement.

We let out our collective breath.

By the end of August, Thomas rarely sat anywhere except in the lounger on the verandah. He was too painful to make it out to under the trees, and could not make the stairs to his bedroom. He lay one quarter turn on his side, with his weight on his hip and his knees pulled part way up to his chest. He was skin and bones, and ate almost nothing. His skin had a faint yellow tinge. He knew there wasn't much time left.

Once he said to me, "Well my dear, we were an odd pairing but we haven't done too badly have we?"

We talked for a while about things we had done, and what we were proud of and what we wished we did differently.

"Do you still blame me for Lawrence Bailey's death?" I asked.

He looked at me. "I'm not sure I ever really did. Anything I said, it was in anger. And looking back on it, perhaps Lawrence wasn't really as important as I thought he was. I have done many good things since then."

I was relieved. It was the only thing we had ever truly disagreed about.

"You know", he continued, pensively, "I'm quite satisfied with my life. I had a great deal to make up for. Previous animosities, damage I did through my own selfishness, and to you, to you I needed to repair the damage. I hope I made your life as wonderful as I could have." He reached out his hand for mine, and I held it. We didn't have a typical love, but there *was* love there, the love of many lifetimes. I held his hand against my cheek as I cried.

His pain was so awful to watch. He looked like he was stretched out tight over the quilting frame in the living room of the farm house. I began to secretly wish for an end to his suffering.

He lingered until the 28th of September. We found him in the morning, he having died in the night. I cried tears, tears of sorrow and relief that his suffering was finally ended. The same morning we found little Silver in his paddock, lying on his side, his lips pulled off his teeth.

Clem and Alastair and I transported Thomas in a simple pine box to Fredericton, a drive we did at night in the cool air in Clem's new truck. We took him to McAdams Funeral home, and they prepared him for a wake in the Irish style at the house on Church Street. And after all the people came and said he looked at peace and then left again, we held a funeral mass at the Cathedral. Clem's new team of horses, big beautiful greys he called Pat and Mike, took Thomas to the Rural Cemetery. We buried him next to Joanie, just as he would have wanted.

It was one of the last times the horse drawn hearse would be used before being sold. Eventually the motorized hearses were stored in Clem and Frances' barn at their new house on Beaverbrook Street in between funerals.

This time in Fredericton's history would presage the ending of the draft horse for use as a drayage animal, to be replaced forever by the car and the truck. Less and less were heard the clop-clop of shod hooves on the streets of town in favour of the roar of the fossil fuel fired engine. Clem and Frank continued with the horses until much later, recognizing as they did that horses possessed more finesse for moving delicate cargo like pianos and household goods. And truthfully, they continued with horses out of familiarity and sentiment, in love with the great animals more than with their women and their children.

After the funeral, Alastair went back to school, and I had the house to myself.

It was so empty with Mrs. McGinn and me. I longed for Mrs. McGuigan. Not a day went by when I had not thought of her since she died, but now I missed her more sorely than ever. She would have come to the house, organized quilting bees, knitting bees, and afternoon teas, and we would have chuckled together after.

In her memory, I did what she would have done. I pieced a quilt in Thomas memory and for the bed in his room, and then invited a group of women to come and quilt it. It was a simple nine patch in Thomas' favourite colours.

Through the church, I organized a charity drive. With all of the people I had come to know, I raised a respectable sum.

I had a tea party. I worked to keep conversation going over the tea cups.

Looking in the mirror one morning I realized that I had become one of the women who organizes teas and quilting bees, I collected money for charity, I gossiped with the other widows. But I was too young to be a widow.

I called Walter that very day and asked if there was room for me to come back to work. I had an option that Mrs. McGuigan had never been able to choose.

April 30, 1934

Ridgeview Veterans Hospital, Saint John

Dear Charlotte;

I didn't want to wait until I came home with this news. The doctors think they know what is causing the pains in my hands and my feet.

They call it Buerger's Disease. It has to do with circulation, but they are not sure of the root cause, any more than it seems to happen to men who smoke. But it could be from having been gassed in the war, or it could be because of other things.

As far as the doctors know, there is no cure. That is hitting me rather hard. The things I do every day all come from my hands. Painting houses, painting pictures, writing poetry, and drawing all involve my hands. What am I to do when I cannot use my hands?

I will be home in a week. It would make me feel much better if perhaps we could get together and play cards or something. Something normal. Perhaps Clem and Frances would like to be dealt in?

See you soon and thanks for "listening".

Love Jack

That summer Alastair graduated from Fredericton High School. He easily gained acceptance into the university up the hill. His first choice was to read history, with a view to progressing to Law, as Thomas had done. He continued to draw, and often showed me his sketch books. One drawing in particular caught my eye. It was a pencil drawing of a man with dark hair, longer than shoulder length and tied back and dressed in chain mail and a suit of armor. He looked familiar to me, but I couldn't quite put my finger on him.

"Do you like him Mother? I made him look a little like Papa. But he is supposed to be a man I am reading about. By all accounts he was ambitious and brutish but he caught my imagination. He was involved in and insurrection against the King and yet somehow came through with his lands and title intact. He died in 1520."

Realizing who he was talking about, I said "That's Maurice Fitzgerald, the 9th Earl of Desmond. Yes, I've read about him. And I don't find this too much like Papa. You have drawn him from your mind's eye, and that's very good."

He was surprised that I knew, but I told him that university wasn't the only way to read books and to learn what came before.

The next time Clem and Jack and Frances came to play cards, I showed them the drawing, with Alastair's permission. Frances commented politely, but Jack and Clem lingered over it, commenting on the way Alastair had framed the face, drawn the fall of the hair.

I would visit Nene regularly during this period. We worked on quilts, knitted, and accepted one another's quiet company. We donated quilts to charity and made some for Nene to sell, baked for churches, and knitted socks for the men who wandered along the railway lines looking for work in depression stricken New Brunswick.

If we visited in the kitchen while she baked, often Jack would visit with us. He sat at a little oval topped table and braced his feet against the spacer at the bottom. Along the skirting under the top on the left hand side, he tacked a piece of sandpaper against which to strike his favourite strike anywhere matches. He would smoke and play solitaire on the table, the surface of which had a biblical scene he had painted there.

We drank gallons of tea in that kitchen. We talked of what we had read in the paper and argued politics. We talked of family, of Frank's constant womanizing and why his girlfriend Helen stood it.

We talked of Frances, her youth and her silliness, but we also talked of how Clem adored her and seemed to have turned the clock back with her, despite the difference in their ages. It was like he had started an entirely new life cycle with her, and we envied them. We were coming to the end of our cycle, and we knew it, with both relief and wistfulness.

When Alastair completed his degree, he made the surprising choice to put off reading Law for a couple of years, and elected to travel to Paris and study art. I was surprised, but I didn't disapprove. Before he left I discussed my intentions for the next few years with him.

"I intend to sell the house and move to the farm. I want to be near the horses, and the growing in the fields. And soon Uncle Jack will move to the Ridgewood Hospital permanently, and I think he needs to have family nearby."

"I have given Mr. Estee instructions of how to care for my estate until you are ready to dissolve it or to take up residence in New Brunswick again. I don't mean to alarm you", I said, noting the startled expression on his face, "I just want you to know you can travel for as long as you want without worrying of your affairs at home."

I had prepared well for this moment. Every letter I had from Jack, from the very moment we met, I had bundled carefully and stored in a shoe box. I gave it to Alastair right before he boarded the train for Halifax to sail for the old world. I gave it to him on the condition that he must not read any of the letters until he was aboard ship. I hoped that in reading them he would love both Thomas and Jack more, and that he would be gentle in accepting their flaws and their weaknesses. I don't know if he waited. But he didn't come back before boarding the ship.

Paris

1939

Dear Mother:

Thank you for the gift of your letters from Uncle Jack. I have known since Joanie and I were small children that Papa was not like other children's fathers, so I am not surprised that he was not entirely what he appeared. I love him all the same and now love him more knowing what he did to protect you and Joanie and me.

As for Uncle Jack, as long as I can remember, he has been a warm, gentle and accepting adult on whom I could always depend. Only once can I ever remember him scolding me, when I dropped the can of strawberry jam on Joanie's foot and she had to see Dr. Chalmers. Knowing that he was our father puts his love for us into perspective.

You must have been very concerned about my reaction to these letters. Rest assured that I love neither of my fathers any less, and in fact I love them more. Here in Paris, particularly in the art community, men with Papa's predilections are much more accepted, although still not open about their activities. It must be so hard to be so different than everyone around you. I do not fault him. I just feel sorrow for what he must have gone through.

Uncle Jack has always been a source of love and support for me. I can't remember him losing his temper with me, not even once. And every time I looked in the mirror, I saw his eyes and his eyebrows on my face, and I knew.

I need to tell you that there is a war coming here in Europe. Shortly I will be heading for London where I can sign up. I am told they are creating a war artist's section, just as there was in the Great War. Please don't worry. I will get to take cover a lot more than the rank and file soldiers.

I will stay in touch. Please give my love to everyone, and especially Uncle Jack.

Love

Alastair

The very idea of another war devastated Jack. "What did I go there for, all those friends I lost, why did we bother if there would just be another war?" Tears glistened in the light from the stained glass lamp as he spoke. We didn't speak of Alastair, of his choice to enlist.

Long before I was ready to lose her, Nene began to exhibit the symptoms of what in later years would be called Early Onset Alzheimer's Disease. At first it was just confusion, but the disease progressed fairly rapidly in her case. Jack and Frank and I all tried to care for her as best we could, but she died much too young.

Just a few months after Nene died, Jack moved permanently into the Ridgewood Veterans Hospital in Saint John. I sold the big house on Church Street, and most of its contents. I took the precious antiques that had belonged to Thomas, and a few more pieces that were special to me, including my brass bed that the McGuigans had brought to the house before I even moved in. And with Frank's permission, I took the little oval table that Jack played cards on and put it in his room in Ridgewood, with the understanding that it would become Alastair's eventually.

Twice a week, I drove my motor car from the farm and did volunteer work at Ridgewood and spent time with Jack. Mr. Monteith didn't like it, thought a woman should not be driving alone, but such ideas had never stopped me.

We would do what we had always done, read the paper together, reminisced and talked about the family. Clem came once a month and we would play cards, just as always. Frances would come too sometimes so we could play a card game that required four hands. The war news would upset Jack, render him silent and sullen, so we didn't talk about it.

As time passed, Jack's condition deteriorated. He would get open sores on his hands where the circulation was so poor that the tissue died. He got the same on his feet, only much worse. After a while he spent most of his time in a wheel chair, because the pain in his feet made walking too difficult.

I got occasional letters from Alastair. Most often he couldn't tell me where he was, or what he was doing, so the letters were most often about himself, how he felt, and if he got leave.

Sometimes I could read them to Jack. Sometimes I couldn't, for fear of upsetting him too much.

I would lay awake at night, worrying about Alastair, where he was, and if he was in danger. Sometimes his letters contained sketches of people he loved, but often the sketches were of a French village or and Italian villa, with a family member framing the image at one side. I had them framed, all of them, and hung them in the farm house.

In 1943, the doctors removed both of Jack's legs due to gangrene. He was philosophical about it. "I guess I will just have to get by without them. Good thing I don't need them to play cards" he said, with that good old Jack grin, wrinkling funny in the scar tissue on his right cheek. By then he knew he was dying by inches. It wouldn't be right away, but typical of Jack, he thought he might as well just live his way through it in the meantime.

On a Sunday afternoon in late 1944, we were sitting together and I was reading The Yearling out loud, when I heard a man clearing his throat.

I looked up and he said "Hello Mother".

Alastair stood there in battle dress uniform, slim but strong, his right arm in a sling, the fingers and palm bandaged thickly. He was right, he looked a great deal like Jack.

I couldn't breathe, couldn't speak. I made a sort of strangled noise, rising from my chair. He held me tight with his one arm, and I cried and cried. Finally I turned to look at Jack. He bore a stricken look, tears streaming down his cheeks.

"You're not going back? You're not going back?" He kept repeating, holding his arms out to his son.

"No Uncle Jack, I'm not going back. I'm to be assigned to a unit here in Saint John". He was hugging Jack fiercely, avoiding Jack's bandaged hands, and his own bandaged hand. "I'm not going back Uncle Jack".

It was Alastair who organized for Jack to come out to the farm the next spring, with a nurse in attendance, to see the horses one last time. It was Alastair who called Clem and Frank, Evelyn and Allie to come visit for the weekend with their families. For a glorious weekend, the farm was filled with the laughter of playing children and the voices of the McGuigans who loved them.

Alastair and I moved Jack's wheelchair out into the paddock where the draft horses were. There were none left that he had known, but there were one or two that recognized him as a kindred spirit. They approached him, sniffed his poor bandaged hands and the stumps of his legs.

The McGuigans and their families sat and watched in stunned silence. Horses in groups can be insanely dangerous when there are humans in their midst, and Jack had no means of self defense. But horses are also second to none as therapy animals, and there were only four of them after all with Alastair and me to fend them away if necessary. Their concentration on him was intense, focused. And then all of a sudden, as if they had agreed on it, they all turned away and resumed their grazing.

That weekend was the first time I noticed that Jack was wheezing, having trouble breathing. I looked at the nurse and she shrugged. She knew no more than we did.

Over the next month or so, the wheezing became worse and worse. Jack slept more without the oxygen he needed to power his frail frame. Family members came and went regularly, knowing the end was near. I read aloud to him often, knowing that he might hear me even if he could not respond.

When he was between dreams and waking, Jack would talk in his sleep, sometimes calling out to any who would listen. He would cry "it's an ambush!" or "don't go!" The nurses assumed that he was dreaming of the war. But I didn't. I was certain it was something else.

One foggy Tuesday in July of 1945 the wheezing suddenly stopped and Jack died. For the first time since I was 19 there was no Jack in the world. Clem was there, and we quietly agreed that he would be buried in the McGuigan family plot. He would receive a military headstone in return for his service in the Great War.

As Clem drove back to his four children and the wife who had urged him to begin his life again, I drove slowly back to Norton. I pulled the car in at dusk, and parked it as usual beside the house.

I stepped into the dark house to find that it was empty. I felt a little weak and reached for a chair to sit on, a chair that just happened to be the medieval chair.

I was back in the same old dream, the dream that seemed to be in and of the chair itself. I was at a wedding, a wedding which seemed to be my own. There was Thomas, beloved Thomas, with his hand out to me, but looking at someone beside me. It was Alastair, my own son, but he didn't seem to know me as a son should. As Thomas and I walked, there were people all around us. Mr. and Mrs. McGuigan, Clem, Allie was there, and there was Jack with a group of other men. Everyone was clapping and cheering. I knew now. I understood.

I woke with a start, and a feeling of nausea and exhaustion. I definitely did not feel right. But instead of heading upstairs to my bed, I ventured outside and over to the paddock with the four draft horses. I opened the gate and carefully closed it behind me.

My chest was feeling heavy now, and the nausea was stronger. I fell to my knees and vomited on the ground, and then fell over onto my side. I felt horses nuzzling me, touching my face and my hands. One lay down beside me, touching me to keep me warm. The others whinnied loudly, until lights began to come on in Mr. Monteith's house.

But it was too late. I saw less and less of the light. The heaviness in my chest was now pain, and I leaned my head into the spine of the horse beside me.

And then it's not that I remember nothing else. It's that there was nothing else.

Bibliographies

To Fly Without Wings

www.orkneyjar.com/history/skarabrae; Orkneyjar, The Heritage of the Orkney Islands – Skara Brae.

www.britainexpress.com/scotland/Orkney/Orkney-Geography.htm; Britain Express, Orkney Geography and Climate

jeremyshiers.com/blog/2oc-warmer-5000-years-ago-orkneys / ; Jeremy Shiers Blog, 2C Warmer 5000 Years Ago in Orkneys

www.wattsupwiththat.com/2019/03/08/; Not Threatened by Climate Change: Orkney Islands by Kip Hansen

Of Dogs and Horses

A Keppoch Song; A Poem in Five Cantos, Being the Origin and History of the Family Donald, Lord of the Isles; by John Paul MacDonald; the Review Office, By James Watt; 1815

Life in a Medieval Castle; Joseph and Frances Gies; Harper; 1974; *ISBN 978-0-06-241-479-3*

Life in a Medieval City; Joseph and Frances Gies; Harper

Notes on the Ruins of Dunluce Castle, County of Antrim; W. H. Lynn, Architect; **Also some Historical Notes of its Builders, the MacUillins and the MacDonnells**; Francis Joseph Bigger, MRIA; Belfast;

McCaw Stevenson and Orr Limited; Linenhall Press; 1905

King Richard II; William Shakespeare; Mineola, New York; Dover Publications; 2015

www.britannica.com/biography/Richard-II-king-of-england; Encyclopedia Britanica Inc; Richard II; 28 January 2021

https://en.wikipedia.org/wiki/Clan_MacDonald_of_Keppoch;

www.finlaggan.org

https://en.wikipedia.org/wiki/Henry_IV_of_England

https://intriguing-history.com/richard-ii-1377-1399-plantagenet/

https://www.britainexpress.com/History/Reign-of-Richard-II.htm

https://en.wikipedia.org/wiki/Clan_MacDonald_of_Keppoch

https://en.wikipedia.org/wiki/Keppoch_murders#:~:text=The%20Keppoch%20Murders%20(Scottish%20Gaelic,of%20the%20MacDonalds%20of%20Keppoch.

Google Maps: Roybridge; the Spean and Roy Rivers; Keppoch Castle, Dunluce

Riding Anyway

The Rise, Increase and Exit of the Geraldines, Earls of Desmond and Persecution After their Fall; translated from the Latin of Dominic O'Daly, OP, with memoir and notes By C P Meehan, CC; Dublin; James Duffy and Co Ltd.; 1878

Medieval Costume and How to Recreate It; Dorothy Hartley; Dover Publications; Mineola, New York; 1931

Fashion in the Middle Ages; Margaret Scott; Los Angeles; J Paul Getty Trust; 2011

Ireland, the Rough Guide; Margaret Greenwood and Hildi Hawkins; London; Rough Guides Limited; 1990

Medieval Ireland; Clare Downham; Cambridge University; Cambridge University Press; 2018

In Pursuit of Saint David, Patron Saint of Wales; Gerald Morgan; Wales; E Lolfa Cyf, Talybont, Ceredigion,; 2017

https://en.wikipedia.org/wiki/Youghal

https://en.wikipedia.org/wiki/Lismore_Castle

https://www.wikitree.com/wiki/FitzGerald-3212

https://en.wikipedia.org/wiki/Maurice_FitzGerald,_9th_Earl_of_Desmond

http://serious-science.org/sex-in-the-middle-ages-6345#:~:text=In%20the%20Middle%20Ages%20they,man%20does%20to%20a%20woman.

https://notchesblog.com/2014/07/29/cunnilingus-in-the-middle-ages-and-the-problem-of-understanding-past-sex-lives/

Google Maps: Lismore, Youghal, Waterford, Wexford, Wales, England and Scotland

Carried on the Back of a Horse

An Irish Heart, How a Small Immigrant Community Shaped Canada; Sharon Doyle Driedger; Toronto; Harper Collins; 2010

Rideau Waterway; Robert Legget; Toronto; University of Toronto Press; 1955

The Capital Builders: Lt.-Col. John By, spending scapegoat; Bruce Deachman; the Ottawa Citizen; August 5, 2019

Military Canals of the Ottawa River; Matthew Farfan; Laurentian Heritage Web Magazine; 2019

Chaffey's Lock Cemetery; Neil A Patterson; Chaffey's Lock and Area Heritage Society; 2006

Algonquin Petition of June 6, 1835; Source Document

Print: **Montreal from St Helen's Island, 1828**; James Gray; McCord Museum

Shipbuilding and Ship Repair; W J Milne, Published online 2006

https://en.wikipedia.org/wiki/Prysten_House

https://en.wikipedia.org/wiki/Royal_Citadel,_Plymouth

https://en.wikipedia.org/wiki/Drenagh

https://www.pc.gc.ca/en/lhn-nhs/on/rideau/

https://en.wikipedia.org/wiki/Lachine_Canal

https://www.tanakiwin.com/

http://parkscanadahistory.com/series/saah/ottawariver canalsystem.pdf

http://www.birchbarkcanoe.net/algonquincanoes.htm

The Ships List, Port of Quebec, 1828

https://www.jstor.org/stable/41613759?refreqid=excel sior%3Adf51431cb63377a79351cb85e84b11e1&seq=1

https://www.chafetree.com/141chaffey.html

http://www.biographi.ca/en/bio/by_john_7E.html

https://en.wikipedia.org/wiki/Technological_and_indus trial_history_of_Canada

https://en.wikipedia.org/wiki/Royal_Engineers

htt https://northamericannature.com/spot-the-difference-between-a-male-and-female-bear/#:~:text=Adult%20bears%20have%20much%20mo re,more%20prominent%20than%20the%20males.ps://e n.wikipedia.org/wiki/Timeline_of_LGBT_history_in_the _United_Kingdom

Reid's Marriage Notices; "29 Jan 1836 (Fri): At Champignon, near Kinston, on Tuesday last, John Haggart, of Perth, to Isabella, youngest daughter of the late John Graham, of the Isle of Skye, Scotland (Rev D Murdock).

Google Maps – The Rideau Canal System, Northern Ireland, Scotland, and Ottawa

The Extraordinary Capacity of a Horse

Fredericton and Its People, 1825-1945; Ted and Anita Jones; Halifax; Nimbus Publishing; 2002

Fredericton Flashback: Stories and Photographs from the Past; Ted Jones; Halifax; Nimbus Publishing; 2003

The Secret History of Soldiers: How Canadians Survived the Great War; Tim Cook; Canada; Random House Canada Limited; 2018

A Family of Brothers: Soldiers of the 26th New Brunswick Battalion in the Great War; J. Brent Wilson; Fredericton; Goose Lane Editions; 2018

Faces from the Front: Harold Gillies, the Queen's Hospital, Sidcup and the Origins of Modern Plastic Surgery; Andrew Bamji; Solihull, West Midlands, England; 2017

Plastic Surgery of the Face Based on Selected Cases of War Injuries of the Face Including Burns, with Original Illustrations; Harold Delft Gillies; London; Henry, Frowde, Hodder and Stoughton; 1920

More Casualties Among Canadians; The Daily Gleaner; Fredericton; 1917-11-21; Provincial Archives of New Brunswick; New Brunswick Great War Project

Sgt. Harry Spare Killed in Action with 26th Batt. ; The Daily Gleaner; Fredericton; 1916-07-15; Provincial Archives of New Brunswick; New Brunswick Great War Project

Two Battalions of 26th in the Fight; The Daily Gleaner; Fredericton; 1917-08-16; Provincial Archives of New Brunswick; New Brunswick Great War Project

Attack on Passchendaele from Battalion point of view; 26th Battalion War Diaries; November 1917; National Library and Archives Collection First World War

Right Front Company, 26th Canadian Battalion; 26th Battalion War Diaries; November 1917; National Library and Archives Collection First World War

Centre Front Company, 26th Battalion, Canadians; 26th Battalion War Diaries; November 1917; National Library and Archives Collection First World War

Operations of "D" Company, 26th Battalion; 26th Battalion War Diaries; November 1917; National Library and Archives Collection First World War

26th Battalion, Nominal Roll of All Ranks Going Into Line; 26th Battalion War Diaries; November 1917; National Library and Archives Collection First World War

26th Battalion War Diaries May 1917; National Library and Archives Collection First World War

26th Battalion War Diaries June 1917; National Library and Archives Collection First World War

26th Battalion War Diaries July 1917; National Library and Archives Collection First World War

26th Battalion War Diaries August 1917; National Library and Archives Collection First World War

26th Battalion War Diaries September 1917; National Library and Archives Collection First World War

26th Battalion War Diaries October 1917; National Library and Archives Collection First World War

26th Battalion War Diaries November 1917; National Library and Archives Collection First World War

The Rum Patrol; Thomas Wayling; Macleans Magazine; October 1 1932

Maritime Drug Smuggling and Rum-Running; John Demont; Online; March 17, 2003; First published in Macleans Magazine May 13, 2002

Attestation papers and personnel Record, Sargent Harry Lynn; National Library and Archives Collection First World War

Canadian Expeditionary Force, 140ᵗʰ Battalion, Nominal Roll of Officers, Non-Commissioned Officers and Men; Embarkation Halifax Nova Scotia; S. S. Corsican; September 25, 1916; Issued with Militia orders 1917

Military Service Act 1917; Issued by the Department of Justice, Military Service Branch; Ottawa; 17ᵗʰ May 1918 – original issue

Irish Travel: Official Organ of the Irish Tourist Association, Dublin; Volume 1, Volume 3, and Volume 4 1928; Bord Failte Library

https://www.bac-lac.gc.ca/eng/discover/military-heritage/first-world-war/Pages/

https://www.bac-lac.gc.ca/eng/discover/military-heritage/first-world-war/passchendaele/Pages/introduction.aspx

https://www.bac-lac.gc.ca/eng/discover/military-heritage/first-world-war/personnel-records/Pages/search.aspx

https://en.wikipedia.org/wiki/York_Street_station_(New_Brunswick)

http://fosterville.ca/anne_articles/index.html

http://www.canadiangenealogy.net/fenian/fenian-convention.htm

https://www.canadashistory.ca/explore/politics-law/seduction-and-the-law

https://www.canada.ca/en/department-national-defence/services/military-history/history-heritage/casualty-identification-military/battle-hill-70-1917.html

https://theconversation.com/what-world-war-i-taught-us-about-ptsd-105613#:~:text=Psychological%20trauma%20experienced%20during%20the,the%20rest%20of%20their%20lives.&text=The%20sheer%20scale%20of%20veterans,our%20modern%20concept%20of%20PTSD.

https://en.wikipedia.org/wiki/List_of_Irish_words_used_in_the_English_language

https://en.wikipedia.org/wiki/History_of_Moncton

https://activehistory.ca/2015/03/sexing-up-canadas-first-world-war/

https://mynewbrunswick.ca/benjamin-wolhaupter-house/

https://www.facebook.com/ForTheLoveOfOldHouses/posts/97-church-street-fredericton-new-brunswickc1858-6500-square-feet-6-bedrooms-35-b/2303166123282761/

https://hekint.org/2019/10/28/the-psychological-impact-of-facial-injury-in-the-first-world-war-outcomes-from-the-queens-hospital-sidcup/

https://www.theguardian.com/world/postcolonial/2014/may/26/broken-gargoyles-the-disfigured-soldiers-of-the-first-world-war

https://www.veterans.gc.ca/eng/remembrance/those-who-served/women-veterans/nursing-sisters

https://geographicalimaginations.com/2016/09/25/the-hospital-raids/

https://en.wikipedia.org/wiki/Partition_of_Ireland

https://en.wikipedia.org/wiki/History_of_rail_transport_in_Ireland

https://www.mayoclinic.org/diseases-conditions/buergers-disease/symptoms-causes/syc-20350658

https://www.hopkinsvasculitis.org/types-vasculitis/buergers-disease/#:~:text=The%20initial%20symptoms%20of%20Buerger's,central)%20parts%20of%20the%20body.

https://www.cdc.gov/tobacco/campaign/tips/diseases/buergers-disease.html

https://www1.gnb.ca/0131/en/heritage/thisweekde.asp

https://nbmediacoop.org/2020/03/21/shutting-the-province-down-the-1918-1919-flu-epidemic-in-new-brunswick/

https://www.warmuseum.ca/cwm/exhibitions/artists/indexeng.html

https://www.warmuseum.ca/cwm/exhibitions/artists/fisher1eng.html

Google Maps – Fredericton, London, Glasgow, Edinburgh, rural Scotland, Saint John and Halifax, Belgium, and France.

Printed in Great Britain
by Amazon